The Dead Don't Speak

Also by Claire Askew

All the Hidden Truths
What You Pay For
Cover Your Tracks
A Matter of Time

CLAIRE ASKEW

The Dead Don't Speak

HODDER &
STOUGHTON

First published in Great Britain in 2023 by Hodder & Stoughton
An Hachette UK company

1

Copyright © Claire Askew 2023

A CIP catalogue record for this title is available from the British Library

Hardback ISBN 978 1 529 34830 9
Trade Paperback ISBN 978 1 529 34829 3
eBook ISBN 978 1 529 34832 3

Typeset in Plantin Light by Manipal Technologies Limited

Printed and bound by CPI Group (UK) Ltd, Croydon, CR0 4YY

Hodder & Stoughton policy is to use papers that are natural, renewable and recyclable products and made from wood grown in sustainable forests. The logging and manufacturing processes are expected to conform to the environmental regulations of the country of origin.

Hodder & Stoughton Ltd
Carmelite House
50 Victoria Embankment
London EC4Y 0DZ

www.hodder.co.uk

In memory of Alan Smith, 1941 – 2022
'Live, baby!'

I

Friday, 12 February, 21:30

Evening was the hardest time. I couldn't settle. The flat came to feel like a series of rooms I was moving through, over and over, like a clockwork toy on a track: chair, hallway, kitchen, hallway, chair. Hallway, bathroom, bed. Repeat. Evening after evening spent not speaking to another person, not even talking to myself, because my voice rang uncanny off the walls of those rooms. It was winter, pitch-black outside before anyone had left work. The city glowed orange and gave off steam, streetlights like coils in a three-bar heater. I was livid all the time. I couldn't stand myself.

That night, I'd gone for a drive. It wasn't late, maybe nine o'clock, but it had been dark for hours. I found myself in the New Town, autopilot driving, not sure how I'd got myself there or why. It was February, the roads greasy, sleet driving slant against the traffic. In spite of this, George Street was busy with Friday-night drinkers. Big groups of coatless girls, whooping and dashing bare-legged through the sideways weather. I parked on the cobbles with my back to the All Bar One. I felt old that night, oddly responsible for those girls. I felt like someone's dad.

The kid in the Honda Civic pitched up like a rock dropped into the middle of the street. I'd let my mind drift, watching the spatter of sleet on the windscreen, de-mister draining the battery. I heard him first, his speakers' bass setting teeth on edge from a quarter-mile away, then closer: the raspy hiss of his air-compressed gears. At the red light sat a single hatchback, driven by a woman – from where I'd parked I couldn't make out her face, but imagined her tired, unwinding from a long shift as she drove home. When the kid in the Civic screeched up on her inside and dead-stopped, revving, bumper over the line, I knew already what he was going to do.

I don't know if I fired my own ignition as it happened, or ever so slightly before. The light turned, and the engine of the Civic roared. The cut-up happened fast, the kid slicing diagonally across the lanes; I watched the woman flick the hatchback's nose in time and narrowly escape a crash. She did what I'd have done, what any of us would, and blasted the horn. He asked for it, I thought: visibility was shit, and it was late and dark on a cold, slick road. It shouldn't have surprised him, but apparently it did. He hit the brakes, skidding a good few yards on the glassy setts.

'What the *fuck*, you fucking stupid bitch.'

The kid had rolled his window down and hauled his torso part way out. His throat was a pale flag in the streetlights' glow, an oversize baseball cap pulled over his eyes. He'd stopped the Civic right in the middle of the road: by now I was out of my space and waiting at the roundabout myself.

'You cunt,' he yelled, over his music's crappy bass. He hooked one arm out into the sleet and made an aggressive *come here* gesture. 'Get out of your fucking car, cunt.'

If the woman blinked, she didn't show it. Neatly, she turned the steering wheel and eased the hatchback out across the carriageway, past the kid and his ridiculous car, the way she might've skirted any obstacle. My light had changed, and as I approached, I saw the boy racer chuck his throat and spit, with enough force even in the February wind to land a gob of phlegm on the woman's passenger door. He moved fast, folding himself back in through his window. This time he didn't rev or spin his wheels, just peeled out with that headache bass cranked up. All she'd done was blow her horn at him, and yet he was going to chase her.

It was surreal, following the two of them down Hanover Street to the Queen Street crossing, which lit up green just as the woman approached. It was a good thing, too, as the kid had glued himself to the hatchback's bumper: I couldn't see exactly, but the gap must have been inches wide, perilously close to a shunt. Had the woman braked at all, he'd have piled into the back of her. He'd flashed his full-beam headlamps up, throwing dazzle in her mirrors. Other motorists bearing witness didn't seem to bother him. His music was so loud it thudded through the road, my own steering wheel buzzing to its beat.

As she headed downhill on Dundas Street, the woman slowed to a near crawl. She might have been trying to annoy him, but I felt it more likely she was terrified. The kid was a bona fide dangerous driver, risking his own safety as well as hers. At low speed, at least, the crash that seemed almost inevitable would be mild. A paint job, maybe. A dent. But I doubted she was thinking of her car right then. She was being menaced: the kid's driving was a clear-cut threat.

'Pass her,' I hissed through my teeth. 'You've made your point.'

But the kid didn't let up. Together, we eased round the long bend at Brandon Street, slow as a funeral cortège, the Honda Civic still practically brushing the bodywork of the hatchback. At the Huntly Street junction, the lights were red, and the woman slowed to a dead crawl in order to force a stop. I saw her indicate left, and then the kid put on his reversing lights. I doubted he knew I was there or even checked for vehicles behind, but I was glad of the few feet of space I'd left between my bonnet and his idiotic spoiler. He rolled back far enough to steer the Civic's nose into the road, then purred into the right-hand lane. His tyres were on the white dividing line, his car's flank right up against the hatchback. In what I hoped was a show of solidarity, I closed the gap between the back of the woman's car and my own.

Of course, the kid zipped down the window on his passenger side. I could see him leaning over, one arm braced against the steering wheel, to yell at the woman whose head didn't turn, who kept on gazing straight ahead. I imagined her knuckles white, her mouth a thin line of grim resolve.

'I told you, get out of the fucking car.'

The woman didn't respond. I saw the kid twist to turn down his music, a gesture so ridiculous I might have smiled, had this been a film I was watching and not an active crime scene.

'Don't *fucking* ignore me, bitch!' The kid put his foot on the accelerator, and I heard the Civic's exhaust rattle underneath the engine's roar. 'I'm gonna fuck you up, you hear? Get out of the car.'

The light was still red. A 27 bus turned right from the box, its two decks full of blue light, like a steamed-up fridge. Still, the woman didn't respond. I remember looking down at my phone, which was sitting propped in the cupholder. I remember thinking I could have dialled 999. Could have done the right thing. The correct thing.

The kid was still yelling.

'You don't *get* to ignore me!' By this time it was practically a shriek, his rage a live, vibrating thing. 'You're *gonna* get out of that car, you cunt. I'm gonna follow you home.'

Almost before he'd said it, I pictured the scene. I hoped this woman had a man at home, some six-foot-four-inch bastard with a mean streak. I thought of him kicking seven shades of shit out of this weaselly kid. That rare thing, instant karma: the idea thrilled me, almost turned me on. I saw that my palms were slick against the wheel.

The light changed, and the woman behaved in a way I hadn't foreseen. From a standing start, she shot off into the night, turning right instead of left, taking the corner on two wheels and very definitely speeding. She was hoping to outrun him, I realised, and it might have worked: the kid wasn't as quick to get off his clutch – I could tell she'd flummoxed him. But I knew he had the superior car, with its souped-up racing accoutrements. She wouldn't lose him easily, and I guessed then that there was no man at home, no one to scare the boy racer off once he caught up with her. My pulse banged about in my head.

'That's *enough*,' I heard myself say.

I lit out of the junction after the Civic. The woman's little car had already pulled ahead, passing the crossing at Rodney Street and toiling on up the hill. The noise of the kid's car turned the heads of the cabbies parked up in their rows at the Canonmills garage: he'd turned his music up once more, its bass a beating I was sick of taking. At Rodney Street the light turned amber but the kid sailed through, already gaining ground on the hatchback. I tried to imagine what he thought he was going to do, thought of the weapons his stupid trussed-up car might contain. Was he carrying a blade, or worse? Up the road, the woman was indicating – a reflex, I assumed, though she was running for her life – to turn left into East Claremont Street. In the beat before the crossing traffic's light turned green, I too flicked on my indicator, and jumped the red. East Claremont Street had speed traps, but Broughton Road did not. I wouldn't even need to push it all that much to beat them to the other end of the block.

At no point did I question what I was doing. There was no voice in my head that said *stop*. In fact, after weeks of scuffing around my flat, I finally felt alive. I'd just run a traffic light, I was picking up speed on a 20mph road, and I had no idea what I'd do with the Honda Civic kid once I caught him. But I was going to catch him. Because this felt good. Because I'd had *enough*.

Broughton Road was quiet, every light green, which felt like a sign I was doing the right thing, like the city itself was on my side. My speedo needle hit sixty and I realised I'd have to ease off if I wanted to make East Claremont Street in one piece.

Thankfully, there was no vehicle coming in the opposite direction as I jackknifed across the carriageway and made the turn. As the wheels came off the tarmac and on to the new street's greasy cobbles, I felt my front tyres skid. Immediately, I made my hands lighter on the wheel, steering into the slide and righting things. I knew how to do this, how to make a car behave exactly as I wanted – I used to love driving, had I forgotten? I realised in that moment I couldn't remember when I last felt so awake.

The kid in the Civic had caught up with his victim: up ahead, I could see the headlights of the hatchback moving slowly towards me, back down at that defensive, crawling speed. As I approached, my own dipped beams caught the female driver's terrified face. Her eyes were on the rear-view, her mouth ragged and chewing on words I couldn't hear. I imagined her chanting *leave me alone, leave me alone*, the kid's aggressive music humming under everything.

They say when two cars collide, the worst part about it is the sound. They're right. I knew what was coming and braced for it, but it still hurt, the screech of bending metal like a toothache. Without really thinking, I'd wrenched the handbrake on and pivoted at some speed into the side of the Civic. I watched as my bonnet ploughed into the driver's door and it crumpled, like a sheet of paper drawn into a fire. In a split second, I glimpsed the kid's shocked face, his eyes shark-black and angry, before the driver's side window gave, the glass crazing all at once to a sheet of TV static. My body was jolted by the impact, making my spine crunch. The Civic slid sideways; I felt its hubcaps shatter as the impact shunted its passenger-side wheels up on to the pavement. My own car was straddling the carriageway. My head buzzed, and as my mouth filled with something slick and sour, I realised I'd bitten my tongue. A long diagonal crease pushed up out of my bonnet, though I could see the Civic had come off worse. The street was quiet, but a hundred residential windows looked down on this length of it. I knew the noise of the crash would have drawn witnesses to those windows, and for the first time, I felt a snicker of fear. I put my car in reverse and backed it out of the collision, the Civic's bodywork making a crumpled-tinfoil sound. I wondered if the kid was hurt, and realised I hoped so as blood trickled into my throat. The Honda Civic was written off: the fundamental structure of it had bent, and I guessed its shove on to the pavement wouldn't have done the suspension much good. Even if the kid was unhurt, he wasn't going to drive away. I felt smug. I'd done it. I'd punished him.

I manoeuvred into position to drive away, but hesitated. I realised the woman's hatchback was nowhere to be seen: in the minute-or-so it had taken to run the kid off the road, his victim had disappeared into the night. I wondered if she'd paused at all, if she'd stopped to watch me ram the Civic and deliver her out of harm's way, or if she'd simply high-tailed it into the dark. I didn't much care – I assumed she felt gratitude towards me, I didn't need to have it explicitly given. Indeed, I was glad she hadn't stuck around, hadn't parked the hatchback with its hazards on and run back in the rain to see if I was okay. It made what came next easier. It helped me commit what I only realised later was a hit and run.

Monday, 12 July, 08:50

Helen Birch had always hated relying on other people. She'd had to train Anjan, her partner, out of opening the car door for her, back when they first started seeing each other. Though he protested it was meant to be charming, part of the way he'd been raised, she argued it made her feel geriatric. People opened car doors for old ladies, not perfectly capable forty-year-old women. Besides, *she'd* been raised by a single mother who'd trusted nothing, double-checked everything, and would have sucked her teeth at anything resembling chivalry.

'I'm led to believe my father was charming, once,' Birch had told Anjan, when he expressed dismay at her inherited cynicism. 'Didn't amount to much in the long run, did it? He left her all on her own with two kids to raise.'

They'd had a half-hearted fight, during which Anjan had agreed to stop opening doors for her. She'd forgotten all about that fight until now, sitting in the pristine leather interior of Anjan's Lexus. She watched as he unfolded himself from the driver's seat, walked around the front of the car, and arrived at the passenger-side door. As he opened it, she zipped off her seatbelt, then handed Anjan her one ugly hospital crutch. It rattled as he juggled it upright on the pavement.

'You don't have to do that,' Birch said, shuffling her still-good leg into position, then hauling herself up out of the car. The crutch teetered as she moved her weight on to it, but Anjan steadied her, keeping one hand on her elbow. 'I'm almost better. I can manage.'

Their faces were close, as though they were dancing. Anjan bent his head and kissed her on the nose.

'Helen,' he said, 'how many times have I said it? You need to learn how to accept help.'

Birch rolled her eyes, but she was smiling back. She leaned forward a little on the crutches, and they creaked.

'I don't *need* help,' she said, 'I'm good.'

Anjan nodded, and stepped away. As he moved, Birch noticed the thin shadow the crutch cast on the pale, flagged New Town pavement. It was still early, the sun just climbing above the neat slate roofs. She'd had a coffee but wanted another – wanted a whisky, if she was honest – to stop her hand from shaking on the stick's rubber grip. She was nervous about the hour ahead of her, wondering even now if there was some way she could back out. Anjan had closed the car door behind her. Now he was beside her again, holding her bag aloft by its strap. Without a word, Birch dipped her head and let him drape the bag over her shoulder. She *didn't* need help, but she'd make this small concession.

'I can stay, if you like,' Anjan said. 'You know I cleared the diary this morning. I can sit right here in the car and wait until you come out.'

Birch snorted.

'We've been over this,' she said, 'and I told you not to be daft. You might have cleared the diary, but you and I both know you've a metric ton of work to do. I'll be fine. It's only an hour, and then I'll call a cab. No need for you to chauffeur me about.'

'I don't mind, Helen. I want to look after you.'

Birch closed her eyes, just for a moment. The July sunlight left a pink print on her retinas as she opened them again.

'I know,' she said, keeping her voice level. 'And I love you for it. But I promise, I can do this. I'll be fine.'

For a second or two, she thought Anjan might argue. But then she saw his shoulders sag, just slightly, and she knew she'd won.

'Very well,' he said, in his lawyerish way. 'But you know, if you need me, then—'

'—don't hesitate to phone.' Birch grinned. *If you need me, then don't hesitate to phone* had been Anjan's mantra ever since she'd been discharged from hospital, hobbling on her hated crutches. Even when she'd proven to him she could manage with only one, he kept on saying it, like he thought she was still an invalid – like he couldn't see the progress she'd made. He wouldn't stop *fussing*. But she kept up the grin.

'I know,' she said. 'And I won't.'

Anjan lifted his hand and brushed a chunk of Birch's fringe out of her eyes.

'Good,' he said. 'I hope it goes well, and she's kind. Don't be overly hard on yourself, all right?'

'All right,' Birch chimed, mimicking his upbeat tone. She liked feeling his hand against her face – wanted to reach up and hold it there, but her own hand was on the grip of the crutch. 'I'll try my best. I mean, how bad can it be? It's just therapy.'

Anjan smiled.

'Yes,' he said. 'It'll help you get better, like any medicine.'

Birch waited until he'd kissed her and they'd said goodbye – until he'd got back in the Lexus, started the engine and driven away – before she let the smile fade from her face. Making Anjan believe she was fine felt more important than actually *being* it, she realised, and it made her frown. That seemed like the sort of thing a therapist might want her to address.

She was relieved to find the entrance to the consulting room was level access: though she'd had a few weeks' practice and had mastered a sort of crab-step up and down, stairs were still annoying. The door of the Georgian townhouse in front of her bore a small brass plaque which read *Dr Jane Ryan, MBACP*. Birch took a deep breath. She was in the right place.

She buzzed the intercom and leaned towards it, expecting she'd need to announce herself. But after a crackle of static, the door made its telltale *thunk* sound, and gave when she pushed against it. The door was heavy, and she was already breathing hard, when she became aware of another person standing close to her.

'Please, let me get that.'

On the threshold was a petite woman with pale, close-cropped hair. As Birch straightened up, she noticed there wasn't much difference between them in terms of age, which surprised her. She'd expected a much older Dr Jane Ryan – someone head-teacherish. The real Dr Jane Ryan looked unexpectedly cool. She looked like someone who might once have been in a band.

'Helen, right?'

Birch clattered into the tiled hallway, the door swinging shut behind her.

'Right. Dr Ryan?'

'Call me Jane.' The woman looked her up and down. Birch wondered if she was going to have to faff around with the stick in order to shake hands, but after a moment, the other woman said, 'Why don't you come through and get sat down?'

Birch followed Dr Jane – *just Jane*, she thought, though the title seemed somehow necessary – into what must once have been this Georgian townhouse's living room. Everything was typically Edinburgh: an elegant fireplace, painted white, dominated the room, and in one corner there was an old press that someone – Dr Jane herself, perhaps – had converted into bookshelves. The many books had titles like *In Therapy* and *A Grief Observed*. A wide bay window looked out on to the street, though the lower panes were frosted for privacy. The carpet was thick, muffling the stopper of Birch's stick.

'Take a pew,' Dr Jane said, gesturing to an armchair on the far side of the fireplace. There was a side table next to it with a box of tissues, and a glass of water Birch almost upended as she half toppled from vertical to seated.

'Sorry,' she said, propping her crutch against the chair's broad arm. 'I'm getting better at this every day, but sometimes my hip just doesn't want to play ball.'

Dr Jane was smiling. Birch noticed she had a dimple on one side of her face, but not the other.

'Don't you worry,' she said. 'I imagine it's frustrating for you. Are you in a lot of pain?'

Birch blinked. She hadn't expected this difficult a question up front. Anjan had asked it a lot when she first came out of hospital, and her response had often been a lie.

'I'm all right just now,' she said. This, at least, was true: it wasn't long since breakfast, when she'd taken her meds. Birch believed it was important to tell the truth in therapy. 'And it's so much better now that it was even a couple of weeks ago.'

'How about walking? How's the physio going?'

Birch laughed.

'I thought I was here to talk about my head,' she said, 'not this useless leg.'

Dr Jane arched one pale eyebrow.

'Well, yes,' she said, 'but I'm pretty sure you know that a physical injury can mess with your head, DI Birch.'

As if prompted, a whisper of pain drifted through Birch's hip. *Don't start*, she thought.

'I guess,' she said. 'I guess it can. But I'm managing it. Like I said, I'm so much better than I was.'

There was a pause, during which she felt as though Dr Jane took a mental note.

'Have you ever attended counselling before?' she asked.

Birch shook her head.

'It was mooted, once,' she replied. 'I worked on the Three Rivers case.'

Dr Jane nodded.

'The college shooting. That must have been hard. You felt like you needed help, back then?'

'No.' Birch worried she'd said it a little too quickly. 'It was offered to me, is all. I turned it down. Decided I could manage.'

She watched as the smaller woman glanced away, reaching for a tablet with a brushed-steel case.

'Well,' she said, 'as you've never done this before, I'll start by asking if you have any questions about the agreement I sent you. Did everything look okay?'

Birch thought back to the Word document Dr Jane had emailed her, and shook her head.

'It all seemed very straightforward,' she said. 'I was more than happy to sign it.'

Dr Jane smiled.

'Good. But you should feel free to ask any questions at any time. That agreement can always be revisited. In addition, I'd like to suggest that we have a sort of review session every so often – maybe once every six weeks? Just so we can discuss your progress, really.'

Birch felt her own eyebrows shoot up. It hadn't occurred to her that she might be doing this for as long as six weeks.

'That sounds fine,' she croaked.

'Great. Final question, before we get started. You saw the part in the agreement where I requested that you keep a therapeutic journal?'

Birch sagged a little.

'I did. That's compulsory, right?'

Dr Jane made a *hmm* face, though she didn't make the sound.

'It doesn't have to be. But I'd like you to try it out, just in between the first few sessions. If you find you hate it, that's okay.'

There was a small silence, into which Birch eventually spoke.

'Will I have to write . . . lots? Are you expecting all my deepest and darkest secrets?'

Dr Jane laughed: a warm, musical laugh that sounded genuine.

'Not at all,' she replied. 'Once you click on the link, you'll see there's a sort of form in there. It asks you to select your mood from a drop-down menu. Then there's a box to write comments. You can write ten words, or a thousand. It's entirely up to you. It's really just a tool I use to track progress. And it's completely confidential, I'd never share the contents of those journals – unless in the specific circumstances outlined in the agreement.'

'If you think I intend to commit a crime,' Birch said, grinning.

'It's that,' Dr Jane replied, 'or if I suspect you of intending to harm yourself or others.'

'Seems unlikely.'

Dr Jane laughed again.

'I agree.'

Birch felt the smile slide off her face. She realised she couldn't put it off any longer: the actual therapy side of things was about to begin. Across from her, Dr Jane opened up the tablet and began to skim down a document.

'So . . . I've got your file here,' she said.

'Uh-oh,' Birch replied. It was meant to be a joke but as she said it, she wished she could bite down on the sound, take it back.

'Nothing to worry about.' Dr Jane was still smiling. *She's nice*, Birch told herself, *this woman is nice, Helen, you can relax.* It didn't really work. 'In fact,' Dr Jane went on, 'I owe you a bit of an apology. I'm sorry it's taken so long to get you here, I know you've been waiting weeks. The wheels of police bureaucracy turn slowly, sometimes.'

'Don't I know it.'

'I'm sure you do.' Dr Jane paused, looking down at the tablet's glowing screen. 'Okay, here we are. Right. Why don't you start by telling me a bit about what's brought you here.'

'I'm sorry?'

'I'd like to know why you've come to see me. What's been going on for you over the past few weeks.'

Birch frowned.

'Isn't that all there in the file?'

Dr Jane's face wore a non-committal expression.

'Of course, but the file has the official version. I want to hear *your* version of events.'

Birch closed her eyes, letting an internal film-reel start up in her mind, jerky but horribly familiar. The cramped, ruined house. A gunshot, then darkness. The thrum of a helicopter. Pain snaking through the lower half of her body like a black vine. Terror so thick she could almost smell it.

'Okay,' she said, opening her eyes again, but curling her hands around the arms of her chair, as though to steady herself. 'Well, as I'm sure you know, on the 4th June, I was part of what became known as Operation Kendall, in the Scottish Borders.'

'Yes. And what was Operation Kendall? What can you tell me about it?'

Dr Jane had fixed her with a still, pale gaze. Birch cast around the room for something to look at, something to focus on so she wouldn't need to meet the other woman's eye.

'It started in the town of Kelso,' she said. 'We got reports that there had been a spree shooting at the Border Union Showground, and that the gunman – a guy named Gerald Hodgson – was at large. A manhunt was launched by some of the Borders divisions, and my team were put on standby to provide support. As the morning went on, we found out that Hodgson hadn't just shot up the showground. Before arriving there, he'd been to his ex-partner's house.' Birch paused. The crime scene photos came to her mind's eye unbidden, as she had known they would. But she pressed on. 'Her name was Sophie Lowther. He'd forced his way into the house and shot both Sophie and her husband. As he fled the scene, he snatched the couple's three-year-old daughter, Elise.'

Dr Jane was nodding. She'd known all of this before Birch even walked in the door.

'So,' Dr Jane said, 'I realise it goes without saying, but . . . this was not a regular day at the office?'

Birch gave a short laugh. She found herself recalling all the times she'd joked to people that there was no such thing as a regular day at the office, not for a member of police personnel. But then she noticed that a silence had opened up in the room, and realised that Dr Jane really did expect her to answer the question.

'Not at all,' she said. 'I mean, it wasn't *the* worst day I've ever had, but it was up there. I ended up personally involved with this particular case in a way I never have been before.'

'Hodgson singled you out.'

Birch nodded.

'After he left the showfield,' she said, 'he ran, but not very far. He took himself off to a place called Seefew, a remote pasture in the hills up the Bowmont Valley. From there, he called to make contact with the police. Or rather, he called to make contact with me.'

'And how did that feel?'

How do you think? Birch thought, though she didn't say it. What was she meant to say? Tell you what, Dr Jane, when it happened, I honestly thought I might throw up, right there in my CO's corner office.

'Terrifying,' she heard her own voice say. 'And bewildering. I had no idea why he'd chosen me to be his contact – in fact, I'm still not one hundred per cent sure. I guess I never will be. But suddenly I was thrust into the centre of this operation. Suddenly I was driving down there, psyching myself up to be sent into a building with this man.'

Dr Jane had glanced down at her screen.

'You conducted the negotiation,' she said, as though reading it.

Birch shrugged.

'If you can call it that. I went in and talked to him.'

'Alone?'

'Yes. Wearing a wire, but on my own.'

Dr Jane flipped her gaze back to Birch's face.

'I can't think of a better way to word this question, but – how did it go?'

Birch winced, looking away.

'Badly,' she said. She could hear the sting in her own voice, the sharpness of it. 'I guess you must know the outcome.'

Out of the corner of her eye, she saw Dr Jane tilt her head.

'I know that you successfully moved the little girl out of harm's way. You negotiated the release of Hodgson's hostage.'

Birch tightened her grip on the chair arms. Another spark of pain – small, but persistent – untethered itself from the wound at her hip and wandered across her abdomen, making her teeth clench. She'd heard this could happen, that stress could make you hurt, but she'd never fully believed it until now.

'It wasn't quite like that, though,' she said. 'She wasn't a hostage, not exactly. She was . . . how can I explain this? Taking Elise was a mistake, he knew that. It was one of a series of mistakes he'd made that day. He claimed he didn't intend to do any of the things he did. He talked like he wasn't in control.'

'Did you believe him?'

Birch tried not to wince at the question. Dr Jane's eyes were still fixed on her, but she couldn't meet them. Instead, she looked at the fireplace. In its grate was a white enamel jug which held a bouquet of pale blue hydrangea blossoms. You had to bury nails at the root to make them grow that colour, she remembered her mother telling her. Acid soil for blue, alkaline for pink. She was aware that silence was slowly filling up the room once more. She was going to have to speak.

'I found that whole thing very difficult,' she said. 'Deciding whether or not to believe him was maybe the most difficult thing of all. I couldn't reconcile the idea that a person could commit murder and then claim it was all a big mistake.' The hydrangea petals were almost too perfect. Birch couldn't tell if the flowers were real or silk. 'I didn't know if I believed that someone could black out, then come to and discover they'd spent fifteen minutes randomly firing a shotgun at people.'

'But?' Dr Jane leaned forward slightly in her chair.

'But . . . I guess he did seem so – I'm not sure what the word is. Unmoored, I guess. Deeply erratic. He was in the room with me, but he was also miles away, both at the same time. There were moments where I looked in his eyes, and I couldn't see anyone behind them.' The words made Birch look back at Dr Jane. It felt necessary to add something more, to underline things. 'As if he'd left his body,' she said.

'That must have been hard, when you were trying to negotiate. Trying to reach him.'

Birch nodded. She realised a lump was forming in her throat, and she tried to swallow it down.

'It was. I don't think I succeeded. I don't think I did enough.'

Now Dr Jane was frowning, her cropped hairline seeming to shift as her face creased.

'What makes you say that?'

'Well.' Birch made a kind of snort noise, though she wasn't laughing. She pointed to her hip. 'I guess you know that he shot me.'

'Yes,' Dr Jane said, softly. 'Yes, I did know that.'

'And you'll also know that he was then shot dead by one of the specialist firearms officers on the scene.' Once again, Birch tried to push down the lump in her throat. I will not cry, she thought. I *won't*. But she could hear the threat of tears in her voice when she spoke again. 'I'd say that outcome indicates a pretty fundamental failure on my part.'

'Just to be clear,' Dr Jane said, her voice still gentle, 'you feel it was your fault that Hodgson was shot?'

'Yes.' The answer seemed too sharp, seemed to puncture something between them. But Birch couldn't help it: that tone was simply the honed edge of her own certainty.

Dr Jane straightened up in her seat.

'But Helen,' she said, '*you* didn't shoot him. Nor did you give the order to fire the shot that killed him.'

Birch looked down at her right hand, hooked around the chair arm. Its knuckles were pale.

'No, but . . . look, you don't get to shoot a police officer and get away with it. It was him shooting me that led to his death.'

Dr Jane let out a short, flat laugh.

'I'm sorry,' she said, 'but . . . you feel it was your fault that *you* were shot?'

Birch felt a shiver at the back of her neck. She bristled.

'Yes,' she said, 'completely. Yes. It feels very obvious to me, in fact, and I'll be honest, I'm not really sure what's funny about it. I made a mistake in the negotiation process. I told Hodgson a lie, and then he found me out and got angry.'

Birch realised her voice had become raised. The fireplace echoed: *angry, angry*. She watched Dr Jane to see how she'd react, but the other woman's face didn't change.

'Helen,' Dr Jane said, gently, 'is it possible that you feel you *deserve* what happened to you?'

Birch blinked. She opened her mouth to speak, then closed it again. She turned the question over in her mind, like a coin whose currency she didn't recognise.

'Yes,' she said, the word drawn out long, distorted. 'Yes, I think I did deserve it. I do deserve it. I deserve all of this.'

'Because you made a mistake.'

'It was a bad mistake.'

'Some people might call it that. Other people might say it was a split-second judgement made in a very high-pressure situation.'

Birch gave her head a short, fast shake, as though trying to dislodge something.

'That's just semantics,' she said, that certain edge returning to her voice. 'A man died. A man died because of a mistake I made.'

Dr Jane glanced down at her tablet, then pointed to it, looking back at Birch.

'I've read up about this case,' she said. 'I know there's been some speculation that Gerald Hodgson actually wanted to die. That it was his intention to commit suicide by cop.'

Birch straightened up, just a little, in her chair.

'I've read those takes, too,' she said.

'You don't agree with them.'

'No, I don't think I do.' She could hear that sharpness still in her voice and didn't like it, but couldn't seem to make it go away. 'And you know, I'm not looking to be let off the hook, here. I don't want to be placated, by you or anyone. Decisions I made led to a man – a vulnerable man, someone who, no matter what he was guilty of, was in crisis – losing his life. That's not something I can just shrug off.'

'Of course not. I don't think anyone would suggest that.'

There was a pause. Birch's hip ached. She realised she felt exhausted, emptied out by this short exchange.

'Well, good,' she said.

'But this is useful,' Dr Jane went on, 'knowing how you feel about Operation Kendall. It seems to me that you're carrying quite a lot of guilt and blame around with you. I don't for one moment believe you should simply shrug that off or try to ignore it. But I do think we can work on it in these sessions.

Work towards helping you reframe that, maybe. Shoulder it a little easier.'

Birch was quiet, though she knew she was going to have to speak. Something had been nagging at her, ever since Dr Jane had told her that she'd read her file.

'I assume you've spoken to my commanding officer.'

Dr Jane nodded.

'Yes. DCI McLeod and I have had a couple of conversations. He's helped in the organisation of these meetings.'

Birch raised one eyebrow.

'That would explain the delay,' she said, almost to herself.

'I'm sorry?'

'Never mind, just a joke.'

Dr Jane fixed her with a look.

'You're not on good terms with DCI McLeod?'

Oh Jesus, Birch thought. Now look what you've done.

'Really,' she said, 'it was just a joke.'

Dr Jane wasn't laughing, but her face softened a little.

'I'm not going to tell on you, Helen. I want you to be able to speak freely.'

Birch gave another shake of the head. *Stop being defensive,* she told herself. But she couldn't seem to stop.

'The guv and I get on fine. I'm a bit of a thorn in his side – sometimes I get out of line and he has to rein me back in.' She lifted a hand and waved it as she spoke, as though trying to bat the whole topic away. 'That's all.'

'It's interesting to note where you're placing the blame, there.'

Birch paused, her hand still held in mid-air.

'Blame?'

Dr Jane nodded.

'I asked if you were on good terms. You answered by telling me the ways in which you think DCI McLeod finds you difficult.'

Carefully, Birch lowered her hand again. She wanted to argue – *no, I didn't* – but realised Dr Jane was right.

'What about the other direction?' Dr Jane asked. 'Do you ever find DCI McLeod difficult?'

Birch wanted to laugh out loud, but knew that would be wrong. If I had a penny, she thought, for every time I've found my boss difficult . . .

'I think everyone finds him a bit difficult at times,' she said. 'But he's my CO. It's not my job to appraise him.'

Dr Jane made an *okay, sure* face.

'I'm not asking you to do an appraisal, though. What do you find difficult about working with him?'

Before she could stop herself, Birch let out a sigh. Why the *hell*, she thought, did you raise the issue of McLeod? Why?

'I'll be honest, I was more comfortable talking about how my actions inadvertently got someone killed,' she said. She aimed for a laugh and just about made it. 'Sentences I never thought I'd say.'

Dr Jane leaned back then, as if to look at Birch from a slightly farther distance.

'That's okay,' she said. 'We don't have to talk about it now if you don't want to.'

Birch let herself exhale, but at the same time she registered surprise, like a light coming on in her head. This was therapy: she hadn't realised not talking about things was allowed.

'I would like to know, though . . .' Birch heard the words come out of her mouth, and realised she'd been wanting to say them ever since she walked through the door. 'I mean, I've been wondering . . .'

She tailed off, looking at Dr Jane. In response, Dr Jane somehow did something that made her face open up, made it say *tell me anything. I'll wait.*

'Wondering what?'

Birch flinched her hands into her lap and looked down at them.

'I mean,' she said, 'I don't know if it's appropriate for me to ask, or if it's something you're even allowed to tell me, but . . . why am I here? When you spoke to McLeod, what reasons did he give for requesting these sessions?'

On the edge of her vision, she saw Dr Jane shift her weight, leaning forward again. For a brief second, Birch thought the other woman might try to take hold of her hand.

'You were badly wounded in the line of duty,' Dr Jane said. 'You were shot, Helen. Operation Kendall was a pretty traumatic event for you. Don't you think that merits being referred for counselling?'

Birch was still looking down at her hands. She didn't know how to feel about the fact that Dr Jane had not, after all, reached over to touch her.

'Maybe,' she said. 'But I'm surprised that McLeod – well, for want of a better phrase, I'm amazed he believes in this stuff. Therapy, I mean. It surprised me that he'd signed off on it.'

'There's a note of something in your voice when you say it surprised you.'

'Is there?'

'Suspicion, maybe. Are you suspicious of DCI McLeod?'

Birch pressed the outside edges of her thumbs together. The nails were bitten down – a new thing, something she'd started doing while she sat awake at night, these past few weeks – and she hated the look of them.

'I . . . think he may have other reasons to send me here. Beyond the fact that I was shot, etcetera.'

Dr Jane did her head-tilt thing.

'What do you think those reasons might be?'

Quiet opened out between them again. Birch wasn't thinking, she was merely pretending to think. She didn't want Dr Jane to know how long she'd spent angsting about this.

'I'm worried he thinks I'm a loose cannon. That I'm trouble.'

'Trouble? In what way?'

Birch buried her thumbs inside her fists, to hide the ragged nails.

'I argue too much,' she said, 'or I don't follow orders, not the way he'd like me to. I make snap decisions. I get too involved.'

Dr Jane was waiting, Birch could tell. She knew there was something more waiting to be said.

'I'm worried he thinks I'm not cut out to be a police officer.'

The sentence hung like a cloud in the clear, high-ceilinged sky of the room. Birch couldn't quite believe she'd said the words, though doing so felt like putting down something heavy.

After a few seconds, Dr Jane spoke.

'Let me take DCI McLeod out of the equation for just a moment,' she said. 'Because really, you can't know what DCI McLeod thinks of you or feels about you, not with any definite accuracy. So what you're really saying is, *you're* worried you're not cut out to be a police officer.'

Birch stared down at her own fists, balled in her lap. She realised this was the pose of a defiant child. She could feel her eyes prickling.

'Correct me if I'm wrong,' Dr Jane said.

The lump in her throat was back, and this time, Birch let it rise. When she finally spoke, her voice was hoarse and wet.

'No,' she said. 'You're not wrong.'

Thursday, 15 July, 16:45

The lighting in the Raeburn Hotel was artfully dimmed, which Amy Kato liked. The loud, upbeat music from the bar was piped into the ladies, which she disliked. Amy stood in the empty bathroom, the edge of the grey marble sink pressing against her thighs as she leaned over to study her face in the mirror.

'Detective Sergeant Amy Kato,' she said, under her breath. She glanced over her shoulder, then looked back at herself and spoke louder. 'Detective *Sergeant*.'

In the function room on the other side of the wall, she could hear the muffled hum of the small gathering DI Crosbie had insisted be put on for her.

'It's not every day you get promoted in CID,' he'd said. 'It calls for a wee dram or two.'

Amy ran a clean fingertip underneath each eye, brushing away a few stray flakes of mascara. She'd tried not to over-think the whole process: studying for the sergeants' exam had been just another thing on her to-do list. She'd managed to stay reasonably calm about it all, though the night before the final exam she'd walked home from work on autopilot and barely slept. The news that she'd passed came without much fanfare, apart from a call to her parents in Japan, during which she listened as her mother cried proud, happy tears down the phone. Work had been topsy-turvy for several weeks: DI Birch had been shot, and Amy – distracted by worry for her friend's welfare – had been moved into DI Crosbie's team. Crosbie

was an old-fashioned man and a decent police officer, someone Amy respected but didn't much like. When she passed
the sergeants' exam, he'd encouraged her to start looking for
jobs right away, and said she should not feel tied to the station
at Fettes Avenue. She tried to see this as encouragement, but
couldn't help but feel he wouldn't mind being rid of her. This
little function he'd thrown felt like a sort of apology: it was
only weeks later, with Amy still swithering, that a sergeant's
post had come up in her very own team. Crosbie's words echoed in her head once again: *not every day you get promoted in
CID*. Like he thought she never would again. Like he thought
she'd hit her ceiling.

She shook her head and straightened up, still watching herself in the mirror. She held her head a little higher and said
again, 'Detective Sergeant Amy Kato.'

'You're damn right.'

Amy spun around, her cheeks flushing with embarrassment. Standing just inside the doorway – or rather, leaning on
a single crutch – was DI Helen Birch.

'It suits you,' Birch said, smiling, 'right down to the ground.'

Amy couldn't help but beam, though her cheeks burned.

'Marm,' she said, crossing the room in two steps. 'I'm so
glad you could make it.'

Birch leaned forward into Amy's awkward, one-armed hug.

'Now, now,' she said, 'don't you *marm* me, I'm not a DI at
the moment. I'm just plain old Helen.'

Amy stepped back, grinning.

'You're neither plain nor old,' she said. 'And we all miss you
loads. I'm so pleased to see you out and about.'

Birch nodded down at the crutch.

'I can't wait to be rid of this bloody thing,' she said. 'I'm
amazed you didn't hear me come clattering in here just then.'

Amy rolled her eyes.

'Whose idea was the loud music? In the *bathroom*. I can't believe you caught me giving myself a pep talk, that's mortifying.'

Birch snorted.

'If that's the most mortifying thing that ever happens to you,' she said, 'you're one lucky girl. Now come on through, will you? I've only been here five minutes and I've already been lectured on how to conduct my recovery by three separate people. I don't want to have to talk to anyone else who isn't you.'

Amy glanced back at her reflection one final time.

'You look fabulous,' Birch assured her, 'as always.'

The two women made their way back to the function room slowly, Amy holding open doors, the stopper of Birch's crutch making soft thuds on the carpeted floor. Amy observed her friend as they walked, noting how tired she looked, the purple shadows under her eyes.

'How are preparations going,' Birch asked, 'for this concert?'

Amy rolled her eyes.

'Honestly,' she said, 'it's the last thing we need. This woman – this Eddison Deas – she apparently has sixty million TikTok followers. We're looking at around nine thousand punters in the venue, but potentially hundreds more just hanging around outside waiting to catch a glimpse. *And* it's being streamed live online, so there'll be tech and vans and entourage everywhere. Edinburgh Castle is one of the hardest venues in the known world to secure, as you well know.'

Birch chuckled.

'Oh, don't I know,' she replied.

Amy sighed.

'It's going to be a circus,' she said. 'You know what we're using as a template for policing this thing? The last royal visit. This is just some kid off TikTok, and she gets as much security as the actual Queen did, can you believe that?'

'Given that I'm not sure what TikTok *is*,' Birch said, 'I don't think I'm qualified to comment. But . . . she's a singer, right, Eddison Deas?'

Amy shrugged.

'Supposedly. But also a model, and an actress, and an influencer.'

'Whatever that means.'

Amy laughed.

'You said it. Honestly, I cannot wait 'til the bloody concert's over, so we can stop having meetings about it. You're lucky you're on leave right now.'

As soon as the words left Amy's mouth, she wished she could take them back. She saw in her friend's face how much they stung. She paused, waiting for Birch's reply. They were just outside the function room now: their workmates' voices a clamour only feet away.

'How do you know,' Birch said, 'that I'm not a huge Eddison Deas fan? I am, in fact, *crushed* that I won't get to breathe the same air.'

Amy grinned. She'd got away with her tactless remark.

'And yet a minute ago, you didn't even know she was a singer,' she said. 'Anyway, enough about Eddison Deas. Let's get a drink.'

Amy pushed open the swing door and held it, so Birch could make her way through. As they entered the gathering with its throng of colleagues, she saw Birch wince, just slightly.

'Let me find you a chair,' she said. 'Whereabouts do you want to be?'

Birch threw her a look.

'You don't have to treat me like an old lady,' she said. 'I'm almost better, you know.'

Amy cocked her head towards the gathering, and watched Birch's eyes scan the room.

'Yeah, okay,' Birch said, her nose wrinkling. 'Stick me somewhere out of sight, where people won't cluck over me. This is your soirée, and I don't want people undermining that by getting interested in me and' – Birch made a kind of shrug gesture – 'this whole *thing* I've got going on.'

Amy rolled her eyes at Birch's self-deprecation, but looked around the room for a suitable spot. There was one on the other side of the bar: a booth seat on the edge of the gathering. However, getting Birch across the room without incident proved to be impossible. Amy had taken only two steps in the direction of the booth when she heard the familiar voice of DI Crosbie.

'Helen, you made it.'

Crosbie was advancing towards them, elbowing his way through his clustered colleagues, not taking a great deal of care about jostling their drinks. Amy glanced over at Birch just in time to see her paste on a smile.

'Alan,' Birch said, 'how are things? Holding down the fort?'

'We're doing our level best without you,' Crosbie replied, in a tone that Amy felt could have been more sincere. 'How are you bearing up?'

Birch cranked up the smile by a few watts.

'Amazingly well,' she said, 'I'm working with a brilliant physio, and I feel like I'm improving more every day. The

Claire Askew

main issue is that I'm climbing the walls. Bored out of my skull most days. That, and I can't drive, of course.'

'Of course,' Crosbie said, tilting his head back and looking at Birch from under the rims of his glasses. 'And you're all the way out in Portobello, aren't you?'

Birch shook her head.

'Not at the moment,' she said. 'I've moved in with Anjan' – Birch glanced at Amy, who grinned – '*temporarily*, only temporarily, before certain people get excited. So I'm living in the Quartermile just now.'

Amy waggled her eyebrows at her friend. She'd long been of the opinion that Birch and Anjan ought to move in together, especially given that Anjan lived in the Quartermile. Amy had been known to go on second dates with men she knew to be dreadful, simply because they lived in the Quartermile.

'Lucky you,' Crosbie said, 'getting to be waited on hand and foot, I imagine.'

Birch slanted an eyebrow at her colleague.

'Not quite,' she said. 'Anjan's caseload is through the roof at the moment. I don't see all that much of him, except at night. Mainly I try to sit still and not disturb any of his piles of paperwork.'

Amy's smile faded. She felt a pang of sympathy for Birch, Quartermile or not. It had to be hard living in a glass-and-steel box with stunning views of the city if you couldn't easily get out *into* the city. DCI McLeod had ordered Birch to have a complete rest, Amy knew. No working from home, no nothing. She realised just how bored her friend must be – and Birch hated little more than having nothing to do.

Crosbie wasn't all that interested: he gestured with his half-full pint in the direction of Amy, who looked away.

'All change here, in your absence,' he said. 'How about our DS Kato, then, eh?'

Birch's smile became a genuine beam as she turned it on Amy.

'I know,' she said. 'I'm terribly proud of her. Hearing she'd got this post was the best news I've had in weeks.' Birch fixed Crosbie with a look. 'She'll be a true asset to the team,' she said, and Amy's grin returned. She could hear the subtext: *you had better appreciate this woman.*

'I don't doubt it,' Crosbie said. 'In fact, I've got just the case for our new sergeant. Something to cut her teeth on.'

Amy winced. Crosbie meant well, but he always managed to make her feel small – a thing DI Birch had never done, as her commanding officer. Lately Amy had wondered if Crosbie had sensed her imposter syndrome and decided to feed it.

'What case is that?' Birch asked.

'Well,' Crosbie replied, 'I don't know if you remember that hit and run we dealt with? It's a few months ago now. A boy-racer type in a naff wee car got rammed off the road on East Claremont Street.' He gestured at Birch's crutches. 'He ended up looking like you – his leg was broken in two places, and his motor a write-off.'

'Yes,' Birch said. Amy could see the *looking like you* comment had set her friend's teeth on edge. 'I remember.'

'We thought at the time,' Crosbie went on, 'that it was an isolated incident. Two daft lads racing each other, or something, and things got out of hand. We got witness statements, but haven't been able to find our man – it looked like it might go cold. But just over the past few weeks, we've begun to suspect that that hit and run might be connected to a couple of other incidents we've been looking at.'

Amy saw Birch's eyes widen, just a little. Her interest was piqued. Crosbie noticed it, too, and glanced over at Amy.

'You tell her, Kato,' he said.

Amy lifted her chin. This felt like a test: Crosbie wanted to hear her talk about the case. See how she phrased things.

'So,' she said, 'a little while ago, we fielded a complaint of stalking. It didn't go very far – it would certainly never have got to your desk, marm—'

'Helen,' Birch cut in.

'Right, sorry. It wouldn't have been passed up because the allegation came from one of our regulars. Dear old Banjo Robin, in fact.'

Birch rolled her eyes, as Amy had predicted she would. Banjo Robin had been a vexatious, almost constant presence at Gayfield Square, the station where Birch herself had been a sergeant.

'Typical,' Birch spat. 'I just love the way that man wants the book thrown at other people for the slightest thing, but insists he's innocent of all charges whenever we have to pick *him* up.'

'Well, exactly,' Amy said. 'It seemed like pretty standard Robin stuff, too. He claimed he'd been followed by a tall, thin man in a black car.'

'Followed *where*? Robin's only journeys are to the Captain's Bar and then to our drunk tank.'

'Perhaps followed is the wrong word,' Amy said. 'I mean, he *said* followed, but I think he meant surveilled. He claimed this black car was always around. Waiting for him outside his place, outside his girlfriend's place. Turning up wherever he went. This tall, thin man was watching him.'

'Let me guess,' Birch said, 'Robin was adamant about this, but couldn't provide anything as useful as, oh, say, a registration number . . . ?'

Crosbie chuckled.

'Got it in one,' Amy said. 'We told him there wasn't much we could do. He then tried to upgrade the complaint, saying this man in the black car had in fact run into him, knocked him down in the road. It all seemed pretty spurious, and eventually he was given short shrift. I don't think anyone thought anything of it.'

'But it turns out,' Crosbie cut in, having apparently had enough of letting Amy tell the story, 'that this tall, thin man in a black car has cropped up in a few witness statements as well as Robin's. It was Kato here who noticed it first, the reoccurrence of that same description. She went for a bit of a dig, and found – how many?'

'Four, total,' Amy replied.

'Four reports,' Crosbie went on, 'detailing threatening behaviour of one kind or another, all within the past six months. A tall, thin man in a black car sitting outside the same address all night. A tall, thin man in a black car approaching local sex workers in Leith, asking questions they didn't want to answer. Robin's report of surveillance and being knocked down. And guess what the witness statements from that original hit and run said?'

Birch was nodding, though it wasn't a yes/no question.

'The other vehicle,' she replied, 'was a black car.'

'Driven by a tall, thin man,' Amy cut in.

'But no make or model on the car? No reg? No further description?' Birch threw Crosbie a look that said, *this is a reach*. 'I mean, I'm guessing there are a fair few tall, thin men driving black cars around the greater Edinburgh area.'

Crosbie was wearing a wry smile, and though Birch's tone was withering, the smile didn't fade.

'Sure,' he said, tipping his pint glass slightly towards Birch, 'the details are sketchy. But what's interesting – what Kato

brought to my attention, really – is not what these witness statements have in common, but what the *witnesses* have in common.'

Birch looked at Crosbie, waiting for him to elaborate. When
he didn't, Amy picked up the tale again.

'They're all small-time perps,' she explained. 'If I told you
all the names, they'd likely be as familiar to you as Banjo
Robin. The kid in the hit and run had a string of priors for
minor drug offences. The address this tall man supposedly sat
outside one night was a house we've previously raided. The
sex workers who say the tall, thin man approached them all
work for one James Able.'

'Oh yes,' Birch said, 'he was another of my Gayfield Square
regulars. Drug offences there, too. Among other things.'

'Right,' Amy said. 'And of course Banjo Robin is an ad hoc
dealer, as you know. So you can see why I got interested.'

Crosbie gestured with his pint glass again, cutting in.

'Basically,' he said, 'if this tall, thin man is the same man
every time, then he's someone who's suddenly taking a keen
interest in the city's small-time lowlifes.'

Amy threw Birch a look that said, *I'm sure you'd figured that
out for yourself.*

'You think a message is being sent?' Birch asked. 'Is this a
bigger fish going after bottom-dwellers who've strayed into
his territory?'

Crosbie cocked his head to one side.

'Could be,' he said. 'That's what I think is happening, to be
honest. It's just the criminal ecosystem doing its thing, and
that's fine. We're used to that, we can deal with it.'

'*My* worry,' Amy said, 'as I've expressed to DI Crosbie,
is that the tall, thin man is a new arrival. I think it's worth
noting that none of our witnesses were familiar with him or
knew where he'd come from. You know how it is, when you

pull someone like Banjo Robin in – they always have a theory, someone they want to point the finger at. But in all these cases, no one had any idea who this guy was or who he worked for. He seems to have no story. And Robin and his pals seem genuinely spooked.'

'They just like it to be *aye been*,' Crosbie said, grinning. 'These small-timers, they like what they're used to. Some new Billy Bigbaws arriving in town gets them jittery. That's all.'

Birch frowned. Amy could tell she was surprised by Crosbie's blithe amusement.

'It'd get me jittery, too,' Birch said. 'We know that finally nailing Solomon Carradice left a big vacancy, for example. We've talked about this, haven't we, Kato?'

Amy nodded, and looked over at Crosbie from under her eyelashes. She'd brought that very concern to him only a couple of weeks before. Solomon Carradice had settled into his twelve-foot-long retirement apartment in HMP Barlinnie almost two years ago, having spent decades running a crime fraternity with links all over Europe and in Russia. Amy knew Birch had been waiting to see if one of Carradice's goons – or one of his rivals – might decide to try and fill the old man's shoes. Crosbie had waved the idea away.

'I did wonder,' Amy said, deciding to try again, 'if this tall, thin man was making a play for Carradice's spot at the top of the pecking order by starting at the bottom. Winning the respect of the small-timers first. These incidents all feel like someone flexing their muscles, don't you think? Someone saying *I'm keeping an eye on you, so don't get out of line.*'

Birch looked convinced, but Crosbie was wearing the same face he had when she'd first spoken to him about it.

'Surely, though,' he said, 'if there was a new bastard on the block, he'd want to make a splash. Do something more decisive, send the message all in one go. If this bloke were a serious threat – I mean a Solomon Carradice – level threat – we'd have found Banjo Robin in bits in a bin bag, wouldn't we?'

Birch was quiet for a moment, considering the two sides.

'Maybe,' she murmured.

'On the other hand,' Amy cut in, 'I'd argue that ramming someone off the road and leaving him unable to walk is no small gesture. This man is clearly willing to inflict serious harm.'

Crosbie shrugged.

'If it's even the same man each time,' Crosbie countered.

Amy swallowed down a sigh. She knew she'd inherited DI Birch's tendency to let a hunch take root, but she also knew Crosbie sometimes let pedantry get in the way of policework. Following a hunch was no bad thing, she felt, even if it didn't lead anywhere.

'Anyway,' Crosbie went on, 'it's early days, and not much to go on, but I think our newly minted Detective Sergeant Kato is the perfect woman for the job. I feel very confident knowing that the mystery is in her hands.'

It was all Amy could do to prevent herself from turning to Birch and openly facepalming. Crosbie had a way of spinning kind words so that they landed like a slap. But Birch was looking at Crosbie.

'Alan,' she said, 'any chance of a drink? I'm parched, and honestly I'm not sure I can face hobbling over to the bar.'

Crosbie's eyes widened.

'How rude of me,' he said, in the same tone he'd used for *we're doing our level best without you*, earlier. 'I should have offered. What'll you have?'

'Just a tonic water,' Birch said. 'With a slice of lime.'

Crosbie snorted.

'You don't want anything stronger? That doesn't seem like you.'

Amy closed her eyes for a moment. Birch nodded downwards, towards the crutch she was leaning on.

'Wouldn't be the best idea,' she said, 'given the painkillers I'm on.'

Crosbie spluttered.

'Oh. No, of course, right you are. Yes. Tonic water and lime, coming up.' He glanced at Amy. 'Kato, anything? It's on me.'

Amy straightened up. It was after five, no one was going back to the office now. She realised she felt irritable: Crosbie's various microaggressions had stung her.

'Well,' she said, 'if you're offering, Alan, I'll have a Manhattan, please.'

She watched as he tried not to wince.

'Dry,' she added, 'not sweet.'

It was clear Crosbie wasn't entirely sure what to do with the information he'd just been given, though in a place like the Raeburn, he knew what it meant for his wallet. He gave a vague nod and reeled away in the direction of the bar.

'You're a wicked woman,' Birch said, righting her course towards the booth.

Amy flipped a section of hair over her shoulder.

'Well,' she said, 'I wanted rid of him for a bit. It'll take them ten minutes to mix that cocktail.'

Birch grinned.

'I need to learn your ways,' she said.

Amy shrugged.

'I just go on a lot of dates,' she said. 'If you're stuck with a tedious guy, you might as well have a decent drink while he bores you to death.'

Birch made it to the booth, and Amy reached out to take the crutch while her friend slid into the seat.

'You okay?' Amy asked. 'You're not in pain, are you?'

Birch laughed.

'I'm fine,' she said. 'I'm telling you, I'm nearly better.'

Amy slipped into the booth opposite Birch, her brow creasing.

'Don't frown at me,' Birch said. 'I promise, I'm fine. But here's a piece of free advice for you: don't ever get shot, yeah?'

Amy was still frowning.

'I'll try my best,' she said.

Birch went quiet. Her gaze seemed to loosen, as though she were looking through Amy, rather than at her.

'It's a weird one,' she said, eventually. 'That case he's given you.'

'I think I gave it to myself, really,' Amy said. She nodded towards the bar, where Crosbie was watching the barman with his eyes narrowed. 'I don't think he was best pleased.'

'No,' Birch replied, 'he wouldn't be. You picked up on something he'd missed, after all. I mean, God forbid any of us actually pay attention.'

Amy laughed. The barman threw an empty cocktail shaker into the air, letting it spin there before catching it again.

'He's not so bad, really,' she said.

Birch nodded.

'No, I know. I'm just salty about being out of action. Be careful, though, won't you? It might be nothing, this case, but it could also be something.'

'You think?'

Birch was still nodding, a slow, contemplative nod.

'I do,' she said. 'Banjo Robin's a pain in the arse, but those kinds of guys do have a function. Crosbie's right: they're set in their ways. Invested in keeping things the way they like them.

When those blokes get loud, or go quiet, or seem spooked, there's usually something to it. Canaries in a mine, you know?'

'I do.'

Birch looked down at the tabletop.

'A tall, thin man,' she said, almost to herself, 'in a black car.'

'Spooky, right? Reading the witness statements, I've started picturing a vampire.'

Birch looked up at Amy again, more present in the room somehow, as though she'd surfaced out of water.

'Arresting a vampire,' she said. 'Now *that* would be a coup.'

Saturday, 20 March, 17:30

At first, I didn't understand what I'd done that night. I drove along Bonnington Road in a sort of trance, not realising one headlight was smashed and the other extinguished completely. I was lucky to make it to where I was going without being stopped, the car banged up as it was, bonnet loose and rattling. My hands shook on the wheel as I crawled up Spey Street Lane and parked in the only available space. In the streetlit dim, I paced the car's length on wet cobbles, appraising the damage. I'd been right: the kid's Civic had certainly come off worse, but I'd need a new front bumper. The headlights would have to be replaced. The bonnet could maybe be hammered out, resprayed, but it would cost. In the distance, I could hear sirens. I realised then why I'd autopiloted my way into Spey Street Lane. I knew a guy: his tiny, one-man body shop was feet away from where I'd parked. It was shuttered at that hour, but I stood in the cold and dark and thumbed a text to him, saying I'd just run into a wall. Around me, hail began to batter down, but I was numb. I knew I couldn't drive home.

Black Golf, I wrote, *parked in the lane. Keys are through your door.*

Needles of ice smattered against the body shop's grille. The lane was a blind tunnel of lock-ups, gutters gubbed with leaf mould, a smell of engine oil. I decided I had no choice, pushing the Golf's keys through the narrow letterbox. They landed on the concrete floor inside with a metallic splash.

That night I flagged a cab and got home soaked and shivering. I walked from room to room for a while, my mind racing, making me do stupid things: the next day, I found my toothbrush in the fridge, laid on the rack at the top of the door beside a tube of tomato puree. I went to bed and lay awake, so wired that I thought I might throw sparks. I was thinking about the kid in the Honda Civic, playing back the evening's mental tape again and again. I was waiting: for the phone to ring, for the heavy knock at the door, two pairs of police-issue boots on the mat and me with the chain still on, deciding whether or not to come quietly. I did nothing for days, waiting. I thought a lot about what I'd say when they came to arrest me, fretted over solicitors and how much they cost. I flinched at every vibration of my phone, though it was never the dreaded call. My acquaintance in Spey Street Lane got in touch about the Golf, texting *head on into a wall, you ok pal?* I paced the floor and thought for an hour before texting back, *aye, just a mental skid, mate. Oil on the road I think.* He wrote back *bonnet needs replaced sorry* and I let myself exhale. *Anything it needs*, I replied, *just do it, and let me know how much.* He told me it might be a week, and I went back to waiting.

It never came, the knock at the door, and I let myself relax, slowly, slowly, one nerve ending at a time. I picked up the car, paid cash and added a handsome tip, hoping the extra notes would say *don't ever tell anyone I was here.* I drove home braced for blue lights in the rear-view mirror, and when they also didn't appear, I let another few nerves uncurl. I got to feel normal again, and then almost proud: I'd done a good thing, after all. I had held a bad guy to account, and gone unpunished. Perhaps the universe was on my side, I thought. Perhaps I really was in the right.

It was an evening in late March when I next ventured out for a drive, sick of being walled up in the flat alone. It was the equinox, blossom just starting on the trees. It had been one of those dramatic Edinburgh days of intermittent rain and shine, the sun turning banks of cloud a volcanic purple, and every half-hour or so, a rainbow. I drove in the last of the light along Lauriston Place, Forrest Road, then hung out to turn right into Chambers Street, waiting for a trio of buses to pass: 27, 42, 23. I was just pottering round the block, I told myself – sticking to the Old Town streets, windows down, blowing the cobwebs off. At the end of Chambers Street, I waited at the light, turned right again, and then left at Black Medicine Coffee on to Drummond Street, the cobbles thrumming under my wheels. I wanted to be off the main drag, away from South Bridge and Nicolson Street – I wanted to dawdle in first gear and look into windows, catch glimpses of other people's lives. St Leonard's police station wasn't far from where I was, but I was pleased to find I didn't much care. I figured if they were going to pick me up for a hit and run, they'd surely have done it by now.

I made a right on to Roxburgh Street, thinking I'd dogleg through and along Richmond Place. I'd lived up this road, years ago, in the first-floor tenement flat on the front of number 8. I slowed the car to a crawl, drawing level with the stair door. It was painted a smart navy now, not the dull, scuffed red I remembered, though the fat brass number 8 was the same. I found myself nosing the Golf into an empty bay and looking back in my mirrors at the dark blue door. It used to stick, I recalled, and was rarely locked as a result. Once inside the stair you could get through into the weedy little back green without a key. I felt a sudden rush of nostalgia, imagining I might be able to stand in that weird little space once again. It must still be the same: an odd rhombus of concrete flags with dandelions in every crack, washing lines on poles and downpipe-crazed backs of the tenements pressing in. I knew that tonight, it would smell of rain, and my whole body yawned towards the thought of standing out there, just for a minute. I'd killed the engine and reached to unbuckle my seatbelt when I heard the shout.

It shook me – woke me, almost – from my deep nostalgia trip. I swivelled to look back along the street, but couldn't see the source of the noise, even when it came again. A yell without words, like a human bark. The angry battle-cry of a drunk.

And not just any drunk. I saw him now, shambling backwards into the road, his face cocked up towards a lit window. Banjo Robin: an Edinburgh legend, for better or worse. I'd known of him for years, run into him plenty of times on the Meadows the same way every local resident had. Sometimes he'd be busking, other times slinging his wares, coat pockets lined with tiny baggies of powder and generic pills. I'd forgotten all about those run-ins, but knew instantly it was him, even before a woman pulled open the sash and leaned out of that second-floor window, yelling *C'mon, Robin, away tae fuck* into the deepening night.

I shifted in the driver's seat until Robin was framed in my rear-view. He was wearing that same tattered coat, and a long pale-coloured scarf with stains I could make out from five yards away. I watched as he swayed on the crown of the road, then righted himself, his head tipped back.

'Fuckin let me in,' he yelled, and the echoes reverberated against the tenements. 'Ah'm no leavin 'til ye hand over ma money.'

'Nae danger,' the woman yelled back. In windows up and down the street, curtains had begun to twitch.

Robin rolled his shoulders back. He stooped, staggered forward, and lifted an object from the gutter. Then he stepped back, raised his arm and pelted the missile up in the woman's direction. It fell short; from the clatter it made as it returned to the pavement, I guessed it was a beer can.

'Ah'll murder ye,' Robin howled. 'Ah'll fuckin murder ye. Yer bairns an aw.'

I felt a fizz of delicious rage pass through me, warming something in my core, the way the first strong dram on a night out can do. I'd felt it before: this was the feeling I'd had up on George Street that evening, watching the Honda Civic kid cut up the woman at the roundabout. I itched to get out of the car, sprint over the road and administer a kicking: I knew Banjo Robin was in no position to put up any kind of a fight. But this was a decent street, inhabited by the sort of people who'd have no problem with calling the police. Someone probably already had, and St Leonard's was only a couple of blocks away. I'd committed a hit and run only weeks ago in the very car I was sitting in. Tempting as a beating was, I had to be smart. And so, with a degree of effort, I stayed put, watching as Robin wheeled and yelled, continuing even after the woman had closed the sash and pulled down the blind. I felt my own vexation spangling in my blood, my pulse hot, hands tight on the steering wheel. I waited for the sound of sirens, but they never came.

'Ah'm no done wi ye,' Robin yelled, his voice cracking with the strain of sustained invective. 'We're no fuckin done.'

He lumbered momentarily out of sight, then reappeared in my driver's-side wing mirror, shambling along my side of the street now, moving towards the car. I could have opened my door and sent him flying, but I stopped myself. As he passed, he must have felt my gaze's angry heat, because he looked down and, just for a moment, we locked eyes. He smirked at me, knowing I must have witnessed the past ten minutes' behaviour, and caring not at all. I was looking at the face of a man who'd always got away with things: a man who'd been a threat, a drag, a nuisance all his life. A siren started up at last, too late, too far away: Robin had already rounded the corner on to Richmond Place. I turned the key, fired up the Golf, and followed.

Friday, 16 July, 20:55

It was a Friday night, the end of a dry, sunny week, and a mauve-coloured haze of barbecue smoke hung low in the air over the Meadows park. Anjan's flat looked out over Coronation Walk, its cherry trees a diagonal green corridor to Melville Drive, and Marchmont Road beyond. Anjan had set up one of his Eames chairs beside the picture window, so Birch could sit with her feet up and watch the comings and goings of the park. She hadn't told him yet that doing this wracked her with longing: down on the grass she could see little gaggles of folk who'd clocked off for the weekend and come to lounge in the warm air with beer and food and guitars. She could see overzealous young men playing frisbee and teetering on slacklines they'd looped around trees. Running between the barbecues were happy dogs. Even trapped behind glass on the very top floor of the Quartermile, Birch was sure she could smell the charcoal smoke, the warm crushed grass. Had she gone down to sit cross-legged on the grass among those people, she'd never – in spite of the hours of physio – have been able to get up again. Anjan wasn't fussed about the great outdoors – and to him, *the great outdoors* very definitely included parks. He wouldn't understand the frustration Birch felt at being shut in, watching the streetlights on Leamington Walk light up all at once like a distant pinball machine.

It was the end of her fifth week at Anjan's place. She sat in the Eames chair and counted the days. It felt like a lifetime, and no time at all, because every day was roughly the same.

She slept badly, partly because of the pain, but also because her brain was busy thinking about all the things she wasn't doing. The emails that must be piling up in her inbox, the paperwork she hadn't done. She also dwelled on Operation Kendall and Gerald Hodgson – on all the things she'd said and hadn't said and should have said. She stayed in bed late every morning, trying in vain to catch up on lost sleep. Anjan forbade her to shower when he wasn't there, frightened she'd slip on the vast stretch of wet-room floor and hit her head. Birch didn't like showering at night, but took his point – she was much steadier on her feet than she had been, but still not one hundred per cent. It took her a long time to feel fully awake, without the shower's warming morning jolt. The whole flat was spotless, cleaned twice a week by a kind but quiet woman Birch made cups of coffee for. She'd promised McLeod – and Anjan too – that she'd relax, not overdo things. But relaxing in a glass-and-steel box was hard. Birch pined for her sagging sofa, its covers worn butter-soft across the armrests. She longed for her scrappy back garden, the peeling bench she'd angled to catch the best of the sun. Watching daytime TV in Anjan's much too classy flat felt wrong. Mostly, she wandered back and forth between the kitchen and the smart Eames chair to make cups of tea and soup and rinse the dishes. In between, she read books she'd ordered online in pairs, one copy for herself and the other for Charlie. In the years her brother was missing, she'd often found herself finishing a good book or film or episode of TV and wishing she could phone him up to gush about it. His being in prison these days meant films and TV were out, but she had come to love the little Birch family book club they had going on. It gave them both something to talk about: there was only so much she could say about work, and Charlie spoke only a little about the everyday inner workings of the jail. He had to be circumspect: having a senior police officer for a sister was a major handicap for him. Charlie had landed in the infirmary once already over accusations of being a grass. A rat. The thought made her flinch, though she knew the various other bad things her wee brother had done. She tried to imagine him happy enough, stretched on his bunk with a book, walking out in his mind through the barred doors, through the high fence, and into an alternate world.

Tonight she was looking forward to reading the next few chapters of a novel by Kirkland Ciccone – *Happiness Is Wasted On Me,* the cover declared. She was liking the book, but she'd promised herself she'd fill out Dr Jane's therapy journal before she went back to it, and the journalling was proving tricky. Her thoughts kept drifting back to Crosbie and Amy and the case of the tall, thin man. Banjo Robin was small fry, but he knew everyone – everyone, apparently, except this guy. Amy really didn't like it, Birch had been able to tell – it didn't sit all that well in her own mind, either. She looked down at the book and wondered idly if her brother might have heard something around the jail – was someone finally planning to challenge for Solomon Carradice's place? And would Charlie tell her, even if he knew?

Giving up, she clicked 'submit' on the half-hearted, half-finished journal entry, closed her laptop, and placed it none too carefully on the rug beside the chair. Her phone had slipped out of her pocket and down the chair's seam. She reached for it, wincing, imagining lint and crumbs under her fingernails, but of course, Anjan's cleaner wouldn't have stood for that. She had no notifications, except for one from the phone's news app: *Eddison Deas breaks records for fastest-selling tour of all time.* Birch rolled her eyes, and swiped the headline away. She found the number she wanted and hit *call*. Amy picked up after only one ring.

'Hey, stranger.'

Birch blinked.

'*You* answered fast.'

There was a pause.

'My phone was in my hand,' Amy replied.

'Hmm. Why do you sound guilty right now, Kato?'

Another pause, this one longer. Birch laughed into the silence.

'Look,' Amy said, 'I was on Tinder, but I was just looking.'

'I told you you'd not be able to stand it for three months!' Birch cackled, and the laughter made her hip hurt.

'I never said no Tinder for three months,' Amy shot back. 'I said no *dating* for three months.'

'And Tinder is an app for what, exactly?'

Amy sighed, but Birch could tell she was smiling.

'It doesn't count,' she said, 'if you don't swipe right on anyone.'

'Oh, I see. You're exempt due to a technicality.'

'Exactly. A loophole, if you will.'

Birch felt a pang of longing then. She wished she could be perched on a bar stool somewhere, Friday-night music in the background, clinking glasses and laughing with her friend. In spite of what her physio had said, right at this moment a bar stool felt like it might be for ever beyond her.

'Anyway,' Amy was saying, 'what can I do you for?'

'Yes, sorry. Don't worry, it's nothing major, I know I'm interrupting your weekend.'

Amy snorted.

'Some weekend,' she said. 'I'm sitting in my PJs with a pile of paperwork.'

'. . . and scrolling Tinder.'

Birch practically heard Amy roll her eyes.

'You don't *scroll* Tinder, you swipe. But of course, you wouldn't know. You don't need to concern yourself with such things, what with having bagged a handsome lawyer, and all that.'

Birch winced. She'd been trying not to think about Anjan unless he was actually in the room with her.

'It's about this case,' she said, raising her voice just a little to emphasise the subject change. 'I've been mulling it over a bit.'

'Too much time on your hands,' Amy replied, 'that's your problem. You ought to discover Netflix.'

'No, seriously. The more I think about it, the more I wonder . . .'

Birch paused. She wasn't sure how to go on.

'What is it?'

'Okay,' she said, slowly. 'This is off the books, right? McLeod can't hear about it, but . . . I'd like to get on board with this. You know, help out a bit.'

She imagined Amy raising an eyebrow.

'Like I said, too much time on your hands.'

'Well, yeah. You're not wrong about that. But also . . . Crosbie thinks this isn't a big deal. He's given it to you because he believes it's probably nothing. Something easy for you to cut your teeth on, wasn't that what he said?'

Amy's tone went cold.

'Something like that, yes.'

'Right,' Birch said. 'And I mean, fine – but what if it *is* a big deal? What if this tall, thin man *is* the next Solomon Carradice? Are we really going to let another bastard of that calibre get his feet under the table in this city, all because we didn't want to properly follow up on a hunch?'

Amy laughed.

'Aha,' she said, 'we have a famous DI Birch hunch on our hands.'

'Oh no, we don't. This is a DS Amy Kato hunch, I think you'll find. It's your thorough policework that has pulled all this up. It's *your* nose we're following.'

'We?'

'Yes, we. I want to get involved a little, if I can. If you'll let me. I think this tall, thin man deserves more scrutiny than he's getting, and heaven knows I could use the distraction, Kato. I'm going out of my mind over here.'

Amy was quiet for a moment.

'I know,' she said. 'I know, and I do sympathise, but . . .'

'C'mon, don't be a narc. I mean it, I'm going mad. Think of this as a bit of freelance consulting work. Just to tide me over, 'til I'm back in action.'

'Did you just say *don't be a narc*?'

Birch rolled her eyes.

'Yes. I know, I'm old and uncool, don't change the subject.'

There was another pause on the line.

'Can you imagine,' Amy said, 'what McLeod would say if he could hear this call?'

'Probably nothing. There'd just be a mushroom cloud go up.'

'There would, and that's what worries me. You're on *leave*, Helen. Besides, there isn't enough work here for two of us to do. I'm literally just cross-checking witness statements and keeping my ear to the ground.'

'There are other things that could be done,' Birch said, 'if I was working on this off the books.'

'Such as?'

'Well, my first thought was that I could go and see Charlie. Find out if he's heard anything. You know what the prison whisper network is like – if this guy has ever been inside, someone will know who he is.'

Amy sighed. She was coming round to the idea, Birch could tell.

'That's true, but—'

'And I could maybe arrange to run into a couple of our witnesses,' Birch went on. 'It would be totally coincidental, of course. Banjo Robin isn't a difficult man to find. It's been a while since I've seen him, we could have a little catch-up. The two of us go way back, after all.'

'Helen, I'm really not sure. McLeod would have my head.'

'If he found out. Which he won't.'

Birch could hear the distant swish of traffic on the other end of the line, and the rattle of Amy's sash windows whenever a bus passed.

'Come on,' she said. 'Give a miserable woman something to do, won't you? I can't just sit around here not doing any work for much longer, it's driving me out of my mind.'

'Speaking of driving,' Amy said, 'how would you get around? You can't do much from Anjan's living room, can you? And I know for a fact that your handsome lawyer will not be aiding and abetting you in this little scheme by taxiing you places.'

Birch closed her eyes for a moment. She didn't love the solution to this problem, but it *was* a solution.

'I thought I could ask my dad,' she replied.

Amy spluttered.

'Seriously?'

'I know, I know. But hey, since the shooting, he's desperate to spend more time with me, make up for his forty years of bad fathering. I think it really rattled his cage.'

'And you're going to exploit that.'

'Absolutely. He didn't teach me much, but he was always the king of exploiting a situation for his own gain, so why not?'

'You're terrible.'

Birch could hear the smile in Amy's voice. She was going to agree.

'Not entirely,' she said. 'He's understimulated, my father, and that's not good for someone who's trying to stay off the drink. It'll give him something to do. Something to think about.'

Amy laughed.

'I guess so,' she said.

Birch's heart fluttered.

'So you'll let me get involved? I promise I won't overreach. You're the boss, this is your case. I'm just helping you out.'

'Honestly,' Amy said, 'it sounds like I'm helping *you* out. I'm only condoning this because I know how nuts you're going. And don't go thinking you'll get to do anything major, okay? You're getting constable-level tasks at best.'

Birch grinned, though Amy couldn't see her.

'Ah,' she said, 'the good old days.'

'And if McLeod gets wind of it—'

'Which he won't.'

'Okay, but if he does, I'll deny all knowledge. We never spoke about it, you just got involved on your own.'

'Great idea,' Birch said, her grin still fixed. 'You try that out on him and see how it goes.'

On the other end of the phone, Amy was shuffling around. Birch could hear the rustling of papers.

'I need to sort some stuff at this end,' Amy said, 'but . . . Monday?'

'Just when you're ready,' Birch replied. 'Email me whatever you think might be useful to look over, and we'll go from there.'

Amy was saying something, but a sound from the doorway behind her made Birch's heart spatter. She twisted around in the chair. Anjan was standing a few feet away.

'Listen,' Birch said into the phone. Her pulse was suddenly gunning: she felt like she had as a teen, when her mother walked in and caught her on the third hour of a phone call to one of her school pals. 'I'm sorry, I've got to go.'

She ended the call without waiting for Amy's reply. Anjan's mouth was a tight line.

'Who was that?' he asked.

Birch swallowed hard.

'My dad.' She didn't even try to make it sound true.

'It was Amy,' Anjan said, his voice flat. 'I only asked to see if you'd lie.'

Birch gritted her teeth. It was something she'd started doing, at the start of her recovery, and it seemed to have become a habit.

'How long have you been standing there?'

Anjan shrugged.

'I heard most of that call, if that's what you're asking.'

He hadn't moved. He looked like a sphinx, immaculate in his heather-grey suit, in his glass-walled, marble-topped flat. Birch turned away again. It hurt too much to keep looking at him.

'I can't believe,' Anjan said, 'that you're taking on work. After all that we've talked about, Helen.'

He clicked across the hardwood towards her, and Birch looked down at the phone in her hands. The screen lit up with a text from Amy: *Everything okay?*

'Helen?'

Anjan was standing in front of her now, demanding her full attention.

'Amy's asking if everything's okay,' Birch said, still not looking up, though the phone screen had faded to black. 'And it's not, is it?' She could feel the prickly heat of tears building. 'Everything really, really isn't okay.'

Anjan sank into the chair opposite her own. She refocused her gaze to look at his brogues, the windows' seam of late light reflected by their shine.

'I know,' he said, 'that you're finding this hard. You're thinking about Operation Kendall all the time – I know you are, even when you say you're not. You're cooped up in this place not able to drive, not able to go about your life. I understand how frustrating it is, I promise, I do.'

'No,' Birch replied. 'I don't think you do.'

Anjan paused for a moment, then went on as though she hasn't spoken – a lawyer's tic, one she particularly hated.

'What I also understand,' he said, 'is that it's tiring. Living this way, walking with a stick, being in pain. Exhausting yourself with physio. And then going to bed and barely sleeping at night.'

Birch looked up at him at last, in surprise.

'You thought I hadn't noticed that,' Anjan said, 'when I'm right next to you?'

'Well, I'm sorry to have disturbed your rest,' Birch said. She didn't sound sorry at all.

'Oh, for heaven's sake. I don't care about my rest. I care about yours. I care that you're secretly taking on work when you're this tired. This isn't nothing, is it? You've been *shot*. Your body is exhausted.'

'Okay,' Birch snapped, 'fine. But what about my mind? I've got absolutely nothing to do, and I'm losing the will to live, Anjan. I can't carry on like this.'

'You can. You must.' Anjan was sagging in his chair. He looked weary, Birch realised, and she wondered what her own face was doing, because after a pause, he softened his tone. 'My love,' he said, 'you could do yourself permanent damage if you don't find some patience. If you don't give your injuries time to heal. I'm worried about you.'

Birch looked down again, at the phone in her hands. Amy's words refracted in the centre of her vision, her eyelashes slimy with tears. *Everything okay?*

'There's this case . . .' she croaked.

Anjan passed one hand over his brow.

'Of course there is. Of *course* there's a case, Helen. There's always a case. Haven't you ever noticed that? There's always something, coming between you and your wits' end.'

Birch's mouth fell open. A single held-back tear escaped down her face, and a moment later she tasted its salty sting.

'Well, yeah,' she spluttered. 'I mean . . . that's just how things are, isn't it? That's my job. It's your job, too.'

He was shaking his head.

'I don't—' Birch blinked, and now her whole face was wet. 'Anjan, we *talked* about this. When we first got together, we talked about how our work—'

Anjan stood, rapidly, his shoes squeaking on the wooden floor.

'I know what we talked about,' he said. 'I know we said some rather stupid things to each other, about both being married to the job.' As he said this, Anjan raised the fingers of both hands and made a bunny-ears gesture in the air. Birch almost laughed – it was a thing she'd never seen him do. But he was still talking. 'Things have changed now, don't you see that? Back then, we were just – I don't know the word for what we were doing.'

Birch swiped at her damp face. When she looked down at her hand, it was streaked with mascara.

'Dating?'

Anjan gave his head a little shake.

'We were . . . exploring a mutual attraction that I think had existed between us for a long while,' he said. Again, had his face not been so stern, and had pain not started to flicker through the lower half of her body, Birch might have laughed at his fastidiousness. 'But now,' he went on, 'things are different. You could have *died*, Helen.'

Birch shook her head. She wanted to tell him not to be so dramatic, but of course he was right. It was a thought she'd had herself, many times, usually in the small hours of the morning. Had the shot been fired a half-second sooner. Had Gerald Hodgson shifted his aim just a little . . .

'That changed everything,' Anjan said. 'It has changed how I feel about you. About us, about everything. I don't want to be so married to my job, going forward. And I don't want you to be married to yours.'

She looked up at him, feeling her eyes widen. She'd always loved how Anjan approached his work: needing to keep his head in the game at all times, even if only a little. Him being that way allowed her to be the same, gave her a free pass to cancel plans or put a pin in her personal life if ever she was called to Fettes Avenue.

'I wish you'd use this time,' he was saying, 'to step back from it all. Figure out if it's what you really want. If it's good for you.'

The remark landed and stung. Under the vague ache of her hip, Birch felt a different pain – a sharp one, somewhere in her chest. A needling feeling, with a voice that said, *he's got a point*. She felt her mouth curl into a snarl, partly in response to that voice.

'I think I know,' she said, 'what's good for me.'

She wanted to stand, but knew she couldn't do it decisively, the way he had. Instead she eyeballed him from the chair, hoping her smeared mascara didn't look pitiful. She waited to see how he'd respond, knowing from bitter experience that the lawyer in him was always keen to win the argument. But after a moment, his shoulders dropped. He raised a hand to his face again and rubbed his eyes.

'Fine,' he said. 'You're right. You're a grown woman, you can live your own life. I've tried to take care of you, since—' Anjan gestured vaguely at her wounded hip, trailing off. 'Because that's what everyone said to me, when you were discharged. The nurses, your father, McLeod. *Take care of her, Anjan.* And I promised I would.'

Birch looked down again at her hands, the phone screen gone dark. The snarl was ebbing away, as quickly as it had come.

'And I've tried,' Anjan said, his voice worn out. 'But you don't like it. You don't *want* help. Don't want it, or can't accept it. So, fine. You know what's good for you.'

'Anjan—'

But he had already stalked away. Birch listened to his footsteps as he moved along the hall to the bedroom, where the hardwood floor gave way to carpet and the sound stopped. Outside, the park was a deep bowl of dusk, punctuated by the little lights of barbecues and lit-up phone screens. Snatches of laughter floated up, and although Anjan was only metres away, Birch felt the familiar tug of her own loneliness. She shuffled forward in her chair, groping on the floor for her crutch. She should get up, go through to the bedroom and apologise, patch things up at least. But just as she'd levered the crutch upright, she heard the boiler fire and the smatter of water: Anjan had got in the shower. She let the stick slide to the floor again, careful to keep it from rattling. The argument had been brief, far less barbed than others they'd had in the past, and yet she felt exhausted. Birch tipped her head back, letting her damp cheek hit the chair's leather back and stick. She closed her eyes to think.

★

When she woke, the flat was filled with pink light. Her neck was stiff, and for a solid minute she didn't know if she'd awoken or was still stuck in a dream. Her bad hip hurt, and though she could feel a chill in the room, she was warm. There was a blanket over her, tucked down into the chair's folds. She blinked. Sunrise: that explained the pink light. The park below was pinstriped by the long, blue shadows of trees.

Birch flailed out of the blanket and knuckled upright in the chair. She'd missed a dose of her pain meds, and her head felt unusually clear. Her phone was wedged against her thigh, and she thumbed it alive: 5.22 a.m. The longest she'd slept in all these weeks.

The crutch was propped near her elbow, and she felt a sudden swell of gratitude for Anjan, for the blanket, for not having to bend and retrieve the wretched stick from where she'd left it on the floor. The words she'd exchanged with Anjan came back to her in flashes, and she winced. What did he mean, he didn't want her to be married to the job? What other option was there?

She stumbled across the living room; the space between it and the kitchen's peninsula unit felt like the length of a football field. On the worktop was a note, in Anjan's elegant hand: *Didn't want to wake you, hope that was the right decision. I'm down in the gym, back soon. I'd like to talk some more. Love, A.* Beside the note was a water glass and a box of Birch's pain meds. She gave the paper only a cursory glance before popping the pills from their blister pack and swallowing two in one go. Her throat felt full of cotton wool, and she remembered she'd been crying.

I'd like to talk some more. She squinted at the words. Pain nudged around in her hip like a restless animal. I can't, she thought, not now. I haven't got the strength.

She stood for five long minutes, considering her options, waiting for the pills to start their work. The urge to run was strong, but she hadn't run – or tried to – since the shooting. She realised almost after the movement began that she was creaking down the hall towards the bedroom, where the few possessions she'd brought lay scattered here and there: clothes in a suitcase, her books on the floor in a haphazard stack, a perfume bottle, jars of pills. She saw how her presence in this place had knocked Anjan's neat and organised world off-kilter. Looking at the crisp, made bed, the nightstand on his side a tidy cube, a new weight settled on her for the first time. She saw the burden of her own care, the job Anjan had taken on, and gasped at her own ingratitude. *I think I know what's good for me.*

Had she been fit, the packing would have been swift, a few minutes' work. It took her twenty, the crutch stubbing little moons into the carpet's pile. She fretted that Anjan might come back before she was done, and half hoped he would. But soon enough she'd zipped the case, made good her tear-stained face with a make-up wipe, and called a cab. The explanation she left for Anjan was just one line, a quick scribble added to his note as she turned for the door: *Can't do this, I'm sorry. H x*

Saturday, 17 July, 06:45

J ane Ryan stood in the little triangular bay of her living room window, her hands wrapped around a mug of steaming coffee, and watched the comings and goings of the street below. Living on the Canongate was a blessing and a curse. Her flat was a beautifully renovated attic space right in the heart of the Old Town: if she happened to be in at 1 p.m., she could hear Mons Meg sound its blast, and on Hogmanay, her roof terrace offered a view of the Castle fireworks that money couldn't buy. However, there was also a taxi rank across the street from her stair door, and even five floors up, the racket of Friday night was sometimes too much to sleep through. Last night had seemed especially loud. Now, bleary but awake, she watched a street-sweeper chug its way along the pavement, sucking up chip pokes and ticket stubs and gum. A see-you-Jimmy hat hung askew on one corner of the taxi rank sign. A woman in last night's lamé minidress picked her way along the pavement, a thick pair of men's sport socks pulled over her feet, stilettos dangling from her hand. Her shoulders were back, her head high: she was daring the few passers-by to think whatever they liked.

'Good for you, doll,' Jane breathed, though she prayed the woman made it home without encountering any broken glass.

From behind her, a familiar sound: the stretchy little meow that Ginsberg, her huge ginger tomcat, only ever made as he woke up from a deep sleep. She gave her head a little shake, and turned just in time to see him slouch into the room, yawning.

'Good morning, sir,' she said, in the same bright voice she always used for Ginsberg. 'It's not often I'm awake before you.'

Ginsberg let out a crabbit little croak.

'I know,' she replied. 'Where's the food, already, woman?'

She crossed the room and squeezed into her little galley kitchen, the tiled floor already warm from the early-morning sun streaming in through the skylight. Ginsberg followed her, his tail a fluffy question mark, and meowed at her as she pattered a handful of tiny, meat-scented biscuits into his bowl.

'There you go, Your Maj,' she said, lifting him on to the counter to eat. This was a daily ritual, but for some reason on this occasion she was reminded of a man she'd dated once, the aversion he'd had to Ginsberg. Cats shouldn't be allowed on kitchen surfaces, he'd claimed. She'd blinked at him and asked just what control he thought she had over this half-wild animal who lived with her. The relationship had fizzled out soon after, and she'd felt relief.

'Love me,' she said, listening to Ginsberg purr as he crunched happily through the kibbles, 'love my cat.'

She wandered back into the living room, her slippers scuffing on the thick carpet, where her laptop was plugged in and charging on the drop-leaf table she called her home office. Realising she'd left her half-empty coffee mug on the worktop next to Ginsberg's bowl, she tutted, and flipped open the laptop's lid. The computer came to life with a pinging sound, and she watched as various notifications began to stack up in the taskbar. Several of her clients had logged their electronic journals in the last twelve hours – more than she'd expected.

She skipped the few steps back to the kitchen, and reached over the still-crunching Ginsberg for her mug.

'Sorry, babe,' she said, as he startled. 'I'm going to need this.'

She settled herself on the old dining chair that went with the table. She'd been meaning to replace it for years: it was too high, and the back too upright, and it played hell with her spine. She bent into that familiar, knuckled curve now, as she clicked on the first of the notifications. The journal host site opened up, and the entry loaded. It was from DI Helen Birch.

'Oh,' Jane said, aloud. Had she been a betting woman, she'd have put money on Helen Birch dodging the task altogether. She was glad to find she'd been wrong.

Birch had sent in her journal around 9 p.m. the night before. As her mood, she'd chosen *frustrated* from the list. The entry that followed seemed rough, sketchy, but Jane reached for her notebook to take down any useful observations it might hold. *Five weeks at Anjan's*, the entry began. Birch had then written the explanatory note *(my partner)*. Ginsberg pat-patted out of the kitchen and wound himself around Jane's legs as she began to read.

'Hello, boy,' she murmured, scrolling with one hand, reaching down with the other to ruffle the cat's soft fur.

Five weeks. Feels like more. Or does it? Feels like for ever I've been here, being fussed over. (I'm beyond sick of being fussed over, I know that's very ungrateful of me.) But only feels like five minutes since Operation Kendall. I think dreams are important in therapy. I think I've read it somewhere, is it true? If so, I should probably record here that most nights I dream that I'm back in that house with Gerald Hodgson. Sometimes I get to do the whole negotiation again and this time I do it better, I do it properly, and no one has to fire a gun or get hurt or die. Those are the good times, until I wake up and I realise I'll never get the chance to go back and actually fix it – it's already done, I already did it wrong. Other times it goes like I remember it in real life, only then something changes and it gets worse and worse and worse. Gerald Hodgson shoots me and then himself, or he shoots me and then runs out and shoots McLeod, or Anjan's somehow there in the house and he shoots Anjan. Often I'm frozen and I can't do anything or even shout for help and I just have to watch everyone get hurt. The worst times are the times when I have the gun and it's me, I'm shooting, and I shoot indiscriminately, at everyone I can see. I don't have that one so much but when I do I wake up in a cold sweat and hope it's the last time. Does this mean I'm out of control? Does it mean I've been really messed up? Because sometimes it feels like it, and that's pretty scary.

Anyway, I didn't mean to write any of that, really. I was going to write about being here with Anjan. It's weird. I understand that it's a good idea to be staying here for now. In theory. I do get that. I get that I shouldn't shower when he's not here, that it's sensible to wait until night-time. I should sit and rest and not do stuff because that way I'll heal faster and better. But I miss being able to do things by myself without someone else telling me it's a bad idea or they're worried about me. I miss driving, the freedom it gives me. I miss my own house and my own stuff. I've even started to miss the dusty skirting boards and all the jobs around the house I haven't done. And Anjan's not here much, he's working hard as usual and I'm on my own most of the time, but I'm somehow missing alone time, too. Does that even make sense? In this house I don't feel truly on my own. Not alone with my thoughts. Or something. I'm out of my element. I don't think it's doing me any good.

I feel mad. Crazy, I mean, not angry. Although if I'm honest, maybe a bit angry, too. Is that because I am *mad? Or is it just because I'm here?*

Thursday, 3 June, 20:08

I'd been tracking Robin's movements for a few weeks. It started that first night: from Roxburgh Street, he'd shuffled up to the junction where Nicolson Street becomes South Clerk Street, then down to West Cross Causeway and into the university's George Square – a pedestrianised block that backs on to the park – so I couldn't follow. Annoyed, I'd revved around the slow bend at Potterrow, down to Tollcross, and hung left on to Melville Drive where, to my delight, I picked him up again. It started then, with that lucky guess at his shambling direction. It made me feel like a spy.

I had time on my hands, and Robin was a thorn in the city's side. It was a game, following him – it tested me in ways I liked. I'd let myself lose sight of him deliberately, then guess at where he was heading. Dog-leg down Guthrie Street and there he'd be, coughed out of a ginnel in the Cowgate. Parked on the Grassmarket I'd get to laugh as I watched him slalom, half-cut, down the treacherous steps past Brown's Place. My sense of the city's map got sharper, the Old Town tenements an endless possibility of rat-runs and switchbacks. What was more, he'd clocked I was following him. He looked over his shoulder now, with furtive eyes. Although we never acknowledged one another, I saw I'd rattled him: I'd seen him spot the car as I slowed to a purr at fifty yards out, the swagger fading out of his gait. It was worth it for that alone, though his routine was largely dull. I got to know the pubs where he drank, and the ones he was barred from. I sat outside his various girlfriends' addresses, sometimes hearing voices raised and objects thrown. And I watched his countless small-time deals: Robin on a pre-arranged street corner, hands in pockets, trying to be nonchalant until the customer pulled up. They'd stop, but never park – just put their hazard warners on and idle while Robin got in the passenger side. I'd time them: twenty seconds max, if all went well. Longer if haggling went on, or for disagreements, of which there were some. But mostly Robin would light out of the car and go, walking as fast as his characteristic shamble would allow, while the driver peeled out from the kerb and they both carried on like nothing ever happened.

I'd started to wonder what I was doing, to question whether I might be going mad. I wanted a confrontation with Robin – passively watching him sweat wasn't doing much for me after a while. I'd thought that the next time he raised his voice to some woman in some flat somewhere, I'd kick in the door and give him a doing – that or interrupt one of his passenger-seat deals. I wanted to feel something. Specifically, to feel the way I'd felt that night with the kid in the Honda Civic: like a vigilante, righting a thing gone wrong in the world. Following Robin had started like that, seeing him shrink back under my gaze. But now I was bored, and itched for something different to happen. Then, as though I'd made a wish, it did.

One evening, Robin led me a merry dance that ended on Salamander Street. This was the furthest from the Old Town that we'd ever been together: a long, slow, stop-and-start tail down Easter Road, across Leith Links, to the street I eventually guessed was Robin's destination.

Salamander Street was still a sort of prostitution-tolerance zone, though not that many girls still worked the kerbs. I scoffed at Robin. Of *course*, I thought – of course he's the sort of john who'd opt for a girl off the street, the cheap bastard. I parked on Bath Road, among the lorries, and watched him, one crooked shoulder propping up the side wall of the Pond pub. It took a while, but a woman appeared, her phone in her hand. It was twilight, but the main road was still pretty loud, and I zipped down my driver's side window to listen to them talk.

'Time d'ye call this, hen?'

I rolled my eyes. Robin straight in there with his classic charm.

'Dinnae start,' the woman fired back. 'I'm havin a *night*, okay?'

I liked her voice. She had an accent, maybe Polish, maybe Russian, but with Scots superimposed on top like paint lashed over a damp wall. It made me smile.

'Fuck's wrong wi yer face?'

I was too far away. Her face just looked like a face to me. I'd put her at thirty-five, maybe forty, her long brown hair a wig or else heat-straightened into static bars.

'It's fine.'

'It isnae. Whit's that oan yer face?'

He reached a hand towards her, and she flinched away.

'It's make-up,' she said, 'will you leave it?'

'Aye, make-up coverin fuckin *whit*? It's aw roon yer mouth, hen.'

The woman reached round, flicked a compact from the back pocket of her too tight denim skirt. She studied herself.

'It's *fine*,' she said again, and though I didn't see the eye-roll, I could hear it in her voice.

'Looks rank,' Robin said.

I felt the insult land in the beat she left before speaking again.

'So dinnae look at it. C'mon, Robin, I've got a half-hour.'

Robin hawked and spat. The woman did a high-heeled dressage step away from the wet star he landed at her feet.

'Ye hink ah'm goin wi ye when ye look like *that*? Ye hink ah'm wantin *herpes*?'

'It isn't—'

I knew what he was going to do, perhaps even before he did. Robin raised both arms and planted his hands on the woman's shoulders, shoving her hard, so she tottered backwards. Her arms windmilled for balance, and she dropped her phone. I heard the inevitable sugary crack as the screen shattered.

'Fuckin skank. Ah walked aw the way doon here, an fer whit?'

Robin's voice was raised. He'd seen me follow him through the town, but seemed to have forgotten I was there. I started the car, in an attempt to remind him.

'It isn't herpes,' the woman was saying, but she could see his mounting rage and was backing away, palms up. 'C'mon, you can trust me.'

'Trust ye?' Robin laughed. The woman backed down off the pavement, on to the cobbled road, and he followed. 'Trust a fuckin worthless hoor?'

I put the car in gear and revved the engine, but Robin was lost in the moment. He was a man whose life held precious little power, and when he could wrest power back for himself, he was energised.

'Okay,' the woman was saying. I could see her glancing over his shoulder, wanting to get back and retrieve her damaged phone. 'Fine, I'm sorry. I'll just go, okay? Just let me get ma phone, an I'll go.'

'You owe me,' Robin snarled, advancing, his hands held out towards her. Something flared in my brain like a match, and my vision flickered. I pulled out of the parking space, tyres squealing on the dusty setts. Robin's head flicked up, terror registering on his face as I gassed the car towards him and then, just as suddenly, braked. I'd misjudged the distance a little: the front bumper buckled his knees and he went down, one arm thumping the bonnet as he went. I expected the woman to scream, but she didn't. As soon as Robin hit the ground, she high-tailed over the road for her smashed phone, to coorie it up in her hands like a baby bird.

I sat in the car, listening to the engine's purr, and Robin as he cursed and roared on the ground.

'That's fuckin attempted murder,' he yelled, putting his greasy palms on the bonnet and hauling himself upright, apparently unhurt. 'What the *fuck*.'

A couple of drunks had filed out of the Pond pub, having heard the ruckus, but I wasn't especially worried. They nudged each other, sniggering, as Robin groped along the car to my open window.

'The fuck *are* you, sunshine?' Flecks of his spit landed on my cheek, but I kept my face calm.

'Sick and tired of your shit, Robin,' I replied, so quietly he had to lean in. 'Sick of people like you.'

He snorted at me, but I could tell he was rattled. On the pavement, the woman was glued to her phone, jabbing the shattered keypad with increasing frustration. I imagined the bruises that must be blooming on Robin's haggard body, and smiled.

'I've had enough,' I heard myself say. 'There's going to be a reckoning in this town.'

Robin put both hands on the car roof and then pushed off like a swimmer, listing back out into the road.

'Attempted murder,' he said again, pointing a finger at my face. I grinned.

'Bullshit. When I decide to murder you, you'll be dead.'

The words surprised me, but I can't have shown it, because I saw Robin shiver.

'Ah'm gaun to the polis,' he said, loping away. He walked sideways, not wanting to take his eyes off me or the car. 'Ah'm fuckin reportin this. An you followin me an aw. Ah'm reportin ye.'

'Be my guest,' I said, though a slight flicker of fear ran up my neck. He wouldn't, surely, I told myself. And if he did, they wouldn't take him seriously. Right? But either way, it was too late. Robin sidled round the corner and out of sight.

The drunks looked disappointed as they drifted back inside. I realised I was still parked in the middle of the road, so shoved the Golf in reverse and backed up to the kerb. The woman was sitting there now, her arms wrapped round her torso, her legs shining bluish-white through chicken-wire fishnets.

'You all right?' I climbed out of the car and rounded the bonnet towards her.

She scowled at me, and held up her phone to show me the ruined screen.

'Vot eto *pizdets*,' she hissed.

I stopped walking.

'I'm guessing that . . . isn't good?'

'Fuck off.'

I felt slapped. Hadn't I rescued this woman?

'Hey,' I said, 'I just did you a favour.'

She didn't speak, but sucked air through her teeth.

'It's only a phone,' I said.

'Oh, *fuck* you.' The Scottish veneer was gone from her voice: I guessed she must put it on for the johns. 'This phone is my business. Without it, I can't work and I starve.'

She flipped the phone out of her hand, as though skimming a stone on to the water of a lake. It scuffed across the cobbles and landed near my feet. I could see the screen was bleeding colours, the whole thing absolutely fucked.

'I'll buy you a new one,' I said, deciding I would only as the words formed on my tongue. 'Give me your address, and I'll order one for you.'

The woman gave me a hard look for a half-second, then threw back her head and laughed.

'What are you, a policeman?' She looked me up and down, amused. 'You must be new.'

'No,' I said.

She snorted.

'Only police expect *shlyukhi* like me to say where they live.'

'It isn't a trick.'

I took a step towards her. Robin was right, there *was* something about her face. Something strange, under the make-up.

'Sure thing,' she spat.

'I wanted to help you, just then.' I gestured back to the spot where Robin had hit the road. 'And I want to help you now. With the phone.'

'I want to help,' she smirked, mimicking me. 'This is what men always say.'

I took another step. Now I could see the gooseflesh on her arms.

'Would a policeman hit a guy with his car?'

She thought for a moment, then shrugged.

'In my country? Sure.'

'Where's your country?' Yes, her skin was puckered around the mouth and down the chin – I could see, in spite of the foundation she'd ladled on. 'You're from Poland? Russia?'

She scowled.

'You're nosy,' she said.

I put my hands up, as though she'd pointed a gun at me.

'Look,' I said, 'I'm sorry. I thought he was going to hurt you.'

She jutted her chin up at me.

'I can take care of myself.'

I paused for a moment, then crossed the rest of the way to the kerb and sat down beside her, pulling my knees up and hugging my arms around them, the way she had done. I felt her flinch, but she stayed put.

'What happened to your face?' I asked.

She turned to look at me. Close up, I could see the ruckled skin was angry, pink under her pan-stick. She blinked, then looked away.

I sighed, then twisted round and pulled my wallet from my back pocket. I felt her watching my hands as I took out a twenty-pound note and held it out.

'What happened to your face?' I said again.

The purple note was pinned between my index and middle fingers. She looked at it, then back at the wallet in my other hand.

'Okay,' I said. I pulled out another twenty, and felt the two notes' papery rub as she took them from me.

'James Able,' she said after a pause, disappearing the twenties into her skirt pocket.

'I'm sorry?'

'You asked what happened to my face. James Able.'

I frowned.

'That's your pimp?'

She laughed.

'He wishes. That's why.'

I didn't understand, and she rolled her eyes at me.

'It's acid,' she said, 'okay? James Able threw acid on my face. He said I'm on his patch, I take punts from his girls. He said he'd make me too ugly to work.'

A ripple of something passed through me then. Something cold, then hot. Disbelief, followed by rage.

'Are you serious?'

She gave me a hard look. Our faces were close together, but she didn't seem to care. She had to be pretty comfortable around men, I guessed.

'You think,' she said, 'that I would joke about something like this? This is my face now. For ever.'

She lifted one hand and ran her fingertips over the skin around her jaw. It looked waxy and numb where she touched it.

'I'll hurt him,' I said, and my voice sounded strange. I didn't know why I was saying it, but it felt true. There was a metallic taste in my mouth. 'I'll hurt him for you.'

She looked at me as though I'd just told her I was Santa Claus.

'Why?'

I blinked. My stomach was turning slow circles. I thought about acid, the slow chew of that pain. Her face.

'What do you mean, why?'

She let out a short, fluttering laugh.

'I mean, why do you care? You're not my father. You're not even a john. I'm just some whore you never met 'til now. So, why?'

I swallowed, but the metallic tang refused to go away.

'Because it's wrong,' I said, aware I sounded petulant. 'Because it's fucking *wrong*, and I'm tired of it. Tired of these guys doing anything they want, and nothing happening. I can't stand it.'

She raised one pencilled eyebrow at me.

'Perhaps you should *become* a policeman.'

I shook my head.

'They're useless.'

She made a sort of chucking sound in her throat, a strange kind of laugh.

'Something we agree on.'

'You reported it, right? This attack?'

Now she laughed properly, but her voice was cold.

'They told me to,' she said, 'at the hospital. But what's the point? They'd drag me to a room and ask me questions, then do nothing – except maybe find some reason to put me in a cell. I know what it's like. I've – how do you say it? I've *helped with their inquiries* before.'

I looked at her thin hands, their immaculate nails.

'Tell me how to find James Able,' I said.

She shook her head, smiling a strange, twisted smile.

'You're weird,' she said.

She pressed both palms on to her drawn-up knees and unfolded on to her feet, the movement smooth and fluid.

'Tell me.'

She was looking at her ruined phone, its splintered screen still glowing faintly in the road.

'I don't know,' she said. 'I don't know where you'd find him.'

'I think you do.'

She shrugged.

'I'm telling you,' she said, 'I don't. I'm not one of his girls. You'd have to ask them.'

She stepped into the road, walked over to the spot where the broken phone lay, and looked down at it. I glanced at the wallet, still nestled in my curled hand.

'Hey,' I said.

She turned and looked at me.

'Can I give you a lift home? I figure it's the least I can do.'

She threw up her hands, laughing.

'I'm still not going to tell you where I live.'

I shook my head, and held the wallet up until she looked at it.

'I'm saying,' I said, slowly, 'that I'd like to take you home.'

I saw that she understood, because she tilted her head upwards and pushed her shoulders back. She glanced one last time at the phone, now lying dark and useless at her feet, and then looked back at me.

'Deal,' she said.

Sunday, 18 July, 10:35

As soon as the cab had arrived, Birch switched her phone into silent mode. For twenty-four hours, she'd watched the notifications stack up: missed calls from Anjan. Anjan: new voicemails. Anjan: seven texts received. She wasn't looking at email, but she guessed he'd probably tried that, too. This was a man who was accustomed to being listened to. She knew from past experience that being ignored was Anjan's kryptonite.

'It's for your own good,' she said aloud, as the eighth text notification in a row flashed up on the screen. 'You're better off without me.' Her voice sounded sad and strange in her empty house. Being home didn't feel as comforting as she'd hoped it would.

The cab driver had taken her as close to her house as he could, making a laboured many-point turn in the narrow lane beside her back gate. He'd prattled to her about Eddison Deas and the concert, the number of visitors it would supposedly draw and how good a weekend of fares it promised to be. Birch had nodded and *yeah*-d until she'd paid and climbed out of the cab and he'd helped her in through the gate. Then she'd closed it, practically in his face, and shoggled down the garden and in through the back door. The little house's familiar rooms seemed stale somehow, dusty from sitting unlived in for five weeks. Though she'd slept through the night in Anjan's chair, Birch took herself to bed and stayed there all of Saturday, watching her phone screen light up and then fade with each of his fresh attempts. She'd lain fully clothed in the sheets, listening to the distant, comforting sound of the sea. She thought about Amy, the case, and the tall, thin man. She thought about her dad: rehearsing the words she'd say when she summoned the strength to sit up and give him a call. She thought of her CID Ford Mondeo, parked for safekeeping in the covered lot at Fettes Avenue, and pined for the way it smelled: coffee and hot dust. She lay there for hours, watching the sunlight move around the walls, because lying still kept her bad hip quiet. At last, when all the light had ebbed from the room, she'd stretched, sat up and dialled her father's number, delivering the words just the way she had planned in order to make him say yes.

The next day was Sunday, and Jamieson turned up late, as Birch had assumed he would. She'd got up early to give herself time to shower and dress – a slower process in her cramped bathroom – then sat on the back garden bench in the sunshine, waiting for her dad to show. Her phone was less frantic than it had been: Anjan had clearly said his piece. From the snippets the preview pane showed her, she could see she'd need to respond: *Helen, I really think we need to discuss* and *I want you to clarify with me what*— It could wait, she decided. She was taking some time. *Time is medicine,* that's what her physio had said. She made a mental note to repeat that phrase to Dr Jane, see what she made of it.

'Sorry, hen.' She'd been on the bench for twenty minutes, ready to leave, the house all locked up behind her. Her father crashed in through the back gate, giving a little start when he saw her there. 'Bastard traffic. An see getting a space doon here, oan a Sunday? Honestly, nightmare.'

'Hi, Dad.'

Jamieson let the gate swing loose behind him, and sauntered down the path towards her. He'd always been a wiry man, but these days he was skinny, worn thin with being off the drink. When he reached her and bent to kiss her on the cheek, Birch saw in the V of his shirt the deep cleft around his collarbones.

'How're you daein, lassie?'

Birch braced one arm against the bench, ready to haul herself upright.

'Can we start with an easier question?'

Her father frowned, but seeing she wanted to get up, extended an arm to her. When she took hold of it with her free hand, she could feel the effort he was making, the tendons tightening as he braced to help bear her weight. Jamieson was in his seventies now – she forgot that sometimes. It was hard to keep track of a man who'd been absent so long.

'We can talk about you first,' she said, as he passed her the crutch. 'How are *you* doing?'

Jamieson shrugged.

'Ach,' he said, as she'd known he would, 'jist daein away.'

'You always say that.'

'It's always true.'

They walked back up the path together, Jamieson hovering closer than she needed, as if he thought that at any moment she might topple over into the grass. As they reached the gate, he skipped ahead a step or two to hold it open for her.

'Any work on at the moment?' she asked, as she passed him.

He followed her out, turning his back on her for a moment to pull the gate shut. Birch noticed, as she always did, the peeling paint she'd been meaning to strip and redo since she moved in, but never had.

They set off up the back lane, her father keeping in step with her. He rubbed the back of his neck with one hand, close enough for Birch to hear the gesture's dry rasp.

'It's aw a wee bit slow the now,' Jamieson replied. 'July. Holidays an that.'

Birch nodded. Her father did odd jobs for a variety of tradesmen friends. She didn't approve of a man his age shifting pallets and mixing cement, but she also liked knowing he was active. Out of the house. Having these feelings surprised her sometimes: she found herself thinking, *so this is what it's like to have a dad.* It was distinctly odd. She wasn't looking forward to the day Dr Jane inevitably asked about family.

'Well,' she said, 'that's actually no bad thing.'

They reached his little van, abandoned diagonally in its space with one tyre up on the kerb. Birch eyed it.

'That's one way to wreck your suspension, Dad.'

Jamieson grinned. He ducked in front of her to open the passenger door, and then stood there as she climbed into the seat. It was like he and Anjan had secretly got together and agreed on the best anxious-hovering technique.

'I can do it,' she said, 'I'm *fine*.' Once she was in and reaching for the seatbelt, Jamieson threw her a wink, before scooping up the crutch and slinging it into the back. She waited until he couldn't see before she rolled her eyes, though whether her frustration was with Jamieson or her own stubbornness, she wasn't sure.

'So.' Her father landed in the driver's seat and slammed the door. 'No bad thing, ye said?'

Birch gave her head a little shake.

'That I've no got much work on. Ye jist said that.'

Jamieson started the engine and swung out of the space at speed.

'Dad.'

'Whit?'

Birch pointed at herself.

'Remember me? Senior police officer?'

'So?'

'So you're still in the thirty limit.'

He squinted at the speedometer.

'Ach right, aye.'

He threw her a look out of the corner of his eye, and must have seen the flat line of her mouth.

'You're no oan active duty, though, are ye? So that's a free pass for yer auld man, is it no?'

Birch sighed.

'C'moan, Helen.' Jamieson prodded her with his elbow. 'Go an cheer up, hen. We're away tae see yer brother. Ye cannae walk in oan a man servin twelve years in the jail wi a face like that, now, can ye?'

Birch held back another eye-roll. She wanted to snap at him, but knew her dad had a point.

'All right,' she said, telling herself she could unclench her jaw: the pain this habit had formed around was nowhere near as strong these days. 'Sorry, it's just . . . I've had a bad weekend.'

They pulled up at a traffic light, and Jamieson glanced at her.

'Ah thought as much,' he said. 'Ah'll admit, ah wis wonderin why I wisnae pickin ye up fae the flat. Fae Anjan's.'

Birch felt herself wanting to flinch at his name.

'We had a row,' she said, her voice small.

'Youse two?' Jamieson's eyes widened. Birch wondered why he was surprised – wasn't it obvious that she'd have spent all these weeks at Anjan's pinballing back and forth between irritation and gratitude?

She shrugged.

'I wanted to get back to doing some work,' she said. 'Anjan would rather I stayed in my sick bed indefinitely.'

She knew this wasn't fair even as she said it, but still, she said it.

'Are ye ready tae work again, hen? Ye still cannae drive . . .'

'No, I know. But this isn't my phased return or anything. This isn't *official* work.'

She saw her father's mouth twist as he suppressed a laugh.

'Och aye,' he said, '*I* see. A wee bit extracurricular, eh?'

Birch tutted at him.

'Not the sort of extracurricular *you*'ve been known to do. It's not illegal or anything.'

Jamieson pressed one melodramatic palm to his chest.

'Illegal? Me? Ah dinnae ken anythin aboot it, officer.'

'Oh, sure.'

He raised an eyebrow.

'So if it's aw above board, then why's Anjan no happy wi it?'

'It's— Look, it's complex, okay? Amy's got this case, and she and I both think it might be a thing. A serious thing, or the start of one. But she's not being supported to investigate.'

'An you thought you'd step in.'

'Pretty much. You have to understand, I was going absolutely barmy in that flat all day with nothing to do. You know what I'm like.'

A brief silence hung in the van, and Birch thought, *oh no, wait, you don't. Not really.*

'An ye're glad I'm no workin, because ye're wantin some help?'

She blinked. Her dad could be pretty with it when he wanted to be.

'I – maybe, yes. Because I can't drive, I thought . . . if I needed to go somewhere, you know?'

'Aye,' he said, 'that's fine. Anythin like that is fine, Helen. Jist call me whenever ye like.'

Birch smiled. He'd liked that, she could tell. He liked being asked for help. Feeling relied on, after all this time.

*

The drive to Low Moss was quiet. Birch had learned that Jamieson generally didn't say much unless he was pushed, and her mind was too distracted to keep a conversation going. He wasn't fussed: once they reached the motorway, her father flicked on the radio and began to sing badly along to a song Birch didn't know. She stared out of the window, trying not to think about Gerald Hodgson, or Anjan, or the tall, thin man. Instead, she thought of Charlie in his cell, counting down the seconds until they moved the route and sluiced the prisoners down out of their halls for visiting. She hadn't been to Low Moss as often as usual since the shooting, and she wondered if she'd see a change in him. She missed him. She found herself wishing she'd finished the Kirkland Ciccone book.

They made it just in time to check in for visiting, Jamieson picking up the twenty minutes he'd run late by speeding on the motorway while Birch turned a blind eye. He was less adept at the check-in process than she was: slower to pass his belongings over to go through the scanner, unsure where to look when they took his photograph. It wasn't that he didn't know the drill: Birch knew her father visited nearly as often as she did. It was maybe the hesitation of the elderly, Jamieson needing more time to process and think – or perhaps it was a symptom of sobriety, his movements slow, each small response a little delayed. Strange, Birch thought, not for the first time – this old man I'm only just getting to know. Strange that he's my dad.

They were the last to file into the Visit Room, and Birch saw Charlie's face relax as he caught sight of them. She felt self-conscious, hobbling through the tables on a stick. Charlie was always in the very back corner, so getting to him seemed to take an age. She liked to walk through the inmates – several of them perps she'd helped put away – with her head high, brisk and businesslike. Her busted hip made that impossible, and she winced with every rattle-click of the crutch, every head she saw turn from the corner of her eye.

'Hey,' Charlie said, smiling widely as she manoeuvred into her seat, 'you're walking better.'

She handed her crutch to Jamieson, who propped it against the table.

'Am I?'

'Totally. Your form's better, or something. Physio must be doing you good.'

Birch smiled. It wasn't like Charlie to be this sweet to her – usually, he'd find any opportunity he could to take the piss. She missed it, in a way, but it was also nice to have a break from the sibling barbs.

'It's good to hear,' she said, 'that you can see a difference. I feel loads better lately. It's working, though I still hate every second I'm on that bloody stick.'

Jamieson made a *pshaw* noise.

'Accentuate the positive, why don't you?' Charlie said, though his tone was not unkind. 'You'll make it, won't she, Dad?'

'Aye.' Jamieson gave her a nudge. 'She's daein grand.'

'And how's the pain?' Charlie asked. 'Still taking the meds?'

Birch nodded. Charlie rubbed his neck, and she saw the gesture her father had made earlier, in the lane, exactly mirrored.

'It sounds like good shit, that stuff they've got you on. If I weren't such a fine upstanding prisoner, I'd ask you to slip me some.'

Birch laughed.

'I swear you're trying to end my career.'

She saw her brother's face change: he'd thought of a zinger but didn't dare deliver it. She rolled her eyes.

'Just say it.'

Charlie nodded at her aching hip.

'Well, just . . . I think you're doing a decent job of *that* all by yourself.'

Beside her, Jamieson chuckled, and sucked air through his teeth.

'Harsh,' he said.

Birch shrugged.

'But fair.' She flapped a hand at Charlie. 'Even if you are a ratbag.'

He grinned. Yes, she thought. *That's* the Charlie I know and love.

Her brother turned to Jamieson.

'How's it going, Dad? Still *daein away*?'

Their father nodded.

'Aye, same auld, ken. Though yer sister's aboot tae gie me an occupation, fae the sounds.'

Charlie looked back at her, his head cocked to one side.

'You finally getting round to some of that DIY?'

She rolled her eyes.

'You're a cheeky swine. And no – it's work. *Work* work. Or . . . kind of, anyway.'

Charlie raised an eyebrow.

'A bit of extracurricular?'

'That's exactly what Dad said.'

They were both grinning.

'Chip off the old block, me,' Charlie said, and Birch felt a strange pang in her chest. I wish that wasn't quite so true, she thought.

'I'm calling it . . . freelance consulting,' she said, 'on the down-low, just 'til I get my phased return. I can't go on doing nothing, I'm losing my mind.'

'She broke up wi Anjan,' Jamieson chipped in. Charlie's eyes went wide.

'We didn't break up,' she said, though her heart glitched as she said the words and a voice in her head said, *oh shit, did we?* 'We just . . . had a fight that has yet to be resolved.'

'Aye, bit she's moved out,' Jamieson said. Birch wanted to elbow him in the ribs, tell him to stop talking about her like she wasn't there.

'I'm getting some space,' she said. 'It's just been a *lot*, being there all the time with nothing whatsoever to do.'

Charlie nodded.

'I get it,' he said. 'No offence, but I've never known how you live with that guy. Bit of a stick up his arse, has he no?'

Birch felt her face flush.

'That's just the thing,' she said, 'I *don't* live with him. I'm not used to it – it doesn't suit me, or something.' She frowned, and saw her brother match her expression. 'But it isn't him,' she said, 'it's me. It's my bloody busy brain.' She gestured at the crutch. 'I'm hating this, that's all. I'm just not managing all that well.'

She'd said it at last, after five weeks of her *I'm fine* lie, and the words made her breath catch. She thought of Dr Jane. Charlie's face was sympathetic, but he shrugged.

'Well, sounds like a bit of work to take your mind off things is just the ticket,' he said. 'I just wonder why you're dragging this lowlife into things.'

He nodded at Jamieson, who beamed.

'Can't drive, can I?' Birch said.

'Yer Da taxi service,' Jamieson cut in. 'Ye might arrive late bit we'll get ye there!'

Birch smiled. Her dad was never so upbeat as when he was sitting with both his kids. She'd tried to give up thinking *you could have had decades of this, Jamieson.*

Charlie put his elbows on the table and leaned in.

'So,' he said, 'is it anything juicy, this work? Anything you can talk about, I mean.'

Birch paused. She already told her brother more than she should – it was a habit she'd vowed to break on several occasions, though she'd never managed to. She felt for him, shut up behind these walls with only bad stuff to think about. More than ever before, she could relate.

'Amy's got a case,' she said, 'but she's not being managed well. Crosbie thinks it's a minor deal, but she and I both think it might be something bigger. He's left her with it, and she needs some help.'

Charlie snorted.

'Crosbie,' he said, 'that guy's a total bam.'

Jamieson's face looked blank.

'He's another DI,' Birch explained, 'at Fettes. He's taken on some of my work while I'm away.'

'Which must be pissing you off,' Charlie said.

She threw him a look.

'I'm trying not to think about it,' she said.

Jamieson still looked confused.

'How does yer brother ken this gadge?' he asked.

Birch laughed.

'Crosbie was the DI in charge of Operation Citrine,' she said, and nodded towards Charlie. 'The operation that landed our kid in this place.'

Charlie rolled his eyes.

'He grilled me for *hours*,' he said. 'Him and McLeod – the fucking odd couple. Crosbie's boring and McLeod's just smug.'

Birch pushed down a smirk.

'I couldn't possibly comment,' she said.

'So what's this case, then?' Charlie cast a glance around the room, presumably to see if anyone was listening in. Birch did the same, but the Visit Room was the usual hum of hushed tones. No one wanted to be overheard here.

'Well,' she said, 'I thought you might be able to help me. Let me know if there's been any talk in this place lately.'

'Talk about what?'

'About the next Solomon Carradice.'

Charlie sat back, putting his palms flat on the table between them. Birch saw his face go slightly pale. Her brother had ratted on Carradice in exchange for an easier term. Unsurprisingly, that didn't make him too popular in jail.

'What do you mean?'

'I mean,' Birch said, 'there's a new scumbag in town. Someone's going after the small fish, and the whole shoal is spooked.'

'He's settling scores, this guy?'

'More like setting up shop, I reckon.'

Charlie frowned.

'And you think it's one of Solomon's guys? I thought they were all inside.'

Birch tilted her head.

'I'd like to think they are,' she said, 'but Carradice had contacts everywhere. I think this is a young pretender.'

'Who's your suspect?'

'That's the thing. These small fish, the ones we've talked to? They don't have a clue who he is. If possible, I like to know the name of every lowlife in my city, and right now I don't.'

Charlie laughed.

'Must be driving you crazy. What's this guy look like?'

'Tall and thin,' she replied, 'that's pretty much all I know. And he drives a black car. A hatchback, maybe a Golf.'

Charlie's eyes were wide.

'That's all you've got?'

'See why Amy needs me?'

'Sure.'

Birch glanced around again.

'So, if there's anything you can tell me . . . has anything been said?'

'This is all news to me, I'm afraid,' Charlie replied. 'If anyone in here knows what this dude's game is, they're keeping it close to their chest. This tall, thin guy – he's white?'

'He is.'

Charlie nodded.

'It's not Iz, then.'

Birch shook her head. Iz – also known as Scissors – had been Carradice's wine-and-dine guy. Mostly, he'd shown high-profile associates a good time, but like all the Carradice goons, he also dished out discreet violence when required.

'It isn't,' she said. 'Besides, Mr Scissors is still inside. You'll be out before he will.'

Charlie raised an eyebrow.

'Don't bet on it,' he said. 'That guy could charm his way out of anything. Mind you, I should have known it wasn't him. Iz wouldn't be seen dead driving a Golf.'

Jamieson laughed, but Birch's attention was caught by a movement on the other side of the room. A member of prison staff – a youngish man bearing the tools and fobs of a regular screw – had clattered into the Visit Room and was advancing through the tables with some speed. He cast around, looking for someone in particular, and even before his gaze landed, Birch knew the someone in particular was her.

'Oh shit,' she hissed.

Charlie turned his head.

'Bloody hell,' he said, laughing as the screw strode towards them, 'Helen Birch, for ever the centre of attention.'

Birch tried to laugh along with him, but she couldn't. She could feel her body flooding with adrenalin: a hot feeling, at the centre of her chest, that spread rapidly outwards into her extremities. Images from the day of Operation Kendall flashed into her mind unbidden: she'd been here, sitting in her car outside Low Moss, when she'd heard the breaking news on the radio that Gerald Hodgson was at large with a shotgun. Only hours later, she herself had been shot and was being wheeled into emergency surgery. Now something else had happened, something urgent, she could tell. She forced herself to pull in a long breath. *Stay calm, Helen.*

The screw arrived at her side. Though her ears were ringing with the adrenalin, Birch was aware that conversation at the tables around them had slowed, or stopped entirely.

'Detective Inspector Birch,' the man said, and she winced.

'Lower your voice, please,' she replied, though she guessed everyone in here knew who she was. Nevertheless, the hush in the room deepened.

'There's a phone call for you, um . . . marm.'

Birch swallowed hard. Yes, something bad had happened. In all her visits, this had never occurred before – not to her, not to anyone else in the Visit Room, as far as she'd observed. She didn't know visitors could get phone calls in the jail. Beside her, Jamieson was already angling the crutch towards her, so she could get up.

'There's been an incident,' the screw said. He glanced at a scrawl of biro on the back of his hand. 'A Detective Sergeant Kato needs to speak with you urgently.'

Birch shot to her feet, forgetting, momentarily, about her hip. Her bad leg twinged, and she flailed against the table.

'Shit,' she hissed, reaching for the crutch. 'Give me that bastard stick.'

'You can take the call at reception,' the screw said, 'but you'd better say your goodbyes. We can't check you in again after this.'

'Will I come with ye, hen?' Jamieson asked.

Birch paused. She looked at Charlie and saw a flash of something pained cross his face. This was his visit, and they'd only just got here.

'It's okay, Nella,' he said. 'You should both just go. You'll need Dad to drive you.'

'I'm sorry, honey.'

'Really, it's okay.' Charlie straightened up in his seat and arranged his face into a resigned smile. 'Good luck.'

Sunday, 18 July, 13:10

'**M**arm, I'm so sorry.' Amy clasped her hands together, making the knuckles white. In spite of herself, she felt nauseous. 'McLeod's on his way, but he's starting from some golf course in the back of beyond, and I can't get hold of Crosbie. I didn't know who else to call.'

She watched as Birch steadied herself against the flank of her father's van, while Jamieson – Amy assumed this was Jamieson, though there wasn't much of a family resemblance – passed her the necessary crutch.

'It's fine, Kato,' Birch said, 'really. You did the right thing.'

The wind off the Forth was unseasonably cold, and Amy was shivering. Her hair – usually worn in an air-hostessy bun – was loose, and she picked wisps of it from the corners of her mouth. It felt weird, being on the job in her Sunday jeans and hoodie. This place, and the chill July day, made it weirder still.

'Better leave your hazard warners on, Dad,' Birch said, gesturing at the van. 'They might think that thing is here to be crushed.'

Jamieson laughed.

'Worked fer a scrapper's once upon a time, ken,' he said. 'An that isnae how it works.'

The scrap merchant's yard was compact, just one corner of a block on the industrial run down the seaward edge of Leith to Seafield. High flats rose up on three sides, and onlookers hung from the balconied walkways, pointing camera phones at the blue flashing lights. On the other side, the crumbling façade of a warehouse, long disused. And all around, twisted spires of metal: car chassis stacked like pancakes, girders in massive, Jenga-like piles.

'Where did they find Able?' Birch asked.

Amy hesitated. She looked over Birch's shoulder, past her, towards Jamieson.

'Oh,' Birch said, 'sorry. Amy, this is my dad, Jamieson Birch.'

Amy did an awkward wave, which Jamieson cheerily returned. He was grinning, apparently delighted to find himself at a crime scene.

'Nice to meet you,' Amy said, 'but . . .'

'Yeah,' Birch cut in. She turned towards her father. 'Dad, you should wait in the van. I'll just be a wee while.'

Jamieson paused, and Amy saw Birch curl her hands tighter around the crutch's grip.

'*Dad.*'

'He can – um.' Amy pushed another strand of hair out of her face. 'You can probably go about your day, Jamieson. If Helen needs a lift home, I can get a uniform to take her.'

He looked crestfallen.

'It's for the best,' Birch said, 'really, you shouldn't be here.'

'Tell ye whit,' Jamieson replied, 'ah'll away an park doon the road fer a wee bit. Go and gie me a phone if ye need me, and if no, ah'll tak masel hame.'

There was a moment of quiet, while Birch considered it.

'Deal,' she said. 'I'll call.'

The two women stood and watched as Jamieson started the van and departed, screeching out of the scrapyard with a spin of his rear wheels.

'Jeez,' Birch said, under her breath. 'He drives like a maniac.'

Amy touched her friend's arm.

'Seriously,' she said, 'thank you for coming.'

'Like I said, it's fine. You okay? You look pretty shaken up.'

'Sorry. I don't know what's wrong with me.'

Birch tutted.

'None of that. I'm guessing you've had a shock, nothing wrong with having a reaction.'

'Okay, but I'm a sergeant these days.'

'Doesn't make you less of a person, y'know. I'm guessing James Able was in pretty fucked-up shape when you got here?'

Amy nodded, swallowing hard, trying not to remind herself in too much detail.

'He was found over here,' she said, pointing, then letting Birch shamble ahead of her. 'Careful how you go, marm. The ground's uneven.'

'Helen,' Birch said, clattering slowly through the yard, 'remember.'

'Whatever,' Amy said, 'we're on the job now. Look.'

They came to a halt a few feet from a scorched patch on the ground. Birch coughed, but Amy tried not to.

'Jesus,' Birch said. 'The smell.'

'I know.'

They stood for a moment, looking at the blackened spot, a rough circle approximately seven feet across.

'So he was doused in something,' Birch said. 'Some sort of accelerant.'

'Must have been,' Amy said. 'We don't know what, yet. But I've texted some photos to Marcello and the lab. Marcello reckons it happened fast: Able didn't really move from this spot, you can tell from the scorch mark. Didn't run, didn't even flail. He just . . .'

'Just burned up.' Birch's face had turned pale, too, which made Amy feel better. 'What did the medics say?'

'Not a great deal,' Amy said. 'They wanted him in the ambulance and gone; it was fast.'

'I'm not surprised. But I mean . . . would you even *want* to survive something like this?'

Amy coughed now, unable to hold it back. The smell was putrid, worse for knowing how it had been made. She wanted to spit, but couldn't bring herself to.

'I'd rather not think about it.'

'He's a big man, Able,' Birch was saying. She was staring at the scorch mark. 'He would have to have been restrained, if Marcello's saying he didn't move about at all, didn't try to run.'

'Restrained,' Amy said, 'or incapacitated.'

'Yes.'

In the back pocket of her jeans, Amy's phone buzzed. As she took it out to read the text, she saw Birch try to look.

'McLeod,' Amy said. 'ETA half an hour.'

Birch looked up at the people above them. The walkways were packed: little kids sat with their legs threaded through the railings, swinging their feet in the empty air.

'He's going to be livid.'

'He is,' Amy said.

'He'll have my head for being here.'

'I know. I'm sorry.'

'It's not your fault,' Birch said. 'It's Crosbie's. Where the hell is he, anyway?'

'It's a Sunday,' Amy said, shrugging. 'Reckon he's the type who goes to church?'

Birch appeared to be considering the thought, but she was still looking up at the flats above.

'That's a lot of witnesses,' she said, after a pause. 'Middle of the day, on a weekend, too. Whoever did this is pretty warped.'

'Someone who wants to be caught?'

Birch shrugged.

'Maybe. Could just be monumental stupidity.' Birch turned to Amy. 'Or it could be something more dangerous. Someone who thinks they'll get away with it.'

Amy frowned.

'You mean . . .'

'Maybe he's got away with other things in the past,' Birch said, continuing as though Amy had never spoken. She pointed at the scorch mark. 'Maybe his behaviour has just escalated.'

'You're talking about our vampire.'

'The tall, thin man,' Birch said. 'We know he'd been show-ing an interest in Able, right? Is *Vampire* what we're calling him now?'

Amy looked back at the scorched earth, tried not to see in her mind's eye James Able's body, still lying there when she first arrived. The smell of it. The terrible sound it made.

'I've been calling him that,' she said. 'But if this was him . . . I dunno. This is less vampire, more executioner, right?'

'Right,' Birch replied. 'This wasn't just a warning. Someone wanted Able dead.'

Amy couldn't look at the black patch any longer. She wanted to walk away, in fact – to walk out of the foul smell's invisible plume, out of the scrapyard, out of the city. She wanted to fol-low the Seafield road until the Firth of Forth rose up to meet her. In spite of the chill in the air, she'd like nothing more than to wade into the sea, feel the salt water scour away the cling of burned flesh and dread.

'If this was the Vampire,' she said, 'then it cements our Solomon Carradice theory. It's real gangland stuff, isn't it?'

'Immolation? Sure.' Birch made a face of pure disgust. 'Very showy.'

'And the audacity,' Amy said, 'of doing it somewhere over-looked like this. I think we were right. The Vampire wants Carradice's seat at the top of the table.'

'It's a calling card, too.'

Amy spun round faster than Birch, recognising Crosbie's voice. She made herself stand up just a little straighter, and then hated herself for it. She wanted to scream *where have you been, I needed you*, right there in the middle of the crime scene, in front of Birch and all the SOCOs and uniforms and gawpers on the walkways above.

Instead, she said, 'Sir.'

Crosbie stepped into the space between Amy and Birch, and Amy heard the creak of a crutch as her friend leaned slightly away.

'He can use this,' Crosbie went on, 'to start building his brand. Inspire fear. Get a crew together, if he hasn't already.' He paused as though for dramatic effect, and Amy tried not to remind herself of their talk in the Raeburn bar just a few days before, when Crosbie had cast doubt on all her theories about the Vampire.

'This is how it starts,' he added.

Amy tried to throw Birch a look, but Crosbie had turned his body in the gap between them.

'I'm surprised to see you here, Helen,' he said. His voice was barbed: Amy hoped he felt guilty for leaving her to set up a crime scene of this scale without her commanding officer, and her only just promoted. 'Isn't DCI McLeod around?'

No, it wasn't guilt, then. Crosbie was stung: he hadn't got there fast enough, and now another DI was on his patch. Worse, probably, that Birch was off the job sick and had still made it there – all the way from Low Moss – before he could. Amy rolled her eyes, not caring if she was in his peripheral vision.

'He's on his way,' she said, her voice cold.

Birch didn't look at Crosbie. She was looking up at the balconies again, the throng of onlookers showing no sign of thinning.

'I answered a mayday call,' she said, 'from a friend.'

Crosbie opened his mouth to speak, but Birch cut him off.

'Though I think you'll agree,' she went on, 'that in the absence of any supervision, Kato has set up a very tight crime scene.'

He closed his mouth, abruptly, like a fish, then opened it again.

'Well,' he said, 'I haven't assessed it yet. I've only just arrived.'

Birch cocked one eyebrow.

'We assumed you must be in church.'

Amy could only see the back of Crosbie's head now: he'd turned to face Birch fully. However, she could see the tips of his ears turning red. Wherever he'd been, it clearly wasn't church.

'I assure you, I got here as fast as I could.' Crosbie rounded on Amy. He was wearing so much aftershave that she could practically taste it. 'Where are we at, Kato? Who are we talking to?'

Amy gestured upwards, towards the walkways, where uniformed officers were now threading their way among the residents, trying to usher everybody back into their homes.

'Uniforms are going door to door,' she said, 'but there must be dozens of properties with lines of sight into this yard. It's going to take a while.'

'Who found the body?'

Amy blinked.

'Sir, Able isn't dead. I mean – sorry to say this, but – not yet. He's in very bad shape, though. I don't think the medics liked the look of it.'

Crosbie coughed. The smell had got the better of him, too.

'Very well,' he said, 'who raised the alarm?'

'A security guy,' Amy said. Birch shuffled a little on her crutch: she didn't have this information yet, and moved in closer to listen. 'The yard's closed on a Sunday, but he was on shift, sat in the Portakabin over there.' She gestured vaguely, without looking. 'He says the first thing he saw was the fire. He thought maybe kids had broken in and torched something.'

Crosbie frowned.

'He wasn't alerted by Able? I would have thought a man on fire would scream like hell.'

Amy shook her head.

'More evidence,' Birch cut in, 'to suggest he was knocked out somehow before being set alight.'

Amy shivered again. This idea was a comfort to her, however thin.

Crosbie was looking down at the blackened patch.

'He did well, this guy,' he said, 'to put Able out.'

Amy nodded.

'It just so happens,' she said, 'he's a retired fireman.'

Crosbie whistled.

'Lucky for Able,' he said.

Birch and Amy exchanged a look that said, *is it?*

'Where's our fireman now?' Crosbie asked.

'Back in the Portakabin. There's a uniform with him. He's pretty shaken up, but wouldn't go to the Royal with the medics. Said he wanted to help.'

Crosbie sniffed.

'Good man. He should be our first interview, I think.'

'Sir, I already—'

Crosbie had turned away, not listening, but he didn't get more than a couple of steps before stopping short. Two uniformed officers were walking towards them across the yard. They guided a woman between them, each steering one of her elbows. She was wearing a long satin kimono, a pair of trainers shoved on to her feet. Amy could see the backs were curled against her heels, like she'd hurried the shoes on without untying them. She was thin, white, and mid to late thirties, Amy guessed. Mascara ran down her face in smears, highlighting what looked like some sort of skin condition that seemed to spread out from her mouth.

'Think we've got something here, sir,' one of the uniforms said. He paused for a moment and looked at Birch. 'Or . . . marm?'

Crosbie flexed his shoulders.

'This is my crime scene,' he said.

The woman in the kimono nudged her elbows out of the uniforms' gentle grip. She leaned towards the officer who'd spoken, but looked straight at Crosbie.

'I'm not talking to him.'

The uniforms shuffled their feet. Everyone looked at Crosbie.

'I hate police,' the woman said. She ran her eyes down Crosbie's body, as though assessing his outfit. Amy noticed it *was* a little haphazard: his shirt was badly tucked at the back. The woman spat. 'Especially *male* police.'

The talkative uniform left his hand hovering in the air, as though ready to take hold of the woman's arm again. He leaned towards her slightly.

'But you *do* want to give a statement,' he said, 'don't you?'

The woman's eyes seemed loose in their sockets. She cast around their small circle of police officers, not seeming to focus on anything. Then she zeroed in. As her gaze landed, Amy felt an urge to step to one side, out of the searchlight of those wild eyes.

'You.' The woman had an accent, one Amy couldn't place. 'I'll talk to you.'

Amy glanced at Birch, then realised too late it ought to have been Crosbie she was looking to. Birch threw her the slightest nod: go on.

'There has to be two of us,' Amy replied. 'I'm happy to interview you, but there has to be two of us.'

The woman sighed a long, ragged sigh. After a moment, she flapped a hand towards Birch.

'The other woman, then. No male police. Not in my house.'

Amy looked again at Birch.

'Your house?'

The woman squinted upwards, then pointed at the topmost walkway, directly across from the yard.

'Up there,' she said. 'That's where I live.' She traced a slow downward line in the air with that same pointing finger, her arm dead straight, drawing an invisible zipwire from the balcony to the oily black star Able's body had left. 'That's why he did this,' she said. 'That's why he did it here.'

★

Amy stood in the woman's kitchen, waiting for the kettle to boil. She looked down at her own shaking hands as she spooned out the sugar she wouldn't normally take. She told herself she couldn't smell the charred flesh smell any more, not here: it hadn't reached this room. And yet it seemed to be everywhere, as though it had snaked into her body and lain down in her lungs like smoke.

The flat was modern, but sparse. Battery-operated fairy lights hanging from drawing-pins pushed in under the kitchen units were this room's only attempt at any sort of décor. Each LED had a red plastic cover in the shape of a ladybird. They cast the plain white bargain-store mugs in a sickly pink light.

Amy had propped the kitchen door open so she could hear as DI Birch began proceedings in the next room: asking the woman's consent to record, stating her own name and Amy's, the date and time.

'Now I need to know *your* name, for the record.'

Birch's voice was kind. Amy felt glad that she was there, instead of Crosbie. He'd insisted on riding up in the lift to the woman's front door, so he could look out over the crime scene – *his* crime scene – from above. He'd hovered as Amy and Birch stepped into the woman's narrow hall, presumably hoping he'd be able to stick around, unnoticed. But the woman had stood on the threshold and held up one flat palm, almost in his face.

'*Nyet*,' she said. 'No policemen.'

'Alyona,' the woman said now, replying to Birch. 'Though the name I use for work is Natalia.'

'It's for your safety, this other name?'

Amy heard the woman make a *meh* noise.

'The clients like it better,' she said. 'Natalia sounds more . . . what word would you say, in this country? More *hooker*.'

Birch gave a soft laugh.

'Personally,' she said, '*I* wouldn't use that word, but I know what you mean. It's okay if I call you Alyona, though, for the purposes of this interview?'

'Please.'

Amy teetered into the room, cursing her still-shaky hands. She clasped the three steaming mugs like a bouquet, their handles gathered, and she could hear their faint rattle. The living room was no less sparse than the kitchen: two leather-effect sofas faced one another across a low, mock-oak coffee table. Birch and Alyona sat on opposite sides, both resting their elbows on their knees and leaning in, like chess opponents waiting for the next move.

'One sugar,' Amy said, placing the first mug in front of Birch. She paused for a moment, as though trying to remember which mug was which, before putting another in front of Alyona. 'Three sugars,' she said. The remembering wasn't necessary: she'd spooned three into her own tea, too.

Alyona lifted the mug in a *cheers* gesture, though her face was twisted, her expression hard. Amy was trying not to stare, but those were such strange marks around her mouth – somehow they were puckered and smooth all at once.

'*Na zdorovie,*' Alyona said.

Amy took a sip of tea, scalding her tongue. She glanced at Birch, who was looking back at her.

'This is your interview, Kato,' she said, once a little quiet had opened between them. 'It's your case. And Alyona chose you to speak to.' She gestured at her phone, which was lit up on the coffee table, the sound recorder running. 'I'm just here to handle tech support.'

Amy let her eyes widen, a kind of silent, useless plea to her friend. But Birch cast her eyes across the table, back at Alyona, so she had no choice but to take a deep breath, and begin.

'Maybe it's best,' she said, 'if you start by just telling us what you've seen today. In your own words.'

Alyona looked down into her mug.

'A bad thing,' she said. 'A very bad thing. I never meant for this thing to happen. I never thought he'd—'

Amy leaned forward. Alyona wasn't crying, but her voice seemed to have dried up. Her mouth hung slightly open, as though she'd been frozen. Amy inhaled, ready to speak again, but out of the corner of her eye, she saw Birch move her hand in a tiny slicing motion. The slightest gesture, but it said, *not yet. Wait.*

Alyona closed her lips, and Amy saw the little marble of bone working inside her jaw. After a moment, she also closed her eyes. Amy glanced at Birch, who carefully raised a finger to her own chin and tapped it. Amy winced, but nodded back: understood.

'What happened to your face?'

She made herself say it, though it was hard – this was a very personal question, and early in the interview, too. She expected Alyona's expression to change as the words landed, but it didn't.

'James Able did this,' she said, quietly.

'He . . . burned you?'

Alyona nodded. Her eyes were still closed.

'With acid,' she said. 'He wanted me to stop working here. On his patch, he said. It was to make me go somewhere else. But this is my *house*.'

'You do incalls? Here, in the flat?'

Alyona opened her eyes again, though she kept her eyes low under their long lashes.

'Mostly,' she said. She pointed one flawless acrylic nail towards the window, beyond which was the crime scene, and the road, and Leith. 'Sometimes I'm out though, if I don't get bookings.'

'Out? Working the kerb?'

'Yes. But not so much. Especially not since—' She trailed off, but turned that same pointed nail towards her face.

'I'm sorry,' Amy said.

Alyona shrugged.

'Wasn't you,' she said.

'Did you report the attack, at the time?'

Alyona gave a grim laugh.

'To the police? No point, honey.'

Amy glanced at Birch, who dipped her head to one side, just once. *Understandable.*

'A minute ago,' Amy went on, 'you said you never thought *he* would . . . do something. Who is *he*? A pimp?'

Alyona's eyes shot fully open.

'I don't work with any pimp,' she snarled. Her manner switched so quickly that Amy held up both her hands, as though the other woman had pulled a weapon.

'Okay,' she said, 'I didn't mean . . .'

'Able didn't like it,' Alyona spat. 'Wanted me to come in with him, be one of his girls. I didn't. Didn't want to. I'm clean, I keep my money. I have a kid. I can't be giving anything to some pimp.'

Amy glanced around the room. It was neat and plain: there was no sign that a child lived here.

'She's back home,' Alyona said, guessing what Amy was thinking. 'She lives with my mother. I send them money, so she can come here soon. Once she's here, I'll give up this work. This is the plan.'

'You didn't want to give up,' Amy said, 'after Able attacked you?'

Alyona shrugged. She still looked irritable after the pimp comment, and Amy wished she could take it back.

'I thought about it,' she said, 'but it's good money. And besides, I didn't want to give him what he wanted.'

'You must have been scared, though.'

'Sure. And it's been harder, with this face. But then . . .'

'Then?'

'A couple of months ago,' Alyona said, 'I got a new regular.'

'A regular client?' Of course, Amy thought as she said the words, what else?

'Yes. I thought he was crazy.' Alyona's face twisted back into the same anguished expression as before: that of someone crying, though no tears came. 'But I didn't think he'd really do something like this.'

Beside her, Amy felt DI Birch sit forward a little in her seat.

'Tell us about this new client. You know his name?'

'Jay.'

'Jay?' Amy repeated it exactly, copying the other woman's inflection. 'As in J-A-Y, the name? Or the initial J?'

'I don't know. I never saw it written down.'

'Okay. Tell us about this Jay. Can you describe him?'

'Tall,' Alyona replied. 'With dark hair. Brown eyes. Very pale.' She gave out a short laugh. 'Though everyone who lives in this country is very pale.'

'What's Jay's build like?'

It was Birch who'd spoken, but Amy had planned to ask the exact same thing.

'Fit,' Alyona replied. 'Like . . . do you say *wiry*? Is that correct?'

Birch and Amy shared a look.

'So . . . you'd say he was tall and thin' Birch said.

Alyona nodded.

'Did he ever come to see you in a vehicle? Do you know what car he drives?'

Amy wanted to relax her shoulders – thankful that her colleague had taken over for a while – but her pulse was kicking up now.

'A VW,' Alyona said. 'A Golf, I think.'

'Colour?'

Amy knew. She knew before Birch even asked the question. 'Black.'

Something passed between the two police officers, like a jolt of static electricity.

'Okay,' Birch said, slowly, 'I need you to tell me everything you know about Jay. Every detail you can recall.'

'I mean . . .' Alyona frowned.

'Not necessarily details of your . . . meetings,' Amy cut in. 'But things like, how did you come to meet Jay? Did he book an incall?'

Alyona shook her head.

'It was strange,' she said. 'I was out that night, I had a booking with someone else, and the guy got upset. About my face. He got kind of rough and broke my phone. Suddenly this crazy man was there, saying he wanted to buy me a new one. Asking me questions.'

'This was Jay?' Birch asked.

'Yes.'

'What questions did he ask?'

'He asked where I lived. I thought he must be one of you people.' Her face twisted as she said the next word, as though it tasted bad in her mouth. '*Police*. I thought he was going to arrest me. But he was strange, too strange to be a policeman. He wanted to know about my face, what had happened. And when I told him, he was angry.'

'Angry how?'

Birch was leaning so far forward in her seat now that her fingertips were brushing the polished top of the coffee table. Amy glanced at her cup of tea, saw a sheen forming on the surface.

'Angry with Able. He said he was going to hurt him.' Alyona's face crumpled once again. 'And now he has. Because of me, this happened.' The look in her eyes changed from one of upset to one of fear: suddenly, she looked the way she had in the scrapyard, when her gaze had barrelled wildly before coming to rest on Amy. 'You have to believe me,' she said, 'I had nothing to do with this thing. It's true that I hated Able, hated him so much for what he did. But I didn't do this. I wouldn't do this.'

'It's all right.' Amy held her hand out, as though Alyona were a spitting cat. 'We know. We're not here to accuse you of anything.'

'You didn't do it,' Birch said, almost at the same time, so their two sentences jangled together, 'but you're saying that Jay did?'

'I'm saying I think so.'

Amy glanced down at the phone, to check the recording was still running.

'He said,' Birch was saying, 'that he wanted to hurt James Able.'

'Yes.'

'This was an act of revenge? Payback for your face.'

'Yes.'

Birch raised her eyebrows.

'He said this the very first time that you met?'

'Yes. Like I said, I thought he was crazy.'

'You didn't think he was serious?'

'No. I hear a lot of *bravada* from men. And he was just some john, I thought. He didn't really know me. And he definitely didn't know Able – didn't know where to find him, nothing.' She made a flapping motion with her hand: *blah blah.* 'I thought it was just talk.'

There was a pause. Birch seemed to be thinking. Amy wondered if she should pick up the thread, but her head was buzzing. She felt sure that the smell of Able's flesh was in the room with them now, thick and bodily.

'And you know,' Alyona added, 'men like Able hurt other people. They don't *get* hurt.'

'You mentioned that Jay became a regular,' Birch said. 'How many times did you meet him, would you say?'

Alyona scrunched her face, thinking.

'I saw him maybe . . . eight times, after that first night. He wasn't obsessive, like some regulars are, but he showed up roughly every few days, I guess.' She curled one manicured hand round the end of the sofa arm, as though she might lever herself on to her feet. 'I can check back in my diary, if you want exact dates.'

'It's okay.' Birch and Amy said the words at the exact same time, and Amy felt herself flush, just slightly. Get it together, Kato, she thought to herself.

'That information could prove really useful, though,' Birch went on, 'in due course. Don't lose those records, if you have them.'

Alyona was nodding.

'So,' Birch said, 'did Jay mention Able again, after that first meeting?'

'Yes. All the time.'

'He talked again about hurting him?'

Alyona made a face.

'Yes. Probably every time he came here, he said Able would pay for what he did to me.'

Birch cocked her head.

'You sound angry about that.'

'Honestly, I was. I didn't want to be saved. So many men, they think we need to be saved, women like me. We don't. I kept telling him, *I'm fine*. And to stop bothering Able's girls.'

'What do you mean, bothering?'

Alyona sighed.

'I said to Jay that I wouldn't tell him how to find Able. I told him I couldn't, that I didn't know anything. I don't think he bought it, but I wasn't going to talk, and he realised that. Suddenly I am hearing from girls I know that this man is asking them questions. A man who looks like Jay.'

'Why wouldn't you give him information on Able?' Birch asked. 'I know you say you don't need to be saved, but . . . wouldn't it have been satisfying? To have Able be hurt, like he hurt you?'

Amy's eyes widened, but Birch wasn't looking at her. Across the table, Alyona was shaking her head.

'I didn't want Able coming back,' she said. 'I was worried Jay would do something, and Able would find out he was one of my johns. The girls were already talking about it. I was scared Able would come and take it out on me. I didn't want him thinking I asked Jay to do something. And I didn't, I promise you. I didn't ask him.' Alyona lifted her left hand and ran the fingertips over her scarred flesh. 'I just wanted to move on.'

'It's okay,' Amy said again, more softly this time. 'We believe you.'

Birch was biting at her bottom lip.

'I'm sorry to have to ask this,' she said, 'in light of what's happened, but . . . did Jay ever talk to you about his specific plans for Able? Did he ever mention, in particular, setting him on fire?'

Alyona seemed to retreat into her own shoulders, just slightly. In a small voice, she said, 'Yes. He did.'

Amy became aware of a new sound in the room: distant, but growing louder. It took her a moment to realise it was the noise of the lift, ascending in its shaft to Alyona's floor. She heard the doors clatter as they opened.

'Okay,' Birch was saying, 'I need you to try and remember exactly—'

Footsteps outside on the walkway, then a banging on Alyona's front door. Amy flinched, but Alyona shot upright in her seat, her eyes wide. Beside Amy, DI Birch closed her eyes, just for a second, as though she knew what was coming.

The room seemed to reverberate with the pounding of a closed fist against the door. After a moment, it stopped, and Amy heard the rattle of the letterbox.

'Birch!' McLeod could have been in the room with them, the way the flat's narrow hallway amplified his voice. 'Outside, now. We need to talk, and I mean *yesterday*.'

Amy felt herself cringe, but Birch's face remained impassive. Professional.

'Interview paused,' she said.

Saturday, 17 July, 23:15

As it turned out, I didn't need to find James Able. In the end, he came to me.

I'd started seeing Natalia. That was how I phrased it, in my head. I was seeing her, as though she was some woman I'd met in a bar and happened to be sleeping with. It didn't matter that I paid her for the privilege. It didn't matter that I knew Natalia wasn't her real name, or that she refused to offer me any details about her life. The other men she saw didn't matter, either – or at least, I tried not to think about them. I felt less lonely, knowing I could go online and book into her company for an hour. Each meeting kept me going for a few days, before I wanted more. And every time I looked at the scars on her face, or thought about them, a wave of rage shuddered through my chest. The injustice of it. Her situation, and mine.

Natalia's flat had a dedicated parking space: a narrow strip of her building's windowless, concrete, basement floor. 'Free parking for clients,' it said on her website, and I always made use of that space. That night, I'd booked a late visit – 10 p.m., Natalia heavy-eyed and gentle with tiredness, which I liked. Somehow it was already July, and the late dusk light turned everything purple: her skin, the plain white walls of her rooms. There was still a faint seam of that light in the sky come eleven, my hands bluish with it as I buttoned my jeans and she counted the notes I'd given her on to the mattress. I rode down in the lift feeling giddy, telling myself, as I did every time, that catching feelings wasn't an option, not in my position, and not with a working girl. Of course, I'd already done it and knew I was in denial.

The basement floor was chilly, though the day had been warm. The space never saw the sun, and its poured concrete walls were thick. I shivered as I crossed the open, strip-lit space to my car. One bulb flickered, the car park like a scene from a silent film.

A few metres out from the Golf I stopped, blinking and confused. I'd been boxed in: a flash, frost-blue BMW X7 had pulled up to my bumper, close enough to touch. Its windows were tinted, but I knew who was inside. For a fleeting minute, I wondered if I was about to die: one of those windows rolling down to reveal the barrel of a gun, the contents of my ribcage spattered Jackson Pollock – style on the concrete. But when nothing happened, I felt myself walking again, trying to saunter towards the X7 as though my pulse wasn't hammering in my throat. Two voices in my head: one saying *this is what you deserve for meddling*. The other was louder: it said, *you did this. Look: you asked for him, and he came.*

The back passenger-side door of the BMW opened, and James Able climbed out. He was shorter than I'd imagined – maybe five-nine with a following wind – but he was also wider, with sculpted arms bulging under his shirt. He was dressed like a stockbroker out on a Saturday night: blue-grey suit trousers too tight in the thigh, a white button-down with the collar popped, and long brown brogues. His neck was red and thick as a tree, the angry, sunburned backdrop for a tattoo of a sacred heart.

He stretched his arms out wide, as though he expected we'd hug, and I saw his hands were blunt and shovel-like, with bitten nails.

'Well,' he said, 'you found me. Now tell me what the fuck you want.'

I looked him up and down, wondering what my chances were. There had to be one other guy in that car, at least.

'You *are* the cunt who's been looking for me, right?' Able asked, letting his arms fall. 'Harassing my girls when they're trying to work? Saying you want a square go? The fuck, man.' He was grinning. His tone was that of a man giving some craic to a pal he knew could take it. 'We don't even know each other,' he added.

I curled both my hands into fists.

'You hurt someone I care about,' I said.

Able cast his eyes heavenwards, as though looking up through the various floors and into Natalia's flat.

'That skank,' he spat, the words curving at the edges, an inflection of surprise. 'The fuck do you care about her, my man? I guarantee she doesn't care about you. You can't reform them, not once they've gone to the dark side. When that bitch opens her legs, there's a fucking echo.'

My vision stuttered out. When it came back, I realised I'd taken two steps forward, swung, and punched Able square in the nose. He was still grinning at me, though blood was streaking his front teeth. He reached out, wrapped one huge hand round my throat, and squeezed. I felt my windpipe flatten, and my body dropped out of fight mode and down into freeze.

'You really want to do this, eh?' He whispered it into my face, and I smelled his blood and the nicotine tang of his breath. My hands hung limply at my sides.

'Yes,' I hissed.

Behind me, the doors of the lift clattered open. I watched as Able refocused his gaze, then heard the hoof-clop of heels on the concrete floor. I writhed in his grip, and he let me turn my head to see the back of a middle-aged woman retreating through the maze of cars, determination not to look back at us clear from the set of her shoulders. Able lifted his hand off my throat, and I wretched.

'Your funeral, pal,' he said. 'But not here.'

★

There were two other guys in the Beemer: when Able approached the front passenger side, the window rolled down and I caught a glimpse. Both huge, of course, with hair buzzed close to their skulls. Designer beards. The nearest had an industrial bolt shot through his ear. My eyes were streaming, the hot ghost of Able's chokehold still burning my throat. He'd turned his back on me blithely, like I wasn't a threat at all. Then he waved the X7 away, watching as his driver backed it up and pulled out of the garage at a slow crawl, leaving us alone.

'Just us,' he said, turning back to me just as I got my own breath under control – as though he'd known exactly how long I'd be useless for. 'I do things the old-fashioned way.'

I snorted.

'What, like burning innocent women with acid? Is that what you call old-fashioned?'

Able shrugged.

'That,' he said, 'was a business negotiation.' He turned his back on me once more and began walking towards the building's exit, the way the BMW had gone. 'I recommend you don't concern yourself with it,' he called back over his shoulder. 'At this point, if I were you, I'd take myself off home. No hard feelings.'

He walked with a swagger I imagined he'd copied exactly from watching John Wayne films. If I'd hated him before, that hate was eclipsed by the loathing I felt for him now. I followed in his wake.

'Where are we going,' I asked, my voice a sneer, 'to *do things the old-fashioned way?*'

As we reached the exit, I felt the air around us change. The dark seemed alive, damp and cool with the early tendrils of a haar. The smudged streetlights painted Able's crisp white shirt a vivid tangerine.

'Not far,' he said, still trotting ahead, not even glancing back. As we rounded the corner of Natalia's block, I began to cast around for something I could pick up and wield. I hated how unbothered he seemed, the way he'd sent away his goons. I was wearing only a T-shirt, my jacket abandoned across the Golf's back seat. I had my wallet, phone and keys in the pockets of my jeans, but nothing more. Able's clothing was tight – I watched the outline of his shoulder blades move as he swaggered ahead of me – but still, I assumed he was carrying a blade at the very least.

'Here,' he said, stopping in front of a peeling black gate in a wall I knew ran along the side of a scrap merchant's yard. Natalia's balcony looked out on that yard: sometimes she'd stand and smoke, looking down at the ripped-out car parts, the miles of looped-up, rusted chain. The gate was fastened with a padlock, the kind with a four-digit code. Able struggled, the spinner too subtle for his knuckled paws. I wondered why I hadn't hit him with something. I wondered why I hadn't run for my life.

'Want me to do that?' I smirked, but he smirked back.

'Don't know the code, do you? And you can fuck off if you think I'd tell it to you.'

Able was bizarre: exactly as I'd imagined him but also not at all. The way he talked, we could have been old friends, bantering down the pub. His confidence was a solid aura he walked around in.

At last, the spinner clicked into place and the bolt came free. Able propped his shoulder up against the gate, and a gap appeared between the bolt and the wall. With some effort, he widened the gap enough that we could both walk through. Though it wouldn't have swung shut, he held the gate for me as though I were his date.

'You own this place?' I asked, passing him.

'A mate of mine,' he said, then laced his voice with a tinge of threat. 'Friends everywhere, me.'

I had my back to him now and didn't like it, but I couldn't show him I was bothered. I strode out across the yard, hearing the gate scrape closed and Able's scuffed footsteps, following.

'Not like you,' he said.

The yard was like a fairground haunted house: the streetlight glinted off oil drums, refracted a million times in splintered windscreens. The shadows were deep, and black, and full of twisted shapes. I pressed on.

'What?' I said, over my shoulder.

'You,' Able replied. He was maybe eight-or-so feet behind, too far away to strike, unless, I supposed, he threw something. 'Billy No Mates. Nobody in this town knows who the fuck you are.'

I looked up then and realised where I was. Natalia's block towered in front of me; I cast my eyes over the identical walkways of the lower floors, then counted front doors until I worked out which was hers. I willed her to come outside for a smoke, to stand on her balcony and spot us, see that I'd done it, I'd tracked James Able down. But her windows were dark, and I thought of her locking the deadbolt, folding my twenty-pound notes into a freezer bag and stashing them in the second drawer, underneath a bag of peas. Natalia peeling her false lashes off at the mirror. Natalia falling asleep in the groove I'd carved in her bed.

'Only that whore,' Able said. 'She's your only friend.'

I walked on, the vaguest shadow of a plan coming together in my head. We had to be closer, so she could see. If I was going to reckon with Able, it would need to be unmistakable.

'You know,' I said, still walking, 'I've met a lot of men like you.' I paused, and when he didn't cut in, went on. 'I'm guessing you never had much power, growing up. Middle child and always ignored, am I right? Always having to clamour for attention, and it was never enough. Maybe your old man beat you up, or maybe your brothers did. And you got sick of that, didn't you? Always being kicked around.'

I passed a hill of tyres, and even in the spooky light I could see that some were newish, deeply grooved, and others smooth and bald and fit only for burning. I paused in my speech, which wasn't so much guesswork as me telling Able about myself, hoping he'd been made the same way. *Fit for burning*, I thought, my eyes still fixed on Natalia's balcony.

'The fuck are you,' Able scoffed, 'my therapist?'

'That means I'm right. Guys like you, it's all attention-seeking, and you don't really care what kind you get. Positive, negative, whatever. As long as someone's looking at you. As long as you're less afraid than the other person.'

'Jesus.' He laughed at me. 'You smoking something, pal? I want some.'

'You had two choices, really,' I said. There was a clear space up ahead, a rough circle rutted with caterpillar tracks, a place where vehicles parked or were turned. 'Wield that power legally, or not. You could've gone in the Army, right? Or the police. But no – I'd guess you're just not a team player, are you, James?' I paced the circle's diameter, then stopped at the far side and turned. 'So, small-time crook it was. Almost like a prophecy.'

Able stopped at the opposite edge of the circle.

'You talk too much,' he said, an edge of genuine annoy-ance in his voice for the first time since we'd met. I suspected the *small-time* comment had stung. He opened his shirt cuffs, struggling with the dainty buttons the same way he'd strug-gled with the padlock. 'We doing this, or no?'

'Doing what?' I watched as he shook out his shoulders and squared up, though we were metres apart on opposite sides of the rutted clearing. I was at least six inches taller than him, but nowhere near as strong. He had brute force, I reckoned, but next to no agility. That would be the card I'd have to play.

'Well,' he said, '*I* was thinking what I'd do is fuck you up sufficiently that you wouldn't come asking my girls – or ask-ing anyone, really – any questions ever again. What were you thinking?'

I cocked my head to one side.

'Me? I was thinking I might set you on fire. See how *you* like being burned.'

Able laced his fingers together, cracked his knuckles.

'You're proper psycho, you are.'

I shrugged. 'Let's see.'

He was advancing towards me across the circle, his body bent into a half-crouch, his balled hands crossed in front of his face. He looked comical, but I didn't smile. Instead, I stood still, hands at my sides, trying to remember the things I knew about fighting, about neutralising another human being. I let Able walk all the way over, until he was close enough to strike. He aimed one darting fist at the centre of my face, but I flinched, and the blow landed glancing on my cheekbone. It wasn't enough to alter my stance – my feet planted in the tracked dirt – but I knew it would leave a bruise. I flattened my palms, then made the same fast motion I might have had I wanted to squash a fly, mid-air. A decisive clap, boxing Able's ears. He reared up out of his boxer's crouch, allowing me to bury my fist in his abdomen and make him sag. I heard surprise in the sound that came out of him: after our tussle in the car park, he hadn't expected any kind of real fight.

'Bastard,' he spat.

He reached up and hooked one thick arm around the back of my neck, dragging me into a headlock. I let myself be bent in two, feeling my throat crush closed once more. For a few moments, Able and I danced around that dry patch of yard, a grunting, scuffling beast with four feet, two heads, conjoined. I tried to ration the breath in my chest: I needed Able's leg just so, just so . . .

Like that. I swiped one foot around his supporting ankle and kicked out hard, buckling his knee and pitching him flat on his front. His grip didn't loosen, as I'd thought it might, and I was dragged down with him, my legs jackknifing awkwardly under my weight. But his weight was greater. As he hit the ground, I heard the air sputter out of his lungs. The heft of his curled arm mashed my face into the ground, and I felt the crunch of scrapyard grit on my lips.

I had to breathe: zigzagging patterns were forming behind my eyelids, my hearing beginning to peter out. At least one of my teeth had been loosened by the fall, the taste of pennies in my mouth. My arms were bent under my chest, but I hooked my right hand out and flailed, beating blindly with my fist on the back of Able's head. I could tell he couldn't get up without letting me go: he'd need to push down with his hands to right himself. Eventually, as I began to worry I might pass out, he made the choice to escape my rain of indiscriminate blows. As soon as he loosened his arm, I wrenched my neck from his grip and rolled, trying to put as much space as I could between Able and myself so I'd have time to haul in some air. I rolled until I hit something: a pile of rusted metal that made an alarming, rippling shift as my body hit it. A four-foot length of starter bar clattered off the top and landed in the dry earth just a whisker from my ear. I'd only made it a metre or so: Able was bent on his haunches a few feet away, spitting, strands of brown saliva hanging from his lips.

'All this,' he panted, meeting my eye, 'for that cheap bitch.'

My chest ached. Lying on my back felt good: I wanted to stay there, camouflaged by the shadows of dead machines and builders' junk, just breathing. The air caught in my ragged throat, but it was sweet. For a moment, I wondered if Able had a point. What *was* I doing here, mouth full of mud and blood, teeth rattling in my head, trying to reinflate my own lungs? All for a woman who wouldn't love me – probably wouldn't think about me ever again if I stopped coming round to her place with my wallet full. But then I thought of her chewed-away face. I remembered the job at hand, the thing I was meant to be doing.

'Come on, then,' I said, my voice an ashen creak. 'Come and finish this.'

Able straightened up. I heard his shoulder blades pop as he flattened them out: first one, then the other.

'Still gonna set me on fire?' he sneered, swaggering the gap between us slowly closed.

'I am,' I said, and he laughed. He was almost upon me.

'That,' he said, 'I would like to see.'

He came to a stop beside me and, as I hoped he would, bent down to better see my face. My breath was still erratic and loud, though I'd got ten it under better control than Able could have known. I wanted him to think I was down and staying there, and it seemed to have worked. He put his palms on his knees and leered at me, his chin now streaked with blood and grime.

'No more questions,' he hissed, and his spittle dripped on to my cheek. 'Ever.'

I pressed my hands down into the gravel, splaying my fingers to make a solid base from which to thrust.

'Deal,' I said. Then I sat up.

I did it fast: as fast as my miserable chest would let me. I'd braced for the impact, but nothing could have prepared me for the rattle-crack of my skull slamming into Able's face. The teeth that weren't already loose scraped together in my mouth, and a bright yellow loop of ache blossomed behind each of my eyes. But it did what I needed it to, this Glasgow kiss: laid Able out on his arse in the dust, giving me time to get up and reach for the starter bar. It was a heavier weapon than I'd expected, and for just a second, I worried he'd get up too fast for me to strike. But I'd felt Able's jaw clamp shut around his own tongue, and heard him howl. Now he bent one protective arm across his face, so didn't see the curled metal rod until I'd lifted it high above us both. His eyes did something then I've never seen before or since: I saw in his face that he believed he was going to die. His limbs reared up as though he were a giant bug, caught on its back, his hands two desperate flashes in the freaky light.

'Please,' he said, just once, the single syllable loud and strident. Blood from his bitten tongue formed a dark ooze on his cheek.

I snorted.

'Karma's a bitch,' I said, and then, 'a cheap bitch, you might say.'

I threw him what must have been a bloody, crooked smile, then brought the weapon down.

*

I don't remember getting out of the yard, but I must have gone back to the gate and scraped it open. Able couldn't have locked it behind us – he hadn't given me the padlock code, and even if he had, I doubt I could have opened it with my shaking hands. I don't remember walking back around the block, retracing the route he'd led me on: I only came to in the car park, standing beside the driver's door of the Golf. My reflection in the window was dim, but frightening: my mouth looked distorted, and my face was dark and smeared. I didn't know what was muck and what was blood, but worse, I didn't know if the blood was mine or Able's. I realised my right hand was still curled around the starter bar: I'd hauled it all the way along the street. Had anyone seen me? I had no idea. How much time had passed between me bringing the bar down on James Able's head and reaching the relative safety of my car? I didn't know. I fished in my pocket for my keys, relieved to find they were still in my jeans and not lost somewhere back in the yard. I dropped into the Golf's enclosed pod of calm, letting the starter bar fall on to the concrete and ring the whole big space like a bell. I closed the door. Took a breath. Took another. Put my hands on the steering wheel and watched them shake. My pulse roared.

I assumed he was dead. He had to be. I'd swung that bar the way you do an axe, when chopping wood – lifting it to its highest apex and then letting the weight of it create its own force. I thought about the human skull, the gentle egg-like shape of it. I'd only hit him once, and that word echoed in my head: *only, only.* As if that made a difference. As if I hadn't just committed murder.

I sat in the car for several hours: in shock, I realise now. My hands were curled on the wheel for so long that the blood ran away from my fingers. Pins and needles prickled my whitening skin, then eventually I was numb to the wrist, but still I didn't move. Did I blink, even? I don't know. The Golf was parked nose-in, the windscreen full of poured-concrete wall, the number of Natalia's flat painted there in flaking white. I sat and stared at the numbers until they became a scrambled glyph of brushstrokes, an eldritch symbol that didn't make any sense. I thought about Able's eyes, the black slug of blood that ran from his lips as he spluttered beneath me in the dirt. How abject he was. How abject he'd been all his life. His life, I thought. His life. How confidently I'd ended it. How easy it was to do.

I don't know what brought me out of my fugue. It might have been the light: though the basement was windowless, I sensed it change. I heard a street-sweeper hiss by outside, and felt – rather than saw – a couple of early-bird residents walk out of the lift to their cars. A new day was starting. My phone informed me it was now Sunday, almost 7 a.m. I couldn't sit here for ever, pretending I hadn't murdered a man. Something had to be done.

Of course, I already had a plan. I'd told it to Natalia several times, while she rolled her eyes and told me I was mad. I'd told it to Able himself, and he'd parroted it back: *still gonna set me on fire?* I had the things I needed: I'd paid for them in cash and stored them in the boot of the Golf. I'd thought through the plan so often it had begun showing up in my dreams, and yet now I couldn't believe I could do it. I *had* to do it, I told myself, and fast. Because fire consumes. It levels. It licks the things it touches clean.

I tested my legs by getting out of the driver's door and standing in the triangular lee it formed. I realised I was cold – that I had been cold for quite some time – and hungry, though I wasn't tired. Adrenaline dazzled in my blood. My legs shook, but I could stand. I could bend. I could lift the starter bar from the floor where it had lain for hours in the shadow of the car. Its weight surprised me once again. The bloodied end left a smear on the chalky white parking space line. I held it with reverence, like a precious sceptre, perfectly parallel to the ground. I carried it around the end of the Golf and popped the boot. I felt the car's suspension register the starter bar's weight as I dropped it inside. I hunted around for a rag, then for screenwash. It was neat, and the tang of it made me cough, but I sponged it gingerly over my face until the rag was streaked with the colour of iron. My eyes streamed. I splashed my hands in the stinging liquid until they came reasonably clean, then I used the pool of blue overspill to wipe up Able's blood from the white line. I wrapped the rag around the business end of the starter bar, knowing that Able's DNA was probably already all over my car. The gallon bottle of screenwash I left on the line. Then I reversed the Golf out of its space and left the engine idling as I returned. I tried not to step back into the marked-out oblong as I swilled the screenwash across it: this wasn't in the plan, I was flying blind, and wondered for a moment if I'd done it, if I'd finally gone insane. Could I leave a tyre print on concrete? If I could, would screenwash go any way to erasing it at all? I didn't have a clue. I just knew I didn't want to make this particular space ground zero: Natalia's address was painted right there on the wall.

I bent down next to the car and cocked the driver's side mirror to look at my face. The blistering wash I'd given it made my skin feel vile, but it had cleared most of the blood and soil. I smiled, then wished I hadn't. One of my canines was hanging loose, the two teeth beside it wobbly and tender, too. My top lip was bruised, my gums bloody. I fumbled in the back seat footwell, found a plastic bottle half full with weeks-old water. I rinsed my mouth, tried to spit the backwash into the bottle. My canine tooth landed with a sparking sound on the car park floor between my feet, and I scooped it up.

'Evidence,' I said aloud. I tucked the tooth into my wallet.

The street outside was quiet: it was Sunday at the industrial end of Leith, and not much doing. The gate in the scrapyard wall was pulled to but wasn't locked. I parked the Golf as close as I could get, hustled my contraband out of the boot and shoved it through the gate. It was fully light by now – July, of course – and the yard looked unrecognisable from the night before. Under streetlight its piles of debris had seemed sculptural, even Gothic. In the hard white light of an overcast Edinburgh Sunday, the yard was simply ugly: a rusty grave-yard. A place where things of no value came to die.

James Able was where I'd left him, his once-white shirt stiff with old blood, his trousers caked with dust. He was camouflaged against the pile of broken metal rods and joints I'd jostled when I'd rolled out of his headlock. I realised he likely hadn't been seen just yet, but knew I couldn't hang around. His face was simply a wound now, and I couldn't look at it for long.

I put on the latex gloves I'd pulled from the box in the boot of the Golf and then stuffed in my pocket. Their insides felt grainy, and in them I had ghoul's hands, too white against Able's bloodied clothes. I had planned to drag him to the cen-tre of the circle we had tussled in, but the weight of him was sapping: I found I could only shift him a couple of feet. I remembered once again that I hadn't eaten anything in hours, and had to be satisfied with what little difference I'd made. When Natalia looked down from her high tower, I told myself, it would be enough. She'd see.

Still wearing the gloves, I unscrewed the child-safe lid on my five-litre plastic jerrycan. The smell of petrol landed like a swift kick, and my eyes watered. I knew I had to be careful here: if I managed to douse myself as well as Able, I could send my own clothes up in flames. I'd always been pissed off by that in films: the villain flinging accelerant in all directions, then flipping a Zippo lighter into the mix and walking away unscathed. I poured the petrol out gingerly, tipping the jerry-can first to lose some of the liquid weight in the dirt. This made it easier to wield: now I could focus on soaking Able's clothes. The petrol stink was solid as a wall, and I moved slowly, afraid that if I caused the slightest spark the whole damn yard would ignite. The scene felt dreamlike, as if this were just another run-through I was doing in my head. Every once in a while I looked up at Natalia's flat, a part of me wishing she'd come out and stand there, watching, from the balcony. I poured the filmy liquid into Able's hair. I doused his shoes. The wetness made the fabric of his shirt cling tightly to his chest – I think that's why I noticed when it moved.

'Able?'

I didn't believe it – couldn't make myself believe it. I'd brought an iron bar down on to this man's head. I'd assumed that act had killed him, but even if it hadn't, he'd been bleeding out for hours. He was dead, I told myself. James Able was dead.

And yet, there it was again – the movement was shallow, but it was there. Able's lungs were still inflating, enough to make his ribcage move. He began to make a strange sound, a sort of low hum through his teeth. He was trying to speak, and the dead don't speak.

'Fuck.'

I dropped to my knees beside him. Yes, there was no mistaking it now, looking closer. I wanted to put my face close to his, but hesitated – partly because of the hideous wound I'd made, but also because some small sliver of me still felt afraid of this man. What if he'd somehow faked all this, and lain in wait for me to come back? What if he ambushed me, once I got near, the way I'd done to him the night before? But as I leaned over his body, prone in the dirt, my chest filled up with the smell of blood – no, of *meat* – the smell of carcasses in a butcher's van. I held my breath, and lowered my cheek over Able's open mouth. I could hear it then, too: the air that seeped out of him was thin, but it rasped.

His eyes were open, and presumably blinking, but I hadn't been able to look at them yet, and I didn't plan to. Instead, I fixed my gaze on Able's chest: in the breast pocket of his once-white shirt, he'd tucked a patterned pocket square. I'd always hated this particular affectation, but now I was glad of it. It gave me a point to focus on while I finished pouring out the contents of the jerrycan.

My last item of contraband was a long-barrelled lighter – one of those things that lights a kitchen gas ring by making a spark. I took it out of my pocket, and nestled it in my hand as though it were a skinny gun. I placed the empty jerrycan on Able's chest: it was plastic, guaranteed to melt. I cleared my throat.

'This is fucked up,' I heard myself say. To my surprise, my voice was clogged. Was I crying? I didn't know why. I looked down at Able's pocket square. 'You deserve to die,' I said.

I didn't know if he could hear me: it was myself I was trying to convince.

My chest hurt. I didn't know if it was the crying, the thick stink of petrol, or simply the after-effects of Able's chokehold from the night before. I looked down at the doused human body before me, and thought of the bright blaze Able was about to become. I thought of Natalia's face, and curled my finger round the lighter's trigger. With my other hand I smeared the tears and snot out off my cheeks, and on to the latex glove.

'You're already dead, anyway,' I said.

Sunday, 18 July, 16:20

'I want to know exactly what you thought you were doing.'

McLeod was yelling. Birch pictured the Sunday skeleton staff of colleagues on the other side of the office wall. She imagined them as a small and silent gaggle, ears pressed to the door, but knew that was overkill – anyone sitting in the bullpen would be able to hear the bollocking she was getting. They wouldn't even need to get up from their desks.

McLeod did not, in fact, want to know what Birch had thought she was doing, as he left her no space to reply.

'You went to a crime scene – you *went* to a *crime scene* – and that was bad enough. But then you proceeded to interview a witness? I knew I'd have to keep an eye on you, Helen, but I didn't expect to be dealing with *this*.'

Birch kept her gaze fixed on the edge of McLeod's desk. Looking directly at him would probably be a mistake right at this moment.

'I went to the aid of a junior officer,' she said, 'who needed help.'

McLeod snorted.

'Oh, trust me,' he said, 'I'll be having words with Sergeant Kato in due course.'

Birch felt her eyes widen, but still, she didn't look up.

'Due respect, sir,' she said, 'you might want to think about having words with DI Crosbie. Kato only called me because she couldn't get hold of him. He's her CO. I'd want to know why he wasn't answering his phone.'

McLeod waved one hand at her.

'It's a Sunday.'

'I appreciate that. I appreciate that it probably isn't the best approach to work-life balance, but . . . we pick up our phones. Don't we? You picked up yours, and you were—' Birch found she needed to pause, and force her face to remain neutral as she said the word. 'You were *golfing*. I was in the Visit Room at Low Moss, and I still managed to take the call. We pick up our phones when a junior officer calls us on a Sunday, because we know they might well be ringing to say listen, a local gangster's been set on fire in a scrapyard and there's nothing in the operational handbook about that. Kato needed help, and her CO wasn't around. If I were you, I'd want to find out why.'

She was glad the desk stood between them. McLeod was pacing back and forth on his side, like a caged cat.

'I didn't call you in here so you could tell me how to do my job.'

'That's not what I'm doing, sir.'

He made an incredulous huffing sound.

'Well, it sounds like it,' he said. 'It also sounds like you're trying to pass the buck, Birch, and that doesn't show a great deal of integrity.'

Birch blinked. In her surprise, she met McLeod's eye, and then realised she'd need to hold his gaze while she said the next part.

'I have to disagree with you, I'm sorry.' McLeod clearly registered the look on her face, because he stopped pacing. 'I'm not trying to pass the buck,' she went on, 'I'm trying to defend Sergeant Kato. In my opinion, she did everything right this morning. She set up a working crime scene, on her own, in very challenging circumstances. I'm sure I don't need to remind you that she's only just newly promoted.'

McLeod broke away from her gaze to roll his eyes.

'I'd rather you didn't remind me. The more I think about it, the more I regret that decision.'

'Sir, she passed the sergeants' exam.'

She realised this sounded sarcastic, though it was just the truth. She waited for McLeod's retort, but it didn't come. Instead, he wheeled his hands in the air between them, as though swatting away some invisible swarm.

'This is all a distraction,' he said, 'from the central issue. Yes, I'll speak to Crosbie. I'm sure he'll have a reasonable explanation for being out of contact. But Kato did *not* do everything right this morning, because *she called you*. This meeting is about *you*, Helen. It's about your decision to involve yourself in this case when you know full well that you absolutely shouldn't have.'

'Sir.'

'Don't *sir* me like I just gave you an order.' He started pacing again. 'I gave you the order several weeks ago, Birch. I said I wanted you to get complete rest – no half measures. You're on leave. You were *shot*, for Christ's sake. The investigation into Operation Kendall is barely even off the ground. I've got five hundred other things to think about, what with the policing of this godforsaken Eddison Deas concert looming over all our heads, on top of everything else. I can't take this as well, truly, I can't. You cannot be here, trying to work, pretending like everything's normal.' He gestured at the crutch, which was propped against the side of Birch's chair. 'I mean, look at yourself. Could you chase a suspect, if you had to, or tackle him? Could you run from a threat? No. And that's before we even get to the prescription medication you're on. I'm sorry to say it, Birch, but right now you are slow, in a whole variety of ways. That makes you a liability. A potential fatality, even. You're a full-blown inquiry waiting to happen. I'm not just fussing because you got yourself hurt. I'm saying you're a danger to yourself and others. Do you understand?'

Birch was silent for a moment. Several thoughts collided in her brain. She realised she hadn't actually considered many of the limitations of her present condition. She'd never thought about the possibility of chasing a suspect: it had been many years since she was in uniform. McLeod's use of the word *slow* had offended her, but she couldn't deny that that was how the medication made her feel, sometimes: like she was pulling her limbs through treacle, especially in the mornings. As if to drive the point home, her hip began to twinge with pain. She realised she'd missed a dose of meds, and immediately craved it.

'I do,' she said, 'I do understand.'

'I don't think so,' McLeod said. He was on a roll now, she could tell. 'I don't think you understand at all. You know why I think that? Because I can see from your face that you're still sitting there thinking about this Jay character. Thinking about this case.'

Birch looked at him, wondering what her face was doing. She wasn't thinking about Jay at all, or hadn't been: she was thinking about that missed painkiller and how she might make up for the break in her schedule.

'We've known each other for a lot of years, Helen,' McLeod went on. 'I know when you've got something in your teeth, and I'm telling you, you have to drop it. If you don't, I'll have to formally suspend you.'

Those words felt like falling into cold water: they shocked her back to the present.

'Okay,' she said, slowly. Saying anything more would be unwise, but McLeod was about to pack her off home again.

She might not get another chance. 'You're right. I have been having some thoughts about this case.'

'I knew it.'

'Just today,' she added, though this was a lie. She assumed McLeod still didn't know that she'd phoned Amy and begged to get involved. 'Just since Able was found.'

McLeod raised an eyebrow.

'Is that so,' he said.

Birch decided to ignore the barb and press on.

'I'm having second thoughts about the—'

'That's exactly my point,' McLeod cut in. 'You shouldn't be having *any* thoughts about this case.'

'But . . . the other day, in the pub, when I talked to Kato—'

'Did you hear me say I'd have to formally suspend you?'

Birch closed her eyes for a moment. Oh sure, she thought, like I'd gloss over the part where you threatened me. She opened her eyes again once she trusted herself not to say that aloud.

'I heard you, guv,' she said, 'but please just let me say this. Let me tell you this, and then I'll hobble out of here and not bother you ever again.'

There was a pause, and Birch thought she saw the slightest hint of amusement cross McLeod's face.

'Don't make promises you can't keep, Helen,' he said. 'But fine. Say your piece.'

Birch let out a breath she hadn't realised she'd been holding.

'Thank you,' she said. 'Okay, so the other day, in the pub, when I talked to Kato, we got very involved with this Solomon Carradice theory.'

McLeod's brow furrowed.

'Solomon Carradice is rotting in HMP Barlinnie, thank Christ. What does he have to do with this case?'

'Nothing, directly. But Kato and I both wondered if our suspect – Jay, the Vampire, whatever we're calling him – might be angling after Carradice's spot at the top of the scumbag pecking order.'

'He's looking to assert his dominance among the criminal fraternity,' McLeod said, 'yes. I mean, he's certainly put his back into it with this latest stunt.'

'Right,' Birch said, 'that's what it looks like, isn't it? But what if that isn't actually what's going on?'

McLeod frowned.

'What do you mean?'

'I mean what if this guy isn't a gangster, or a wannabe gangster. What if we jumped to that conclusion too quickly?'

'I don't see what other conclusion there is.'

'My worry,' Birch said, 'is that we've all spent the past two years anticipating that this would happen. Waiting for someone new to step into Solomon Carradice's shoes. I think everyone in this building would agree it's a *when* situation, not an *if*. We've all feared it was coming. And isn't it the human condition to try and explain a problem by assuming it's the thing that you feared all along?'

McLeod was frowning. His eyes didn't seem to be focused on anything.

'One therapy session,' he said, 'and you're in here talking like this.'

Birch tried not to dwell on that comment. She didn't want to think about Dr Jane right now.

'I'm just saying, we might be leaning towards this theory because in a way, it's what we all want. To have caught the problem early. To be dealing with it before it gets out of hand. I'm saying, it'd be easier for us if this guy *was* a gangster.'

McLeod threw up his hands.

'This is what I mean about you being on medication, Birch. We've just found Edinburgh's most arrogant fancy man bludgeoned and burned to a crisp. You're trying to tell me this Jay isn't a gangster?'

Birch cocked her head.

'Wait – bludgeoned?'

McLeod nodded.

'Notice that you weren't in possession of that particular fact, because you're not supposed to be on this case. But yes, James Able had suffered a blunt force trauma to the forehead, prior to being set alight.'

'Shit.'

'Indeed,' McLeod sniffed. 'You're telling me that isn't the behaviour of a man hoping to build himself a career in mindless violence?'

Birch closed her eyes again. The pain in her hip was mild, but thickening.

'Listen, I get it,' she said. 'I know all the evidence points in that direction. But something doesn't add up. Why aren't we hearing about accomplices? Why does no one know who this guy is? There's something more to this that we aren't seeing.'

McLeod gestured towards the closed door of the office, indicating the bullpen beyond it.

'Well, if that's true,' he said, 'then we'll find it. We're all quite good at our jobs round here, you know. Has it ever occurred to you to give the rest of us some credit?'

'Sir, I'm not trying to – look, I just think Alyona's testimony—'

McLeod brought his palm down hard on the desk between them. The blow landed with such force that the pens on the tabletop scattered and rolled to the floor.

'Enough!' His voice bounced off the walls. 'I've held back from asking you this many a time over the years, DI Birch, but just who the hell do you think you are? You behave as if this place would fall down around our ears without you here to steer it in the right direction. You act like we're all just bumbling fools. We've all had the same training as you, and there are officers here with far more experience, into the bargain.'

Birch felt stunned. The words seemed to detonate around her: they hit and stung. She'd had bust-ups with McLeod before – probably more of them than anyone else in the building – but he'd never said anything like this before.

'We don't need you on this, Helen.' His tone was a little softer, like he'd realised he'd gone too far. 'We need you to get better, instead, and come back one hundred per cent, so when we need to catch the next bastard, you're ready to help. I promise you, we can handle this one on our own.'

She dropped her hands into her lap and looked down at them. *Who the hell do you think you are?* She didn't know the answer.

'Message received,' she said, 'and understood. Thank you for listening to what I had to say.'

She fumbled with the crutch, her palms slippery, and cursed in her head. She wished more than anything that she could simply have got up and removed herself from the room. She must have looked abject, because McLeod spoke again, his voice even softer now.

'I'm sorry,' he said, 'if that was hard to hear. But I need you to understand that you're not a serving police officer right now. People are talking, Birch. Your colleagues are worried about you. The way you're behaving, it's . . . well, it doesn't seem entirely rational. It's important to everyone here that

you move past this and get well again. Mentally, not just phys-
ically. I *need* you to understand.'

Birch steadied her grip on the stick and tried to stand up
straight. Her commanding officer thought she was crazy – not
just annoying, not just insubordinate. Crazy.

'I understand, guv,' she said. 'Don't worry, you have been
perfectly clear.'

*

She'd expected that when she opened the office door – determined she wouldn't be helped by McLeod – she'd find every
eye in the bullpen turned her way. But instead, her colleagues
looked more intently focused on their work than she had ever
seen them before: everyone was studiously ignoring her. You're
not a serving police officer right now, she thought, McLeod's
voice echoing in her head. Maybe that means they can't see you.

She clattered past the bullpen as fast as the crutch would allow,
and made it to the lift. Not yet, Helen, she said to herself, even as
the doors shut her inside the grim reflective box alone. She fixed
her reflection in the lift's mirror with a steely glare, and tried not
to blink until she'd ridden all the way to the ground floor. When
the doors opened, the small knot of officers waiting to go up
parted to let her through, a little too dramatically, as if she might
be contagious. Perhaps I am, she thought, hearing McLeod say
again *just who the hell do you think you are?* Perhaps they're worried about catching my bad attitude. She nodded hello to those
who made eye contact, though only a couple did, and she felt the
fact of that sting in a way it wouldn't do, usually.

At the main door, Birch balanced on her good foot, raised
the crutch and used its rubber stopper to push the pad on
the automatic exit. The disabled door, as her colleagues called it –

she realised she'd never noticed before what was wrong with that particular phrase. Once outside, she pulled in a long huff of air, then wished that she hadn't: the lump that had been rising in her throat only grew. Her eyes began to sting.

'Just make it off the premises,' she hissed through her teeth, and began to smatter across the car park. Halfway over, she paused, and heard herself let out a single, quiet sob. Parked in front of her, in a space clearly marked *Police Vehicles Only*, was Jamieson's van.

'Dad.'

Seeing her approach, her father climbed out of the passenger seat. He had a tightly rolled cigarette stuck to his bottom lip and a guilty grin on his face. Birch was still several metres away, but he called out to her.

'She said I could park here.'

'Who?'

Jamieson nodded in the direction of the car park attendant's kiosk: little more than a fibreglass box from which the barrier arm was manually operated.

'Yon wifey.'

Birch drew close to him, and saw him register the look on her face.

'I seriously doubt that,' she said, pointing to the words on the ground. Jamieson spoke at almost the same moment.

'What's wrong, hen?'

There were tears in her eyes now, it was too late, but nevertheless she tried to plaster on a smile.

'Nothing,' she said. 'I mean, I got a bollocking from McLeod, but it's not like I didn't know it was coming.'

Jamieson puffed out his chest, and then spat on to the tarmac. This was a habit Birch usually abhorred, but in that moment it was the gesture of solidarity she was looking for.

'A bastart, that gadge,' Jamieson declared. 'Have I no always said it?'

'You have.'

She was crying now, there was no getting away from it. She hated herself for not being able to stop.

'Said some pretty mean shit tae ye, didn't he?'

She nodded, sniffing.

'How did you know?'

Her father cocked his head to one side.

'Helen, we havnae really kennt each other aw that long, but ah ken ye're a strong lassie. Ye dinnae get this upset fer nothing.'

He watched her for a moment, but she could tell he wanted to speak again. He gave her a gentle nudge with one elbow.

'Want me to gie him a doin?'

Birch couldn't help it: she laughed.

'Dad!'

He made a dramatic, whole-body gesture of *what, me?*

'Whit? Ye think yer auld man's past it? Ye think ah cannae malkie a bastart due tae ma advanced years? That's *ageism*, ken.'

Birch was smiling now, too: wan and wet, but a smile nevertheless.

'I don't know what you're doing here,' she said, 'but I'm glad you came.'

Jamieson patted her on the shoulder.

'Ah wisnae havin ye driven hame in the back of a polis car,' he said. 'Yer neighbours might've decided ye were a criminal!'

Birch prodded the front tyre of her father's van with the stoppered end of her crutch.

'Of course, no one would get that impression if I turned up in *this* fancy vehicle.'

Jamieson shrugged.

'Cheaper than a cab, though, eh?'

He slung an arm around her shoulder. Normally, Birch avoided hugging her father: it felt forced, somehow too awkward after all these years. But this time she appreciated the warm weight of his arm there, the care in that gesture.

'C'mon then, darlin,' he said. 'Let's get ye hame.'

★

By the time they got back to her little house in Portobello, it was late afternoon. The weather was still a little chilly for July, the last wisps of a haar drifting over the water out towards Fife. The seafront was beginning to empty out: café owners pulling down their shutters, families packing windbreaks into the backs of their cars. It didn't feel like the same day Birch had set off into earlier: her visit to Charlie felt like it had happened weeks ago. Jamieson parked as close to the house as he could get, but the walk to her front door was slow. The pain in her hip had begun to swell and break, a persistent wave. It hadn't been this bad for weeks, and she felt an undertow of worry over her progress, whether she'd undone something. And almost as much as she wanted her meds, Birch wanted to lie down in her own bed, stop thinking, and go to sleep.

Instead, she let Jamieson fuss over her for a while, largely because she was too tired to argue. He fixed her a cup of too milky tea, and forced her to eat a cheese sandwich before she swallowed her pills.

'It's true,' he said. 'Doesnae matter whit the medicine is. Ye line yer stomach first, that's the rule.' Birch laughed, he asked her why, and she didn't have the heart to say how strange this sounded coming from a man who'd spent the last forty years or more upending bottle after bottle of whisky into himself.

'I don't know, Dad,' she said, 'I'm just exhausted. So fine, give me the sandwich. I'll do whatever you say.'

She'd eaten, and felt better for it, and told him so. She'd swallowed the big, dry pills with such relief that she felt an almost immediate effect: her muscles relaxing, she guessed, and taking a little of the tension away. It took fifteen minutes or so for the meds to really kick in, and during that time Jamieson clucked around: her phone was on charge, the TV remote in reach, a blanket retrieved from the airing cupboard and laid at her feet, should she need it.

'Mum would have loved this,' Birch said, sure now she could feel the soft melt of the drug in her veins. Her father made a face she didn't understand, and she added, 'Seeing this, I mean. You taking care of me.'

She realised too late that she'd wounded him. When he replied, his voice was quiet.

'Aye,' he said, 'mibbe so. More likely she'd have said it wis much too little, much too late.'

Birch felt her cheeks flush. She'd had that particular thought many times herself.

'Sorry, Dad. I meant it as a nice thing.'

Jamieson reached down and squeezed her hand.

'Ah ken, lass. An ye're right. Jist wish ah'd straightened things oot sooner, ken? While she wis still alive.'

They stayed like that in silence for a little while: Birch reclined on the couch, feeling the meds chip away at her pain, Jamieson standing beside her, holding her hand. Her mother's inscrutable photo watched them from the mantelpiece. Outside, the constant slow exhale of the sea.

Birch waited a while after Jamieson left, to make sure he'd really gone. She didn't want him popping back in, having forgotten something. She didn't want to think too much or have to explain herself to anyone. Her phone had been on silent since she'd sat down in Alyona's flat, but she was aware there were new voicemails there from Anjan. Texts she didn't want to read.

'You're not a serving police officer right now,' she said aloud, copying McLeod's inflection as she opened up her contact list. Amy was right at the top, and Anjan just below her. For a moment, her thumb hovered between the two names, but she knew who she was going to choose. She looked at the clock as she counted the rings: nearly 6 p.m. The phone rang once, twice, thrice.

'This is Kato.'

'It's me,' Birch said, as if she didn't know her caller ID had come up on Amy's screen.

'Hi. How are you doing?'

'Uh-oh,' Birch replied. 'You've been told not to take calls from me, haven't you?'

'Yes,' Amy said, her tone unusually blithe. 'Yes, that's right.'

'And you're in the bullpen right now?'

'That's correct, yes.'

Birch's heart rate clicked up a notch. Amy sounded for all the world like she was talking to a random caller, someone she'd never spoken to before in her life.

'I'm guessing McLeod isn't far away?' Birch hazarded.

'Yes, I can confirm you've got that right.'

'Okay. I'm guessing you've been told not to pick up any calls from me, so you're disobeying a direct order right now, Sergeant Kato.'

On the other end of the line, Amy paused.

'That's still under review,' she said, 'I'll be able to tell you more about that in due course.'

Birch smiled. She wasn't sure what she'd done to deserve such a good friend.

'Say no more,' she said. 'Call me back when you're able to talk. I hope your dressing-down from McLeod wasn't too horrendous.'

'I'm afraid not,' Amy said, and Birch winced.

'Shit, I'm sorry. You get on, and we'll talk in a bit.'

'That's great,' Amy said, and then, with a little more genuine warmth, 'thanks for calling.'

The line went dead. Birch reached out for the blanket Jamieson had brought her, and pulled it up over her legs. She didn't so much fall asleep as spark out, regardless of the full July daylight, or the fact that her shoes were still on.

She woke to the phone vibrating off the chair arm and on to her face. It was almost dark: the clock now read 9.45. Birch's mouth was dry and tasted like tinfoil. In spite of Jamieson's cheese sandwich, she felt ravenous.

Rubbing the cheekbone her phone had hit, she swiped to pick up the call.

'Hi, Amy,' she said.

'Oh shit. You were asleep.'

'Jesus. Is it that obvious?'

On the other end of the line, Amy balked.

'Sorry. You just sound . . . croaky.'

Birch had to admit, she did.

'My dad put me to bed on the sofa, like I'm a kid off sick from school.'

'That's cute. He called the station earlier to say he was picking you up. Wouldn't hear of a uniform taking you home.'

Birch laughed.

'He said he thought the neighbours might think I was a criminal.'

'Oh, bless.' Amy's voice was the same one she used when looking at photos of her colleagues' dogs. 'He seems like a sweetie.'

Birch made a sputtering noise.

'Sweetie is pushing it,' she said. 'I think mostly reformed arsehole is closer. Anyway, I'm awake. Are you still at work? You sound like you're moving.'

'I'm walking home. Literally just clocked out.'

'Jesus. It's nearly ten.'

'Yeah.' Amy drew the word out, long and slow. 'There's been a development.'

'Anything you can tell me about?'

Birch felt the import of what she was about to hear in Amy's pause. The horrible adrenalin feeling returned: the same one she'd had earlier, sitting with Charlie.

'We got a call from the Royal. James Able died this evening.'

Birch closed her eyes, forced herself to breathe. She felt strangely affected by the news and was surprised – James Able was a scumbag, and if anything, the grisly end he'd met was only proof that karma did indeed exist. But this was the first time since Operation Kendall that she'd heard about the death of a perp. The news landed differently this time: some-how, it was harder to hear.

'Okay.'

It wasn't much of a response, but it was all she could man-age to say.

'I mean, having seen the state of him, earlier . . .' Amy trailed off.

'It was probably inevitable.'

Amy didn't reply. Birch recalled how ashen-faced the younger woman had looked at the crime scene, how carefully she'd carried the mugs from Alyona's kitchen. The tremor in her hands. Amy was struggling with this too.

'So that means . . .' Birch didn't finish the sentence. She wanted to encourage Amy to speak. It worked.

'That means our vampire is now a bona fide murderer,' she said. Then she added, in a quieter voice, 'Shit just got real.'

'You're not wrong. How's McLeod's blood pressure?'

Amy made a high-pitched hum, as though weighing up the question.

'Down a bit from earlier,' she said, 'though not by much. Murder by immolation is a splashy crime, he knows the papers will be all over it. We've tracked down Able's wife, though.'

'He had a wife?'

'Turns out, he did.'

Birch felt her eyes widen. She always found it hard to imagine the women whose life choices included legally attaching themselves to known psychopaths.

'You did the visit?'

'Crosbie and I. He wanted to come, though he didn't say much. I think he's pretty determined not to let me out of his sight again.'

'I'm sorry, Kato. McLeod gave you hell, too, I imagine?'

'To be honest, it all descended into a rant about Eddison Deas after a while, and I zoned out. It wasn't anywhere near as bad as the pasting you got, from what I hear.'

Birch sucked air through her teeth.

'It wasn't the best half-hour of my life, I'll admit. But we both survived. And if you did the visit with Able's wife, that means you're still on the case?'

Amy passed by a beer garden or the open door of a bar: Birch could hear the filmy spill of music in the background of the call.

'Yeah. I thought he'd pull me off it, too, but I've basically written the entire file.'

Birch made a tutting sound.

'That's what happens when Crosbie gives you a little project to keep you busy, not realising what he's dealing with. I hope that guy got hauled over the coals, too?'

She could hear the slight smile on her friend's face as she answered.

'A chat was had.'

Birch smiled back.

'Fucking *good*,' she said.

Amy went quiet. The music in the background faded, but the ambient sound of the city filtered down the line: voices. The slam of a cab door.

'What's Able's wife like?'

'Timid,' Amy replied, 'you'll be unsurprised to learn. Living in precarious luxury. They've got a heart-shaped swimming pool in the basement.'

'Classy.'

'Yep. All the more so for being financed by Able's cut from his girls.' Amy's voice was tinged with disgust. 'She seems to know about it all, the wife. Didn't seem especially surprised that he'd ended up dead. Almost like she was expecting us.'

'How the other half live, eh?'

'Well, quite.'

'Must have been a hard visit to do, nevertheless.'

Amy tilted her head. Birch could tell, because she heard the clack of the other woman's earring against the receiver.

'I've done worse. The Three Rivers shooting, telling the parents – that was tough. Those kids going off to college and then never coming home. I mean, you remember.'

Birch tried not to. She was tired of remembering bad things.

'We all do.'

There was a sound on the line, and it took Birch a moment to realise her colleague was stifling a yawn.

'Sorry,' she said, 'you must be exhausted. Let me say my piece, and then you can get to your bed.'

Amy snorted.

'I wish. Work still to do before tomorrow, when the Able news breaks.'

'Oh God. Just hydrate, okay? Not too much coffee.'

Amy laughed, and the laugh had another yawn in it.

'Really? Never known *you* follow that advice.'

'But I'm a senior officer, honey, different rules for me.' Birch winced before she'd even finished the sentence. *You're not a serving police officer right now.*

'Okay.' Amy was still laughing. 'So go on, then. Say your piece.'

Birch paused. It felt hard to switch gears away from banter and back into work mode, especially when Amy was clearly so tired.

'You might have already had this second-hand, from McLeod,' Birch ventured. Maybe she wouldn't need to say very much at all.

'I don't think so,' Amy replied. 'He didn't really say much about the talk you two had.'

Damn, Birch thought.

'I wouldn't exactly call it a talk,' she said. 'More like a verbal sandblasting. But okay – the short version is, what if we're wrong about the Solomon Carradice thing? What if this guy isn't some pretender to the scumbag throne?'

The question registered with a moment of surprised quiet.

'Um . . .' Amy said.

'I know, I know. But hear me out. Why no accomplices? Why no leads? This guy's like a fucking ghost. It's making my teeth itch. Something doesn't fit.'

'I thought you were pretty convinced.'

'I was,' Birch said, 'until . . . well, until I wasn't. Until today, I guess.'

She imagined Amy frowning, maybe even rolling her eyes as she walked.

'But surely,' Amy said, 'this Able thing is the biggest indicator yet that this is gang-related? Or someone wanting to get in on that world?'

'Yes, I admit that. I admitted that to McLeod. I just can't seem to stop asking myself the question, *what if it isn't that?*'

'You've got a hunch?' Amy laughed. 'What am I asking for? Of course you've got a hunch. So, what – you think these crimes are all related in some way? Linked by something none of us are seeing?'

'I . . . feel like that's what I ought to be saying. But no, that isn't what I'm saying.'

Amy was still smiling, Birch could tell, but there was an edge of something else in her voice. Impatience, perhaps.

'Helen, I have to be honest – you're not making a whole load of sense.'

Birch pressed one palm to her forehead. Her hip hurt. Her hip always hurt.

'No,' she said, 'I know. Let me organise my thoughts a bit. So, whenever a violent incident occurs, and you're looking for motive, what are you assuming?'

'Something personal,' Amy replied. 'A family connection. Sex. Jealousy. All that stuff.'

'Right. And those motives aren't there for our perp, our vampire. He isn't known to the people he's gone for. Robin had no clue who he was, for example. So we can basically rule that out.'

'Well, yeah.'

'But say we run with the gangster theory. This is some new Billy Bigbaws seeing a gap in the market and wanting to start his empire. What motives are we looking for in a case like that?'

There was a short pause before Amy answered.

'Money,' she said. 'I mean, drugs, larceny, protection rackets – all that stuff boils down to money, doesn't it?'

'It does. So here's the thing: where's the money in this case? Our guy runs a kid off the road, he stalks Robin, he kills James Able. But how does he profit? What does he get out of it?'

'I mean . . . reputation? Power? Other people's fear? He's building a brand, isn't he?'

'But why kill Able out of nowhere? Wouldn't a smart guy get into his crew, get the goons on side, get the girls on side? Then when he took out the king, he could claim the whole kingdom.'

'I see what you're saying,' Amy replied, 'but maybe he just isn't smart? I'm sorry, marm, I'm just struggling to see what other motive there might be.'

Birch decided to ignore the *marm* and barrel on. She was committed now.

'I'll tell you what I'm starting to think this is. I think this is revenge.'

Amy fell silent. In the background, Birch heard the rattle-crash of a shopfront shutter being pulled down.

'Think about it,' she said. 'Before McLeod so rudely interrupted, Alyona was trying to tell us about this Jay bloke – who, unless a pretty hefty coincidence is involved, is our vampire, right? I asked her if she thought Able being set on fire was an act of payback for her face. She thought it was, and it certainly seemed set up that way: it happened right outside her house, for one thing.'

'Also,' Amy cut in, 'Jay booked an incall with Alyona last night. He was there – we've got him less than a block away from the scene – around the time Able was attacked.'

'You brought her in?'

This wasn't really surprising, but Birch heard herself sound surprised.

'We did,' Amy said. 'That was the most significant thing she had to say.'

'Pretty significant.'

'Yeah. But anyway – revenge?'

'Yes.' Birch felt Amy's desire to get on with it, her tiredness palpable on the line between them. 'Able was a vengeance killing. What if the other incidents were acts of revenge, too?'

Amy made a *pshaw* noise, which made the phone line crackle.

'I dunno, Helen,' she said. 'I see what you're getting at, but if this Jay isn't a gangster and is in fact just an ordinary guy . . . who has that many enemies? Who among us feels the need to get revenge on that many people?'

Birch closed her eyes.

'Okay, listen,' she said, 'stick with me, because I'm about to get weird.' She opened her eyes again, trying to push the pain in her hip to the back of her mind. Trying to make sense. 'I know we're trained to look for the personal motives, we're trained to look for connections between victim and perp. I know those connections are there almost every time. But what if this guy wasn't getting revenge for himself? Alyona's not family, after all – he hasn't even known her all that long. What if he was getting a more nebulous kind of revenge? Just getting revenge generally?'

Amy had stopped walking. Birch guessed she must be in her street now, keen to put down the phone, take out her keys, get home.

'I'm sorry,' she said, 'it's been a long day, and I might just be being slow, but . . . what are you saying?'

'I'm saying I think we might be dealing with a vigilante.'

Why didn't I just say right at the start? Birch wondered. Because she'd have dismissed it, she thought. She's probably going to dismiss it anyway.

'Think about it,' Birch went on. 'The people our vampire has gone after have one thing in common: they're all lowlife bastards. They've all done bad, or at least highly questionable, things. There's an argument to be made that the world would be better without these guys in it, right? So what if this Jay decided to clean up the streets?'

Amy still didn't speak, and Birch felt a spike of annoyance.

'Come on, Kato. I know it's only a theory, but it could have legs, no?'

'I don't know,' Amy said, at last. 'I mean, I've read about vigilante cases. They're pretty rare. And there needs to be a catalyst. People don't just wake up one day feeling all Robin Hood. Something happens to traumatise them, or galvanise them.'

'So something happened to our vampire. We just don't know what it is yet.'

Amy's pauses were increasingly uncomfortable. Birch could feel it.

'You said all this to McLeod?'

'I didn't. I just said the Solomon Carradice theory needed another look. That I wasn't convinced.'

'Okay, good.' Amy sounded genuinely relieved.

'What do you mean by *good*?'

The other woman took a deep breath.

'Helen, I'm your friend, so you have to know I say this kindly, but . . . you sound a little wrung out right now. You sound like you've maybe run a little too far with this, in your head. I'm starting to get worried.'

Birch winced. Once again, words of McLeod's echoed in her head: *people are talking, Birch. Your colleagues are worried about you.*

'I get that, I do, but I'm telling you—'

'I can't go to Crosbie with this,' Amy said, 'and McLeod would hit the roof. I wouldn't even know where to start with building a case around this.'

'But it makes sense. You have to admit, it makes sense.'

'I think it makes sense in a narrative sort of way. As a story, it works to neatly link these crimes. But how often are things neat, in real life? And as far as motive goes, I'd need a lot more actual evidence before I could be convinced.'

Birch closed her eyes again. She was still tired, though she'd slept a good few hours on the couch. She realised Amy wasn't going to help her.

'And that's why you're a damn good officer, Sergeant,' Birch relented. 'You should have been promoted years ago.'

Amy's tone lifted.

'You're not upset with me?'

'God, no,' Birch said. 'You know what I'm like, Kato. I need the voice of reason to bounce my mad ideas off, sometimes. I'm grateful you're always around. Especially when you've been ordered not to talk to me.'

Amy scoffed.

'I think McLeod knew that order was futile even as he gave it, to be honest.'

There was a moment of tense quiet between them.

'So you won't be saying we've spoken?'

Amy nodded, or maybe shook her head: Birch heard the patter of the earring once again.

'I will not.'

'Good. Thanks for listening to the wild theories of a frustrated woman. Just keep it in mind, okay? Just think about it.'

'I will. I'm at my door now, Helen.'

I knew you were, Birch thought.

'Good stuff. You get inside and put your slippers on. Don't work too far into the wee hours, please.'

Amy smiled then, Birch could tell.

'Fingers crossed.'

Birch hung up the call, and sat in the dim grey box of her living room. Her mother's face was a whitish smudge on the mantelpiece. Her hip didn't hurt any more, as such, but it felt weird: stiff, perhaps, from her lopsided sleep. She ought to get up and cook something – eat something more substantial than a cheese sandwich. She ought to hydrate herself, brush her teeth, wash the metallic taste out of her mouth. She ought to get into soft clothes and take herself off to bed, try to sleep in spite of the pain, in spite of McLeod's barbs from that afternoon echoing around in her head. Instead, she threw Jamieson's blanket on to the floor and sat up. *Your colleagues are worried about you:* McLeod's voice rewound and replayed in her head like a broken record. She rolled her eyes. She was going to have to do this on her own.

'Fuck*sake*.'

She fished around on the rug for her crutch and levered herself upright. Rather than putting on table lamps, as she might do normally, she shuffled across the room and hit the switch for what her family had always called 'the big light'. The living room lit up like the inside of a fridge, and she saw the weeks she'd spent at Anjan's written in the thin film of dust that covered almost everything.

'Life's too short,' she said to herself, 'to *dust.*'

She stepped out into the hall, where the sound of the sea filtered louder through the front door, punctuated by the *pat-pat-pat* of night-time joggers out on the prom. She put the light on here, too, then shifted her weight fully on to the crutch. With her free hand, she got hold of the knob on the understairs cupboard door. She took a deep breath, expecting a tsunami of possessions she wasn't sure she could bend to pick up. Then she pulled.

'Oh, Jesus.'

To her surprise, the cupboard's packed stuffing of boxes and bags had held, but it was more chaotic than she'd remembered. It took some effort to rearrange the junk, balanced as she was on her good leg's foot, and working slowly and gingerly to avoid an avalanche. At last she saw, wedged in the back, the item she was looking for. She stuck the crutch into a gap, and worked at the cheap wooden frame of the pinboard until it moved. If she stretched, she could reach an arm in and manoeuvre it up and over the piles of stuff.

'Okay, Helen,' she said, her voice bouncing up off the old-fashioned pot-tiled floor. 'This is going to hurt.'

It did. She lunged for the pinboard, figuring it made sense to do things quickly. Her fingers closed on one corner and held on, though she yelped at the hot bolt of pain her bad hip sent flashing down the back of her leg. She was bending in ways her physio would surely have advised against, but the pinboard was coming free. She gritted her teeth and gave it a final tug, almost falling backwards on to the tiled floor as it shot out of the cupboard's grip. Her bad leg felt fizzy now, and she guessed she'd be in trouble from someone for working it wrong. But she had her prize: she swung the hanging string on the back of the pinboard over her shoulder, flapping the sheet of chipboard and cork on to her back. She slammed the cupboard door, retrieved the crutch, and shambled triumphantly through the living room and into the kitchen. A stack of Post-its sat next to the fridge, ostensibly for writing shopping lists, though usually she used them to leave notes for Anjan or scribble down details from phone calls she took at home.

'And a pen,' she said, unhooking her arm from the crutch and leaning on the worktop while she swung the pinboard down on to it with a splintery crack. Her cutlery drawer was perpetually full of crap, and she found a biro wedged among the bottle openers and paring knives.

'Right,' she said. She peeled a Post-it from the top of the stack and wrote *VIGILANTE CASE* in block letters across it. She stuck it to the pinboard with the pad of her thumb, where it fluttered.

'McLeod is going to *love* this,' she whispered, 'when he finds out.'

Sunday, 18 July, 10:00

I figured I had to get rid of my car.

The blaze made by Able's body sent a plume of smoke up over the scrapyard wall. I watched it in my rear-view as I drove away, trying to stay calm. I wondered how many CCTV images there were of the Golf at the scene. I'd been lucky with the kid in the Honda Civic, but now it was different. Now I'd killed someone, luck wasn't enough. I was going to have to be smart.

I didn't drive back to my flat. Instead, I considered the petrol gauge, wavering at just over half a tank, and tried to think of the most remote place I could take the car to on that, and be able to get home on public transport, undetected. I drove seawards, passing Portobello and Milton Road, hanging a left at the Jewel on to the A1. It was quiet, still early on a Sunday, and it felt good to speed up to seventy, feeling the car putting miles between myself and the thing I had done.

I drove in a dwam, my hands pale on the wheel. The road was a straight line I largely ignored, giving my head a shake at the roundabouts, but otherwise zoning out, my brain on cruise control. Somewhere near the Coldingham turn a realisation came: I'd never be able to see Natalia again. I'd never know if she'd watched James Able's body burn. I'd just have to hope that she had. I hoped she was watching it now.

I made it to Berwick, the sea to my left almost hidden by a solid white wall of haar. Gulls hung over the tarmac, wailing. I turned on the radio, but not for long – its idle prattle annoyed me. I hated that the world wasn't changed, the sky hadn't fallen. Didn't everyone realise I'd killed a man? Didn't everyone know?

I didn't go into town: I imagined a camera mounted on every building's corner, the Golf tracked like a fox along every street. Instead, I turned right and took the bypass, burning off Sunday drivers in the crawler lane. The A1 signage told me I could go on to Alnwick, if I wanted, or to Newcastle beyond, but I knew this place. I'd come here on teenage holidays, camping and swimming on Scremerston beach with pals who'd long since drifted away. I'd walked the fretwork of single-track roads that zigzagged between the A1 and the sea, laden with tent poles and underage beers. The fact that it was touristy July wasn't ideal, but I reckoned I'd find a hiding place somewhere in that web. A place to dump the car and run, buy myself time to work out what I ought to do next. Right then, I hadn't the faintest clue.

I followed an ancient memory off the main road, round a sweeping right-hand bend, beyond a farm with camping pods, and then left. The trees gave way and the sea opened out like a sail, the horizon still muffled by haar. That would help, I thought: those sea mists were notoriously freezing, which meant there'd be fewer people around.

Between my car and the beach was the East Coast Mainline, and around a quarter-mile out I saw the level-crossing lights flash on and the barriers jerk down. Something told me I needed to stop: those barriers would have cameras, and I didn't want the Golf to be recognised this close to my proposed dump site. I hit my hazard warners and pulled into the verge, thankful the road was quiet. When I climbed out of the driver's door, I felt the haar's cold pulling the hairs on my arms. The air was damp and salt-thick and tasted like those holidays I'd spent here as a stupid kid. I walked to the back of the car and looked at the number plate, the seamless plastic rivets that held it in place. I had no idea what tool might be used to remove them. I tried to prise them out using my fingernails, but made not a whisper of difference. I wracked my brains, wishing for a can of black spray paint, a marker pen, anything I could use to obscure the letters and numbers that linked this godforsaken car directly to me. A Land Rover clattered past, its canvas shell a throng of dogs. The woman driving it looked at me oddly as she passed, and I watched until she pulled up at the crossing, making sure she didn't plan to turn around.

I didn't hear the train until I saw it, the sound of its approach submerged beneath the ambient roar of the sea. But as it crashed past the crossing, the blur of it impossibly fast, I had an idea. The barriers lifted. I waited for the Land Rover to cough away and out of sight. Then I popped the boot and retrieved the iron starter bar.

The rag I'd wrapped around the gory end was stuck there, mud-coloured now and crusty. I flipped the bar in my grip and swung the cleaner end at the centre of the number plate. I felt it dent the metal behind, and flinched, thinking of the pride I'd once taken in this car, how much had changed in the months since my life went awry. But what mattered now was the yellow plastic plate, which shattered into a satisfying maze of bits. The pieces came away easily; I gathered them up in my palms and threw them into the Golf's open boot. They lay beside the rumpled latex gloves I'd worn to offer Able's body to the fire. The gloves made the whole car smell of petrol, but I was glad of them – I'd need them, soon.

The front plate smashed as easily as the back. I walked in a circle, picking up any fallen shards, inspecting my handiwork.

The car could now be any black VW Golf, fresh from a dealer, perhaps, or awaiting personalised plates. I couldn't have taken it any distance like that, but it would pass under the level crossing's eye. I drove on, rattling over the sunk tracks. Birds ribboned in and out of the haar.

The road descended into a long spine of dunes. I passed a series of gravelled alcoves that served as car parks for the beach. I'd guessed right: the haar was keeping folk away. The Land Rover was there, and a couple of other, smaller cars. Atop the headland, a deserted ice-cream van sat wreathed by fingers of mist. I passed it, remembering old summers, the communion-like taste of wafer cones.

The memories were ancient now, but I recalled my way along the road until a seam of grass appeared at its centre. I passed a crumbling concrete shack, the shell of a WW2 lookout post, and thought back to climbing into its piss-reeking dark with my pals to drink cans and make a racket. And somewhere beyond it there'd been a track . . . hadn't there?

I almost missed it, choked now by years of weeds and marram grass. I hit the brakes and swerved, sand spraying up from the wheels. The hard-standing fell away and I felt the Golf skid, steering wheel juddering in my grip. Yes, this was it – no longer a track but a faint path that fell away from the road. I wrestled the car to a manageable speed, then eased down into this natural bowl in the land. I'd camped here once: I remembered lying stoned outside my tent in the dark, hemmed in on all sides by the protective walls of dunes. Now this place was a fly-tipper's dream: I steered around an ancient fridge, a bike frame, weather-blackened mattresses. I brought the Golf to a stop, having crunched over a bottle and felt one of the tyres give. I couldn't have driven out of that place anyway, even if I'd changed my mind. The car was beached, wheels heavy with sand. I tried not to think what I'd spent on it – or what it had cost me, which was more.

I waded knee-deep in the scattered rubbish and marram, searching for anything flammable. I lay on my stomach in front of the Golf and reached in as far as I could, under the front bumper. There I stuck bits of driftwood into the sand, making a pyramid shape: dried white, the sticks were perfect for tinder. I found a couple of aerosol cans, and a plastic lighter that didn't spark but still contained liquid. I tucked these into the pointed cage of sticks. At the centre were the petrol-soaked latex gloves. As I stretched the gas-ring lighter in to ignite the pile, I hoped it would be enough.

The walk back to town was around three miles, give or take. The sun was high now, the haar beginning to shrivel back, more cars trailing down the tiny roads towards the beach. I kept my head down, skirting the dunes until they ran out. As I walked back over the railway tracks, I covered my face with both hands, and felt absurd. I imagined the glare of the CCTV on my back as I climbed the hill I'd driven down, back towards the treeline.

At the top, I turned and looked back the way I'd come. A roil of black, gauzy smoke was rising from the dunes. A camp-fire, I hoped the locals would think: an optimistic barbecue in the haar. That wouldn't wash for long: I thought of the Golf giving up to the flames, its various petrochemicals setting the whole makeshift dump ablaze. I'd lain there, not even sixteen, staring up at the star-specked, cloudless glass of the sky. I couldn't believe what had happened to my life, to the man I'd been.

On the edge of town was an ASDA, housed in a massive, anonymous hangar. I filled a basket with face wipes and dry shampoo, two chicken and bacon sandwiches I planned to wolf on the station platform while waiting for my train. A two-litre bottle of water, disposable razors and a travel-sized can of shaving foam. Toothpaste, a toothbrush, a miniature bottle of mouthwash. From the clothing aisles I bought a small wheeled suitcase and a cheap polyester suit, a plain white button-up shirt, unremarkable tie. The shoes I was wearing were generic casual boots – I figured they would do. I chucked it all in a bag-for-life, glad I had cash left over after my evening with Natalia. I carried the whole lot to the customer toilets, and locked myself in the disabled cubicle.

The man who emerged after thirty minutes or so was far less dishevelled than the man who went in. His face was no longer smeared with soot and screenwash, the memory of someone else's blood. Up close, his head looked a little odd, like its close shave had been done partly blind, with only the help of a greasy mirror in a toilet stall. But his hands were clean, his dirty clothes balled up out of sight in a bag-for-life and zipped inside a suitcase. He wore a suit that wouldn't last long, but fit. He'd brushed his teeth. He looked for all the world like a businessman making an overnight trip. I was him, and he was me, and we were walking to the station to get on the next train home. Then we'd figure out what in the hell we were going to do.

II

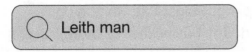

Q Leith man

Top   **Latest**   **People**   **Photos**   **Videos**

Breaking News @edinburghevenews 35m
BREAKING **Leith man** in critical condition following
brutal attack: edinburghevenews.co.uk/leith-man-critical-
condition-following-brutal-attack-3594892
Breaking News @edinburghevenews 34m
Replying to @edinburghevenews
The attack appears to be gang-related and local residents
are urged not to panic. Live reporting at the link above:
more updates as they come in.
Leila @leilababyg 31m
Bet all the money in my bank this #Leith attack is football
related #sectarianism #scotlandsshame **#leithman**
Irina in Scotland @irinabeks 29m
Replying to @edinburghevenews
keep Leith safe for our kids!!!! Gangs not welcome here!!!
Leith Man jonnomcb79 26m
I know who it was got set on fire in Leith and let me tell
youse all whoever did it should get a medal
hibsfan886 @hibsfan886 25m
Replying to @jonnomcb79
aye james able local scumbag seen him round lots
Edinburgh Police Incidents @edinburgh_999 22m
Police Scotland appealing for information on brutal attack
in #Leith early this morning. The victim has been identified
as **Leith man** James Able. Call Crimestoppers 0800
555111
Graham W @get__tae 19m
Replying to @jonnomcb79

Good riddance, Able pimps vulnerable women on Salamander St & has dodgy businesses in Leith. Ruining the community.

hibsfan886 @hibsfan886 18m

Replying to @get__tae

an hes a jambo lol

Alison Ross @alibalyalibalyb 16m

Replying to @edinburgh_999

I don't agree with violence but Leith is safer because this has happened. Kinda hope the police don't catch who did this . . .

Mary-Ellen McG @earymellen 15m

Replying to @alibalyalibalyb

I hope it was his wife!!!!!!!!!!

Monday, 19 July, 09:05

'So, Helen. How has your week been?'

Dr Jane was wearing a cashmere jumper today, oatmeal-coloured, with a slash-style neck. Birch coveted it, though she suspected such a garment would look far more haphazard on her.

'Honestly,' she replied, 'I'm not sure where to start.'

Dr Jane looked down at her iPad.

'Well . . . towards the end of the last session, we got to something I thought was quite interesting. You said you were dealing with worries that you weren't cut out to do your job.'

'Yes, I remember.'

'But in your therapy journal entry from Friday – thanks for having a go at that, by the way – you say you're also missing the job, that perhaps you feel less *yourself* without it?'

Birch felt her face flush. With all that had happened since she'd written it, she'd actually forgotten about the journal entry.

'I wondered,' Dr Jane was saying, 'if you might like to explore all of that today.'

Birch shuffled in her chair. She'd stayed up late, scribbling on Post-its, hunting out drawing-pins. Her pinboard was full of half-formed thoughts and questions. At the centre was a hot-pink Post-it she couldn't stop thinking about. It read, *hit and run: witnesses.*

'You seem a little distracted,' Dr Jane observed, and Birch realised some time had passed since anyone had spoken.

'I am,' she said, 'I'm sorry. I didn't sleep very well last night.'

'More bad dreams?'

Birch blinked.

'I'm sorry?'

Dr Jane gestured vaguely towards the iPad on her lap.

'You mentioned in your journal entry that you've been having recurring dreams.'

Birch shook her head.

'Last night it was more a case of busy brain,' she replied, inwardly cursing the whole damn electronic journal idea. 'Getting to sleep was the problem, not staying asleep. It's like that sometimes.'

'Always? Or just since Operation Kendall.'

'The latter.'

The other woman nodded.

'So what is it that your brain is busy with?'

'Just . . . thinking about things. I mean, it depends.'

Dr Jane uncrossed her right leg from her left, then crossed them again, the other way around. The movement was elegant, and Birch envied it. She felt as though she hadn't sat elegantly in a chair since she came out of hospital.

'Tell me some of the things you think about, when you're lying awake at night.'

Birch was quiet for a moment. Dr Jane put on her *I'll wait* face.

'Well, I think about my brother a lot. I think about all the things he's done, what it feels like to be in the jail. How long it is 'til he gets out. That sort of thing.'

'That's understandable,' Dr Jane said. 'But I don't think that's what's keeping you up nights, is it?'

Birch blinked. She knew she wouldn't like this part of therapy: she'd expected to be seen through, but dissembled all the same.

'I've been doing this job a while,' Dr Jane said, smiling. 'I'm pretty good at telling when I'm being fobbed off.'

'Sorry,' Birch said. The word seemed to fall out of her mouth unbidden.

'It's okay. You don't know me very well, and the truth is uncomfortable. Especially when you have to share it with a stranger.' Dr Jane bent her body forward: the same gesture Birch had mistaken last week for a bid to reach out and take hold of her hand. 'Things like sleeping better,' she said, 'I think we can work to improve without much difficulty. But I can only help in a meaningful way if you tell me what's really going on. You can trust me, Helen. Like I said last week, none of what you say will ever go beyond this room.'

'Is that true?' Birch felt herself frowning. 'I don't mean to call you a liar, but I know you have to provide reports to DCI McLeod. You do have to feed things back.'

Dr Jane was nodding.

'Sure,' she said, 'but those reports are formalities, they're quantitative data. I have to feed back whether or not you attend sessions, how many you've had, things of that kind. I literally fill out a form. There's no detail written into it. DCI McLeod will never know anything specific about what you've shared with me. Neither will anyone else. I give you my word.'

'Okay,' Birch said. 'Okay, I understand.'

'You seem a bit preoccupied by DCI McLeod. What he may or may not think of you.'

'Oh, trust me,' Birch said, 'I'm now under no illusions about what DCI McLeod thinks of me.'

★

She felt a strange sensation, travelling home from the session in a cab. She'd been exhausted when she first got out of hospital six weeks ago, convinced she could feel the wound in her hip drinking up every unit of energy she had. Though the hip had got better, her sleeping hadn't, thanks to the busy brain she'd now begun to empty out all over Dr Jane. Now she felt another layer of tired, one that seemed to settle over her like a veil. She couldn't remember the last time she'd talked at such length with anyone, not even Anjan. Dr Jane had listened patiently, wearing a look of kind, professional concern. When Birch had finished recounting her dressing-down in McLeod's office, Dr Jane had waited a while before replying. Birch found that short silence comforting: she admired the way the other woman didn't leap to say what she thought, the way most people might have done.

'Do you think,' Dr Jane said, eventually, 'that it was fair for DCI McLeod to go about things that way?'

'No,' Birch had replied, so quickly she'd surprised herself. 'Not entirely.'

'As he spoke to you, did you feel that he was fully in control?'

Birch had hesitated a little at this question, though the answer felt clear and loud in her mind. She was surprised to find that the more she said to Dr Jane, the more she wanted to say. The more she let herself tell the truth, the more easily it came.

'Not entirely. Not towards the end of the conversation.'

'Okay,' Dr Jane replied. 'I think it's important that you just notice that. Just note that the things said about your character – the ones you found most hurtful – were not said by someone who was being fully rational and fair. They were said by someone who wasn't in full control.'

Birch had frowned at this. She'd hoped for a little more than just *noticing*.

'Sure,' she said, 'but that stuff was still said. I still heard it.'

'I know. And those remarks have come at a bad time for you, haven't they? You're already struggling with low self-worth, intrusive thoughts, and bad sleep, *and* you're still managing your pain. You're trying to survive in a situation where your markers of success and stability are largely absent. You set a lot of store by serving others, I think – by being good at your job, by focusing on that. Without that, your identity feels less certain, doesn't it?'

Birch felt her own eyes widen.

'I guess that's true.'

'Right,' Dr Jane replied. 'And that's a very difficult position to be in, especially when your present physical health prevents you from doing a lot of things that might potentially combat that feeling. So to be in that difficult position, and *then* have to hear the things DCI McLeod said to you yesterday – that has to have had an effect. Far more of an effect, I'd say, than if you'd sat in that room and had that conversation under normal circumstances.'

Oh Jesus, Birch heard herself thinking. She really does know things, this woman. She isn't just bullshitting me.

'So, what do you propose I do?'

Dr Jane seemed to zero her gaze in on Birch's hands. Birch was picking at her cuticles with a thumbnail, a thing she seemed to do when she was nervous. Realising Dr Jane had noticed, she stopped.

'I can't tell you what to do in your relationship with DCI McLeod,' Dr Jane said. 'It isn't my job to give that kind of advice. But again, I'd say to you – practise noticing. Notice that you're depleted right now, that things have a more profound effect on you than usual. Notice that your self-worth isn't great. Remind yourself that, although you're much better than you were, you're still living with an injury. Notice, and act accordingly. See if you can't give yourself a bit of a break.'

★

The driver helped her out of the cab, and offered to walk her the few yards along the prom to her door.

'I'm fine,' Birch said, handing over a decent-sized tip. 'I promise.'

As the cab roared away, she considered all the things she'd said to Dr Jane, and realised she hadn't once made mention of Anjan.

Is that bad? she thought, as she closed the gap between the cab and her front door. She still hadn't listened to his voice-mails, though a couple more had appeared. She hadn't replied to his texts. He swung in and out of her thoughts, along with McLeod's barbs, Dr Jane's careful remarks, Gerald Hodgson and the things he'd said before he fired hot metal into her hip. But mostly she thought of the tall, thin man, the almost mythic quality he'd taken on. The case felt like a western: unknown stranger walks into the local tavern and rattles out the bad guys. There's a new sheriff in town, but he doesn't show his face. Birch knew that Alyona would be asked for details of Jay's appearance, so an identikit picture could be made up. Realising she wouldn't get to see it made her livid. She wanted a copy of that picture for her board.

She made a beeline for the kitchen as soon as the door was closed. That same pink Post-it was still preying on her mind: *hit and run: witnesses.* That was her plan for the rest of the afternoon: go back to the first known incident involving the Vampire. Read absolutely everything in Amy's file. The case file would have been updated; Birch only had the old version she'd been emailed on Friday night, after pleading with her colleague on the phone. There'd be more officers accessing it now, not just Amy adding her diligent notes while Crosbie ignored her. It would have Alyona's testimony filed, alongside the statement of the security guard who found James Able and put out the fire. It would have notes of Amy's meeting with Able's timid wife, and witness statements taken by uniforms from the people on balconies who'd ogled at the scene. But there shouldn't be anything new pertaining to the hit and run, and that was the bit Birch cared about. She assumed McLeod still didn't know she had this file, and what he didn't know she was up to wouldn't hurt him. She decided this was a sentiment Dr Jane would surely sign off on.

'I'm *noticing*,' she said to no one, 'that DCI McLeod can go to hell.'

She pottered around the kitchen on her crutch, taking longer to do things which, before the shooting, would have taken seconds. She cooried a flask out of the cupboard for tea, filled the kettle with both hands while balancing on her good leg. With a little difficulty, she carried her laptop out to the garden and set it on the ratty coffee table she'd consigned to the patio. A return trip was required for the flask of tea and a mug.

'Sick to the back teeth of this, Dr Jane,' she said, rattling the crutch at nothing in particular. 'I can't tell a lie: being almost better but not *better* is still pretty shit.'

Finally, she was settled on her garden bench. The day was warm but overcast, a fact she didn't mind. There'd be no glare on her screen as she read the file, and being outside was a treat after such a long time spent in Anjan's flat.

Amy had organised things immaculately, a fact for which Birch immediately gave thanks.

'Oh, Kato,' she said, seeing each document clearly dated and named, laid out in chronological order, new to old, 'Crosbie really doesn't deserve you.'

She scrolled past the newer entries in the file: Amy's observations on Robin's complaints, and then the complaints themselves. The first of Amy's notes on the hit and run was a profile of the kid who'd been run off the road; more out of nosiness than anything else, Birch opened it.

Christopher Dale McGill, goes by Dale
D.O.B. 12 August 1997
Given address is 63 Riccarton Pl, Currie, EH14

Prior offences
IN10 Using A Veh. Uninsured Against Third Party Risks (2014, no charges brought, points added to licence)
DR50 In Charge Of Veh. While Unfit Through Drink/ Drugs (2016, caution issued)
S5(3) Misuse of Drugs Act 1971 Possessing a controlled drug with intent (2016, caution issued)
S4(1) / S4(3)(b) Misuse of Drugs Act 1971 Being concerned in the supply of a controlled drug (2017, one year suspended sentence)
S4(1) / S4(3)(b) Misuse of Drugs Act 1971 Being concerned in the supply of a controlled drug (2019, two year custodial sentence, HMP Edinburgh [Saughton], 396 days served)

Interviews: 1, conducted by Det Sgt Amy Kato, DC Li Park at Edinburgh Royal Infirmary
Full interview transcript and witness statement available

Summary

McGill's vehicle (2018 Honda Civic, registration [personalised] D41 EMC) struck on driver's side flank at high speed (relative to 20mph zone). Approximate time of incident 21:30, location East Claremont Street, EH7.

Honda Civic mounted pavement on passenger side. Driver's door, window and footwell collapsed. Driver's side airbag failed to inflate. Considerable damage to bodywork and suspension. Vehicle subsequently declared written off.

McGill injuries sustained: right leg broken in two places and lacerated; right elbow shattered; collarbone broken on right-hand side, facial lacerations, general minor lacerations from flying glass.

Other vehicle was a VW Golf, black, possible partial registration SM65, SN65, SM66, SN66. McGill claims driver was erratic, the crash deliberate and unprovoked. No known link between suspect and McGill. Suspect described as male, thirties, Caucasian.

Relevant offences and codes

S1(A) Road Traffic Act 1988 Causing Serious Injury By Dangerous Driving

AC10 Failing To Stop After An Accident

AC20 Failing To Report An Accident Within 24 Hours

DD10 Driving In A Dangerous Manner

SP30 Exceeding Speed Limit On A Public Road

'McGill claims driver was erratic,' Birch read aloud, 'the crash deliberate and unprovoked.' She raised her eyebrows. 'Yeah, I bet he does. Let's see if our witnesses agree.'

She clicked back to the main file and scrolled. Documents with names beginning 'Witness' began to appear, but Birch didn't open them. Her eye was caught by a video file, titled Witness_ECStGreekCCTV.

'It was filmed?' she whispered. 'Thanks for glossing over that one, Kato.'

However, as soon as Birch opened the video, she could see why it hadn't been mentioned. The angle was bad: the video had been captured by the CCTV of a Greek restaurant on East Claremont Street – she could see the stainless-steel café tables stacked on the pavement outside – but the view was partially obscured by a hanging basket filled with blue and white flowers.

'Brilliant security measure, there, lads,' Birch muttered. 'Top class.'

The video was only a few minutes in length. A couple of cars – the second of which was McGill's Honda Civic – seemed to appear out of the depths of the hanging basket. Seconds later, the Civic was violently shunted on to the kerb. The café tables toppled to the floor – the clip was without sound, but Birch imagined the racket the incident must have made. The Vampire's car sat motionless for maybe a minute after the impact, before performing a three-point turn that happened mostly off camera. Birch saw the few frames where the car's number plate was ever-so-nearly in view – this must have been how those guesses at a partial registration were made. The black Golf sped off, and the last part of the video showed the aftermath: the dinged-up Civic, witnesses emerging from their stair doors and crossing the street. People beginning to film the scene on their phones. Presumably some of that phone footage was in the file, too, but it wouldn't show very much more than McGill sitting trapped in his vehicle, waiting for the cavalry.

Birch clicked back to the beginning and played the video through again.

'Hang on a sec.'

The footage had been clipped at the start, so it didn't appear for long, but yes: now she watched again, the car in front of the Civic stood out in a way that it hadn't before. Namely, she noticed how closely McGill was following it: his front bumper closer to that little hatchback than if he'd been being towed. Birch minimised the video and scrolled through Amy's clearly named files to see if she could identify a witness statement made by the hatchback's driver. When nothing stood out in the filenames, she opened each of the documents one by one. None of them matched: there were statements from local residents who'd looked down from their windows at the scene; a statement from a pedestrian who claimed he'd seen a black VW Golf driving at speed a few moments before. Statements from the attending officers, and a rather short, terse-sounding statement Amy had taken from the injured McGill. Nothing from the driver of the hatchback, though that person must have seen it all.

Birch itched to ring Amy and ask what the deal was. Hadn't that lead been followed up? Was a statement taken and just misfiled? That didn't seem like the Kato way. The hatchback was only visible for a few short frames. Could it just be that no one had noticed it?

But no, she couldn't phone – she'd got Amy in quite enough trouble already, and if she was going to disobey orders, she would have to do that alone. Or nearly alone: she replayed the video another few times, trying to hit pause as soon as it started to capture a clearish image of the hatchback's number plate.

After several attempts, she got it. It was an older car, and though the freeze-frame was blurry, she was almost sure the number was Y807 BRM. Were she at work, she could run a check on it, see what came up. Oftentimes, nothing in the PCN system – on those occasions she'd obtain a warrant and approach the DVLA. Stranded at home, she couldn't do either, but she suspected she knew of someone she could call. Nearly alone, she thought again. Just a wee bit of help.

She still knew the number off by heart. As she listened to it ring, she counted the years she'd spent working in the building at the other end of the phone.

'Gayfield Square custody desk.'

Birch grinned.

'Is that Al?'

She didn't know why she was asking. Al Lonsdale's Wakefield accent was both familiar and unmistakable.

'Depends who wants to know.'

'Al, it's Helen Birch.'

'Ye gods, I didn't recognise the voice! How're you doing, love? We've been worried about you round these parts.'

She cringed. *Your colleagues are worried about you,* McLeod had said.

'I'm doing fine,' Birch lied, smiling. 'I got the flowers you lot sent, they were beautiful.'

'Should have been a bottle of whisky, was what I said. Who wants geraniums when you can have Glenfarclas?'

Birch laughed.

'Usually,' she said, 'I'd agree with you. But I'm off the drink right now, with these painkillers I'm on.'

'Bloody travesty, that. The whole thing. I envy whoever picked off the bastard who shot you, Helen love. I'd have liked them to bring him in so I could have smacked him about on your behalf.'

'You're a sweetie, Al, but you know full well that sort of thing isn't allowed.'

'Well.' He tutted down the phone. 'Most unsatisfactory state of affairs, if you ask me. But you're keeping well? On the mend?'

'I am. Physio every week.'

'They're working you hard?'

'At times, but I need it. Mind you, I think I had more physio last night trying to get something out of my understairs cupboard than I've had at the Royal in the past five weeks.'

Al guffawed, then stopped himself.

'You're back at your own manor, then? Not staying with your fancy lawyer any more?'

Birch sighed.

'There's been a lot of talk about me over in Leith, it seems.'

'Oh, chuck egg, never anything bad.' Al sounded stung, worried he'd hurt her feelings. 'You know we all love you down here. We'd have you back from those pen-pushers at Fettes in a heartbeat – I speak for the whole team when I tell you that.'

'Be careful what you wish for. I might transfer back.'

'Lass, I'd hold you to it. Anyway. Did you just ring for a gas, or can I do something for you?'

'Okay, so . . .'

'O-ho ho,' Al said. 'That's a guilty-sounding tone.'

Damn, Birch thought, he's good. Al Lonsdale had worked on the custody desk for longer than she'd been alive. He knew when a person was lying, when they were scared and trying to hide it, when they were carrying something concealed on their person, when they were high. Al could guess with near-total accuracy if the fresh-meat inmates he admitted to the cells were innocent or guilty.

'Jesus. You ever think about cold-reading, Al? You could make a fortune as a medium.'

He snorted.

'Nah,' he said, 'couldn't be arsed with the ectoplasm, and all that jazz. Now, spit it out, love. You're after something off me, and I've a sneaking suspicion it's something you're not supposed to have.'

'Well . . . listen, you know I'm on leave.'

'I do.'

'And you know how I hate to be idle.'

'Oh yes. Yes, indeedy.'

'So . . . there's this case.'

She practically heard his eyes roll.

'Aye, of course there is.'

'To which I am very, very definitely *not* assigned.'

'Well, no.'

'But in which I might have something of a passing interest.'

'Helen,' Al said, 'just stop right there, and let me translate. You're bored shitless – pardon my French – sitting at home, and you've poked your nose into summat, the way you like to. That prat James McLeod won't let you be doing, so you're ringing me to see if I'll send you over some file or other. Something to keep you busy. Am I right?'

Birch grinned.

'You're remarkably close,' she said, 'but it's not a file. Just a number plate you can maybe run for me. A wee speculative check, that's all.'

'Oh bloody hell, that's nothing. I was hoping you'd get me in far bigger trouble than *that*.'

'Sorry to disappoint. But . . . you'll do it?'

'Can't see it causing any harm, and if it's behind His Majesty's back, then all the better. What's the plate?'

'I'm pretty sure it's Y807 BRM.'

'Right. Now, before I run it, I want you to promise me something, Helen.'

'Anything for you.'

He made a huffing sound.

'Aye, you've said that before, but I'm still waiting on you accepting my marriage proposal.'

'Al . . .'

'Don't say it, I'm old enough to be your dad, I bloody well know. No, the promise I want from you is this: you promise me you're not going to go doing anything stupid with this information, all right? If this is the reg of some hard-nosed bastard, you are *not* to go picking a fight with him, do you understand?'

'I think it's unlikely.'

'I didn't ask if it was likely, kid. I'm saying, you're sniffing around at something or other because you're bored, and that's fine. I'd be the same in your shoes, and no mistake – you of all people know I could never retire, I'd go spare. No, I'm just saying, if this is violent crime or anything risky, just behave. No messing. No getting yourself shot again. You promise me.'

'I promise. Trust me, getting shot is something I never want to have happen again.'

'Right. I'm taking that as your word. If you break it, I'll be mightily displeased.'

Birch realised she hadn't smiled so much in a long time.

'I wouldn't dream of it.'

'Hmm. All right, then. Give us that number plate again, Y807 what?'

'BRM. Bravo, Romeo, Mike.'

'Aye aye, don't come all that phonetic stuff with me, young lady. Right. Let's see what I can find.'

Birch waited in silence, listening to Al's breath on the line. It sounded raspy as always, and she wondered if he'd ever come good on the assertion that one day he'd quit smoking once and for all. *I could if I wanted to*, he'd declare – happily reeling off the old cliché – *I just don't want to.*

'It's coming,' he said, into the quiet. 'But then, so's Christmas. Much use as a chocolate fireguard, this system.'

'Happy to wait,' Birch replied.

She listened to him breathe some more.

'Bingo,' Al said, at last. 'Ye gods, you naughty, naughty girl.'

'Who, me?'

'No, not you, Helen, you're an angel. A meddling angel, don't get me wrong. But no – I mean the lass who owns this 2001 Renault Clio. She only went and got herself an MS10, back in 2011.'

Birch frowned.

'I don't know that particular code, I have to admit. Blame the painkillers. Is it a serious offence?'

Al adopted a tone of faux-shock.

'Doesn't know the code,' he said, 'and her a detective inspector, too. No, you wally. An MS10 is the code for leaving your vehicle in a dangerous position. Three penalty points. In other words, this lass can't park to save her life.'

Birch cackled. It made her hip twinge, but she didn't care.

'That's it? That's all that's on file.'

'The full length and breadth of it,' Al replied. 'Sets my mind at rest about you getting shot again, anyroad.'

'Doesn't seem likely, does it? You okay to give me her details?'

'Aye, like I said, if doing so would piss off His Nibs, I'll give them out gladly.'

Birch poised her hand above the laptop, ready to type in whatever he said.

'There really ought to be more old-fashioned coppers like you, Sergeant.'

Al made a noise of derision.

'That's not what they say on these training courses the top brass keep sending me on. Anyway, here's your woman. You've got a pen?'

'No, but I'm ready.'

'Of course,' Al said, 'it's all technology now, isn't it? Okay. Your MS10 offender is one Josephine Stewart. Stewart spelled the *e-w* way. She lives at 15 Boat Green, EH3. Nice spot down there.'

Birch was typing.

'Is it?'

'Aye. Right by the Water of Leith, I think. It flooded badly round that way back in 2000. Maybe before your time.'

Birch found herself grinning again.

'I remember the year 2000, Al.'

'Aye, but you'd have been knee-high to the proverbial. Know where I was, the night of those floods?'

Birch knew the answer: it was the correct response to many of Al's questions, as anyone who worked at Gayfield Square soon learned.

'Behind that desk?'

'Behind this godforsaken desk, you are not wrong. And they'll have me to shoot, you know. I'll always be here.'

'I hope that's true.'

'For anything you need,' Al said, 'I mean it.'

Birch felt almost teary. She really missed Al and her old station, but more than anything, she just missed *work*. Being out there. Getting things done.

'You're a gem,' she said, 'and I owe you a pint.'

'Several, I'd say. We'll go on a hot date, once you're feeling better.'

'I'd love that.'

The phone line made a scuffing sound: Al was moving.

'All right,' he said, 'steady on. I've got to go now, Helen love. My vast expertise is required elsewhere.'

'I'm not surprised,' Birch said. 'Take care.'

She ended the call, locked her phone, and then stared at Josephine Stewart's details on the screen. She'd written *15 Bt Grn EH3*.

'Boat Green,' she said, trying to picture the place that belonged to the words. She couldn't, quite, but she knew roughly where Al meant when he said *right by the Water of Leith*.

'Okay,' she said. She opened up her phone again and dialled.

'This is Jamieson,' said the voice on the other end, and Birch had opened her mouth to speak before she realised the call had gone to voicemail. 'Ah'm busy the noo. Leave a message, or gies a phone back.'

Birch chuckled as she waited for the beep.

'Dad,' she said, when it came. 'It's Helen. You busy tomorrow? If not, I could do with a lift.'

Monday, 19 July, 21:10

'Ye're awfie laden there, darlin. Huv ye nothin tae read at hame?'

Amy dumped the heap of newspapers on to the counter.

'Just trying to keep up with the news,' she said, her voice far brighter than she felt. She watched as the man rang them up: *Scotsman, Herald, Daily Record, Edinburgh Evening News.* She tried not to look at the chocolate bars stacked up by the till in their jewel-coloured wrappers. She seemed to be craving sugar, and assumed it was a side-effect of working late.

'Is it no a bit scary, this?' The man tapped his finger lightly on top of the *Record*, which happened to be on top of the pile. Along the header, beneath his finger, ran a colourful banner: *Eddisonburgh: the capital counts down.* Amy frowned, but then the newsagent spoke again. 'A guy getting set oan fire. Ye dinnae like tae believe there's gangs in a city like Edinburgh, eh?'

Amy looked at the headline then, though she already knew what it said: *Organised crime: murder investigation launched after Leith man burned alive.*

'Scary,' she said. For just a brief second, she imagined she could smell it again: the horrible stench of the crime scene. She shivered. 'Yeah, it is.'

The man shook his head, and pushed the papers towards her, as if he wanted rid of them.

'Anythin else, hen? Fancy the Euromillions this week? Big rollover Wednesday, they're sayin.'

Amy tried to straighten her face out. She stifled a yawn.

'Tempting,' she said, 'but I'll give it a miss. Never have any luck.' She gestured at the papers, the correct change already counted out in her hand. 'Just these.'

'Well,' the newsagent said, 'see if ah win? Ah'm takin ma grandkids tae Disneyland.'

Amy smiled.

'That's perfect,' she said. 'I'll keep my fingers crossed for you.'

She turned to leave, the papers wedged under one arm, and the man called after her.

'Thirteen million!'

Amy held her free hand aloft as she slipped out of the shop door, setting off the electric bell. Her fingers were crossed. She really did hope that he won and got to visit Mickey Mouse with his grandchildren. She just wanted to get inside her flat and take off her shoes. It was hard to think about anything other than that.

The little licensed newsagent was the last shop open on Amy's block. She'd often nip in for a late-night pint of milk, a bottle of wine, or – once – a box of condoms, which she'd paid for without ever meeting the shop assistant's eye. She didn't normally buy papers, preferring to scroll through the news on her phone. But this wasn't an ordinary day: for the first time ever, she was in print.

They hadn't held a press conference – not yet. McLeod wouldn't have allowed it. They could hold a press conference when they'd made an arrest, he said, and not before. But Amy had sat and written a brief from which a press release would be rapidly prepared. She'd emailed it to Crosbie and the media team, and Crosbie had forwarded it on to McLeod. The papers already had the story, but sending the release meant the details were a little more likely to be correct. It also meant that Amy would be named. *Sergeant Amy Kato, speaking on behalf of Police Scotland.* She planned to clip the articles and post them to her parents in Japan, though she did wish the story in question wasn't quite so grim.

Amy let herself into the flat, and placed the stack of papers and her handbag on the table in the hall. She locked the mortice behind her, slid the chain on, then slipped off her high heels while still on the mat, so as not to walk on the laminate in them. She carried them into the bedroom, found their box, and placed both shoes gently inside. Her bed, though neatly made, looked incredibly inviting – too inviting, she decided, to even sit down on it, in case she should topple over and fall asleep. She peeled her tights off awkwardly, standing first on one foot, then the other. Dropping them in the laundry basket, she padded out of the room at a lick, not looking back at the bed – trying not to even think about it. Her tired feet left quick ghost prints on the shiny floor. She realised she fancied a beer, and wished she'd bought herself a couple of cans from the shop.

Amy retrieved the bag and papers from the hall. The *Record* and the *Evening News* had put the story on the front page. She felt a strange kind of reverence, carrying them into the kitchen, scanning the topmost paper for her own name. Her eyes were heavy, and the small text swam and blurred. She laid the papers out in a row along her breakfast bar, tempted to draw up a stool and make the clippings then and there. But no: she looked up, in the direction of the fridge. It was already late, she should eat something. The idea of cooking made something inside her wilt.

'Pizza it is,' she said, fishing in her handbag for her phone. She'd skipped dinner the night before, sitting up late to write the release brief, eating crackers and jam to keep herself going. 'I deserve it,' she added, her voice firm.

The app's algorithm knew her too well: it suggested Civerinos' Scarface pizza, the one with walnuts and honey. Amy reckoned she could eat that pizza every day until she died, and never tire of it. She placed the order, then instantly swiped to her Gmail to check it was confirmed. She'd been ignoring her personal inbox, thanks to work: it was full of emails from skincare brands and letterbox flower companies with subject lines like *we miss you!*, offering her coupon codes if she came back. There was an email from her mother, with the subject line *Typhoon season has started early here!* She felt a shudder of worry and swiped the email open, only to find her mother had sent her a jokey video of her father pointing a hairdryer at their Bichon Frise.

'Thanks for the heart attack, Mum,' she muttered, but laughed as she watched the dog luxuriating, its fur blown into a flat, sleek cloud. The inbox pinged, and the pizza confirmation came.

She had no sooner put the phone back down on the countertop when it rang. She felt her face twist into a grimace: work call or not, she didn't really want to talk to anyone right now. But her expression switched to one of surprise when she saw who was calling. Anjan Chaudhry, the caller ID informed her.

'Hi – Anjan?'

'Yes, I'm afraid so.' Anjan sounded as tired as she felt. 'How are you doing, Amy?'

She frowned, unable to figure out what he was calling for. She tried to run through the station's live cases – was Anjan assigned as solicitor somewhere?

'I'm okay, thanks.'

She couldn't think. Her brain felt fried.

'Busy, I'd guess,' he was saying, 'with this immolation case.'

'You've seen the papers?'

'Yes. You're quoted.'

To her own annoyance, Amy found herself blushing.

'I know,' she said, 'it's a first for me. Not the greatest print debut, though, is it? Local man is set on fire, on Sergeant Amy Kato's watch.'

Anjan laughed.

'It could be worse. In a few months, I might be getting dragged through the mud for defending the man who lit the match.'

'True. You're used to this.'

'Occupational hazard. I knew what I was letting myself in for.'

There was a pause on the line. Amy waited for him to cut to the chase, but he didn't.

'So, Anjan,' she said. 'What can I help you with this fine evening?'

'Oh yes,' he said, as though he'd drifted into his own thoughts and forgotten she was there. 'I know it's late to be calling. And it's about a personal matter, too. I'm sorry.'

'That's okay. What's up?'

When he spoke again, he sounded a little bashful. Hesitant, even, a thing Amy had never imagined him being.

'It's about Helen,' he said. 'But . . . look, you might think this is inappropriate, and please do tell me if you'd rather not, but – you're in Stockbridge, aren't you? I wondered if we could maybe chat over a drink?'

Amy closed her eyes. Her feet ached. She still had things to do before she could finally surrender and get into bed. The idea of putting her tights and shoes back on made her whole body sag. Besides, she and Civerinos already had plans.

'Normally,' she said, 'I'd say absolutely, yes. But I've just ordered a pizza, and need to be in. I'm sorry.'

Anjan seemed to straighten up then – she practically *felt* him pull himself together at the other end of the phone.

'It's quite all right,' he said. 'I was just passing, and wondered. But don't let me interrupt your night any further. Forget I even called.'

Amy tried to fight what she was about to say, though she knew it was inevitable. *You're too nice*, her mother used to tell her. *You never say no to anything*.

'Anjan – wait. If you need to talk to someone . . .' She paused, seeing in her mind's eye her mother's *told you so* face. 'If you need to talk to someone, and don't mind if that someone is stuffing pizza down her neck, then why don't you come over? Let me give you the address.'

'No, really, I don't want to impose.'

Amy rolled her eyes.

'I wouldn't have suggested it if I thought it was an imposition. Tell you what – you can stop at the shop across the street and get a couple of beers, if that makes you feel better about it.'

Anjan was quiet for a moment.

'I really appreciate this, Amy.'

She tried to keep her voice light, shiny.

'No worries,' she said, and then, 'Budvar, if they have it.'

★

Anjan looked haggard, standing on her doormat, though his clothes were as uncreased and high-end as ever. Amy had always recognised him as a fellow Type-A person, and admired him from afar for his unruffledness. Tonight, although he was clearly tired, he hadn't so much as loosened his tie. When she opened the door, he held up a blue translucent carrier bag, its handles strained by the weight of the bottles inside.

'Budvar,' he said, by way of greeting.

'You're a lifesaver,' Amy said. 'Come away in.'

As she followed Anjan through to the kitchen, Amy glanced around, unsure what she was looking for. Evidence, perhaps, though she wasn't sure of what. It just felt bizarre, having a lawyer in her flat – and intimate, having a man there. Amy went on plenty of dates – DI Birch would often make fun of her Tinder addiction – but very few of them ever ended here.

'Have a seat,' she said, gesturing to the sofa that stood against one wall. It didn't often occur to her, but she suddenly felt self-conscious at not having a proper, separate living room. Birch had told her about the grandeur of Anjan's Quartermile flat, which didn't help.

'Nice place,' Anjan said, as if he'd guessed what she was thinking. 'Handy for everything.'

Amy nodded.

'It's nice to be able to walk to work,' she said, 'though sometimes it feels a little *too* close, you know.' She rifled in a drawer for her bottle opener, then lifted one of the slippery, frosted beers. 'You want one?'

Anjan held up his hands.

'No thanks,' he said, 'I'm driving. Just been to a function round at the Grange.'

Of course you have, Amy thought. Though it was only down the road, she'd never set foot in the Grange Club – the home of Scottish cricket, venue for many a high-end soirée – and imagined she never would. She felt embarrassed now, drinking newsagent lager in front of this well-to-do man . . . but she'd had him bring it for her, so she had to. She popped the cap, fetched a glass from the cupboard and poured out the pale gold fizz, though drinking beer from the bottle was usually one of her favourite things.

'Okay,' she said, crossing the room. She arranged herself on the far end of the sofa, trying not to feel slovenly in the absence of tights or shoes. She sent up a quiet prayer of thanks that she hadn't changed into PJs yet. 'Tell me what's on your mind.'

'Helen,' Anjan said. 'Helen's on my mind.'

'Has something happened between you two?'

He threw her a pained look.

'Oh,' he said. 'She hasn't told you? You don't know?'

'I don't know anything,' Amy replied. 'The two of you haven't split up, though, have you?'

'I didn't think so at first. But now I think we might have done.'

Amy felt stung. She wanted to comfort Anjan, but more than that, she wanted to know why her friend hadn't mentioned this development.

Anjan seemed to have the same thought.

'I'm amazed she hasn't said anything,' he said. She saw him think of something then that widened his eyes: a jolt of panic. 'Wait,' he added, 'have you seen her since the two of you spoke on the phone, on Friday night? Has anyone seen her?'

Amy flapped one hand, as though flagging something down.

'Easy, Anjan,' she laughed. 'She isn't lying in a ditch somewhere. I saw her yesterday, and spoke to her on the phone last night.'

This seemed to set his mind at rest, though only for a moment.

'In that case,' he said, 'I don't know why she's ignoring me.'

'Friday night was the last time *you* saw her?'

'Yes. We had a fight.'

'Oh, shit – because of her conversation with me? That's why she hung up the phone so suddenly?'

'I'm afraid so. I didn't think it was appropriate for her to be taking on work. To be perfectly frank, I still don't. But she won't call me back or answer my texts. I've emailed her. I've left voicemails. I don't know if she's even seen them. I went round to her house yesterday afternoon, but there was no one home. She seems to have ghosted me, to use the appropriate neologism.' He gave a sad smile. 'And you know,' he added, 'for someone in my line of work, it's exceptionally difficult when you're not given any right of reply.'

'Okay, look,' Amy said, 'I can shed a little bit of light, but you have to promise not to be mad at me, or at Helen. Can you do that?'

Anjan frowned.

'I can't make a promise based on information I don't yet have.'

'Spoken like a true lawyer.'

He sighed.

'I'm certainly not going to get angry with *you*, Amy. Helen is a grown woman and can make her own decisions – knowing her as I do, I'm fairly certain she'd do whatever she wanted regardless of how you tried to influence her. But I'm already more than a little angry with *her*, so any promise I made on that score would be a lie. There, how about that?'

Amy laughed, though the laugh was hollow. She wanted to say *it's weird, talking about her like this, behind her back.* Instead, she took a deep breath.

'Well,' she said, 'there's this case.'

'The tall, thin man.'

'Yes.'

'This is the case she's doing some work on for you, behind McLeod's back?'

'She told you that?'

'No. But I overheard most of what was said on the phone on Friday night.'

'Well,' Amy said, nettled by the judgement she read into *behind McLeod's back,* the way he said it, 'you'll be happy to hear that's all over now. Things escalated.'

Again, panic registered in Anjan's eyes.

'The case,' she added, hastily, 'the *case* escalated – Helen is in good health, as far as I know. But McLeod did find out. He gave us both an absolute pasting, as you might expect. Be sure your sins will find you out.'

'Indeed.'

Amy gestured over at the papers, still lined up on the breakfast bar.

'The immolation case,' she said, 'and the tall, thin man case are one and the same.'

'I see. That's quite some escalation.'

'Yeah.'

'But Helen's off it now? You promise me? Because this is serious, Amy. This isn't just some overdue paperwork you're passing on to her. This is a serious investigation into violent, organised crime.'

Really? Amy thought. I hadn't noticed.

'You said you wouldn't get angry with me,' she said, and heard the petulance in her own voice.

Anjan let his shoulders drop, just slightly.

'Apologies,' he said. 'I'm just worried. We haven't spoken in three whole days, and it's not for want of trying. I don't have a clue what's going on.'

Amy mirrored his body language, relaxing just a little, though her brow was furrowed.

'If I'm honest,' she said, 'I'm worried about her, too, and I only saw her yesterday. I think everyone's a bit worried about her. She seems . . .'

'. . . to be making rash decisions?'

Amy tipped her head to one side.

'Maybe. I was going to say *erratic*. A bit out of control. You think she's ghosted you, for real? Because that *would* be a rash decision.' Her frown deepened. 'It doesn't seem like her. Maybe she's just taking some space?'

Anjan shrugged.

'I don't know why she wouldn't just ask for space,' he said, 'if that was what she needed. But really . . . I don't know, Amy. I can't help but think it's the *work* she needs space from. She needs rest. Not to be chasing around after this tall, thin man.'

'I was told,' Amy said, 'that McLeod warned Helen yesterday that he'd suspend her if she carried on. He's ordered her to take her leave in full. I promise you, she's done now. Done with the case.'

'She was at Fettes yesterday?'

Amy winced.

'She came to the crime scene.'

Anyone else might have raised their voice, but Anjan Chaudhry lowered his. Amy found his incredulous whisper harder to deal with than a shout.

'She *what*?'

'It was my fault. I called her. I couldn't raise Crosbie, and I was trying to set up this crime scene all by myself. My first one, since the promotion. I thought I was doing things right, but I couldn't be sure. I needed a CO, just to run things by. That was all I wanted her to do, was stand there and say *have you remembered to do this thing?* I swear, that was it.'

Anjan's eyes were cold.

'You couldn't have done that on the phone?'

Amy looked at the floor.

'She was at Low Moss,' she replied, 'visiting Charlie. They wouldn't let me speak to her, they just passed on a message.

And you know Helen. Once she heard what it was, she just set off.'

'And where was McLeod? Why couldn't he have come?'

Amy rolled her eyes. She couldn't help it.

'It was Sunday,' she said. 'McLeod was golfing.'

Anjan whispered something under his breath that Amy didn't quite catch. She didn't imagine it was especially complimentary.

'That man,' he said, a little louder. 'It's my opinion – and Helen knows this – that she'd never have been shot in the first place if it wasn't for DCI James McLeod.'

Amy frowned.

'I don't know if that's true.'

He didn't care what she knew or didn't know, she could tell. He'd said he wouldn't be angry with her, but he was.

'Be that as it may,' he said. 'I'm sorry she was given a pasting, as you put it. But I'm glad it happened, as harsh as that sounds, if it means she'll stop and focus on getting better.'

Anjan shifted his weight and elegantly levered himself up off the couch.

'I'll be going,' he said. 'I appreciate you seeing me at this late hour.'

Amy also stood, feeling the pain in her feet once again as they took her weight.

'Anjan,' she said, 'you don't have to go just yet. We can talk some more. Perhaps I can help? With the ghosting thing, I mean. Get Helen to call you, or something.'

He tilted his chin up. She'd disappointed him, and Amy Kato hated disappointing anyone. Outside in the hall, her buzzer rang.

'Your pizza's here,' Anjan said, ignoring her question. 'That's my cue.'

He turned and walked out into the hall, and Amy followed.

'Anjan,' she said again, in the same plaintive tone. She felt like a child. He reached the front door and opened it. For a second, she thought he wasn't going to look back, but then he turned, his body already halfway into the stair.

'I'm sorry, okay?' Amy said. 'Won't you please let me help?'

His face softened, ever so slightly.

'Don't worry,' he replied. 'I'll handle it from here. You've done plenty, tonight. You've set my mind at ease. Everything's window-dressing, really, as long as Helen is no longer anywhere near this case.'

'She isn't. McLeod's seen to that.'

Amy lifted the entryway receiver and pressed the button. The spring of the lock, and the sound of the pizza man elbowing the main door open, floated up from below them.

'I just wish,' Anjan said, his voice echoing in the stair, 'that she'd learn to accept help. Not even necessarily from me. At this point, anyone would do.'

Tuesday, 20 July, 09:30

'You know you've no control like that.'

From the passenger seat, Birch nodded at the steering wheel of the van. Jamieson was driving them through the chicanes of the Boat Green estate like a boy racer, one hand on the gear lever, the other flat on the wheel, turning it with his palm. He flashed her a grin.

'I mean it,' she said, 'if a kid ran out in front of you now, you'd never swerve in time.'

The grin didn't move.

'Nah,' he replied, 'see ma reflexes? Ah could've been Nigel Mansell.'

'Oh yeah? But you chose to be a handyman instead?'

Jamieson shrugged.

'Had to. Too tall fer wan o they wee F1 cars, ken?'

He braked sharply, making Birch jump, then spun the van into a parking space.

'There ye go,' he said, pointing through the windscreen. 'Fifteen.'

She looked up. The modern-looking tenement block was brown brick, three storeys high. Many of the windows were propped open in the already hot July day. It was 9.30 a.m.: Birch could feel the double espresso she'd drunk on the way beginning to go to her head.

'It's a stair?' She looked down at the maps app on her phone screen, hearing the dismay in her own voice. 'Al never mentioned that. I don't have a flat number.'

'Disnae matter,' Jamieson said. 'Can ye no jist ring aw the buzzers, an ask fer the wifey 'til ye get the right wan?'

Birch winced.

'Not the most professional approach, is it?'

Her father shrugged.

'Huv a wee look at the stair door, then. These new-type flats, they often huv the names oan, do they no?'

Birch hesitated, peering at the building's front door. It was wood with glass panelling, the reinforced kind, with a tiny wire grid running through the panes.

'Tell ye whit,' Jamieson went on, 'ah'll dae it. A wee recce. Saves ye gettin oot the van fer a wasted journey.'

He unclipped his seatbelt.

'Thanks, Dad.'

He grinned at her again.

'Jist sit tight,' he said, then rose from the driver's seat and slammed the door behind him.

Birch watched her father daunder across the pavement to the door. There clearly were names marked on the entry system, because he bent his face close to the panel and peered at it. McLeod's incredulous voice had run through her dreams all night, and now Birch heard it again: *you proceeded to interview a witness*. She gave her head a quick, fast shake.

'I did my job,' she said, as though addressing the messy dashboard console of the van. 'That's all I want to do, is my job.'

At the stair door, Jamieson straightened up, and threw her an A-okay sign. He bounded back to the van triumphant, and flung open the passenger door.

'She's there,' he said, 'I seen her name! *Stewart, J.*, it says. That has tae be her, does it no?'

Birch laughed.

'Look at you, doing detective work.'

Her father puffed out his chest, not realising she was teasing him.

'Aye, get that bastart McLeod tae get me oan the payroll.'

She felt the laugh die in her chest.

'Not likely,' she shot back, trying to keep her voice light. 'He barely puts up with *me*. I think he'd say another Birch around the place would be over his dead body.'

Jamieson snorted.

'Fine by me,' he said. 'She lives in flat two, the wifey. Will ah wait here for ye?'

'If you don't mind? I shouldn't be ages.'

'Take yer time,' Jamieson replied, 'ah'll just read the paper.'

Birch glanced at the fresh copy of the Scottish *Sun* Jamieson had bought at the petrol station, along with her grainy espresso. There was a picture of Eddison Deas on the cover.

'Great,' she said. 'Just try not to believe any of it.'

He stuck his tongue out at her, then bent his arm for her to lean on as she clambered out of the passenger seat.

'Will ah walk ye tae the door?'

Birch looked up – the distance was maybe five yards, give or take – but resisted the urge to roll her eyes. Her father still acted like she was fresh out of hospital – like the weeks of physio meant nothing. Nevertheless, she smiled at him.

'I've got it,' she said. 'I won't be long.'

Birch didn't let the smile fade until she reached the front step. She'd been hoping for a house, or at least for a main-door flat: a building where Josephine Stewart would come to the door herself, with no entryphone acting as a go-between. She didn't want to have to say the words 'Police Scotland': ideally, she'd be let in through the door voluntarily, without having to state her business first. She'd worn her Police Scotland lanyard, her photo ID for access to Fettes Avenue clearly hanging from it. She'd hoped that this would be enough to get her through Josephine Stewart's door, without her warrant card needing to be involved. This was splitting hairs, she knew, but in her head, it made the difference between conducting a formal interview – a thing she very definitely was not allowed to do – and just calling in.

Her hand shook as she pressed the buzzer marked *Stewart, J.*, then waited. There was a crackle on the line and a woman's voice said, 'Hello?'

Birch shifted on her crutch, bringing her face closer to the panel's receiver.

'Josephine Stewart?'

'Yes?'

'My name is Detective Inspector Helen Birch.' She could say that, right? It wasn't a lie. She paused for a moment, wondering what might be reasonable to say next. 'I wonder if I might have a few moments of your time?'

The words were barely out of her mouth before the door made that familiar tenement noise: a thick buzz followed by the clunk of the electronic bolt sliding back. Birch pushed her way in. The stick rattled against the door frame. The door had swung shut again behind her before she thought to cast a glance back at Jamieson and the van, but she could see through its smeary glass panels that he was already out of sight behind the spread pages of the *Sun*.

The stairwell was cool and dark, with brown wall-to-wall carpet and a stainless-steel banister. Birch noticed right away that the fire exit was blocked by bikes, in spite of a homemade, laminated sign which yelled *FOR THE LAST TIME!!!!! BICYCLES MUST NOT BE STORED IN THIS STAIR IT IS A HAZARD!!!!!* In spite of her nerves, she smiled, feeling many an Edinburgh tenement memory spool out into her brain. None had time to settle: the door to flat two was already ajar, a narrow slice of someone's face hanging in the gap above the brass security chain. She was being watched.

'Josephine Stewart?'

Birch sounded like a robot, saying the name the exact same way she had on the entryphone.

'Yes,' the woman behind the door replied, though with an upward inflection, as if she wasn't sure. 'You're a detective?'

Birch shuffled a little closer to the door.

'Helen Birch,' she said, trying not to say her title again. She pointed at the lanyard. Please don't make me get the warrant card, she thought.

Josephine Stewart didn't seem fussed about identification: Birch could only see one of her eyes, but her gaze didn't shift.

'Am I in trouble?'

Should you be? Birch wondered.

'Not at all,' she replied. She was trying to keep her voice low, knowing as she did that Edinburgh tenements often had ears: listening ears pressed against adjacent flats' front doors. 'I'm following up on an incident from a few months ago. I have reason to believe you might have been a witness.'

Through the gap in the door, she felt the other woman relax.

'Oh,' she said, drawing the single syllable out in a kind of relieved sigh. 'You're here about the car thing.'

Birch frowned. This woman had a prior motoring offence. How many *car things* might there be?

'I think so,' she replied, trying to smile. 'Do you mind if I come in for a minute? We can see if your car thing is the same as my car thing.'

There was a pause, then the gap in the door narrowed, and Birch heard the rattle of the chain.

'Sure,' the woman said, opening the door to reveal a narrow hall, a bright but tiny flat beyond. Her tone was warmer now, but still carried an edge of mistrust. 'Come on in.'

Josephine Stewart stood back, so Birch could pass through the hallway and into the little living room. Birch registered for the first time that the other woman was wearing pyjamas, her hair a little mussed.

'I'm sorry if I woke you,' she said, clicking over the shiny wood-effect floor.

Behind her, the front door rattled closed.

'Oh,' the other woman replied, 'I wasn't asleep yet.'

Birch came to a stop in the centre of the living room. The flat was a studio, the whole space not a lot bigger than her office at Fettes Avenue. It was L-shaped, with a double bed tucked into the short leg of the L and obscured by a voile curtain that hung from a rail with oversized rings. A short section of worktop ran along one wall: underneath it was a slimline fridge, a built-in oven and hob, but no washing machine. A sofa wouldn't have fit in the space: it took Birch a moment to identify that if Josephine Stewart ever sat down, she'd have to do so on a loveseat in one corner, currently piled high with laundry.

'Yet?'

The woman was blushing.

'I'm a nurse,' she said, brushing past Birch and crossing to the seat, where she began pushing the balled-up clothes aside. 'On nights, just lately. I'm not long home.'

'Don't worry about that,' Birch said, gesturing as best she could, crutch in hand, that she was fine. 'I don't need to sit, I won't take up too much of your time.'

Josephine Stewart turned her head, and fixed Birch with a look that reminded her of her mother.

'Like I said, I'm a nurse. I don't know exactly what your injury is, but I can see from your mobility that it would be better if you sat down.'

Birch opened her mouth to argue. She wanted to say *listen, it's been less than an hour since my meds, I've had a coffee, I'm fine.* But then she thought about how she might feel after standing for twenty minutes leaning on a crutch, and relented. She allowed the other woman to make a clearing on the seat for her, then she lowered herself into it.

'Tea? I can put the kettle on.'

Birch shook her head. She saw it now: though this woman couldn't be that much older than her, she looked motherly, and had large, steady-looking hands. She was a born nurse.

'Really,' she said, 'this won't take long – Josephine? May I call you Josephine?'

'Josie.'

'Okay, great.'

Birch fumbled her phone out of her trouser pocket. The other woman was watching her, as though performing some sort of appraisal.

'Car accident?' she asked.

'I'm sorry?'

Josie gestured towards the crutch, which Birch had balanced against the laundry.

'Your injury. You're hurt somewhere in your pelvis, right? I can tell from how you walked in here. Was it a car accident?'

Birch shook her head. I'll ask the questions, she thought.

'No,' she replied, 'just got myself into a scrape on the job, that's all.'

Josie looked as if she wanted to know more, but to Birch's relief, she didn't speak again. Birch balanced her phone on the arm of the loveseat, partially visible now.

'I'd like to record this conversation,' she said, 'if that's okay with you?'

Josie cocked her head. Birch didn't like that the other woman was still standing, but there was nowhere else in the tiny living space for her to sit, other than the floor.

'Depends,' she said. Her voice was small, uncertain: Birch saw in her face the familiar look of someone who's dealt with police personnel before and not enjoyed the experience. 'Who's going to listen to it?'

'Just me,' Birch replied, a little too fast. 'I'll listen back later and type up a witness statement.'

Josie didn't reply.

'I promise you're not in trouble,' Birch added. 'You're a witness, you're not under suspicion of anything.'

'Okay,' Josie said. This wasn't strictly consent to record, but Birch figured she was already bending the rules. She opened up the app on her phone and hit record.

'Tuesday, 20th July,' she said, '9.42 a.m.' She paused, not wanting to say the word *interview* on the recording. 'Detective Inspector Helen Birch, visiting Josephine Stewart in her home, to take a witness statement.'

This was by no means the official wording, but then, this wasn't official.

'Right,' Birch said, looking back up at Josie. The other woman was eyeing the pulsating red dot in the phone's screen. 'Just ignore it, if you can, and speak freely.'

Josie nodded.

'I'll try.'

'Great. So, I'm here to talk to you about an incident that happened on the night of Friday, 12th February, around 9.30 p.m. I know it's a few months ago now, but I'm hoping you can cast your mind back to that night.'

Josie blinked at her: once, twice.

'So this *is* the boy racer thing. I can't remember the exact date it happened. But it was around then, I guess.'

Birch set her jaw, but tried to keep her face neutral. She really didn't want to lead this particular witness.

'The incident I'm investigating,' she said, 'is a hit and run. It happened on East Claremont Street. Although you weren't involved, I have reason to believe your car was very close by when the incident happened.'

Josie frowned.

'I was involved,' she said. 'I'd say I was involved.'

Birch felt her eyebrows lift, almost involuntarily.

'To be honest,' Josie went on, 'I'm really surprised it's taken this long for someone to get in touch with me. I expected one of your lot on my doorstep the very next day.'

There was a hint of annoyance in her voice. Birch glanced at the phone, to check it was still recording. Her hunch was going somewhere: there was clearly more to this hit and run than she or Amy knew.

'The best thing,' she said, 'might be for you to give me your version of that night's events, to the best of your recollection. Do you think you can do that?'

'I can try.'

'Fantastic.'

Josie turned her back on Birch, and crossed the short stretch of floor to the bed. She pulled the voile curtain aside, and the rings rattled on their pole. Birch watched as Josie secured the voile with a makeshift tie-back made from a hair scrunchie. Then the other woman sat down on the edge of the bed, facing the loveseat.

'I'd been on the twilight shift,' Josie began. Birch hoped the phone's mic would still pick her up, now that she'd moved. The room was only small – it would, right?

'I remember I was really tired,' Josie went on. 'It was a bit of a wild night, very wet. I drive back and forth to the Royal all the time, but when you're tired and there's weather, you know . . .'

She tailed off. This woman feels guilty about something, Birch thought. She's justifying something to herself.

'I probably wasn't paying enough attention,' Josie said. 'I probably messed up somehow.'

'Messed up at what?'

The other woman sighed.

'Okay, so . . . I got to the roundabout on George Street. You know, where the statue is? And I was in the left-hand lane and this other car pulls up next to me. I noticed it because the guy's music was really loud. Obnoxiously loud. I was so tired, and it really went through my head. It annoyed me.'

'This car . . . it was a Honda Civic?'

Josie shrugged.

'Probably,' she said. 'I'm no expert on cars, but it was something like that, yeah. It was all tricked out, though, you know how these boy racers do. Fancy paint job, all iridescent. I remember thinking, why would you paint your car the colour of a bluebottle?'

Birch smiled at the comparison. She knew the exact colour Josie meant.

'Anyway,' Josie went on, 'something happened at the roundabout. I thought this guy cut me up.'

'You thought?'

'I mean . . . yeah. I replayed it a lot in my head, afterwards, trying to figure out if I did something wrong. I pulled out to go round, and he was in the right-hand lane, so he should turn right, shouldn't he? But he didn't – all of a sudden he was cutting across in front of me, pushing in. I thought he was going to hit me.'

'Yeah,' Birch said, visualising the roundabout, thinking about the rain, the wet-cobble dazzle of headlights, the slippery setts. 'That's cutting you up, no two ways about it.'

Josie's face fell into a look that seemed to combine intense relief and gratitude, though she wasn't looking directly at Birch.

'Well,' she said, 'I blew my horn at him. I know I shouldn't have, but I did. Like I say, I was tired, and his music had pissed me off. And he'd just wanted to be in front, hadn't he? He'd used the roundabout to try and overtake me.'

Josie was still staring into the middle distance, not meeting Birch's eye.

'You know you didn't do anything wrong, don't you?' Birch asked. 'It seems to me like you sounded your horn in order to alert the other driver to your position on the road, and prevent a collision.'

She knew she shouldn't be doing this: shaping the events Josie was describing into a narrative of her own. This woman had undoubtedly just been pissed off and wanted the guy to know about it. But Birch had been in her shoes many times: having to deal with someone else's bullshit while tired, irritable, and just trying to get home. Besides, she found herself warming to this hard-working woman with her bijou flat full of laundry and houseplants. She found herself thinking of Anjan's chic penthouse, how much more at home she felt *here* – in this room she'd walked into only minutes ago – than there.

'Maybe,' Josie was saying, 'maybe it was fine, what I did. But I still wish I hadn't. I wished, almost immediately, that I'd just let him do it, let him get in front.'

'Why?' Birch tried to shake the thoughts of Anjan out of her head. 'What happened next?'

'He stopped his car,' Josie replied. 'He just slammed his brakes on and stopped, right in the middle of the road. I'll be honest, I freaked out. I thought he was going to get out, and come and hurt me.'

'And did he?'

'No. He rolled down his window and yelled at me. He said some pretty horrible things. Words I'd rather not repeat.'

Josie looked up from under her eyelashes, and just for a moment, Birch saw the shy little girl she might once have been.

'It's okay,' she said, 'you don't have to. But these things he said – they were threatening?'

'Yes. Oh yes, definitely. He said he was going to follow me home.'

'And how did you respond?'

Josie's gaze dropped to the floor.

'I didn't,' she said, her voice small again. 'Maybe I shouldn't say this to you – to a policewoman – but I really, really wish I had. I've replayed that night so many times in my head, like I say. And a big part of me wishes I'd got out of the car like he asked, gone over and given him a bloody good talking-to. He was just some scrawny kid! I'm old enough to be his mother, for Christ's sakes. And yet I was afraid of him. I was terrified; it was pathetic.'

Birch leaned forward on the chair, though it made her hip click. She wanted Josie to meet her gaze again, but she didn't.

'I promise you,' she said, 'it wasn't pathetic at all. Not engaging with this man was absolutely the right thing to do. After all, he could have been armed. He was threatening you.'

Josie straightened her shoulders: a brisk, nurse-like gesture.

'Yes, well,' she said, 'he'd parked himself in the middle of the road, in front of me, so in the end I just drove around his car. Then he started to follow me.'

Birch nodded.

'I've seen CCTV,' she said, 'of the incident on East Claremont Street. The Honda Civic was driving very close behind another car. You were the driver of that car?'

'I was. And he was *so* close behind me. He put his full-beam headlamps up, and it was raining, so my mirrors just filled with dazzle. I couldn't see a thing behind me other than that light. And he was inches off my back bumper; I had to slow to an absolute crawl, or he'd have hit me. I was sure he was going to. I was driving on absolute tenterhooks, just waiting for the bang.'

'You did the right thing,' Birch said again, feeling like an automaton. She was lying: the right thing would have been to call the police. She wanted to shake this woman, demand to know why she hadn't reported the incident. Threatening behaviour, dangerous driving – all caught on CCTV. But none of it mattered, without an initial report.

'It's the hardest bit of driving I've ever done,' Josie was saying. 'I was scared, and I was having to concentrate on not braking sharply, or he'd hit me. But I was also thinking, how does this end? How do I get rid of this guy? How am I ever going to get home? A couple of times I tried to get away from him, but it didn't work. Then, all of a sudden . . .'

Josie stopped speaking, and in the quiet that hung between them, Birch heard the sounds of the other tenement residents going about their lives. Footsteps on the floorboards above them. The distant static of daytime TV.

'All of a sudden? I'm sorry, Josie, I can't fill in the gap for you. I need to hear your version of events.'

The other woman nodded.

'Well,' she said, 'I heard the noise of it, first. This terrible loud crunch of metal. I thought, well, that's it, then, he's run into me, it's happened. But I realised I hadn't *felt* any impact.

And when I looked in the rear-view mirror, I could see this other car had swerved into him and was basically ramming him off the road.'

'What did you do?'

Josie's eyes swivelled downwards again.

'Something I'm not proud of,' she said.

Birch glanced down at the red dot on her phone screen, praying the microphone was picking all of this up.

'And what was that?'

Josie closed her eyes.

'I drove away,' she said, her voice so quiet it was almost a whisper. 'Honestly, I barely even braked. I saw what was happening, and I couldn't quite believe it, but I'd been so scared. So afraid that I wasn't going to be able to outrun this man, and eventually, he'd hurt me. So I didn't stick around to see what came next. I took the opportunity to run.'

Birch wasn't sure what to say. Josie's fingers twisted in her lap, her face a mask of guilt. It was tempting to reassure her, but Birch had already done too much of that as it was.

'I drove home,' Josie went on, 'and parked my car all the way over on the other side of the estate, as far from this flat as I could, in case he came back somehow and found it. I walked back here like this.' She held out one hand, flat, palm down, and made it shake. 'Terrified. I had three stiff drinks, went to sleep, and never told anyone about it. Not until now.'

When Birch still didn't speak, Josie finally lifted her head and met her eye.

'I spent weeks,' she said, 'expecting a visit from you people. Expecting to be arrested. I should have known you'd come along eventually.'

Birch almost laughed.

'Arrested for what?'

Josie blushed.

'Failing to report an accident,' she said. 'Isn't that a crime? Or . . . wasting police time? Withholding evidence? That sort of thing.'

Birch tried not to smile.

'You witnessed the accident,' she said, 'but you didn't cause it, so reporting it wasn't your responsibility. I can't deny, it would have been useful to have your testimony earlier, but then, we should have reached out to you sooner.' The other woman was shaking her head, as if she didn't believe what she was hearing. 'Josie, you were the *victim* of a crime, not the perpetrator.'

They were both quiet for a moment. Outside, the slam of a car door. Birch thought of Jamieson, leafing through his paper in the van.

'What happened,' Josie said, 'to the driver of the Honda Civic?'

Birch blinked.

'I'm sorry?'

Josie was twisting her fingers again, as though tying a knot in some invisible string.

'It looked like a pretty bad crash,' she said. 'Was he okay?'

'He was hurt,' Birch replied, 'but he's recovering.'

The other woman looked alarmed.

'Recovering? It was months ago.'

'I'm sorry, Josie,' Birch said, 'that's all I can really tell you.'

She felt the familiar tug to wind things up: it was generally easy to tell when a witness had finished saying anything of use, even if they were still talking, which Josie wasn't. She perched on the end of her bed across from Birch, looking wrung out.

'Last question,' Birch said. 'Can you tell me anything about the other vehicle you witnessed? The one that struck the Honda Civic?'

Josie was already shaking her head before Birch had even finished the question.

'I didn't see it at all, until I heard the crash,' she said. 'I was so focused on driving, on trying to figure out how to get out of that whole mess. All I can tell you is it was a dark-coloured car, and you probably already knew that.'

'Yes.' Birch tried to keep her tone gentle. 'That's okay, though, Josie. You've been incredibly helpful, and I really appreciate you letting me take up some of your time.'

It was one of those moments where Birch wished she could just stand up and move towards the door. Instead, she reached for her phone and ended the recording, before reaching for her godforsaken crutch. She realised, not for the first time, how much she missed being able to convey her intentions through decisive movement.

'Need a hand?' Josie was standing now, and reaching out her hands towards Birch.

'No, no.' Birch rattled upright and steadied herself. 'Thank you. But my physio tells me I have to do these things by myself.'

For the first time in their entire interaction, Josie smiled.

'Your physio is right,' she said. 'But you're getting plenty of rest? Managing to sleep?'

'Mostly,' Birch lied, moving towards the door. She could tell Josie didn't believe her: apart from anything else, the purple shadows under Birch's eyes were unmistakable. 'I'm getting there.'

Before Birch had a chance to fully get out of the tenement's main door, her father had leaped from the van and run – or as close to *run* as Jamieson Birch could manage – to help her.

'How'd it go?' he asked, bracing the door open with one locked arm and breathing hard.

Birch was frowning. She may need him to drive her around, but she didn't need him to open damn doors for her. She realised this was partly residual annoyance towards Anjan, and *his* door-opening habit, so she ignored it.

'Pretty well,' she said, 'I think. But now I've discovered there's someone else I am absolutely not supposed to go and interview.'

Her father stepped back to let her out, grinning as she passed him, then letting the stair door swing shut.

'Jist tell me the address, hen,' he said, 'an ah'll take ye there.'

James Aynsome had his own private, custom-designed consulting room, which he'd converted himself from the basement of his vast West End townhouse. Walking along Grosvenor Crescent and stopping on the pavement in front of the house always made her feel inadequate: plain little Jane Ryan, whose practice room was rented by the hour and probably always would be. Aynsome's basement had its own door, down a stone staircase whose cast-iron handrail was painted with shiny black Hammerite. The door had a brass plaque which read *Jas. Aynsome, FRCPE,* and an old-fashioned brass bell pull. Every time she stood and waited for her supervisor to answer the door, Jane felt like she'd been sent to the tradesman's entrance. She wondered if his clients felt that way, too.

For such a large man, Aynsome moved quietly: when he opened the door, she jumped a little in her skin.

'Janey!' he boomed, beaming at her, as he always did. 'Janey, Janey, Janey. Get yourself indoors, my girl, it's *fright*ful hot.'

He wasn't wrong. Jane stepped gratefully into the basement's shady hallway.

'Lovely to see you, James.'

This was both true and not true. Jane liked spending time with her supervisor. He was a big grey bear of a man, strident but affable; deceptively uncle-like, with a mind sharp as cheese wire. Their supervisory sessions usually consisted of a careful chat over tea and fancy boxed fig rolls James mail-ordered from Fortnum's and ate by the half-dozen at a time. It wasn't a bad way to spend a morning, not usually. But today . . .

'Why don't I believe you?' Aynsome asked, and not for the first time, Jane wondered if he really could hear people's thoughts. 'That's quite the frown, Janey.'

'Sorry,' she said, and gave her head a small shake. 'Lots to talk about today, I'm afraid.'

He placed a paw-like hand on her shoulder, ushering her in.

'Precisely what I'm here for,' he said. 'Do come through. I *had* thought we could sit out on the patio, but this weather is rather ferocious. We'll see how we get on.'

Jane made her way through the familiar corridor, coveting as she always did its deep, cream carpet and tasteful artwork. The door to the consulting room was closed: they wouldn't sit in there today. Instead, she carried on to the far end of the house, where the corridor opened out into a small kitchenette with two internal doors: one led to a bathroom Aynsome's clients could use; the other led to the back stairs that connected the basement to the rest of the house. Jane knew her supervisor was fond of her, but she also suspected she'd never gain admittance to this building's upper floors.

'Go on out,' he said, clattering around at the kitchenette. 'I've put the brolly up, so we'll have shade.'

The basement's back wall boasted French windows that opened out on a stone patio, beyond which was Aynsome's lush but immaculate back garden. Jane always wondered if he tended it himself or hired a gardener. Either way, the beds and troughs and hanging baskets were stuffed with gorgeous, coloured blooms. Jane took a deep breath in as she stepped from the cool shade of the basement into the warmer shade under a massive canvas parasol. The air smelled like honey and green, and she could hear bees at work in the nearby plants. James had positioned two teak Adirondack chairs in the lee of the parasol, and as she sank into one, Jane smelled the hot teak scent of the wood.

'I'm afraid I can't stand tea on a day like this.' He'd already finished the sentence before he appeared on the threshold and grinned at her. 'It's dreadful weather for a man of my stature . . . and yet, we get so little sun in this country that I feel it's our duty to be outdoors. I was thinking a cold rose lemonade?'

Jane realised she was actually licking her lips.

'That sounds ideal,' she replied. He nodded, withdrew into the kitchenette, and reappeared with two tall glasses clinking in his hands. Jane reached for hers and almost dropped it: the glass was slippery with condensation, and her hands greasy in the July heat.

Aynsome made a sort of breathy creaking noise as he flopped into the chair opposite, lemonade spattering on to the flag-stones. The Adirondacks had cupholders, because of course they did. Jane took a few sips, then placed her fizzing pink drink into its slot. Her supervisor took the top of his in one long gulp.

'Just the job,' he said. 'Now then, to business.'

He shuffled around in the chair, getting comfortable. Jane hooked her handbag over the arm of her Adirondack and fished out her notes.

'How have you been,' Aynsome asked, 'first of all? You know, in yourself.'

Jane smiled. He always asked it this way: *how have you been? You know, in yourself.* She guessed this was his way of showing that he wasn't just asking how she was in a passing-the-time-of-day sort of way. He was asking after her in his professional capacity.

'A little frazzled, James, I can't lie.'

He raised one bushy eyebrow at her.

'Frazzled is a word that covers a multitude of sins. Can you be more specific?'

Jane screwed up her face. She knew she'd been vague.

'Anxious, then. I've got a lot on my mind.'

Aynsome rubbed his hands together, warming them up in anticipation of the work ahead.

'That's more like it,' he said. 'Well, first of all – and you know what I'm going to say, Janey, I'm sure – it'd be useful for us to figure out what's causing that. Is it a resilience thing? Are you feeling less able than usual to carry that mental load?'

Jane cocked her head, considering the question.

'I'm *busier* than usual. I was approached by Police Scotland again – you know I did some work with some of their personnel during lockdown?'

He nodded.

'I remember.'

'Well, I've taken on another handful of contracts. That's on top of my usual private practice.'

'Very well, I'll ask roughly the same thing again: does that mean you now have too much work? Are you regretting taking on the extra?'

She realised her head was still cocked to one side, like a dog's. She righted it.

'Not so much that. It's summer, so, you know, my regulars are quite quiet. Lots of holiday breaks and such. I weighed it up pretty carefully before I said yes to the police.'

'So it's not a case of working too many hours, being stretched too thin?'

She lowered her eyes. On her lap was a matt-card folder labelled Police Scotland. It contained client notes, process notes, client preference surveys. Copies of the contract she'd signed with the police, of the contracts between herself and the clients that everyone had had to sign.

'No,' she said, 'no, it isn't the workload. It's the *content* of the workload.'

Aynsome pointed towards the folder she was holding.

'These police contracts, specifically?'

She looked up at him.

'One of them in particular,' she said.

'I see. Well, I think there *might* still be a conversation to be had about resilience, Janey, but let's get into this client and see what we can see, shall we?'

She let out a small, relieved huff of breath, not loud enough for him to hear.

'That would be great, if you don't mind.' She flipped open the folder and began sifting through the documents. 'Obviously, because it's the police, it's all a little more sensitive than usual. I feel like I have to be extra careful around the confidentiality stuff.'

'Good girl. How would you like to refer to this client? I'll take your lead.'

Jane fished a single piece of A4 paper out of the stack.

'Here's the client's Core-10 form. They've only filled out one for me, so far – we've only had a couple of sessions.' Aynsome was already reaching for the paper, and Jane had to crane her neck to read the client ID at the top of the sheet. 'PS for Police Scotland,' she said, 'and the ID number 7770386.'

'That's a bit of a mouthful. PS7, for brevity?'

'Perfect.'

'Hmm.' He was peering down at the sheet of paper in his hand. The sun bounced off it, rendering it impossibly white. 'Client PS7 has a very low Core-10 score.'

'Yes. This one's a smart cookie. They filled it out quite cyn-ically, I think.'

He was already nodding.

'I suspected as much. Trouble sleeping is all they'll really admit to?'

'At the moment. But I think they've been dishonest about a couple of the others in particular. In spite of what they've ticked for question two, I don't believe this client has anyone to turn to for support – or rather, *they* don't believe they do. They're a member of police personnel – in truth, they have a whole support system. But they can't see that.'

'They also have you.'

'Yes. But Client PS7 seems rather alone. Wilfully so, I think. Unwilling to ask for help. Unable, even.'

With his free hand, Aynsome took a swig of his pink lemon-ade. Ice clattered in the glass. When he spoke again, his voice sounded damp.

'How are they in session? Distant? Quiet?'

Jane paused for a moment before answering.

'Not so much distant,' she said, 'as just very, very controlled. Wary, I'd say. I get the feeling that everything Client PS7 says has been carefully thought about before it is said. I'm being given a narrative, rather than the truth.'

'You've had how many sessions with this client?'

Jane flinched a little. She'd had a feeling he might say she was rushing it.

'Two,' she replied. 'I realise it's early days.'

'It is. Time is, as we know, one of the most useful tools at our disposal. It might just take a little while for that guard to come down.'

Jane closed her eyes. Aynsome was looking down again at the Core-10 form in his hand. She wanted to say *there's more to it than that*, but didn't have any evidence that there was.

'You said there was another category on here that was causing you concern?' Aynsome asked.

'Yes. The *unwanted images or memories have been distressing me* question. Client PS7 ticked zero for that question – *not at all.* That doesn't match with what they're saying to me in session, nor does it match with the therapy journal they've submitted.'

She watched her supervisor's eyes as they scanned down the paper.

'You made clear to the client that the Core-10 scores wouldn't be shared with Police Scotland?'

'Yes. I sent them the contract by email, then went over it with them at the start of the first session. It was clear they'd read it.'

Aynsome shrugged.

'Nevertheless,' he said, 'I understand the hesitation. Apart from *I have made plans to end my life*, the unwanted images or memories question contains maybe the most frightening wording on the form. Admitting to *that* means admitting you're mad, in the eyes of a lot of clients.'

For just a second, Jane's mind wandered to James Aynsome's own clients. She didn't know much, but she knew he offered therapy to some pretty powerful people. One of his regulars was an ex-Army field marshal.

'And no one wants to admit they're mad, do they?' he was saying. 'Especially not to a therapist who's been paid for by their boss.'

'You think the client is paranoid?'

He passed the form back to her. Where his hand had been, the paper felt a little damp.

'I can only think anything based on what you're giving me,' he said. 'And so far it seems like you don't think the client trusts you yet. Does that seem accurate? You don't think you've connected with Client PS7.'

'Yes, I suppose that is what I'm saying.'

Aynsome leaned back in his chair, and Jane heard the slats shift under his weight.

'This brings us back to a familiar place, doesn't it?'

Jane placed the form atop the pile of papers on her knee. She looked down and scanned it, as though she didn't already know what it said. *I have felt tense, anxious or nervous: 2, sometimes. I have felt panic or terror: 0, not at all. I have had difficulty getting to sleep or staying asleep: 4, most of the time.*

'Yes,' she said, quietly.

'That's understandable, you know,' Aynsome replied. 'We all have our patterns. I've been at this lark for forty years, and *I* still have them. One of yours is that you like to bond with a client early. You feel like if you can't, that's a failing.'

Jane realised she was nodding.

'I know that it isn't,' she said. 'My logical brain knows that it isn't. That different clients move at different speeds. Sometimes that connection *never* happens. It's par for the course.'

'Yes. And it certainly isn't your fault. Isn't anyone's fault.'

Jane straightened up, and took a sip of her lemonade. The ice had melted, watering it down.

'Yes,' she said, 'you're probably right. It's less that something's off with this case, I imagine, and more that Client PS7 is setting off some of my own stuff. Things around validation.'

Aynsome was smiling at her, the way she would sometimes smile at clients when they figured something out for themselves.

'Being trustworthy is very important to you, Janey,' he said. 'That's an admirable quality. But what you have to realise is—'

'—is there's a difference between a client not trusting me, and me not being trustworthy.' She filled in the blank, enjoying his approval.

Aynsome raised both hands, pressing the tip of each middle finger to its neighbouring thumb. He looked like he might be about to begin conducting an invisible orchestra.

'Ex*act*ly,' he said.

She returned his smile now, but was aware it felt watery. She *wanted* him to be right about this: it was her stuff, not the client's, that had created the uneasy atmosphere in her consulting room. But she still wasn't totally sure. Was she bothered by the fact that Client PS7 didn't trust her? Or was she bothered by the fact that – somewhere in the back of her mind – she didn't quite trust *them*?

'Give it time, is my advice,' Aynsome was saying. He closed his eyes and tipped his head backwards, looking every bit like a grizzly bear basking in the sun. 'In some cases, all we can do is give it time.'

Tuesday, 20 July, 11:15

Riccarton Place, Currie, was the picture of suburbia. Jamieson dawdled the van over the speed bumps, passing neat gardens with pampas grass and hanging baskets, bedding plants in the neon pinks and purples of a bad headache. The houses were 1960s Wimpey boxes, two-up, two-down and pebble-dashed, identical. Birch put her face close to the glass of the passenger-side window, counting up through the numbers on the uPVC front doors.

'Sixty-three,' she said, pointing. 'There it is.'

Jamieson braked, and brought the van to a stop. Birch grinned. If Dale McGill lived here, then he surely still lived with his mum. The living room windowsill was crowded with Royal Doulton lady figurines, and in the well-kept garden were granite statues of cherubs. The curtains in the front bedroom window were closed, though it was almost lunchtime.

'Yep,' she said, 'this is the place.'

Jamieson pulled the handbrake on, but Birch held up a hand.

'Don't park here,' she said, her voice a little too sharp. 'I can't be seen getting out of *this* thing, not by this particular witness.'

'Eh? Whit's wrang wi ma van, then?'

Birch rolled her eyes.

'I mean, I could give you a list. But right now, I'm just worried about how belligerent this kid might be. I need this to look above board, so he doesn't think to raise a complaint. I've told you what'll happen if any of this gets back to McLeod.'

Jamieson made a face, but he took the handbrake off and eased the van back out into the crown of the road.

'That gadge,' he said, the corners of his mouth turned down. 'McLeod. He wants tae take the stick oot his arse.'

They parked around fifty yards up the street, adjacent to a front garden dotted with decorative gnomes. As Birch did her now familiar dance with the crutch, she kept her eyes fixed on one in particular: it wore a pointed red hat and held up a sign that read *gnome is where the heart is*. She thought of some of the neighbourhoods she'd worked in over the years, and couldn't quite believe that thing was still there, sitting among the busy Lizzies only inches from the pavement – that it hadn't yet been stolen and used to pan a windscreen in.

She rattled her way along the street and down the garden path of number 63. The front door had glass panels inset, with fake-leaded tulip motifs in red and green. The doorbell played 'Frère Jacques'.

Birch sent up the same silent prayer she'd made at Josephine Stewart's front door: please don't make me get my warrant card out. But she needn't have worried. The woman who answered the door looked only briefly at Birch's face before clocking the lanyard around her neck. The change in her face was almost alarming: Mrs McGill looked immediately exhausted.

'Oh my goodness,' she said, her eyes fixed on the lanyard, 'what is it now? What's he done?'

Birch tried for a reassuring smile.

'Mrs McGill? I'm Helen Birch, I—'

'You're with Police Scotland.' Her tone was one of disappointed resignation. 'And you'd like to talk to Dale. Don't worry, I know the drill. Come away in.'

Birch followed Mrs McGill into the hall, picking carefully over the threshold step on her stick. Mrs McGill gestured to the right, and Birch walked into the living room. The eyes of around three dozen Royal Doulton ladies were immediately upon her.

'Please,' Mrs McGill said, 'sit.'

She was an older woman than Birch would have expected, given that her son was only twenty-three. She reminded Birch of her own mother, wearing a pinny and moccasin slippers, keeping the house clean and trig. Birch chose a spot on the mock-velvet sofa, and to her surprise, Mrs McGill sat down in the armchair opposite.

'Listen,' she said, leaning forward, her voice low. 'I'd like you to tell me first, if you don't mind. Tell me what sort of trouble he's in. I don't want to be sent out of the room and then have to hear it from him later. He won't tell me the whole truth, you see. He never does.'

Birch winced.

'Mrs McGill, your son—'

The other woman let out a short, mirthless laugh.

'Son? Oh, bless you, hen, how flattering. Dale is my *grand*son.'

Birch kicked herself, inwardly. She might have known that, had she had full access to the case file. Had this visit been legit, she'd have been fully briefed.

'I'm sorry,' she said. 'I just assumed—'

'Don't worry,' Mrs McGill replied. 'It's refreshing, if anything, to meet someone who doesn't know all our family's business. No, my daughter – Dale's mum – she . . . ended up with a bad man. I mean a *really* bad man.'

'You don't have to tell me,' Birch said, 'it's okay.'

Mrs McGill nodded, and there was gratitude in the gesture.

'The short version is, she ended up with a bad man, and I ended up with Dale.'

'I'm sorry.' It was the wrong thing to say, but the words came out of Birch's mouth before she could stop them. Mrs McGill didn't seem fazed.

'It's been hard,' she said, that same exhausted expression on her face, 'I can't tell you a lie.'

Birch shifted her gaze. A lady figurine in a fancy blue and pink frock sat on the coffee table between them.

'That's Rebecca,' Mrs McGill said, watching Birch. 'Your name is Helen, you said?'

'It is.'

'I have a Helen, somewhere.' Mrs McGill cast around the room, her eyes eventually alighting on the mantelpiece. 'There she is.'

She pointed to a figure in a dark blue dress, her hair painted mid-brown, very much like the brown of Birch's own hair. She was carrying a bouquet of yellow flowers under her arm and appeared to be frowning.

'She's lovely,' Birch lied.

'Hmm. Rather plain, actually, compared to her sisters. But I like her.'

Birch nodded, politely.

'I've been collecting them for years,' Mrs McGill went on. 'I've even got the balloon lady, but she's up in the bedroom.'

Birch didn't know what this meant, but she kept nodding.

'Anyway.' The other woman's face darkened. 'You were going to tell me about Dale. What it is he's done.'

Birch smiled in what she hoped was a reassuring way.

'Nothing, actually,' she said. 'I'm not here about anything you don't already know about. Dale was involved in a hit and run incident earlier this year.'

'Yes,' Mrs McGill cut in. Her guard was still up, as though she were still waiting for a bombshell. 'I very definitely know about *that*.'

'Well, I've come across some new information about what happened that night. I'd like to discuss it with Dale.'

Mrs McGill leaned forward again, almost too eager to hear about her grandson's misdeeds.

'There's more to it, isn't there?' she asked. 'More than he's been saying, I mean. You're not telling me that a boy like Dale gets side-swiped like that out of nowhere, totally unprovoked.'

'That was how he described it to you?'

'Yes.' Mrs McGill snorted. 'He said the other person must have been jealous of his car. That noisy monstrosity! I ask you.' She lowered her voice to a near whisper. 'I have to say, I was delighted when we found out that thing was no longer roadworthy. I'd been just waiting for him to come a cropper in it. The way he drives around, it's a blessing he's still on this earth, frankly.'

Birch held back a grin. She liked this weary woman, so clearly and thoroughly sick of her grandson's shit.

'I'm afraid there is evidence to suggest that the hit and run might have been . . .' Birch hesitated. 'Retribution,' she said. 'For . . . something.'

'I knew it.' Mrs McGill levered herself up out of the arm-chair, and crossed the room with some alacrity. Then she was out in the hall, calling her grandson's name.

'Dale?'

There was silence.

'*Christo*pher Dale Mc*Gill*!'

Still no answer came from upstairs, but Birch thought she heard a shuffling overhead: the sound of a body turning over in bed, perhaps.

'Dale,' Mrs McGill called again, louder this time. 'There is a *policewoman* here to see you.'

Now there was movement. From the room above, Birch heard a gruff but audible 'fucksake', followed by the creaking of floorboards.

Mrs McGill put her head round the living room door, but before she could speak, there was a shout from the top of the stairs.

'Is she hot?'

Mrs McGill rolled her eyes.

'Excuse his vulgarity,' she said, keeping her voice raised, so Dale could hear.

'Don't worry,' Birch said. Her palm already itched to slap this kid, and he wasn't even in the room yet.

Overhead, more creaking.

'He's a little slow moving at the moment,' Mrs McGill said. She glanced at Birch's crutch, propped beside her against the sofa. 'But then, it seems you'd know about that.'

It was almost a question, Mrs McGill's head cocked to the side as if she wanted Birch to tell her what had happened – why she was on a crutch, but still coming to interview her grandson. Birch kept her face blank, listening as Dale McGill began making his heavy-footed way down the stairs.

When he appeared in the living room doorway alongside his grandmother, Birch almost laughed. Thanks to the scant information in the file, she'd been left to build up her own picture of this young man. She'd imagined someone tall and lumbering, an overgrown boy with big fists. The real Dale McGill was a weed – he looked more like a teenager than a man in his mid-twenties. He was wearing grey joggers and a T-shirt, both of which looked pretty lived-in, and his white, freckled arms were dotted with tattoos clearly designed to assist with his image. On one forearm was a flaming eight ball above a banner that read *death wish*; the other arm sported a black wrap-around dragon design, older tattoos underneath raised and faint beneath its wings. Both arms bore the scars of his accident, pale pink streaks among the dubious artwork. McGill wore a stud earring with a sparkly CZ on the bezel. In his eyebrows were little nicks of bare skin he'd shaved visible.

'Nice shades,' Birch said. He'd walked into the room wearing wrap-around Oakleys, a yellowish sheen on their lenses.

'Hungover, aren't I?' McGill replied. His voice had a high-up register, like a girl's.

'Take those glasses off, Christopher,' his grandmother said. Her cheeks were flushed: she was embarrassed by this man, Birch thought, and no wonder.

'It's fine,' Birch said.

'Make us a coffee, Nan,' McGill commanded, not taking his eyes off Birch. 'I'm dying, here.'

Mrs McGill looked across the room.

'Helen?'

'No, no. Nothing for me.' She waited until the other woman had bustled out of the room, and then looked at McGill. 'Dale, or Christopher? Which should I call you?'

His face was sullen, but he began to shamble fully into the room.

'Dale,' he said. 'I fucking hate Christopher.'

Birch saw for the first time that he walked with a stick: a wooden walking cane with a curved handle, its length too long for his small frame. It gave him the look of a degenerate shepherd. He flopped into the armchair where his grandmother had just been sitting, raised the stick, and aimed its stopper at the nearest Doulton figurine. Birch flinched. It was the Helen.

'These wee pottery women, eh?' McGill prodded the ornament lightly: Birch could tell he knew better than to truly mess with these treasures. 'Creepy as fuck. They're everywhere in this hoose, even the bathroom. They watch you when you pee.'

He was showing off. Birch kept her face impassive.

'You could always move out,' she said, 'if you don't like it. A proper grown-up like you? You ought to have your own place.'

He narrowed his eyes at her.

'Can't afford it, can I?'

'Really? I thought you were a man about town, Dale. Fancy car you had, eh? All those modifications.'

This was a gamble: Birch had only seen the car on the crap CCTV from the Greek restaurant, but she guessed if it had a spoiler that high, there had to be other bells and whistles.

'Look.' He lowered the stick, realising she wasn't there to play. 'I know you're not here to get me on anything, okay? Know how I know that? Because I haven't fucking *done* anything.' He made a long, sweeping gesture with his left hand, along his right-hand side. 'Not been able to leave this fucking house, have I? Not like this.'

'Of course. How are you healing?'

He wrinkled his nose at her.

'Better than you, by the looks.'

Birch wanted to laugh. He thought she'd rise to *that*?

'Got you on tramadol, have they? Leg broken in two places, elbow smashed . . . can't have been nice.'

'Nah, it wasn't. So . . . what? You've caught the bastard that did it? Is that what you've come for?'

'You're close,' Birch replied, 'but not quite there.'

'You're really gonna make me guess what you're here for? The *fuck* kind of polis are you?'

'The kind that knows what really happened that night, Dale.'

He snorted.

'I've told you lot everything I know. I've no fucking idea who that guy was, the guy in the Golf. He just came out of nowhere and side-swiped me. Almost like one of you lot. PIT manoeuvre, or whatever.'

Birch smiled.

'You've been watching too much American TV,' she said. Then she went quiet. Silence, she knew, could be the perfect rope by which to have a suspect hang himself.

It worked. McGill began to get agitated.

'Seriously,' he said, after a moment. 'Fuck's *sake*. I'd never seen that guy before in my entire life.'

'No,' Birch replied, 'I believe that's probably true.'

'Then what *is* this?'

She raised an eyebrow at him. She'd have liked to be able to shift position in the chair, take her time about it, make him squirm. But her hip was hurting enough as it was.

'I've read the statement you made immediately after the incident,' she said, 'and I'm not especially interested in anything you said that night. I am, however, very interested in what you *didn't* say.'

McGill screwed up his face and pushed his tongue down under his lower lip. Birch had always hated that gesture, what it represented.

'Is this, like, a riddle?' He was trying to mock her. He clearly couldn't quite tell whether she had anything on him or not. 'I'm seriously meant to guess what the fuck you're on about?'

No, idiot, Birch thought. It's called not leading the witness. She carried on as though he hadn't spoken.

'What were you doing,' she asked, 'at the time the incident occurred?'

He laughed a disingenuous laugh.

'Driving,' he replied. '*Ob*viously.'

'How would you say you were driving?'

His smile weakened a little.

'How?'

'Yes. In what sort of manner.'

She saw his throat move as he swallowed.

'Dunno. I was just driving.'

Birch wondered, for a moment, what she was doing here. She didn't really need McGill's testimony – not if all she wanted to do was strengthen her theory that the tall, thin man was indeed a vigilante. She realised she was partly here for Josephine Stewart: this kid had followed and threatened an innocent woman, and thought he'd got away with it.

'Any other motorists around? Any you interacted with, I mean, other than the driver of the VW Golf?'

He looked at her through his stupid glasses and didn't speak. The colour was draining from his face now, and his freckles stood out dark against the pale skin.

'A Renault Clio, maybe,' she went on, looking down at her nails, 'with an older reg. Blue. Female driver. Ring any bells?'

This time, when he swallowed, she heard it.

'I didn't do nothing,' he said.

'That's a double negative.'

'A what?'

Birch looked back up at him, and he flinched away from her gaze.

'Why don't you take those glasses off,' she said, through her teeth, 'like your grandmother asked you to.'

When McGill reached up to remove the Oakleys, she thought she saw his hand tremble, just a little.

'You were caught on CCTV, *Christopher*,' Birch said. 'So you can protest all you like, but we know exactly how you were driving that night.'

Suddenly, he was animated.

'Listen,' he said, his voice raised, 'she was a bitch, all right? I was just driving, minding my own fucking business, and all of a sudden there's this bitch honking me. Like, what the fuck?' He wheeled his left arm, narrowly missing the mantelpiece of fragile women. 'Isn't *that* an offence? Sounding the horn without due . . . fucksake, without due *some*thing?'

This time, Birch did laugh.

'That's your defence, is it? A mean lady in a wee blue car blew her horn at me, Your Honour, and I was frightened?'

His eyes widened.

'Fuck you,' he spat.

'You want me to haul that woman up on charges of sounding her horn without due *something*, and ignore the various offences you went on to commit?'

'*What* offences?'

He lurched forward in the chair, hitting his right elbow off the arm, and Birch saw how much it hurt him. His eyes went blank for a moment, and he sank back, limp.

She held up one hand and used the other to count off on her fingers.

'Well,' she said, 'let's see, there's threatening behaviour, for a start. There's driving without due care and attention, which I believe escalated to dangerous driving pretty quickly. And you announced your intent to follow her, and then you followed her, which is essentially stalking, isn't it? So all in all, it's not looking great for you, kid.'

'Don't call me kid,' he hissed. 'Don't you fucking come in my house, and—'

'Your house?' Birch cut in. 'Oh, I beg your pardon. So these are *your* porcelain dolls, are they? These are *your* doilies on the chair arms?'

This wasn't an interview any more, she realised. It had never been an interview. Now she was in a room with McGill, she didn't care if he made a complaint to McLeod. This had always been about administering a much-needed come-uppance.

'You can't prove *nothing*.'

He wheeled his good arm again, and this time, it made contact. The Helen figurine toppled over on to the mantelpiece, then rolled off the edge and smashed on Mrs McGill's marble-effect hearth. Its decapitated head ricocheted into the carpet.

Mrs McGill had been outside, listening: Birch could tell by how quickly she entered the room. Her grandson sat frozen, staring at the blue painted shards, his arm still raised.

'I'm so sorry,' Birch said, when he didn't speak. She could have sworn Mrs McGill had tears in her eyes.

'It wasn't you, was it?' she said, not looking at either of them. 'It was this reprobate.'

McGill spluttered.

'Nan, I—'

His grandmother stabbed her index finger in his direction.

'*Don't,*' she said, in a voice so forceful that even Birch jumped. 'Just don't say a word.'

The air in the room crackled. McGill had the good grace to hang his head.

In the thick quiet, Birch shuffled herself to the front of the plush sofa. For about the thousandth time, she cursed the way her injury prevented her from making meaningful physical gestures. Instead of standing up decisively, she knuckled upright on to her crutch. Neither Mrs McGill nor her wretched grandson looked up: Mrs McGill was looking down at the Helen figurine's shattered remains; Dale was looking down at the ridiculous yellow glasses in his lap, confronted, Birch imagined, by his own reflection.

'I'm sorry to have disturbed you, Mrs McGill,' she said, clicking her way across the soft carpet.

'Mind your feet,' the other woman replied, her voice heavy. 'There are always wee shatters you can't see.'

Birch nodded, and exited the living room as fast as she could. In the hallway, she fumbled with the security chain, wondering if Mrs McGill would follow her, see her off the premises. But there was no noise from the room behind her, and as she wrestled open the door, Birch imagined the two of them still frozen there, each silently resenting the other.

Back in the van, Jamieson was once again obscured behind the *Sun*. When Birch opened the passenger-side door, he gave a little start.

'All okay, hen?'

She landed heavily in the passenger seat.

'Not really.'

Jamieson closed the paper, then creased it in half and wedged it on to the dashboard.

'The kid wis . . . whit did ye say earlier? Belligerent?'

'He was. But . . .'

'But whit?'

Birch shook her head.

'I don't know, Dad. I'm just not sure what it was I went in there for. I ended up just giving him a telling-off. And then . . .'

Jamieson turned his torso so his was facing her more squarely.

'Lassie, are ye okay? Did he dae somethin?'

She could see a protective anger building in her father's eyes, and she held up her hands.

'No, no, don't get excited. His granny was there the whole time. I just . . .' Birch closed her eyes. Her hip was hurting, all of a sudden. She couldn't think. 'Oh, I don't know. It just wasn't great.'

Jamieson snaked an arm around her shoulders and squeezed.

'You'll fix it, hen,' he said, 'whatever it is. Or it'll fix itself. Things dae that.'

Birch nodded, slowly at first, and then with more conviction.

'Yes,' she said. 'You're right, I'll fix it. But not right now. Right now, I need to . . .'

She tailed off, rummaging in her pocket for her phone. She'd felt a flutter in her stomach that she instantly recognised: the on-to-something feeling, she called it.

Jamieson started the engine as she thumbed to Amy's number.

'Kato?' she said, not waiting for any kind of greeting. 'Don't say anything, okay? And don't hang up until I'm done. This vigilante theory of mine . . . it's got legs. I can prove it. Any chance you're free to meet up this afternoon?'

'They said you were here to see me.' McLeod stood in the doorway, jacket on, his morning Starbucks clutched in his hand like a missile he wanted to throw. 'I assumed that was some sort of dreadful joke.'

'Wishful thinking, I'm afraid, sir,' Birch replied. Beside her, Amy winced. She could tell Birch was trying not to grin, which she found slightly worrying.

'I'm trying to think what possible explanation you could have for being here, Birch.' McLeod crossed the room, rounding his desk and setting the coffee cup down. Amy eyed it with envy: she'd already had two this morning, but they'd barely made a dent in what felt like a wall of fatigue.

'And you, Kato.' McLeod pinned her with a filthy look. 'I thought the orders I'd given you were crystal clear.'

Amy squirmed in her chair. She hadn't even liked the idea of coming into McLeod's office before he'd arrived, but she'd felt guilty about keeping Birch leaning on her crutch outside the door.

'They were, sir.'

He snorted.

'Oh, I see. You understood them, you just decided not to follow them.'

Birch cleared her throat.

'Kato followed your orders to the letter, guv,' she said. 'If you need to bollock anyone, it should be me.'

McLeod let out a sigh.

'Thing is, Helen,' he said, 'I tire of bollocking you, as you put it. I seem to spend a hell of a lot of time doing it, and it never makes the blindest bit of difference. Would one of you like to tell me what the hell is going on?'

Amy was still cringing. She hadn't liked this plan one bit, but she hadn't been able to help being pulled in. Like Anjan, she didn't think it was desperately good for her friend to be involved with this case, but – it couldn't be denied – Birch's theory was getting interesting.

'Just a minute,' Birch said. 'I've invited DI Crosbie to join us – this is his case, after all.'

McLeod threw up his hands.

'I knew it,' he said. 'You're here about the case I expressly said you were not to be part of.'

'Marcello's heading up, too.' Birch had clearly decided to ignore his remark. 'It'd be handy to have an analyst view on what I'm about to say.'

Amy found herself nodding: Marcello would be a calming presence. He always was.

And McLeod was livid, as she'd known he would be. She could see two dark red spots appearing high up on his cheeks. His nostrils flared. He began to crash around behind his desk, opening drawers and rifling, then slamming them again.

She tried to look at Birch, but the other woman was watching their boss, wearing the slightest hint of a smile. Amy couldn't believe anyone could be enjoying this.

'Sir,' she said, 'are you . . . looking for something?'

'The *form*,' McLeod blustered. Another drawer slammed. 'The bloody suspension form. I got it printed out, ready for this very eventuality.'

Amy's mouth fell open.

'Sir . . .'

'Don't, Kato.' He straightened up, and jabbed a finger at Birch. 'We talked about this. She cannot say she wasn't warned.'

Amy was aghast, but Birch's expression hadn't changed.

'All due respect, guv,' she said, 'I'd save your energy for now. You haven't even heard what I'm here for, yet.'

McLeod looked like he might flip the entire desk.

'I have no doubt,' he said, 'that I'll be unpleasantly surprised.'

Amy felt like the awkward party guest who gets stuck in a room with an arguing couple. She wanted to be anywhere else: sitting at her desk running number plates from cars parked in the streets around the scrapyard. Dialling the numbers of Able's known accomplices and getting voicemail every time, everyone gone to ground. She'd rather be tackling her terrifying inbox than sitting here. When a knock came on the office door, she jumped, but also felt relief. More bodies in the room might dilute the gathering storm.

Marcello and Crosbie had arrived together. Crosbie slipped into the room first, wearing a scowl, opening the door only just wide enough for his body to slide through. He didn't speak. By contrast, Marcello strode in confidently after him, pushing the door open wide, and crossing the room to his favoured spot beside the window. Crosbie took up position in the back corner: a place from which he could look daggers at Birch without her seeing, Amy realised.

'Lovely morning,' Marcello announced, to everyone and no one.

McLeod rolled his eyes. He gestured towards the open door.

'If you don't mind,' he said.

Birch was closest, but these days it took her a while to get out of a chair. Amy sprang up.

'I'll do it,' she said. When she reached for the door handle, she saw her own hands were shaking, just ever so slightly.

'Right,' McLeod said, once Amy had sat back down. He'd made his hands into fists and rested them, knuckles down, on the desk. He stood like that, his weight braced on his arms, looming at Birch. 'We have been summoned, and we're here. I warn you, Birch, this had better be good.'

Birch cleared her throat. It sounded fake, theatrical. She was baiting him. Amy knew how much her friend had missed being away from work – the thrill of the chase, and all that – but this was crazy. Her theory, though worth looking at, was at the moment built on only the flimsiest evidence. McLeod could well throw it back in her face, and suspend her into the bargain.

'It's my belief,' Birch began, 'that James Able's murder was *not* gang-related, as we've all been assuming. I'd like to apologise to Sergeant Kato for encouraging her to pursue a line of inquiry that suggested we were dealing with an aspiring gang leader. Since Solomon Carradice was put away, I've been preoccupied by the fear that he'd be replaced. I was guilty of presuming that because this case could, from a certain angle, look that way, that was what it must be.'

From the corner, Crosbie snorted.

'*Look* that way? All the evidence points towards—'

Birch held up her hand, but didn't look back at him.

'Not *all* the evidence,' she said.

Amy's eye was caught by Marcello cocking his head to one side, just ever so slightly. He was interested.

'I'm assuming,' McLeod said, his eyes closing as he spoke, 'this means you've gone out and found additional evidence? Something we were unaware of?'

Birch straightened her spine.

'Yes, I believe I have.'

McLeod's eyes were still closed.

'And you did that after I told you in no uncertain terms that you were to do absolutely no work whatsoever, including and perhaps especially on this case?'

Birch gave one short nod.

'Sir,' she said.

McLeod's eyes snapped open. He seemed to be about to speak again, but Marcello cut in.

'What is this evidence, please?'

In the corner, Crosbie sneered.

'As this is *my* case,' he said, 'I'd also like to know.'

Amy sat very still, watching Birch, who took a deep breath.

'There was a key witness,' she said, 'to the hit and run incident in February, whose testimony was missed. One Josephine Stewart.'

Crosbie made a noise of derision.

'The hit and run? Birch, that was months ago! This has grown arms and legs since then. I don't know if you noticed, but a man was just set on fire.'

This time Birch did turn and look at him.

'By the same person,' Birch replied, speaking almost as one might to a child, 'who committed the hit and run in February.'

Crosbie shrugged, but didn't speak again. When Birch straightened up, Amy thought she could perhaps see just the smallest flicker of doubt written on her face. But the other woman continued speaking.

'In the case file,' she said, 'was a short snippet of CCTV from a restaurant on East Claremont Street. It shows the black Golf hitting the side of Dale McGill's car.' She looked up at Marcello. 'You'll have seen this,' she said.

Marcello nodded.

'Briefly,' he said. 'Not a lot to see.'

'I agree,' Birch went on, 'it's a pretty useless piece of video. However, in the first few seconds of the clip, I noticed something. McGill was following very close behind another car – a hatchback.'

'Yes,' Marcello said. 'Driving badly. He's a – boy racer? That's how you say it?'

'He is,' Birch replied. 'But the more I looked at the clip, the more I thought, this isn't just your standard boy racer tailgating. There's more going on here. So I ran the number plate of the hatchback through the system.'

McLeod made an abrupt sound, and Amy jumped.

'You didn't,' he said. 'You did not. Know how I know that, Birch? Because after I sent you packing on Sunday afternoon, I temporarily suspended your PCN access. So I know you didn't do anything of the kind. You had someone else do it for you.'

He levelled his gaze at Amy.

'Didn't she, Kato?'

Amy opened her mouth, but found no words would come out. She knew he was wrong, but felt her cheeks flushing with guilt all the same.

'You've got the wrong end of the stick, there, guv,' Birch said, holding up both hands as though to try and stem a tide. 'Kato knew absolutely nothing about this, not until I briefed her yesterday afternoon. But you're right, I didn't run the plate myself. I had help.'

McLeod was still looking at Amy. She wanted more than anything to melt into thin air.

'You expect me to believe this, Kato?'

Birch sighed.

'*Sir,*' she said, 'I'm telling you, Amy had no knowledge of what I was doing. I got Al Lonsdale to run the plate for me, if you must know. Perhaps you'd like to take it up with him, when we're finished here?'

McLeod's eyes boggled, and Amy hiccuped down a nervous laugh. She knew what would happen if Sergeant Al Lonsdale was called in to be hauled over the coals. McLeod knew it, too.

'It has been noted,' he said, icily. 'You may as well carry on. I have the horrible feeling it's all about to get worse, anyway.'

'You'd be right,' Birch said. 'The plate returned a result for Josephine Stewart: a single prior for a minor driving offence. Since her details were on the system, I decided to pay her a visit.'

There was another derisive noise from the corner.

'You *did*n't,' Crosbie said.

Birch didn't turn to look at him again.

'She's a key witness,' she said, still looking at McLeod, but very definitely speaking to Crosbie, 'who was overlooked by everyone on your team.'

Amy saw Marcello look down at the floor. She felt tempted to do the same. How many times had she watched that CCTV footage? Twice, maybe? She'd thought the same as Marcello: that the footage simply showed a boy racer, driving the way boy racers do. She wished she'd paid more attention. On the other side of his massive desk, McLeod was massaging his temples.

'Stewart informed me,' Birch went on, 'that my hunch was correct. McGill wasn't just tailgating her. He'd cut her up at a junction, and when she blew her horn at him, he yelled at her, threatening to follow her home. What you see on the CCTV clip is him making good on that threat.'

'How would you possibly prove that?' Crosbie asked.

'I could corroborate it,' Birch said, 'by speaking to McGill himself.'

McLeod dropped his hands.

'Let me guess,' he said.

'Yes,' Birch replied, 'I went to his house and had a word.'

McLeod began casting around himself again, running his eyes over the surface of the desk.

'I swear to God,' he said, his voice dangerously quiet, 'I had that form printed out.'

'McGill's new testimony,' Birch went on, ignoring him, 'confirmed Josephine Stewart's version of events. When the Vampire drove his Golf into McGill's car, it was an intervention. Nothing to do with gangs or drugs or Solomon Carradice. The Vampire intervened in Ms Stewart's predicament. In his mind, he was rescuing her.'

Crosbie let out another snort. His attitude was making Amy's teeth itch.

'Again,' he said, 'this is all very interesting, but there's absolutely zero concrete proof.'

'That's fair,' Birch said. She was still looking at McLeod, whose face was by now a kind of mauve colour. 'But think about the interviews we have with Alyona – or Natalia, however we're referring to her. She felt the Vampire's attack on Able was motivated by vengeance. He was settling a score on her behalf, not trying to claim Able's territory or anything like that.' She looked at Marcello now, and for the first time, Amy saw something imploring in her friend's eyes, as though she'd realised what thin ice her theory was skating on. 'Gentlemen,' she said, 'as I've said to Kato – I know it sounds unlikely, but I really think we're dealing with a vigilante here.'

The room was quiet for a long time. Amy felt a thin seam of sweat form in her hairline. McLeod placed both hands palm down on his desk and, for the first time since he'd entered the room, sank slowly into his chair. She didn't dare turn to look at Crosbie, brooding in her peripheral vision. Instead, she watched Marcello. Ever the analyst, she could see him turning Birch's revelations over and over in his mind. Eventually, he spoke.

'It makes sense,' he said. 'From a profiling perspective, I can see it.'

McLeod looked up at the ceiling.

'Oh God,' he said, very quietly.

'Yes . . .' Marcello had developed a thousand-yard stare. He began brandishing the index finger of his right hand. 'Yes, Natalia – she was burned. So he, this Jay, this Vampire . . . he burned Able back. McGill, he was driving dangerously, he was going to crash into the hatchback, and so . . . the Vampire crashed into him. Banjo Robin, he makes a nuisance of himself. The Vampire was a nuisance back.' Marcello seemed to snap back into the room, his eyes focusing on Birch's face. 'Yes,' he said, clapping his hands together, just once. 'DI Birch, I tip my hat to you. You should be in my job.'

'A vigilante,' Crosbie said. 'Are you lot for real?'

Birch was looking to McLeod for a response.

'It checks out, sir,' she said. Amy felt the edge in her voice – she was pleading with him. 'It makes sense. It isn't much to go on yet, but if we were to switch even some of our attention to this angle, we could—'

McLeod held up a hand, and Birch shut up immediately. Amy blinked. This wasn't like her friend at all. By the window, Marcello had begun to pace, his brain working fast behind his eyes. McLeod, too, was ruminating. Amy could see he was weighing it up. She tried not to think of the suspension form, the words it must say. Beside her, Birch shifted her weight in the chair, as though trying to shuffle away from her bad hip.

'Marcello,' McLeod said, after a long knife-edge of silence, 'I'm going to need your input here. I'm afraid I can't be carried along on another Helen Birch goose chase unless you can set my mind at rest. How credible is this theory?'

Marcello stopped pacing.

'Credible,' he replied. 'It makes a great deal of sense. In my opinion, it is an avenue very much worth pursuing.'

McLeod closed his eyes for a moment: Amy felt he knew what Marcello had been going to say, but hoped nevertheless that he might say something different. When he opened his eyes again, McLeod was looking at Crosbie.

'Alan,' he said, 'this is your case. What's your view on all this?'

'*Is* it my case?' Amy could tell Crosbie was looking at her. She made her spine rigid. 'Is it? Doesn't feel like it, these days.'

She could feel Birch holding back the urge to roll her eyes.

'It is,' McLeod said, his voice a flat line. 'If you think there's nothing to this, just say the word, and it'll be the last any of us speak of it.'

Across the room, Marcello's eyes widened. Amy held her breath. This was Birch's career, essentially being handed over to Crosbie. Surely McLeod couldn't—

'I don't know,' Crosbie replied. 'I don't know what to make of it.'

'Alan—' Marcello took a beseeching step forward, but McLeod held up a hand for quiet.

'I'm asking you,' he said, still looking at Crosbie, 'do we pursue this line of inquiry or not?'

There was quiet. Amy wanted to reach out and squeeze Birch's hand, but knew she couldn't, not in front of McLeod.

'Alan.' Marcello said Crosbie's name again, very softly this time, his Italian accent making the L into a kind of springboard between the vowels. 'I think this is worth considering.'

Behind Amy, Crosbie sighed.

'Listen,' he said, 'if this turns out to be garbage, Birch . . .'

'Don't worry,' McLeod cut in. 'If this turns out to be garbage, I'll have plenty to say on the matter.' He took a deep breath, as though dredging up the very last ounce of patience he had. 'So, Marcello. What's the angle?'

Marcello was quiet for a moment. Amy could tell he was weighing up what to say next.

'If it's okay with all of you,' he said, 'before I comment, I'd like to hear what DI Birch thinks.'

At the sound of her title being used, Birch's chin flicked upwards. She looked at McLeod for a moment with her head on one side, as though waiting to see if he'd prevent her from speaking. He didn't, though he wouldn't meet her eye.

'Well,' she said, slowly, 'this is why I wanted Marcello to be here. He knows about profiling, so he can tell me if my idea will actually work. The rest of you can tell me whether or not it constitutes entrapment in the eyes of the law.'

McLeod was looking upwards again. Amy wondered if he might be praying.

'Dear God, Birch,' he said, 'I'm regretting this already. What exactly is it you want to do?'

Birch glanced at Amy. Amy nodded in encouragement, though she'd already heard the plan.

'So,' Birch began. 'How do you draw out a vigilante?' She looked over at Marcello, who raised an eyebrow. 'You give him something to go after, right? Something to avenge.'

Marcello smiled a slow smile.

'DI Birch,' he said, 'I believe you're talking about bait.'

Wednesday, 21 July, 18:55

'Honestly.' Birch let go of her crutch and flopped on to the couch, letting Jamieson catch the stick and lean it against the arm, so she could reach it easily. 'I can't believe Marcello convinced them. For a second there, I really thought McLeod was going to have my head.'

Jamieson rubbed his hands together.

'Wish ah could've seen his face,' he replied. 'Ah dinnae ken whit ye said, bit . . . ah bet it wis priceless.'

Birch smiled. She knew when her father was fishing.

'I can't tell you, Dad. I'm sorry. But it was absolutely nuts; the whole plan is nuts. If it turns out I'm wrong about this, it might be the end of my career with the police.'

Her father crossed the room, heading for the kitchen door. He made a *pshaw* noise.

'Well, okay,' Birch went on, 'maybe not the end of my career. But we're talking serious punishment from McLeod. He's going to make me a traffic cop. I'll spend the rest of my life in a van on a motorway bridge, getting the Vicky from passing motorists.'

'He willnae,' Jamieson called back. He was in the kitchen now, clattering mugs. 'He widnae dare.'

'Trust me, Dad – he would.'

There was a crash. Her father had found the cupboard that, unless opened carefully, avalanched baking trays on to the floor. Birch had been meaning to sort it out for years.

'Fucksake,' he hissed, and then called back to her, 'but he willnae *have* tae. 'Cause it'll all be fine, whitever this plan o yours is.'

Birch frowned. It had been a long day, and her hip hurt. Not as much as it once had, but hurt was hurt.

'I really hope so,' she said. Her father was boiling the kettle now and couldn't hear.

When he returned to the living room, Jamieson was carrying a tray.

'Ah found a tinned soup in the cupboard, hen,' he said, setting it down on the coffee table in front of her. 'An did ye toast, an a wee bit o cheese.'

Birch had been lost in thought, only vaguely aware of her father moving around in the next room. It was comforting, she realised, to have him in the house, just doing his own thing. It felt like how the father – daughter relationship was meant to be.

'Oh, Dad. You didn't have to.'

Jamieson lifted a steaming mug from the tray and handed it to her.

'An a spot o tea,' he said.

Birch wrapped her hands around the mug, feeling the sting of the heat.

'You're a total star. Honestly, you're the only person in my life these days who doesn't treat me like I'm a lunatic woman who needs to be watched like a hawk and worried about. These past few days, I don't know what I would have done without you – all the driving, you know? You've been such a help.'

Jamieson beamed, straightening up.

'Dinnae worry, hen,' he said, 'it hasnae been a chore. Ken, ah like tae be useful. Jist dinnae eat that soup ower fast, it's hot.'

Birch frowned. He was shouldering on his jacket.

'You're leaving? You don't want to stay for a cuppa at least?'
He shrugged.

'Cannae,' he said. 'Wid love tae, but . . . cannae. It's ma meeting the nicht.'

Birch smiled. She'd been sceptical, when Jamieson first came back into her life, announcing he was clean and sober and attending AA. Charlie had reprimanded her for not believing their father capable of change. Thus far, he'd proven her wrong: he wouldn't miss AA for anything.

'Of course,' she said. 'Sorry, I'd forgotten. I hope it goes well.'

'Ye'll be okay?'
She nodded.

'Just fine. Thanks, Dad.'

'Jist wait 'til that soup's no so hot.'
She laughed.

'Okay,' she said, 'maybe you're worrying about me a *bit*.'

Jamieson was still grinning. As he rounded the sofa to get into the hallway, he paused, and placed one hand on the top of her head, just for a moment. It felt unexpectedly heavy: warm and calming. Birch didn't generally like people touching her hair, but the feeling was pleasant. She felt a little sad when he took his hand away.

From the hall, her father looked back as he opened the front door.

'Ah'll pick ye up the morn,' he said. Then he was gone.

Birch balanced her tea mug on the sofa arm beside her, reached out, and lifted the soup bowl off the tray and into her lap. Her dad was right: the contents were scalding hot. She balanced the bowl between her knees, letting it warm her like a hot-water bottle. Her head felt light and buzzy. She couldn't quite believe McLeod had signed off on her plan.

She knew she owed Marcello a pint – or several – once all this was over. Without him, she'd almost certainly have been suspended.

In her trouser pocket, her phone began to ring. She jumped, and a hot slop of soup scalded her leg.

'Fuck.'

Birch lifted the bowl again and tried to move it rapidly back to the tray. She made it, but in doing so, cocked her elbow and knocked the cup of hot tea off the sofa arm and on to the floor. She heard the gush and seep as the liquid made its way across the rug.

'Fuck!'

The caller ID read *Alan Crosbie*. Birch dithered, unsure how she was going to clean up the spilled tea while on crutches. Her pelvis ached. She figured she may as well answer the call.

'Hi, Alan.'

'Helen? Are you all right?'

She sighed, realising she'd answered crossly.

'Yes, sorry. I'm fine. Just dropped a cup of tea all over the shop, is all.'

Crosbie made a small, strangled sound on the other end of the line. He didn't know how to respond.

She rolled her eyes.

'What can I do you for?'

Crosbie coughed.

'Look,' he said, and the tone of his voice made something in Birch's chest go instantly cold. 'I'm calling to ask that you reconsider this ridiculous charade you've got planned for tomorrow. I can't believe James approved it.'

Birch felt her eyebrows rise, almost unbidden. *James?*

'Okay,' she said, 'listen, I know it's your case, but—'

'I suppose,' Crosbie ploughed on, as though she hadn't spoken, 'he probably just wants you out of the way. He knows this little stunt will keep you busy – you and Kato – while the rest of us get on with the actual policework.'

Birch didn't move, and didn't reply. She couldn't quite believe what she was hearing.

'But it's a shameful waste of resources, when we're busy enough as it is. This ridiculous concert – the First Minister has decided to attend now, did you know that? So that's a whole extra raft of work. On top of a perp out there setting fire to people. I ask you, Birch, have you even stopped to consider what you're doing?'

When she eventually replied, Birch's voice was quiet.

'I could ask you the same thing,' she said.

'What exactly does that mean?'

Birch peered over the arm of the sofa. The mug had rolled when it hit the floor, and a brown arc of liquid was slowly soaking into the rug.

'I just . . . I don't know why you'd call me. Why you'd say these things.'

Crosbie snorted. It crackled on the line.

'You're going to be wrong, you know,' he said. 'And it's going to be bad for you. Not just for you, for everyone. Me, Kato. Marcello, for all his ridiculous enthusiasm. It's going to be embarrassing. Wouldn't you rather call off this whole idea, and not put yourself through that? Put all of us through it?'

'Seriously,' Birch said, louder this time. 'Why are you calling me?'

'Aren't you listening?' Crosbie raised his voice, too, the tone of irritation more pointed. 'I'm concerned, is all. I don't want you to lose your job. Do you want to lose your job?'

There was something about the way he was talking that wasn't quite right. Birch sat in silence, trying to figure it out.

'Alan,' she said, the realisation dawning on her. 'I have to ask. Have you been drinking?'

Crosbie made the same snort noise again.

'No,' he said, the single syllable fast and staccato. She thought he'd express anger at her assertion, but he didn't. Just that single *no*.

Birch's eyes widened.

'Oh, wow,' she said, the words coming out slowly, though her thoughts were racing. 'I get it now. Everything suddenly makes sense.'

'What makes sense? What the hell are you talking about?'

'I'm talking about Sunday,' she replied, 'when Kato was calling and calling you, and you couldn't be raised. I'm talking about things being overlooked in this investigation. Josephine Stewart and the CCTV, for example.'

On the other end of the call, Crosbie was so silent that Birch thought maybe he'd placed his mobile down and walked away.

'Are you there?' she asked. 'Please, tell me I'm wrong. I'd love to be wrong. Reassure me.'

There was a pause, and in it she could hear his breath, faint, but there. He was still listening.

'You've just made a very serious allegation,' he said.

'I'm aware of that. But I'll ask you again: have you been drinking?'

Suddenly, Crosbie was shouting.

'I don't have to put up with this,' he yelled. Birch flinched, moving the phone away from her ear. 'You've no idea what you're talking about. Call off tomorrow's humiliating exercise, I'm telling you. Call McLeod right now and tell him it's not happening.'

When she was sure he'd finished, Birch brought the phone closer again.

'Or what?'

Nothing. Another few seconds of silence, and then the line went dead. *Call ended,* her screen informed her.

For a while, Birch simply sat. The phone screen went dark in her hands, and she saw her own face reflected back at her. The longer she sat there, the more she became convinced that Crosbie had definitely been drunk – she could think of no other explanation for the erratic call. It had only lasted a couple of minutes, but it had shaken her. She began to worry that she'd done the wrong thing, confronting him – that he might raise a complaint about her, and then she'd end up embroiled in a fight with him on top of the trouble she might be about to get into with the Vampire case. She was convinced she was right – the Vampire was a vigilante, and they'd never get their hands on him unless they treated him that way. But her conviction was based on nothing much more than the undeniable feeling in her gut that she was still learning how to trust. A hunch. Intuition, Amy would say. It felt harder these days to listen to that instinct – she blamed the pain meds and being off the job for dulling her senses. Did Crosbie have a point? Was that gut feeling enough to risk embarrassing herself and her colleagues? To risk her whole career?

When she snapped out of her anxious reverie, Birch saw that a slimy film had formed on the surface of her soup. The arc of spilled tea had established itself in the rug. She thought of what it would take to get up, move through the house, bring a cloth and carpet cleaner and sort it out. She thought of having to stand at the microwave and wait for the soup to reheat. She wasn't sure she could do it – not tired and filled with doubt and with her bad hip gently throbbing. She couldn't call her father back: it was AA night, and AA was sacred. She looked at the mantelpiece, and her mother's photograph.

'I want my maw,' she said aloud, and then burst into tears.

Nothing happened, of course. It was impossible to summon one's dead mother for help, no matter how deep the need. Birch heaved up snotty sobs and listened to them reverberate off the walls of her empty house. She cried for the weeks she'd spent cooped up, bored and miserable. She cried for the pain that had slowly eased but never stopped, no matter what position she slept in or sat in or how recently she'd taken her meds. She cried for her own stubborn stupidity, her endless need to get her own way. If it weren't for that brattish streak, she thought, she'd still be at Anjan's, looking out over the park from an Eames chair. She probably wouldn't have been shot, even – none of this would have happened. Her mother looked back at her from the picture on the fireplace, her face inscrutable.

Birch's phone was still in her hand. She barely had to look at it in order to navigate to Anjan's contact, she'd done it so often.

He answered after only one ring.

'Helen?'

'Anjan,' she spluttered, through tears. 'That was quick.'

'I had my phone in my hand. What's wrong? Are you all right?'

Birch paused.

'Not really,' she said, 'no. Oh God, Anjan, I'm a mess. I'm so sorry.'

'Hey.' He made his voice softer, drawing out the single vowel. 'There's no need to apologise, it's fine. Just take a breath. Tell me what's happening.'

'I'm sorry,' Birch said again, in spite of herself. 'You're probably busy, this is daft.'

'Never too busy for you.' She could hear relief in his voice: she'd called him. He was pleased. 'Do you need me to come over? I can come right now.'

Birch paused, shocked. These were words she'd never once heard Anjan say. She'd resigned herself early on in their relationship to the fact that he wasn't the drop-everything type.

'Aren't you working?'

He laughed.

'It's seven thirty at night. On a Wednesday.'

Birch tried to smile.

'Oh, like you've never worked after five. Tell me you're not sitting with a brief in front of you right now.'

Anjan went quiet.

'Fine,' he said, 'you got me. But seriously, this isn't anything I can't put down. Let me come round, Helen. Please? I've been very worried, and I'd really like to see you.'

She gulped back tears, then hoped he hadn't heard.

'I'd really like to see you, too,' she said, her voice small.

'Give me half an hour,' he replied. She could hear he was already moving.

Thirty-two minutes later, Anjan knocked at the front door. In that time, Birch had managed to stop crying, get off the sofa, hobble to the kitchen, and sponge the spilled soup off her clothes. She'd been unable to remove the tray from the coffee table – walking on a crutch and carrying with both hands just wasn't an option – and the skin on the now cold soup had become thick and stomach-turning to look at. She'd hooked the tea mug up off the floor and sprayed carpet cleaner on to the stain, but hadn't yet scrubbed it. Unsure she could bend enough, she had contemplated trying to do the task with one foot, but worried that this new, untested movement might somehow undo all her hard work in physio. She'd washed her face in the kitchen sink, not wanting to tackle the stairs for such a small task. Her eyes were pink, her cheeks puffed. She'd cried all her make-up off. She hoped she didn't look too off-putting.

Anjan let himself in.

'Helen?' he called, from the hall. 'It's me.'

'I'm in the kitchen,' she called back. A moment later, Anjan appeared in the doorway.

'What are you doing?'

Birch had wedged herself against the fridge. She was trying to extract a bottle of wine from the rack on top of it.

'For goodness' sakes.' Anjan crossed the short space between them, and then he was beside her, close enough to touch. He reached up, and extracted with smooth ease the bottle she'd been sweating over for a good sixty seconds. 'It's this you wanted? What about your meds?'

Birch felt her face flush. He smelled great.

'I thought you might want some,' she said. 'I'm trying to be a good host.'

Anjan looked at her, his brow furrowed. She seemed crazy, she could see it in the blatant worry on his face.

'I'm driving,' he said, gently.

Birch looked at the floor.

'Of course. Sorry.'

'Helen,' he said. 'You're upset. You look exhausted, too. I've been so concerned. Tell me what's going on.'

She opened her mouth to speak, but before she said even one word, her face creased, and the tears returned.

'I'm so sick of it, Anjan,' she said. She gestured downwards, at her useless hip, then flailed the same arm more broadly at the kitchen in general. 'Sick of this. Of everything. Sick of not driving, not working. I can't stand it.'

Anjan switched to the same soft voice he'd used on the phone.

'Come on,' he said. 'I know how frustrating it is. How hard. But you're doing brilliantly.'

'I'm not.' Birch had the bizarre desire to stamp her foot, a thing she hadn't done since she was a small child. She didn't do it, because she knew it would hurt like a bitch. 'I've messed up literally everything. I'm on McLeod's absolute last nerve – he's printed out the form to order my suspension, it's that bad. I messed things up with us. I'm a total burden on my poor old dad. People hate me. You hate me. *I* hate me. Everything's wrecked.'

Anjan held out a tentative hand and placed it on her shoulder. When she didn't flinch away, he curled his fingers around the top of her arm and gave her just the slightest shake.

'Listen to me,' he said. 'I hate to tell you this, because I know you don't like hearing it. But Helen, you're wrong. Wrong about me, at least. I absolutely do not hate you.' He laughed. 'I'm not sure what you think you possibly could do to make me hate you.'

For the first time since he'd entered the room, Birch met his eye.

'I'd like to give you a hug,' Anjan added, in his slightly stiff, lawyerish way. 'If you would like me to.'

Birch didn't reply – she just allowed her body to sag against Anjan's. He wrapped her up in his arms, and stayed still while she spluttered and sobbed.

'I'm sorry.' She said it over and over again, though she wasn't entirely sure what she was apologising for.

'It's okay,' Anjan replied, each time.

After a while, she realised she needed to get it together. She put one palm on Anjan's chest and used it to lever herself back upright.

'Thank you,' she said, 'for coming here.'

'Of course. I think you should sit down and let me look after you a bit.' He watched her face, and as she opened her mouth to speak, held up a hand. 'No arguments,' he said. 'Get your stick, go and sit down on the couch. I'll make us a cup of tea. Have you eaten?'

Birch shook her head. The thought of the cold, scummy soup made her want to cry again.

'My dad made me soup,' she said, 'but I got a phone call, and it went cold.'

Anjan smiled at her.

'Isn't that one of your idioms in this country? No use crying over cold soup?'

Birch attempted a watery smile back.

'You know very well it isn't,' she said.

'Well.' He grinned at her. She could still see worry in his eyes, but the smile was genuine. 'Something like that, anyway. Go. Sit. Get comfortable, if you can. I'll be through in a minute. Then you can tell me all about how you're back involved with work and it's backfiring on you, exactly like I said it would, and you can say *Anjan, you were right, as you always, always are.*'

She laughed, and the laugh was wet and thick, but sincere.

'Would you like to stay tonight?' She blurted the words out before she'd really thought them through. 'I . . . I've just really missed you.'

Anjan was still smiling, but there was something else in his expression now. Something a little sad, alongside the worry.

'How about we have some tea and a talk,' he said. 'Then we'll see how you feel.'

★

Birch drank the tea – strong, with extra sugar, at Anjan's insistence – while he pottered around the house. She pointed out the tea stain on the rug, and watched in amazement as he rolled up the sleeves of his Tom Ford shirt and got on his hands and knees to scrub it out. He whisked the tray of cold soup and toast away, replacing it a few minutes later with more of the same, only fresh. Birch felt wrenched back and forth between extreme gratitude and total embarrassment. She never wanted anyone to see her this dejected – especially not Anjan.

'That was great,' she said, chewing the very last mouthful of toast. 'I hadn't even realised how starving I was.'

Anjan was slumped in the armchair, diagonally across from her. His shirtsleeves were still rolled up, and Birch couldn't stop admiring his forearms: one of her favourite things about him. Her mother's picture seemed to glow on the mantel.

'You're not taking good enough care of yourself, Helen,' he said. 'I've been saying you're not fit to be in this house on your own. Not yet.'

'I know.' Her voice was small. He meant well, but she felt like a chastened child. 'But I *want* to be. It's been weeks. I thought I'd made so much progress.'

'That's just recovery for you. You were shot, remember. Not that long ago, really.'

'I know.' She said it again, in the exact same small voice.

'But,' Anjan roused himself from the chair and picked up the tray of empty dishes from the coffee table, 'we don't have to talk about any of that just now. I'll get rid of these plates, then you can tell me what got you so upset. What happened tonight.'

Birch nodded, partly to herself, as he carried the tray to the kitchen. She heard him set it down, and then the sound of the dishwasher door being opened, the wonky top shelf rattling out.

'Don't you do that!' she shouted. The dishwasher wasn't yet full, but she'd been slowly adding dirty dishes to it for several days. As a result, it had started to smell.

Anjan ignored her. She listened as he rinsed out her soup bowl and stacked it in the machine. She heard the crackle of plastic as he unwrapped a tablet and placed it in the slot. Eventually, she heard the quiet hum of the dishwasher starting up. She felt hot and flushed: with mortification, but also with a deep gratitude she didn't think she'd ever quite felt before.

Anjan appeared in the kitchen doorway.

'Done,' he said. He was rolling his sleeves back down, fastening the cuffs as if getting ready for a day's work, though it was almost dark outside. 'Do you need anything else? Is there anything more I can do?'

Birch thought for a moment. A smile crept across her face. Anjan matched it.

'What?'

'I'm just thinking about the layer of dust on everything in this house. Wondering when the last time was that I cleaned the loo.'

Anjan froze, as though he might roll his sleeves back up again and go in search of the bleach.

'I mean,' he said, 'I absolutely can . . .'

She laughed.

'Please don't,' she replied, 'I was joking. I'm mortified enough as it is that you're having to wait on me hand and foot. Just come and sit down. I so appreciate you being here.'

Anjan crossed the room and settled back into the armchair. Birch had hoped he'd sit down next to her on the couch, but tried not to look too disappointed. She'd done this, after all. She'd walked out on him.

'The time has come,' Anjan said, still smiling at her. 'It's time for you to tell me what's going on with work.'

'So you can say you told me so,' Birch replied, 'I know. It's going to be the biggest I-told-you-so in history, too.'

He raised a *go on* eyebrow at her. She took a deep breath, and began.

A my had always found visits to prisons disturbing. There was something so profoundly uncanny about them, especially the ones that had expanded rapidly, with shiny modern add-ons being built on top of old bones. HMP Edinburgh – or Saughton, as it was less-than-affectionately known – was one of these. This prison had been here for over a century, though its history was obscured by angular façades and acres of glass panelling. As Amy was led into the centre of the prison's maze, she felt a paradoxical claustrophobia in spite of the buildings' wide sprawl. One minute, she was standing on the smart carpet of the lobby, having her photograph taken by a tiny webcam. The next, she was inside a cold stone corridor with whitewashed walls that smelled like church: floor wax and old dust. Then she was whisked through the education block with its all-mod-cons barber salon and radio studio. She felt lost, confused – the name of the female prison officer she'd been assigned had fallen immediately from her head. The woman led her through an endless series of sheet-metal doors, prattling happily over her shoulder. On her hip, the woman wore a radio that whirred and buzzed.

'It's good you've come so early,' she said, as Amy half listened, her bearings shot. 'We haven't moved the route yet. They're having their breakfast just now.'

Amy imagined the prisoners queued up and blinking, still numbed from sleep as the food was piled on to their trays. She wondered what they ate, how good or bad or bearable it was – the food, but also just life in this warren. She reminded herself the people here – men and women alike – had done bad things. This place was what happened when you did bad things. This was how justice worked. She was part of it.

'You off to this concert tomorrow night, then?'

Amy blinked. She'd largely tuned out the screw.

'I'll be there for work,' she replied. 'Though I have to admit, I don't really know who Eddison Deas *is*.'

The other woman laughed.

'I guess you don't have kids,' she said. 'I've got a daughter, Ashley. She's fifteen, and in our house, it's Eddison Deas this, Eddison Deas that. What Eddison Deas is wearing, who she's dating, where she's been. We had a stand-up row the other day about her, in fact – I had to outlaw the drinking of weight-loss tea under my roof.' The screw put on a petulant, teenage voice. 'But *Mum*, it's *totally* safe – otherwise Eddison wouldn't *ever* promote it! Absolute eyewash. If you ask me, some eighteen-year-old shouldn't be allowed to sell dodgy weight-loss crap to her however-many-millions of followers. Not when they're impressionable weans.'

'Hmm,' Amy replied, only half listening. It wasn't yet eight thirty, and although she'd drunk a large coffee, she was realising she still had some waking up to do.

'Here we are,' the woman said, coming to an abrupt stop. Amy looked around. They were now in a corridor that could have belonged to just about any anonymous office building in the city. A little plaque on the door read *Meeting Room B*.

'Your colleague is already here,' the screw said, knocking gently on the door.

There was a pause, then Amy heard Birch's voice inside. 'Hello?'

The screw pushed open the door.

'Just us,' she chirped, shooing Amy into the room. Birch was sitting in one of four seats arranged around a large square table.

'Morning, Kato.'

'Marm,' she replied, then nodded in the direction of Birch's bad hip. 'I was sure I'd be here before you.'

Birch grinned in reply. Amy saw her friend's crutch propped behind the meeting room door. Beside it was a folded-up wheelchair.

The screw cut in.

'We zipped DI Birch through the prison on wheels,' she said, 'to make sure she'd be here before the route moved.'

Amy was beginning to feel irritated by this woman's early-morning cheer. She decided to focus on Birch, cocking her head in the direction of the wheelchair.

'And how do you like it?' she asked. 'Fancy getting one?'

Birch let out a sigh.

'I'd bloody love one, sometimes,' she said, 'but the physio people tell me I'm not allowed. It would get in the way of pro-gress.' She glanced up at the screw, who was in the process of moving into the room and closing the door behind her. 'I'll make the most of the luxury while I'm afforded it.'

The screw nudged Amy, a little harder than was necessary, and she jumped.

'Have a seat, hen,' the woman said. 'I just need to brief you both a little.'

Amy obliged, wishing someone would get her another cof-fee. It was a bad idea, given how jittery she felt, but she wanted it anyway.

The prison officer settled herself into a seat on the other side of the table. The smile was gone from her face now, and her voice dropped from airy to sombre, as though a button had been pressed.

'Now,' she said, 'I'm sure you're aware of who Lennox Whitelaw is, and why he's here.'

Birch nodded.

'I was part of the team who had him put away,' she said. 'That's how I knew he'd be a good fit for our operation.' She glanced at Amy. 'But that was all before DS Kato's time, so maybe fill her in a little.'

Amy leaned forward across the table. She'd read up about Whitelaw the night before, but she'd been sleepy and wasn't sure how much of the information had stuck. An extra briefing couldn't hurt.

The screw shifted her body slightly, so she was facing Amy.

'Okay,' she said. 'The short version is, Whitelaw was convicted seven years ago on three counts of rape, one count of statutory rape, and two counts of sexual assault. His youngest victim was fifteen.'

Beside Amy, Birch snorted.

'Nice guy,' she said.

The screw continued speaking, without reacting to the comment.

'Subsequently,' she said, 'another couple of women have come forward, so additional sexual assault charges have been added. Whitelaw is currently appealing those charges, so lately we've done a fair bit of pulling him out of the pack for court appointments and whatnot. We don't think the other inmates will particularly notice he's gone, which is handy.'

Amy made a polite *go on* face.

'He's a clever so-and-so,' the screw said. 'No matter what you say to him, he's always got an answer for you. He worked in finance, before he ended up here – I mean big finance, stocks and shares, all that. He loves to talk about how when he gets out of here, he'll be wealthy again within a week because he's so good at playing the markets. Insufferable, really, but he winds the other inmates round his little finger. They believe his bullshit.' The screw put one hand down flat on the table between them, checking she had Amy's full attention.

'Let me warn you now,' she said, her voice becoming more stern, 'that this man is a master manipulator. Especially of women. He knows how to turn on the charm, and when to go for the jugular. He had a female solicitor ask to be taken off his case, even. If you're not careful, he'll get in your head. So just be careful.'

She sat back in her chair.

'Not that he's ever charmed *me*,' she said. She looked Amy up and down. 'But I'm not a pretty quean like yourself. You'll be just his type.'

Amy pushed her shoulders back.

'Don't worry about me,' she said, sounding more confident than she felt. She was glad Birch was doing this with her, rather than DI Crosbie.

'We need to get our stories straight,' Birch was saying to the screw, 'for the media. I spoke to Whitelaw's legal team late last night, and they've agreed on the line we're taking. We're telling the press that Whitelaw is filing for a mistrial on the basis of new evidence just come to light. They're happy to issue a statement saying they've negotiated bail.'

The screw clicked her tongue.

'There'll be a bloody outcry,' she said.

'That's what we're hoping for,' Birch replied. 'We need this to be very public. We have to make sure our vigilante hears about it.'

'Be some story,' the screw said, 'if it was real. Is anyone going to buy it?'

Birch shrugged.

'We only need a couple of days,' she said.

'And then what?'

'Then Whitelaw comes back here,' Birch said. 'However this goes, he's coming back to serve his time.'

'He just gets a couple of days out,' the screw said. She rested her elbows on the table so she could raise both hands and make bunny ears in the air. 'On bail.'

'Precisely.'

Birch seemed confident, Amy thought. She could tell the screw wasn't keen on the idea, but was doubtless just doing as she was told. McLeod played golf with a lot of the bods high up in the SPS. Amy wondered how many favours he'd had to call in just to get this mad plan of Birch's to float. It would have to work.

The prison officer looked down at the tabletop, as though studying a sheet of invisible notes.

'We unlocked Whitelaw early this morning,' she said, 'seven thirty, ahead of everyone else. As far as anyone knows, he's meeting with his solicitor.'

'And what does *he* know?' Amy asked. 'How much has he been told?'

The screw gave Amy a slow blink.

'Nothing,' she said. 'He's clueless. We've fed him and put him in a holding cell, and I hear he's complaining to high heaven because no one will tell him what's going on.'

From the corner of her eye, Amy saw a slow smile cross DI Birch's face.

'Great,' she said, 'that's great. We'll catch him on the back foot.'

The screw nodded. The radio at her hip crackled, and Amy listened to the patchy message it picked up.

'That's them moving the route,' the woman said, rising from her chair, 'which means we can go and get Whitelaw. You ladies ready?'

Birch looked at Amy, who tried to keep her expression calm.

'As we'll ever be,' Birch replied.

The woman nodded, and crossed to the meeting room door.

'Five minutes,' she said, opening it and stepping out. 'Give or take. You two need anything?'

Coffee, Amy thought again. An ejector seat. A career change. But she didn't speak – only shook her head in unison with Birch.

'Right you are,' replied the screw, and closed the door. The two women listened as the plod of her heavy boots faded down the corridor.

Birch raised her eyebrows at Amy.

'You definitely all right with this?'

Amy lifted one hand to her collarbone to touch the lucky locket her mother had given her.

'Fine,' she said, trying to sound breezy. 'You think Whitelaw will go for it, though? What if he refuses?'

Birch shrugged.

'He'd be an idiot to refuse. He's getting a damn good deal here, for free and gratis.'

Amy zipped the locket back and forth on its chain.

'Well,' she said, 'in exchange for being human bait for a murderer.'

Birch laughed.

'Minor detail.'

Outside in the corridor, there were voices. Several sets of footsteps, growing louder. Amy dropped the locket and straightened up in her chair. Beside her, Birch cocked her head first to one side, then the other, cracking her neck, as though she were a prize fighter.

'Showtime,' she said, throwing Amy a wink.

The door to Meeting Room B opened, and the same female screw walked in. She kept her eyes on the door as she sidled past Birch's chair, positioning herself behind it. Amy had assumed Lennox Whitelaw would trudge in after her, sleepy perhaps from being woken earlier than usual, and disgruntled. But the man who strode into the room was confident and upright. Though he wore the standard prison uniform of heavy-duty black trousers and pullover, he looked for all the world like he was walking into a business meeting. His hands were cuffed, but the way he moved seemed to make up for this obvious signal of criminality. He was fiftyish, compact and handsome, his hair buzzed short. He made eye contact with Birch, and then with Amy, and flashed a deal-closing smile.

'Well,' he said, 'good morning. To what do I owe the pleasure?'

A male prison officer had followed Whitelaw into the room. Now, he gave the handcuffed man a gentle push, manoeuvring him in the direction of the chair that his female colleague had just been sitting in.

Amy saw Birch grin.

'Have a seat, Lenny,' she said. 'I can call you Lenny, right? As we've met before.'

Whitelaw sat down, lifted his hands and placed them on the table in front of Birch. They were clasped, as though in prayer, and the handcuffs clattered on the wooden surface. Amy watched as the two prison officers communicated via a series of looks: *am I okay to leave? Yes, I can handle it. Right, I'll be just outside.* The interaction took less than five seconds, and then the male screw shuffled out of the room, closing the door behind him.

'Lennox,' Whitelaw was saying, 'would be my preference.' He arranged his face into an incredulous, open-mouthed smile. 'I'm sorry to say that I don't remember you.'

'That's all right,' Birch replied, 'it's been a few years. Detective Inspector Helen Birch. I've been promoted, since last we spoke.'

'Why, congratulations,' Whitelaw said. He didn't look at Amy, but the way he studied Birch's face showed he was waiting for an introduction.

'This is Detective Sergeant Kato,' Birch said. Whitelaw turned his fake, white smile on Amy, and Birch held up a hand. 'And she's about as interested in your charm school schtick as I am, so I suggest you save it.'

Whitelaw ignored her.

'Delighted to meet you, Sergeant Kato,' he said. In spite of his perfect teeth, Amy noticed that when he said the word *sergeant*, he had a slight lisp. He struck her as the sort of man who liked to convince clever women that he was vulnerable, really, underneath the bravado – that he needed their help. She allowed herself to relax a little. She'd met men like this before.

'So, are either of you going to tell me the purpose of this meeting, or am I going to have to guess?'

Amy looked at Birch, who looked down at her own hands.

'Oh, we were just passing, really,' she said. 'Thought we'd drop in and see if we could interest you in a two-year reduction to your sentence.'

Whitelaw laughed.

'DI Birch,' he said, 'don't be a tease.'

Birch eyeballed him.

'I'm dead serious,' she said. 'Aren't I, Kato?'

Amy nodded. She paused for a moment before speaking, wanting to check that her voice, when it came, would be strident.

'Absolutely,' she replied. 'Two years' reduction to your custodial sentence, already signed off by your legal team, effective immediately.'

'In exchange for what?'

Amy didn't allow herself to blink.

'Co-operation,' she said.

'With a little something we're calling Operation Stake,' Birch cut in. Amy tried not to smile: she'd been delighted when her slightly jokey name suggestion had been approved. McLeod had clearly been tired, and just wanted the paperwork signed off.

'Delicious,' Whitelaw quipped. Amy hated his face.

'S-t-a-k-e,' Birch said. 'We're hoping to catch ourselves a vampire. And we thought, who better to help us with that than a ghoul?'

Whitelaw blinked, rapidly, several times. Amy wanted to laugh: he was fluttering his eyelashes.

'Can I just confirm,' he said, 'that I'm awake, and not, in fact, having a fever dream? A vampire?'

'Turn of phrase,' Birch said. 'The man's a vigilante. He's even more enthused about fixing up scumbags than I am. You might have heard, he set a man on fire the other day.'

Whitelaw tilted his chin upwards, but didn't take his eyes off Birch.

'Oh, I'd heard about *that*. A vigilante, you say?'

'Yep. Real nasty piece of work. Your kind of guy.'

Whitelaw looked at Amy.

'I hope you don't believe this slander, Sergeant Kato. I hope you're able to make your own mind up about me.'

I already have, Amy thought. The nerves in her stomach were gone now – she'd figured this man out. He was like so many moneyed career-men she'd been on dates with: he'd been told he was special so many times that he'd come to believe it completely, and learned to convince other people, too. In truth, he was simply a scumbag, and Amy had tangled with plenty of those in her time. She cleared her throat.

'We're here,' she said, 'because we know our vigilante is looking for his next target.' She tried to remember the things Marcello had told her, the day before, about how the Vampire might be thinking. 'We know he'll want to strike again, to keep his streak going. And as far as he knows, he's just got away with setting somebody on fire. And hey, we *could* sit and try to figure out what he's going to do next . . .'

Amy paused, lifted one hand, and shifted her long, shiny sheet of hair from one shoulder and on to the other. She watched Whitelaw follow the gesture with his eyes.

'Or,' she said, 'we could be more efficient about it and just ask for help.'

'*My* help?'

Amy simpered, just ever so slightly.

'Of course,' she said. 'Who else?'

He'd been smiling the whole time, ever since he walked in the door, but now Whitelaw's smile took on a different quality. It was the smile of a shark scenting blood.

'If I can be of service to you, Sergeant Kato,' he said, 'you just tell me how.'

Birch banged the flat of her hand on the table, and Amy tried not to jump.

'We're saying we want to dangle you in front of this psychopath like you're a prize fish,' she said, her voice jangling with edges. 'We reckon you're just the sort of menace he'd delight in fucking up, and we want to let him.'

Whitelaw unhooked his gaze from Amy's face for long enough to roll his eyes.

'You know,' he said, 'this Good Cop, Bad Cop act is terribly old-fashioned.'

Amy wished Birch hadn't spoken. She'd felt like she was making progress.

'Lennox,' she said, trying to draw him back in, 'we know you're embattled at the moment. We know you're midway through a new appeal, and that if you lose, you're facing an extension to your already lengthy sentence.'

Whitelaw snorted, but didn't speak.

'You're in a position to get a pretty good deal out of us.' She tucked a strand of hair behind her ear, trying once again to draw his eye. 'When was the last time someone asked you for help?'

She saw his pupils dilate, just slightly. She'd done it, she had him back.

'I'll admit,' he said, 'you're intriguing me, Ms Kato.'

Amy could feel Birch's eyes on her. Her flirtation was winning out over Birch's intimidation.

'Here's what we'd like to have happen,' she said, clasping her own hands and placing them on the table, mirroring Whitelaw. 'If you agree to our terms, you'll be released later today. The media will be informed that new information has come to light in your case, an application has been filed for a mistrial, and bail has been awarded.'

Whitelaw raised an eyebrow.

'Lucky old me,' he said. 'Is that how things actually work?'

Amy gave a short laugh.

'Sadly for you,' she said, 'it isn't. It's intended to appear outrageous and unfair, so the papers will pick it up and run with it.'

'So it becomes visible.'

'Exactly. So *you* become visible. So our vigilante hears about it, and—'

'And is tempted to put a stop to it.'

'Yes.'

Whitelaw laughed a put-on laugh, and glanced at Birch.

'Like a prize fish?' he asked. 'More like a flashy lure to *catch* a prize fish.'

Birch narrowed her eyes at him.

'Whatever metaphor works for you, Lenny.'

Whitelaw made a face, as though Birch had just put a bad smell under his nose. He turned back to Amy, and his smile flashed up again, like a neon sign.

'Forgive me,' he said, 'but it sounds like you're trying to get me killed.'

Amy shook her head.

'We'll attempt to draw our vigilante out,' she said, 'by letting him think he can get close to you. But we won't actually let him do that. You'll be installed in a police safe house, and accompanied at all times by a plain-clothes surveillance team.' In her mind's eye, Amy saw McLeod's face, heard again the crackle in his throat as he'd lectured Birch on how *the cost of all this, Helen, had better be bloody well worth it.* She widened her eyes at Whitelaw. 'We guarantee your safety,' she added.

He laughed, as she'd expected he would.

'You're terribly sweet, Ms Kato,' he said. She'd tried not to bristle at his first use of *Ms* in place of *Sergeant* – the second time, it took more effort. 'But you're not making any sense. How is your vampire meant to find me if I'm locked up in a safe house?'

Amy smiled, showing all her teeth.

'Because,' she said, 'tomorrow night, you're going to go and see Eddison Deas.'

'Eddison . . . who?'

'She's an influencer. An online celebrity. And she's playing a concert tomorrow night at Edinburgh Castle.'

Whitelaw sniffed.

'Doesn't really sound like my scene.'

Birch snorted, but Amy carried on.

'We guessed as much,' she said, 'but it's going to be a hell of an event. The First Minister will be in attendance, as well as, we believe, a fair number of celebrities. Tickets to this gig sold out in minutes.'

Whitelaw's eyebrows were creeping upwards. Amy glanced at Birch.

'In fact, it sold out so fast, I believe it broke some kind of record . . . right, marm?'

Birch had folded her arms. She didn't look away from Whitelaw's face.

'Right.'

'Anyone who's anyone is going to be there.'

Whitelaw leaned forward. Amy could see he was looking at her hair.

'The question is, Sergeant,' he said, 'will *you* be there?'

Amy could see it in his face then: the ugly need to break another person, remove their power. She took a deep breath, and closed up her throat in case the words that followed made her retch.

'If you'd like me to be,' she replied.

Whitelaw beamed.

'So you're telling me,' he said, 'that I'm to be let out on bail and taken to a concert so an attempt can be made on my life . . . then what?'

'Then you come back here,' Birch cut in, 'and pay the rest of your debt to society. Minus two years.' She flashed him a thoroughly hollow smile. 'Because we're generous like that.'

Whitelaw hadn't looked at her. His eyes were still fixed on Amy's shiny hair. She was glad she'd washed it that morning and worn it down. She realised he was waiting for her to speak.

'Two years,' she said, 'and our gratitude.'

He seemed to snap out of some internal reverie then. She saw his pupils shrink back again, and the shark-like look intensified.

'Five,' he said.

'I'm sorry?'

'Five years,' he replied, 'not two.'

Next to Amy, Birch let out a noise of derision, and Whitelaw's smile widened.

'I don't know what DI Birch expected,' he said, not moving his eyes from Amy. 'I do this for a living.'

Amy wanted to gauge Birch's reaction. She wanted to look at the female screw, who was only feet away but still and silent as a pillar. She knew she couldn't look at them, because it would show weakness – but what she said next would need to be right. Whitelaw could still walk away.

She leaned forward. Now, she could smell his breath: toothpaste and the ghost of bad coffee. Underneath that, the smell of prison detergent. The smell of his body: the smell of a taut, evil man.

'Look at me,' she said, though he already was. 'Look at my face. I know you know how negotiating works, that you've done this dance a thousand times before. I know you can see the cards I'm holding. I am authorised to offer you two years. That's it, that's all I have.'

He watched her, his face only inches away. She thought of his mouth, pressed down on the mouth of a fifteen-year-old girl, his hands on her throat so she couldn't scream. She felt the flesh on the back of her own neck creep upwards in disgust.

'Two years,' she said, into the silence that hung between them like a guillotine. 'Look at me, and tell me that's not a good deal.'

The silence widened. Whitelaw didn't seem to blink. She could tell he'd read books on this stuff, understood that generally, if you were quiet, the other person would crack. But she'd read those books, too, so knew she couldn't speak again, or look away, no matter how long this took. She thought of the women Whitelaw had hurt, the way they'd feel when they saw the ridiculous news of his bail. Family liaison officers were being arranged to let them in on the plan, and support them through the next couple of days, but Amy could only imagine the anger they'd feel. She knew she was betraying them, sitting here offering a bribe to this man who by rights ought to rot for the rest of his life in this jail. A part of her hated DI Birch for making her do it – she couldn't face the idea that Birch's theory might be wrong, that she might be sitting here sweet-talking a convicted rapist based on absolutely nothing at all. And the gall of him, asking for more! She looked at his eyes. She wanted to lunge across the table and claw at them.

'You've the makings of a good little negotiator, Sergeant,' he said. He let his shoulders drop, and Amy clenched her jaw to prevent relief from flooding her face. She'd won. 'Two years. And I'll go anywhere I'm told, on one condition.'

Amy still didn't blink.

'Which is?'

'That you'll accompany me.'

Beside her, Amy felt something in DI Birch loosen and uncurl. They'd done it, they'd cleared the first hurdle. She had to say yes to this now – it was all that stood between them and Operation Stake.

It took every nerve Amy could muster to smile at the odious man seated opposite her.

'You, me, and Eddison Deas,' she said, her jaw so stiff it hurt. 'It's a date.'

JournalPortal / Clients / Dr Jane Ryan
Client: Helen Birch
Date: Thursday, 22 July
Time: 20:56
Mood selected: Worried

Journal entry text: Hi Dr Jane. I thought this was as good a time as any to check in, as I think I'm as close as I've ever been to getting suspended from the police force. I've set in motion an extremely risky chain of events. If even one thing goes wrong, then I'll be suspended and probably fired. McLeod says he has the form printed out and ready to go, and I don't think he has any reason to lie about it.

I'm getting ahead of myself: maybe I should explain that I've got involved with this case at work, even though I'm supposed to be on leave. I think I've made clear to you and to everyone that I've been going slowly out of my mind these past few weeks, and I just wanted something to keep my mind occupied. Or rather, to keep my mind occupied with something that wasn't thinking about Operation Kendall, and Gerald Hodgson, and all the things I said and didn't say that night, and all the ways it might have gone differently.

I'm sitting here writing this and realising that maybe this whole thing is just me trying to run away from that night – Operation Kendall, I mean. I'm a fixer, I've always been a fixer – I want to go back and do it differently, make it better. If I can't do that, then I at least want to shove it aside, not think about it any more, think about something else, anything else. Fix something else, so I scratch the fixer itch. But instead

I've set up something that might not be a fix at all, it might make everything worse. And what will I do then, to make things better?

I'm sure that as a therapist this is all sounding major alarm bells for you. I know that the purpose of therapy is the exact opposite of what I'm talking about here. Your job is to *make* me think about things, isn't it? To make me confront things and deal with them, not just slap a plaster on them and shove them aside. I just don't know if I can. I'm so tired. Not just lack-of-sleep tired, but weary, in my head. Weary of thinking all the time. I threw myself at this Vampire case because I thought changing the channel in my head might help. It hasn't helped. Now I'm just thinking about the two things in stereo. My brain is even noisier than before. Operation Kendall was a fuck-up, Operation Stake might well also be a fuck-up. And it's me, I'm the common denominator. *I'm* the fuck-up.

We talked about this in our first session and I've been thinking about it ever since: you said it seemed like I was worried I'm not cut out to be a police officer, and you were right. I *am* worried about that, since Operation Kendall. If I'm totally honest, something about that night has changed the way I feel about everything: not just the job, but me, who I am as a person. There aren't many moments when my thoughts quieten down enough for me to see things clearly. But just occasionally, it happens, and the question I find myself asking is not just 'am I still cut out for this?' It's 'do I still want to do this? Do I still want to be this person?'

It's a terrifying question, Dr Jane. I got into this game fifteen years ago because I wanted to find my missing brother. I was looking at the police missing persons investigation and thinking 'you lot are useless, I can do this better'. McLeod was right when he asked me the other day, 'Who the hell do you think you are?' He said I act like I believe the place would go to hell in a handcart if I wasn't around – or words to that effect. And I'm ashamed to admit it, but maybe he's right. I got into the police thinking I was going to show them all how it was done, and when I think about it, I've kind of had that attitude ever since. I got fast-tracked: into CID, then DS, then DI. I was the blue-eyed girl of Gayfield Square. I believed my own hype. But Operation Kendall changed something. I fucked up, big style. Because of me, a man died.

How can I carry on doing this job, after that? Do I even want to? Maybe I don't. But oh God, that's a terrifying thought – I can't imagine even saying it out loud to myself, let alone anyone else. Who would I be, if I wasn't a policewoman any more? I haven't the faintest clue. But I guess if Operation Stake goes badly, then whether I like it or not, I'm going to find out.

Friday, 23 July, 16:00

'I think I might have made a terrible mistake.'

Birch was sitting in the back of a cramped surveillance van, her hands pressed together, palm to palm, between her knees. Marcello was a couple of feet away, typing so fast into a tiny laptop that his fingers moved in a blur.

He glanced up at her.

'Don't say that now,' he replied, gesturing vaguely around at the van, and the tech she knew he was delighted to be meddling with. 'I think we are committed.'

Birch shifted her weight. There was no way to sit in this cramped space that didn't make her hip ache, but she was determined to be at the centre of things. McLeod may have preferred her to, but there was no way was she waiting in her office for the phone to ring – not on this operation. He'd relented, and sent her with Marcello – so she'd have a babysitter, she suspected.

'I know,' she said, 'but if the Vampire doesn't show, I'll be fired.'

Marcello turned back to his screen.

'He will show.'

'You're always so confident in me. We both know we're only here because you convinced McLeod.'

'That's not true.'

'It bloody is. He was literally hunting for my suspension form until you backed me up.'

'That was a bluff. DCI McLeod is – how does one say it? He likes the melodrama.'

Birch laughed.

'I'll tell him you said that.'

Marcello looked at her again and gave a slow blink.

'I know,' he said, grinning, 'that you won't.'

Birch stared down at her feet, and the non-slip floor of the van, its raised circles like small black moons. She felt sick, and the smell in this windowless box wasn't helping. New car smell, Jamieson would have called it: disinfectant and cheap rubber.

'You know,' Marcello said, 'I'm confident in you because you have never been wrong.'

Birch snorted, but he went on.

'Genuinely,' he said, 'I only ever back the winning horse. Helen Birch is a safe bet.'

The van was parked on a cordoned wedge of Johnston Terrace, nose to nose with the Eddison Deas tour bus. Ostensibly, this unmarked grey van belonged to a security firm that came as part of the entourage. In truth, it was Birch's command post, one of several positioned around the venue. It was four in the afternoon, and the Castle had closed early to prepare for the concert. Eddison Deas – Birch couldn't help but refer to this woman by that full, ridiculous name, even in her own head – was already inside, tucked safely behind the centuries-old walls. Birch imagined her standing in some plush, tapestried room, entourage milling about while she did vocal exercises and picked over her outlandish rider. The woman she'd Googled to see what the fuss was about looked like a doll: fake lashes, perfect teeth, and a faint Glaswegian accent that came out only once in the video Birch watched, when Eddison Deas said the word 'homepage'. Almost nine thousand people had bought tickets to this gig, with more expected to congregate in the surrounding streets to try and listen in. Such a fuss for this tiny, birdlike woman who'd apparently made herself famous by singing along to pop songs and reviewing lipsticks in fifteen-second videos. Birch didn't get it, but she'd use it: a splashy, once-in-a-lifetime chance their vigilante would have to take.

'He *will* take it, won't he?' she said, aloud.

'I'm sorry?'

'The Vampire. He'll take the chance to do it. To get near Whitelaw.'

'I don't know,' Marcello replied, still typing, 'I can't tell you.'

Birch nibbled at a sore piece of skin beside her thumbnail. It was sore because she'd been bothering at it since this morning and couldn't seem to stop.

'I've realised,' she said, 'that if he can't get into the gig without a ticket . . .'

Marcello was trying not to sigh, she could tell. He looked up from his screen, twisting at the waist so he could face her.

'He won't be interested in the gig,' he said. 'We've been over this. The gig would be too difficult anyway – too many bodies in there. Too many witnesses, and no clean exit. He would be stupid to do anything in there, and if we know one thing about him, we know he is not stupid. I doubt he'd even think about going in.'

'Inside the concert would be a big deal, though. The First Minister's going to be in there. Tons of press. Don't vigilantes want to be famous?'

Marcello shook his head.

'Only the ineffective ones,' he said. 'Notice our vampire has never come forward anonymously to speak to the press or claim his crimes. Notice he's never written a manifesto. This is precisely the reason we need to take him seriously. He isn't doing this for notoriety. He's doing it quietly, on his own, because he genuinely believes what he's doing is right.' Marcello curled his top lip. 'Idiots who write manifestos on the internet always get caught. The Vampire is smarter than this.'

'Bad luck for us.'

Marcello was on a roll, thinking aloud – he went on as though she hadn't spoken.

'Plus,' he said, 'the First Minister means more security. More police. The First Minister means *armed* police. And the Vampire isn't committing suicide by cop. He's not one of those types, either.'

Birch was nodding, not because she necessarily understood this for herself, but just to show she was listening.

'So he'll try to get to Whitelaw when, then? Before?'

Marcello cocked his head to one side.

'Probably not. He'll arrive in the area before Whitelaw – in fact, I would not be at all surprised if he's already out there, somewhere, waiting on Castlehill so he can scope out the scene, watch Whitelaw arrive, weigh things up, you know? I suspect he'll wait outside for the duration of the concert, let Whitelaw leave, and then follow. Try to separate him from the herd, get him somewhere alone.' Marcello shrugged. 'But you know, I can't guarantee that. That's only what *I* would do.'

Birch let out a laugh, but it sounded hollow.

'Hey,' she said, 'don't you be going to the dark side. We need you.'

Marcello cocked his thumb at the computer screen and grinned again.

'No life of crime for me,' he said, 'don't worry. This job is much more fun.'

He began to turn away again, but Birch saw that he'd caught her frowning.

'Helen,' he said. 'Stop worrying. Like I said, we are committed now.'

'And he'll strike after. After the gig.'

'That would be the most likely time.'

'You're one hundred per cent sure.'

He held up his hands. When he spoke, she sensed the slightest edge of irritation in his voice.

'I am a profiler,' he said. 'When do we ever say we're one hundred per cent sure?'

'Never.'

'Okay. So, I have told you all that I can.'

Birch closed her eyes.

'Fine,' she said, and her throat felt thick. 'I'll shut up now.'

Marcello was quiet for a moment, then he spoke again.

'Anyway,' he said, 'if you get fired, then I do too. We go down together.'

Friday, 23 July, 18:00

Amy's post for the evening – the whole of the evening – was at Whitelaw's side. She and three male undercover officers would flank him at all times, from the moment he left the safe house to the moment he went back into it. Amy had stood for a long time in front of the mirror the night before, trying to decide what to wear. She needed to look like a concert-goer, like someone who knew who Eddison Deas was, who cared enough to buy a ticket to be in her presence. But she also needed to wear something she felt strong in – she wanted clothing that felt like armour, clothing that Whitelaw's odious energy couldn't seep through. After almost an hour of trying on different combinations of skirts, tops, jeans, jackets, Amy realised that what she really wanted was a flak vest. A riot shield, like a missile-proof wall between Whitelaw's body and her own. What she really wanted was to never have to be in the presence of that man ever again. But she'd said yes. She knew that if she hadn't, he'd have walked away from the deal.

Now she sat alone in the passenger seat of an unmarked police saloon car, one of two parked up on the pavement outside the safe house. This house looked for all the world like a standard family home: double-fronted, pebble-dashed, with a tarmacked drive. It had been chosen carefully: no house directly opposite, no line of sight from any neighbouring properties into the windows or back garden. A high fence had been erected around three sides, and at the back of the plot, the ground fell away down a steep

bank. The front drive was decorated with troughs filled
with bright bedding plants, which Amy couldn't stop looking at. She wondered whose job it was to replenish those
when they withered, and made a mental note to ask Birch
if *she* knew. There were patterned blinds at the downstairs
windows and blackout blinds on the first floor: Whitelaw
had drawn them all. For all his swagger, he clearly didn't
want to take any chances.

The front door opened, and Amy's colleague, DC Oliver
Bow, stepped out. A tall, greying man in his early fifties, Bow
was far too old to be going to an Eddison Deas concert, Amy
thought. But then, so was she. People would probably assume
Bow was someone's dad, sent to stand apart from his teenage
kids so as not to embarrass them. Whitelaw too, she realised,
might be read that way, and the thought made her stomach
turn. She tried not to let herself return to the thought of
the fifteen-year-old he'd attacked, the things she must have
experienced.

Bow rounded the bonnet of the car, opened the driver's
side door, and got in.

'His Majesty was asking why you weren't going in to collect
him,' he said. 'Had a bit of a paddy about it, in fact. Hence
the delay.'

Amy rolled her eyes.

'Jesus. Do I need to get in there?'

Bow smirked.

'Nah,' he said. 'Bastard doesn't understand the word *no*. It's
time he fucking learned.'

'True.'

Bow glanced down at Amy's jeans. She'd chosen a lilac pair,
in the end – she'd worn them exactly once before, too afraid
of spilling anything on them to put them into the regular

weekend rotation. On her top half she wore a black top with long sleeves and a high neck – the idea of showing any flesh around Whitelaw was unbearable – under a denim jacket. Trainers, of course. She was so used to working in heels that she kept having to glance at her feet, feeling every so often a spike of fear that she'd left the house in her slippers.

'Nice fit, as the young ones say.'

Amy blushed.

'Oh God,' she said, 'I had no idea what to wear. What do you wear to go and see an eighteen-year-old internet celebrity sing? I wanted to look . . . I don't know, young, I guess. Young and hip. Instead I seem to have dressed as a kids' TV presenter.'

Bow barked a laugh.

'You *are* young, you do know that, right?'

Amy lifted one hand to her face.

'Well, thanks. But there's young and then there's . . . Eddison Deas young.'

'Listen, how do you think I feel, going to this thing? I look like someone's granddad.'

Amy opened her mouth to reply, though she wasn't sure of the appropriate thing to say. But before she had the chance, Bow turned his face towards the house and made a quick, upward nod.

'Here we go,' he said. 'Here comes His Nibs.'

Amy followed Bow's gaze. Lennox Whitelaw was stepping over the threshold of the safe house, one officer in front of him, the last of their team bringing up the rear. He seemed to linger on the shiny driveway, dragging his feet, looking around.

'Oh,' Bow whispered, 'don't you dare, sunshine.'

Amy was already reaching for the car door handle.

'You think he's going to run?' She could feel her heart rate ticking up.

'He'll regret it if he does,' Bow said, but Amy could feel how tense he'd also become. 'Malcolm there, behind him, he's a positive track star, he'd catch him in no time. No one wants to come down hard on concrete then have three six-foot coppers land on top of them.'

Amy was watching Whitelaw, but she still found a moment to be stung. What made Bow think *she* couldn't catch up to a fleeing perp?

The officer at the back – Malcolm, Bow had called him, though Amy only knew him as DC Johns – said something; she saw his mouth move. Whatever it was seemed to work: Whitelaw stopped casting about, picked up his feet, and walked over to the car. DC Johns stepped around him and opened the back passenger-side door. Whitelaw climbed into the back seat, behind Amy.

'Ms Kato,' he said, as Johns slammed the door. 'I'd have thought you might come in for a moment and see the place. It's a basic sort of arrangement, I must say.'

'*I'd* have thought,' Bow cut in, 'this place'd seem like luxury after a few years in the big hoose.'

Amy watched in the wing mirror as Johns and the other officer got into the car behind. Johns was driving. She saw him flash the headlights, once, twice, a signal to Bow. Let's get going.

'I still remember the taste of good food, Officer Bow,' Whitelaw snapped. 'I still remember how good high-thread-count sheets feel.'

Bow started the engine.

'If you thought we'd be providing any fancy bedding in a safe house, pal,' Bow spat back, 'you're more touched than I'd taken you for.'

Whitelaw sniffed.

'I ask for nothing,' he said, 'but a greeting from Ms Kato, here. Amy, are you going to speak to me?'

For a split second, at the use of her first name, Amy's vision flickered, and she literally saw red, as people say they sometimes do. She hauled in a deep breath to steady herself, even as her mind raced to figure out how he knew. One of the other officers must have mentioned her by her full name, and he'd overheard. Or perhaps he'd asked outright, and one of them had been stupid enough to tell him.

'Good afternoon,' she said, her teeth on edge, 'Mr Whitelaw.'

'Not so courteous today, Ms Kato?'

Amy spun round in her seat and fixed her eyes on him. It startled him: she saw him shrink back, just slightly.

'You will address me,' she said, her voice icy, 'as Sergeant Kato. I will not answer to anything else. Is that quite clear?'

The car was moving now, but beside her, Amy heard Bow let out a low whistle.

Whitelaw rallied. He tried the same eyelash-flutter he'd thrown at DI Birch in the prison meeting room the day before.

'But Amy,' he said, 'we had a deal. You, me, and Eddison Deas, remember? It's a date.'

Amy didn't shift her gaze, but she did smile.

'I thought you were a world-beating negotiator, Whitelaw.'

He blinked.

'I'd like to think I am, yes.'

She allowed her smile to widen – she thought of this as her *I'm too good for you* smile, the one she reserved for men who took her on dreadful first dates then asked to see her again.

'In that case, you ought to realise,' she said, 'it was me who closed the deal, not you. Surely you get that I said what I needed to say to bring you on board this operation?'

He was frowning at her now, just a little.

'Now you're with us,' she said, 'I'm under no obligation to treat you any sort of way. It's my job – mine, and DC Bow's, here – to see you don't get killed. That's it. That is *literally* it.'

She looked him up and down, letting her eyes linger on his hands, cuffed and laid in his lap.

'Beyond that,' she added, 'you're nothing more than a bargaining chip.'

Out of the corner of her eye, Amy saw Bow cock his head to look at Whitelaw in the rear-view mirror. In response, Whitelaw's face contorted into a smirk. He still thought he had the upper hand.

'I could still refuse to co-operate,' he said, his voice low and snake-like now. 'I could simply refuse to be part of this operation.'

Bow laughed.

'You don't have a choice, sunshine,' he cut in. 'The only thing you can refuse to do at this point is get out of this fucking car. And I'm sure Sergeant Kato would agree to my suggestion that in that event, we simply call for some more surveillance units, then leave you in it with the doors unlocked. Somewhere nice and public. A lovely sitting duck for our vigilante.'

He nudged Amy, who was focused on keeping her gaze locked with Whitelaw's.

'Hell,' he added, 'I bet we could sell tickets to that.'

Amy became aware she was channelling DI Birch: trying on for size a kind of toughness that had rarely been required of her before. But she was a sergeant now: what happened to Whitelaw, in the absence of a superior officer, fell to her. She flashed the *I'm too good for you* smile once more.

'Now, there's an idea,' she said.

Whitelaw held up his cuffed hands, a fake, beseeching gesture.

'Goodness, but this is out of character, Ms Kato. Yesterday, you—'

Amy held up a hand, and to her surprise, Whitelaw fell silent.

'I am this team's commanding officer,' she snapped, realising her voice was raised only after the words began to form. 'You will address me as such, or not at all.'

Beside her, Bow nodded.

'Damn right, Sarge,' he muttered.

Whitelaw's eyes had widened. He was quiet.

'Good,' Amy said, turning back round in her seat. 'We understand each other.'

Friday, 23 July, 20:30

The Esplanade was packed with bodies. People – most of them under the age of twenty-five – stood shoulder to shoulder, swaying in time to Eddison Deas' patchy vocals. The music, blasted out of speaker stacks the size of city buses, reverberated off the buildings on Castlehill and Ramsay Gardens. The evening sun shone long over the Esplanade, flashing off watch faces on hands held aloft, and contraband bottles of alcohol passed among gaggles of concert-goers. It glittered on the skin-tight, sequinned jumpsuit Eddison Deas wore to strut the length and breadth of the stage, a giant screen behind her copying her every move with a second-or-so's delay.

'I love you, Edinburgh!' she yelled, as the tail-end of one song bled into the ramp-up of another. 'It's good to be home!'

Her fans sent up a collective cheer in response, every hand in the place shooting into the air. McLeod clocked the bottles that went up with them: vodka, beer, neon-coloured liquid in plastic bottles scrubbed clean of their labels.

'More underage drinking in here,' he muttered, 'than in the Cav on a Saturday night.'

'Sing this one with me!' Eddison Deas yelled into the mic, and McLeod's voice was lost amid the immediate atonal yell-song of the crowd.

Crosbie was standing with his arms folded, his elbow nearly touching McLeod's own. They'd chosen a spot near the back of the crowd, where a few other older adults – parents of the younger kids in attendance, McLeod both assumed and hoped – stood, mostly staring down at their phones. He and Crosbie looked to all the world like dads whose tweenage daughters were somewhere up front, gripping the edges of homemade pillow-case banners painted *Eddison is my hero* or *Queen D*. They were here to diligently chaperone and taxi – that was the story, if anyone asked. So far, no one had. No one so much as looked at them.

Though he hadn't moved his eyes from the distant stage, McLeod saw Crosbie's lips moving.

'I can't hear you, Alan,' he half shouted.

Crosbie leaned closer.

'I said, I wonder if Lennox Whitelaw is enjoying this as much as I am.' When McLeod raised an eyebrow, he added, 'Which is to say, not in the bloody slightest.'

McLeod scanned the crowd. If he let his vision blur, the throng of bodies seemed to move as though it were one thing: a slow but constant ripple, like wind passing over a pond. He was glad the First Minister had been persuaded to watch the concert from the wings. Having her amid all this would have been a whole other layer of anxiety.

He let his gaze come to rest on Amy Kato's blue denim jacket, then picked out Lennox Whitelaw sitting beside her. They were up in the bleachers, nearish the stage, placed strategically to put Whitelaw on display. McLeod was too far away to see clearly, but Whitelaw didn't look especially engaged. He slumped in his seat, his arms folded much the same way Crosbie's were.

'Looks like he's having a whale of a time to me,' McLeod smirked.

He felt, rather than heard, Crosbie cleave a heavy sigh beside him.

'I'm telling you, James, this is all going to turn out to be a hiding to nothing. A very costly one.'

Crosbie's voice was raised against Eddison Deas' amplified croon, though the crowd had quietened a little. She was singing a ballad now, her voice wavering on the longer notes.

'Why,' McLeod replied, his voice weary, 'do you think I'm spending my Friday night here with you?'

Crosbie snorted.

'The answer to that is fairly straightforward, guv, if I may speak plainly,' he said. He was half shouting, and McLeod felt mildly self-conscious, though no one appeared to be listening. 'Helen Birch.'

McLeod raised one hand and touched his own forehead, as though feeling for a pain there.

'I'm here,' he shouted back, 'because I've sunk a hell of a lot of resources into this Operation Stake. The aftermath is going to be a nightmare, no matter how it goes.' He gestured vaguely around at the mooning, swaying crowd. 'As much as I dislike it,' he added, 'it's better if I'm here, on the ground.'

Crosbie looked away, screwing up his eyes as though trying to focus on something onstage, some detail.

'That's just another way of saying what I just said. Hiding to nothing. Very costly.'

McLeod took a long breath in.

'We need to catch this particular perp, Alan. His behaviour has escalated fast, and since he killed James Able, he's gathered fans. You know there are now hundreds of tweets out there praising the guy? Encouraging him, even. There are people suggesting which local arsehole he ought to pick off next. We don't want another charred gangster on our hands, and we definitely don't want the public thinking that acts of vigilante justice can go unpunished.'

Crosbie didn't look back at his boss. His eyes followed the movements of Eddison Deas, but he shrugged.

'I still don't buy this vigilante angle.'

'You've made that abundantly clear.'

At this, Crosbie raised his chin and met McLeod's eye.

'Every shred of training I've ever had says it's the least likely explanation,' he replied. 'Crime is personal. If you're going to be murdered, chances are it's going to be by someone you already know. Not some Robin Hood character. I'm telling you, it's a goose chase.'

'It's a line of inquiry we are exploring.'

'It's a fairy tale, dreamed up by a woman high on heavy pain medication.'

McLeod's face twisted, then stilled. Though he made sure Crosbie could still hear him, he lowered his voice.

'Kindly remember who it is you're speaking to, Detective.'

'Sorry, guv, but with all due respect—'

McLeod leaned inwards and put his mouth close to Crosbie's ear.

'I'm not talking about me being your commanding officer, Alan. I'm talking about me being the guy who covered your arse not all that long ago.'

Crosbie tensed, and made his face go blank, but the expression was not entirely genuine.

'I suggest,' McLeod went on, 'that you're not really in a position to question anyone else's mental clarity right now.'

Crosbie flapped a hand, as though McLeod's words were smoke he wanted to clear. The senior officer straightened up, but they were standing closer now than they had been.

'I'm fine now,' Crosbie huffed. 'It was a one-time slip, that's all.'

McLeod frowned.

'Are you sure about that? I want to believe you, truly. But I do find it worrying that key evidence in this case was missed.'

Crosbie looked back at the stage. Eddison Deas had raised her arms above her head and was leading the crowd in a slow clap. Only about half of them were clapping anywhere near on-beat.

'I don't know what it is you're referring to,' Crosbie said.

'That CCTV footage. McGill and the dangerous driving.'

Crosbie snorted again. When he spoke, there was a sting in his voice.

'It's Kato you need to speak to about that. The hit and run case was her responsibility.'

McLeod's eyes widened, though Crosbie couldn't see it.

'Kato is a brand new sergeant, still finding her feet,' McLeod replied. 'I haven't always been her biggest fan, as I'm sure you know. But she did well to link the early activities of this Vampire character and take it higher up. A more seasoned officer would have revisited that footage – *should* have revisited that footage. But *you* are that more seasoned officer, Alan. As head of the team, the responsibility falls to you.'

This time, Crosbie wheeled round, turning his entire body to face McLeod.

'So she can make a mistake, but I can't?'

McLeod was quiet. Nearby, a couple of faces flicked round in response to Crosbie's sudden movements. Seeming to realise he'd gone too far, Crosbie spluttered. He held up his hands.

'I'm sorry, guv.'

McLeod stayed quiet for a moment. Around them, the noise of the concert throbbed. The slow clap was subsiding to a smatter.

'I'm starting to wonder what happened last Sunday – the day Able's body was found.'

Crosbie's own hands were still held up, defensive.

'What do you mean?'

McLeod cocked his head.

'Kato wasn't able to raise you. She had to set up the crime scene largely alone.'

'It was a Sunday.'

McLeod nodded.

'And that's what I've said, in your defence, to anyone who's raised it. But Alan, *I* could be reached that Sunday. Birch was meant to be on sick leave, but she could be reached. We keep our phones on, don't we? That's part of the job.'

Crosbie dropped both hands to his sides and balled them into fists.

'Who's raised it?'

'I'm sorry?'

'You said, that's what you've said in my defence, to anyone who's raised it. Who has raised it?'

McLeod stiffened.

'That really isn't the point.'

'It was her, wasn't it?' Crosbie hit one curled fist against his thigh. 'Fucking Birch. What has she told you? What did she say I'd said?'

McLeod blinked slowly, once, twice.

'Why don't *you* tell me what you've said.'

'Nothing. She's lying.'

'Lying about what?'

Crosbie repeated the same gesture, hitting his own leg with his right fist, as though banging a gavel.

'About my drinking! About my calling her, drunk! I tell you, it didn't—'

This time, McLeod held up a hand. He did it slowly, so people wouldn't look. The conversation was getting out of hand. This was a public place, after all.

'I need to stop you there, Alan, because DI Birch hasn't mentioned anything at all to me about you calling her, or you being drunk, or any of this. But having listened to you just now, I can see we might have a problem on our hands, don't you think?'

'No, this is outrageous. I'm absolutely capable of—'

McLeod closed his raised hand, then pointed the index finger at his colleague's face. Crosbie's mouth closed hard, like a trap.

'Capable of coming to my office at nine thirty on Monday morning, to discuss this further. I don't think talking about it any more right now is desperately wise.'

Crosbie didn't reply. He looked down at his still-balled fists, which, McLeod noticed, were shaking slightly.

'Alan,' McLeod said, his voice still half raised against the concert's din, but his tone gentler now, 'I can help you. There are systems in place that we can use to help you. But you have to be willing to co-operate with me. We can't let this escalate any further.'

Still, Crosbie studied his hands.

'Don't you agree?'

In the pause that followed, Eddison Deas belted the final note of her ballad, and a cheer rose up across the Esplanade like a tidal wave. The noise seemed to build a wall between the two men – between them and everyone around them.

When Crosbie eventually spoke, McLeod only knew it because he saw the other man's lips move.

'Yes, guv. I do.'

Friday, 23 July, 23:15

It was dark now. As the concert ended, the last of the sun had turned hazy behind clouds that Amy hadn't seen drifting in. As the fans trickled out between the barriers of the Esplanade, drizzle had begun to fall: the soft, drifting kind of drizzle that soaked anyone who went out into it almost immediately. The Castle Esplanade felt huge – somehow even larger now that the crowd had cleared out of it. The massive scaffolds of tiered seating rose like weird statuary into the wet night air. A clean-up crew of six or seven people in hi-vis vests were picking their way along those vast bleachers with heavy-duty bin bags and grabbers, gathering litter. The Eddison Deas road crew moved back and forth onstage, beneath the lighting rig, dismantling sound equipment. Industrial floodlights overhead rendered everything too bright, too sharp around the edges, like film footage with the contrast turned up high. Uniforms still manning the cordon waved the command post vans into this spotlight glare. DC Bow brought up the rear in his black, unmarked car.

Lennox Whitelaw sat on the front row of the now-empty bleachers, handcuffed, but – in defiance of a warning from DC Johns – smoking. A member of the cleaning crew had bummed him a cigarette before anyone had had chance to get cuffs on him, and now he sat, awkward but gleeful, cupping both bound hands in front of his face and blowing out smoke.

'You'll regret that,' Amy said, 'when you get back inside and there aren't any more.'

Whitelaw smirked at her. Having learned she would no longer respond to his charm, he'd been openly hostile to her – borderline abusive, at times – for the duration of the night.

'Shows what you know about fucking prison,' he snapped.

Amy had no strength left to fight with him. After nothing had happened during the concert itself, she and her team had spent the last hour tailing the odious bastard on foot, parading him up and down the Royal Mile, along George IV Bridge, even into some of the dark, narrow closes of the Old Town, hoping for an encounter with the Vampire. Amy had kept her teeth clenched the whole time, willing Whitelaw not to run, then hoping he would; hoping the Vampire wouldn't turn up, then hoping he would; hoping she and the team could inter-vene in time if there was a struggle, but also hoping she'd see Whitelaw die in front of her before she could stop it. Sergeant Kato was sworn to guard and protect this man – that was her entire role in Operation Stake. But *Amy* Kato – the person she was when not at work – was willing Whitelaw to meet the vigilante, to walk into traffic, to fall down an open manhole. Anything – after only a few hours in his presence – to get him out of her life again.

At last, McLeod had called an end to the charade, and one by one the various command units gathered on the Castle Esplanade. Officers who'd been watching approaches to the site – Castlehill, Castle Wynd North, and Ramsay Lane – reported no one matching the Vampire's description. Indeed, no one suspicious had been seen at all. The uniformed officers in attendance – whose team had been charged with policing an Eddison Deas concert – were delighted with how *their* operation had gone. The First Minister's team had already contacted McLeod to congratulate him on the event's smooth running. And yet, as the command unit vans emptied, everyone involved in Operation Stake looked dejected – even, to Amy's surprise, DI Crosbie.

McLeod waved everyone into a huddle alongside what had been Command Unit 2. Amy watched as Marcello helped DI Birch out of the back of their shared van, then walked beside her to the edge of the gaggle, tense and watchful of her movements. His face looked grave. Birch looked a little drawn – Amy wondered about the pain in her injured hip, given that she'd sat in the cramped back of a van for what must have been almost seven hours. But of course, with Operation Stake having seemingly failed, Amy knew Birch would also be thinking of the suspension form in McLeod's desk drawer. She'd gambled with her own career, and lost.

Amy's trainers were soaked, and her feet felt numb and crinkled inside them. She took hold of Whitelaw by the elbow and hauled him to his feet. He dropped the final draw's worth of his cigarette, and it hissed on the wet ground.

'Bitch,' he spat. DC Johns clapped a hand down on his shoulder.

'Dinnae start,' he warned.

'Lads,' Amy said, making eye contact with Johns, 'get this clown in the car, would you, please?'

Johns nodded, and began to steer Whitelaw in the direction of DC Bow and the unmarked saloon. As he passed the gaggle, Whitelaw jerked to a stop. Amy watched him seek out Birch with his eyes.

'No sign of your vampire, DI Birch?' he called out. Amy saw Marcello lay a hand on Birch's arm: *don't rise to it*. Johns nudged Whitelaw, and he swayed but didn't move away. Instead, he made a show of looking over the command post vans. He whistled.

'Must have cost a pretty penny, eh? All this. Quite the bet to put on some distant odds, *marm.*'

Johns nudged Whitelaw again.

'Shut the fuck up, scumbag,' he hissed, 'get moving already.' Marcello's fingers curled around Birch's forearm.

'Is your CO here?' Whitelaw went on. He was laughing now, a studied laugh that set Amy's teeth on edge. 'I want to see this person – him or her. I want to see what sort of idiot signed off on such a hare-brained scheme.'

Johns raised a hand and gave Whitelaw one swift, hard push.

'I said, get moving.'

Amy couldn't tell if Whitelaw really was knocked off balance, or if he found the time to calculate the move, then fall. Either way, he crumped forward on to the Esplanade's wet tarmac, and she watched as his cuffed hands twisted awkwardly, and his face hit the ground. Whether or not the fall was fake, the sharp wail he let out surely wasn't. Johns stood over Whitelaw's prone body, aghast.

McLeod broke away from the gaggle and strode the three paces or so to stand beside Johns. Amy, who felt somehow responsible, came up on DC Johns' other side. Part of her felt the urge to grab his hand, or at least to show solidarity in some way – another part of her wanted to yell at him for doing something so stupid. At their assembled feet, Whitelaw wailed again. In her peripheral vision, Amy could see the rest of the officers' faces turned towards his twitching form.

McLeod cleared his throat and looked at Johns.

'That wasn't ideal, was it?'

Johns' eyes were wide.

'I'm sorry, sir,' he stammered. 'I didn't— he wasn't—'

Whitelaw twisted on the ground and let out another cry of pain.

'Assault!' he yelled, and although he was face down, Amy could tell from his voice that something bad had happened to his teeth on impact with the ground. 'I'll sue you, you animal!'

McLeod winced, then turned and looked back at the gaggle.

'Would someone get a medic for me, please?'

Amy saw Marcello throw Birch a *you okay?* look. She nodded, once, and he nodded back. Then he turned and half jogged away, in the direction of the Castle buildings, to seek help.

Johns was watching McLeod's face.

'Guv—' he said.

McLeod waved him away.

'I don't think you should make a comment at this time, do you, Johns?'

Amy tried to prevent her mouth from falling open. She knew McLeod was now on high alert – with Whitelaw writhing at their feet, anything they said could be used in a future lawsuit, should he come good on his threat to sue, which Amy had no doubt he would. But nevertheless, she wanted him to say something comforting – not for Johns' sake as much as for her own. She waited until she could be sure McLeod wasn't looking, then she raised one hand and rested it gently on Johns' shoulder.

'Come with me for now,' she said, and steered him back to his original trajectory, towards DC Bow and the car. He stumbled beside her, eyes not really focused on anything, and she knew from her own past, bitter experience that all he could do right now was replay over and over the mistake that he'd just made.

'It's okay,' Amy said, once she was confident they were out of Whitelaw's earshot. 'We've all fucked up, Johns, trust me. You did good today.'

His eyes seemed to zero back in.

'Yeah,' he said, a bitter tang in his voice, 'until right then.'

DC Bow was out of the car now, and came to his colleague's side.

'Don't sweat it, kid,' he said. 'There were witnesses. That wasn't you. Bastard dived like fucking Ronaldo.'

Johns lifted his head.

'You swear?'

Bow nodded.

'Swear blind, son. I'd swear it to any disciplinary panel in the land.'

Amy frowned. She also wanted to comfort Johns, but she didn't like how blasé Bow was being. She'd seen the incident, and from closer up than Bow had. *She* wouldn't have been able to swear that Whitelaw had definitely engineered his fall.

'Don't worry,' Bow was saying. 'Come on.'

He threw Amy a wink, then put an arm around Johns' shoulders, taking him off her hands. 'I'm pretty sure you're off duty now – is that right, Sergeant?'

Amy was still frowning, but made herself smooth out her face again. She didn't know what the official line ought to be, but she knew McLeod well enough to know that he wouldn't want Johns involved in much else for the time being.

'Sure thing,' she said.

'Thought so,' Bow replied. He grinned at Amy. 'Don't tell the guv over there, but I've got a hip flask in the dashboard. I reckon this kid's earned a wee nip, don't you?'

Amy forced a smile. None of this was really okay, but she felt tired and defeated, and more than a little bit glad that Lennox Whitelaw had just smashed his face against the tarmac.

'How about we all just pretend I didn't hear that?' she said, after a pause.

Bow winked again.

'Sure thing,' he said, mimicking her.

Amy turned back towards the gaggle. Seeing Whitelaw still on the ground made the uneasy smile fade on her face. Marcello must have located a first-aider: one of the clean-up crew was kneeling on the ground beside Whitelaw now, with McLeod standing over her.

Amy drifted to Birch's side, almost without thinking.

'She's the medic?' she whispered.

Birch's teeth were chattering.

'Hope so,' she hissed back, trying to smile.

'Marm, are you cold?'

Birch shook her head.

'Honestly? I think it's adrenaline. I know this has all been a spectacular fuck-up, but *God* it feels good to be back at work.' She paused, and then added, 'I ought to enjoy it, eh? As I'm about to be fired.'

Amy's face crumpled.

'Helen—'

'Don't,' Birch hissed, 'let's not dwell on it. There's bigger fish to fry right now.'

Amy wanted to speak again, but she saw Birch's gaze shift. The first-aider – a wiry woman in her fifties – had levered Lennox Whitelaw into a sitting position. Amy watched as he made a show of spitting blood on to the concrete, then raising both his hands – still cuffed – to touch his swollen mouth.

'You've lost a couple of teeth, pal,' the first-aider told him. She clapped him hard on the back with the flat of her hand, then stood up. She looked at McLeod. 'Otherwise,' she added, 'no harm done.'

McLeod nodded once in thanks, and the woman made to leave, but Whitelaw seemed to be settling in for a tantrum.

'No harm done,' he parroted. 'No harm done! I've just been assaulted by a police officer!'

He looked wildly around at the various officers clustered around him.

'I want to press charges!' he yelled.

McLeod looked at the first-aider.

'Does he need further medical treatment, would you say?'

The woman shrugged. Amy could tell she was beginning to resent the situation she'd been put in.

'Get him checked over, maybe,' she said. 'But if anything, what he needs now is a cosmetic dentist, not a doctor.'

Amy realised Crosbie was standing behind her, because somebody let out a low laugh, and she recognised it as his.

'I hear the standard of cosmetic dentistry in Saughton is second to none,' he muttered, apparently to her. She didn't turn her head. She was distracted by Birch, whose teeth were still chattering.

McLeod was waving a hand in the direction of Bow's car. After a moment, both Bow and Johns climbed back out of it and approached the group. Amy hugged her denim jacket around herself. It wasn't all that cold, but she could feel the drizzling rain making its way through her various layers of clothing. She longed to be away from this place – to let herself into her tiny nest of a flat, close the door, and try to forget the events of the past few hours. Total *lack* of events, more like, she thought to herself.

McLeod was speaking now.

'Bow, let's get Mr Whitelaw back to his accommodation, shall we? I'm told there are scene guards stationed on the premises to receive him from you.'

Bow stepped closer.

'Yes, guv.'

McLeod looked around, and Amy felt his eyes come to rest on her.

'Kato,' he said. Just that, just her name. He looked tired. Everyone did.

'Yes,' she said, hoping she'd understood correctly. 'I can go alongside DC Bow.'

McLeod gave a tight smile.

'Good.' He looked over at Johns, who was still hovering beside the car. 'DC Johns, you're relieved of your duties for now. We'll speak.'

Johns didn't reply, but Amy saw him drop his shoulders.

'Oh, sure.' Whitelaw was still sitting on the wet ground, his legs splayed in a triangle – the way a toddler might sit, Amy thought. He made a show of gathering bloody saliva in his mouth and spitting once again. 'I bet you'll speak. You'll circle the wagons, like you fuckers always do. Get your stories straight.'

Bow strode over to Whitelaw, brushing Amy's elbow as he did so.

'Och, woe is you, eh?' he said, grabbing Whitelaw by the elbow and hauling him to his feet. Whitelaw looked startled to be suddenly upright, as though he wasn't sure how he'd made the shift.

Amy leaned towards McLeod.

'Sir,' she said, 'I'm sorry, but . . . I do think we should get him checked over. Concussion can be—'

McLeod sighed heavily.

'Ever the girl scout, aren't you, Kato?' He didn't look at her, but Amy was grateful for Birch's *just ignore him* glance. '*Yes*, we'll get a proper medic out. They'll meet you at the house, I imagine.'

This was enough for Bow.

'Right then, sunshine.' Still holding Whitelaw's elbow, he spun the odious man on his heels and began to march him away, towards the car. 'Let's get you back to your palace, shall we?'

Whitelaw looked at Amy with wide eyes as he passed her. His face and hands were flecked with blood. She winced.

Birch listed over on her crutch, and nudged her friend with her shoulder.

'You going to be okay?'

Amy looked Birch up and down.

'Me? I'll be fine, marm. But what about you?'

'What about me?'

'I mean . . . I don't want to be rude, but . . . this operation has definitely failed. I don't know if you ought to be around McLeod right now. How are you going to get home?'

Birch shrugged.

'Cab, probably.' She struggled to raise a smile. 'Got to enjoy life's luxuries before my salary gets cut off.'

'I mean—'

Birch eyed McLeod.

'I sense we're about to get a debrief,' she said, as though Amy hadn't tried to cut in, 'and it isn't going to be pretty. I know you don't exactly *want* to go with Whitelaw, but it has to beat sticking around here.'

'Never mind me, marm. *You* need to get home. The debrief can wait. Tell him you're in pain.'

Behind Birch, Marcello stepped into Amy's line of sight.

'Don't worry, Kato,' he said. 'I can drive DI Birch back home, after we're finished here.' He met Birch's eye and grinned, though Amy could tell his heart wasn't in it. 'We can commiserate,' he said, 'about both losing our jobs on Monday.'

Amy frowned. Her feet were soaked. Her hair was dripping at the ends, and she felt as though, once she fell asleep, she might just remain comatose for the whole of the weekend. Her first case as a sergeant, and it had failed. The Vampire hadn't come. They'd wasted time and resources, and let a dangerous rapist out of jail, all for no result. Birch must have been wrong, and the Vampire wasn't a vigilante at all – or he was, but Whitelaw was too much of a risk, or he suspected he was being drawn, or . . . *something*. Something else she'd need to figure out, and on her own, too. Because on Monday Birch would be gone – suspended, or back on leave awaiting suspension. Amy would have to face Crosbie, would have to go back to her desk and start again from square one. The tall, thin man named Jay was still at large. It was still her job to find him. But moving on from an operation of this scale – no, from a *failure* of this scale – just wasn't something she really knew how to do.

Over by the car, Bow whistled, and Amy jumped. Whitelaw had been folded into the back seat, and Bow had rolled the driver's window down to summon her. She looked around, but realised she couldn't see Johns. She assumed he must have simply turned his collar up against the rain and walked away.

'Let's get this show on the road, eh, Sarge?' There was a note of urgency in Bow's voice – presumably he too wanted to avoid the inevitable speech from McLeod.

Amy took a step towards the car, and Bow, but paused beside Marcello, and lightly touched his arm.

'Take care of her, will you?'

He nodded.

'Of course, of course.'

Birch rolled her eyes.

'You two,' she said, 'I'll be fine.'

Marcello gave her a look. All three of them knew she was flagging, including Birch herself.

'Take your meds,' Amy replied, 'and get some rest, okay?'

Birch tried to smirk.

'Yes, Mum,' she shot back.

'Good. I'll call you tomorrow.'

Birch glanced over at McLeod. He was holding a hand up for quiet, preparing to speak.

'Get the hell out of here,' she hissed, 'while you still can.'

Amy nodded, and made a dash for the car.

III

Subject: Client PS7, serious concerns

Dear James,

Apologies for the missed calls to your phone. I assume you're asleep and won't see this until the morning. I'm trying to reach you because I'm really quite worried, and I'm in need of some advice.

I received a phone call just now from Client PS7, the Police Scotland client we discussed at our supervisory meeting on Tuesday. Obviously, their decision to contact me outside working hours is in itself a concern, but it was the client's manner that really alarmed me. They were erratic on the phone, shuttling back and forth between sounding by turns animated and then nihilistic. They talked about feeling like their career in the police force has been completely jeopardised as a result of actions they've taken, and said that as a result, nothing matters any more. Although they were vague on the details, I am now worried that they may be at risk of coming to harm, or possibly even harming others. The client didn't seem intoxicated, just very agitated. The call was quite short: after only five minutes or so, they hung up. Although I don't usually have a policy of speaking to clients out of hours – as you know – I did try calling back, but to no avail. The number now goes immediately to voicemail.

I've tried calling the number I have for DCI McLeod, my senior contact at Police Scotland, but I believe it's a direct line to his office, so also goes to voicemail.

I feel quite shaken, and also conflicted. Was the client just blowing off steam? Or do they really intend to harm themselves? What further action should I take, if any? I'm really not sure.

Do let me know what you think, once you see this. I've left you a voicemail, too. Call me back whenever: I don't imagine I'll be getting much sleep tonight.

All best,

Jane

Saturday, 24 July, 01:25

The rain was heavier now: Birch lay awake listening as it spattered against her bedroom window. Her teeth were clenched, but she knew she ought to force herself to relax her muscles while she waited for the pain meds to kick in. She'd missed two doses – a thing she'd never done before – but the pain in her hip barely registered, her brain was so busy. Marcello had walked her as far as her front door – trudging beside her at the speed of an exhausted woman on one crutch – even though she hadn't wanted him to. It was probably a good thing: had he not seen her safely into the house, she might have allowed herself to topple off the promenade and on to the damp sand of Portobello Beach. The idea of being washed out to sea felt incredibly appealing right now.

Instead, she lay and thought about everything. McLeod's debrief on the Esplanade had been pretty underwhelming: he'd basically paraphrased what they all already knew. Operation Stake had failed, their perp was still at large, they'd need to redouble their efforts, etc. Birch hadn't been listening to, as much as watching, her commanding officer. He didn't look at her, not even once, while he spoke. It was as if he'd already got rid of her. He didn't mention her or the fact that the operation had been almost entirely her own stupid idea. She guessed from his face that he was having the same thoughts as she was: why did they ever think this would work? They didn't even know if the Vampire had seen the news of Whitelaw's release. What if he'd fled? He could be in Brazil by now, for all they knew.

They'd run a costly operation off the back of Birch's iron-clad belief in a hunch and Marcello's profiling: two things which, in the past, had never failed.

'Well,' Birch said aloud into the darkness of her room, 'there's a first time for everything.'

McLeod had come up to her, once the debrief was over and the gaggle had begun to disperse.

'Guv,' she'd said, the one syllable all she could manage.

'I trust,' McLeod replied, 'that you understand you're done.'

He'd kept his voice low – only Marcello, standing beside her, could hear – a fact she was grateful for.

'Done with this case,' he went on, 'at the very least.'

'I do.'

He drew himself up.

'We can talk about your future more generally,' he said, 'in due course. But as of right now, you're relieved of your duties. I don't want to hear of any more meddling, is that clear? You're back on sick leave, and you're to take it seriously. Because I won't only suspend you, Helen. I *will* bring disciplinary proceedings.'

'I know.'

He'd leaned back then, appraising her. When he spoke again, his tone was softer.

'I should never have entertained the idea,' he said, 'of you being on the ground with us this evening. I regret it – you look dreadful.'

He looked over his shoulder then – for the first-aider, Birch assumed.

'I don't need a medic, sir,' she said, trying as hard as she could not to be offended. 'I actually feel fine. I just need to go home.'

McLeod didn't look convinced, but he nodded.

'Okay then,' he said. 'Get plenty of rest, and go to your appointment on Monday morning as usual. And please, I'm asking you – put this case out of your mind.'

Birch had flinched. She didn't appreciate him mentioning her therapy in front of Marcello. She didn't appreciate him mentioning it at all: she had no idea how she'd face Dr Jane, come Monday morning. Indeed, she felt the strong urge to call the therapist's number and tell her she was never coming back to see her ever again.

'Yes, guv,' she said.

★

The bed was too warm, and she couldn't get comfortable. She could feel the painkillers beginning their slow, familiar seep into her bloodstream. But she knew there was still no chance at all of her falling asleep. *Put this case out of your mind*, he'd said. As if it were that easy.

'I can't get suspended,' she said. Her voice sounded somehow creepy in the empty room, but she wanted to talk – it helped her to think. On her phone was a text from Anjan which read *call me when you're done, it doesn't matter how late, I'll be awake*, but Birch knew this was a lie. Anjan had many skills, but the one she most envied was his ability to fall asleep as if on cue. It was half one in the morning: the empty room was the only listening ear she had.

'I just *can't*.'

She raised a fist and brought it down hard on the bed beside her, and felt the coiled springs of the mattress reverberate with the impact.

'If I get fired,' she said, 'what am I going to do? Where will I go?'

She thought of herself wiping tables in a restaurant, her hip healed but aching as she stacked up dishes, carried trays. She'd survived working waitressing jobs for years as a younger woman, but knew she couldn't live like that again. To her surprise, she felt a lump rising in her throat.

'I guess I found Charlie,' she said. 'That was my whole reason for joining the police. I guess I did that, at least.'

Birch realised who she was talking to. In the dark, she imagined Dr Jane sitting with her notes on her lap at the end of the bed, her head cocked, listening.

'I found my brother,' Birch said, 'and then I helped put him away. Twelve years, minimum sentence.'

What would Dr Jane say? What would the other half of this conversation be? Birch wished she knew.

'I guess I've done a lot in this job,' she said. 'Years in uniform, policing Easter Road on match days and filling the drunk tank on a Saturday night. Fast-tracked into CID, back at Gayfield Square with Al behind the desk, *aye been*. Getting my pips, and then Three Rivers – an actual fucking college shooting that very same week. McLeod nearly suspended me then as well – I bet he wishes he had done, now. Then I found Charlie. And then . . .'

The words dried up. Her own dim room became the cave-like dark of the ruined cottage at Seefew. She was barricaded in with Gerald Hodgson once again, about to say the wrong thing and send Operation Kendall in entirely the wrong direction. About to get up and try to run, while Hodgson levelled the shotgun at her, waiting for her to still. And then her hip exploding, rifle fire, a helicopter, her name being shouted over and over.

Birch brought her fist down on the mattress a second time.

'No,' she said. 'I *won't* be suspended. I won't. Not without a fucking fight.'

And yet, she had no idea how to fight it. The effort it had taken just to lie in bed and have one half of an imaginary conversation felt considerable. Her brain churned with an intensity she was beyond sick of. Operation Stake had been her idea. McLeod had humoured her. She guessed he felt bad that she'd been shot, that Operation Kendall ended how it did – so he thought he owed her one. But she also knew he wouldn't be able to present it like that before a disciplinary panel: he, too, would have to answer for the failings of Operation Stake. Hers might be the head that rolled, but privately he'd be hauled over his own set of coals. Not even privately – the press would love it. Lennox Whitelaw snuck out of jail for a sting operation that flopped. She thought of Solomon Carradice – of all the bad people she'd helped put away – hearing the news in their jail cells. She thought of the women Whitelaw had attacked, of the statements they'd be well within their rights to give to click-bait journalists eager for a scoop. She thought of her own name – printed, Googled, hashtagged, discussed. She thought of Alyona in her high flat in Leith, a man's body scorched into the ground outside. The distrust – or perhaps it was disgust – Alyona had made clear she reserved for the police. A woman who'd tangled with James Able and lost. A woman who'd surely met some of the worst men in this city, if not in this world – and yet the people she hated most were police. A woman who remained the key witness in the Vampire case, having met and talked to the elusive Jay more times, it seemed, than anyone else.

Birch's thoughts were a merry-go-round, spinning and spinning: Dr Jane, Gerald Hodgson, McLeod, Charlie, the Vampire, Solomon Carradice. Crosbie and his drinking. Anjan and the uneasy truce the two of them had begun to build. She thought of Amy, getting home completely beat after delivering Lennox Whitelaw to his safe house. She thought of Whitelaw himself, and wondered how it felt to be sleeping in a comfy double bed tonight, knowing that tomorrow he'd be returned to jail. She thought of Josephine Stewart and the hit and run. Dale McGill and his grandmother, the miserable life they lived together under the watchful eyes of Mrs McGill's figurines.

Birch screwed up her face. Jesus, Dale McGill was a hateful kid. She recalled him looking at her through his ridiculous iridescent glasses.

'The Venn diagram,' she said, imagining Dr Jane would appreciate a Venn diagram reference, 'of appalling drivers and men who wear mirrored sunglasses? It's a circle.'

As if on cue, a car roared past the back of the house, flying towards Joppa in the thirty zone at what must have been sixty, if not more. Birch heard the hiss-clunk of an air compressor, the squeal of tyres. Had she not seen the physical state of McGill only days ago, she could believe it was him, back out on the road in some new souped-up vehicle. Chasing an innocent woman through wet streets. Ending up written off on the pavement by a man who wanted to set things right.

PIT manoeuvre, or whatever – that was what McGill had said. *Almost like one of you lot.* Birch rolled her eyes in the darkness. UK police weren't trained in the PIT manoeuvre, though anyone with the Advanced Driving Certificate could probably perform one. It was too dangerous to be used: a PIT manoeuvre could cause fatalities in the targeted car. The aim was to carry out a safe—

Birch's eyes widened. She felt as though a flywheel somewhere in her brain had suddenly begun to turn. Her pulse ticked up.

'Hang on . . .'

She struggled upright in bed, then swung her legs over the edge of the mattress. The pain in her hip sank its teeth in once again, but she barely registered it. She reached for the bedside lamp and flicked the switch. Her alarm clock told her it was 01:47.

'Almost like one of you lot,' she said. McGill's voice was clear in her mind: an adolescent sneer. The kid was an idiot, no doubt about that. But . . . hadn't Alyona said basically the same thing?

Birch's phone was charging on the bedside table. She clawed it up and fumbled with the unlock code, her hands suddenly shaking. This is nothing, she thought, it's nearly 2 a.m., your brain is playing tricks on you. But if Alyona and McGill agreed on this . . .

Heart thudding, Birch opened up the sound file she'd recorded in Alyona's flat. Her own voice drifted out, and she shuddered at its uncanny familiarity. She hit the skip button, almost reflexively, and then Alyona was speaking . . . 'what word would you say, in this country? More *hooker*.'

No, it was further on than that. Birch skipped though, stopping at fifteen-second intervals to listen to a snippet, then carry on.

'Suddenly this crazy man was there,' Alyona's voice said, and Birch paused. 'He asked where I lived. I thought he must be one of you people.'

There was a moment of quiet on the recording, and then Alyona's voice again: a single, hard word, almost spat out into the air: '*Police.*'

Birch stopped the recording. She looked down at the lit screen of her phone, then at the bedside table with its mess of pain pills, tubes of chapstick and hand cream, discarded notes from the case scribbled on to Post-its. She heard McLeod's voice in her head, clear as day: *I don't want to hear of any more meddling, is that clear?*

'Of course,' she said, and the urge to laugh bubbled up from somewhere in her chest. She felt as though someone had just hit her, hard, over the head, and dislodged something. 'He's a policeman.'

She stared down at her phone again, doing nothing for long enough that the screen auto-locked, and she caught sight of her own face in the now- black glass. She looked knackered – her hair sticking up at angles, mascara she'd forgotten to clean off smudged across her cheeks. Everything hurt – everything. There wasn't really much for her to lose.

Since her mother had died, Birch had resigned herself to not having anyone left she could call for help – not at 2 a.m. on a Friday night, when what she needed to ask for was tantamount to madness. Her mother was dead, Charlie behind bars. Anjan had surprised her over Operation Kendall, walking through ploughed fields to the crime scene – but if she called him now and told him what she was thinking of doing, she knew she'd get nothing more than a fight. That left only one person, and Birch felt a lump in her throat as she scrolled through her phone to his contact, and dialled.

'Dad? Sorry, it's— no, no, don't worry, it's okay. I'm *fine*. No, nothing's happened, I promise. But I'm afraid I do need to be driven somewhere. I'm sorry. Yes. Yes, right now.'

Saturday, 24 July, 01:25

By process of elimination, I worked out where he was. I had the cab driver drop me a few streets away, then I set off on foot to do a recce. It was fully dark by then and had begun to rain. I felt like a homeless man, carrying everything I owned on my back. The Cameron Toll shopping centre rose up by the road, closed for the night but lit up like some brutalist beacon. I thought about the things I'd miss if I went to prison, then realised that all of them were things I couldn't have anyway, not now I'd murdered a man. A bad man, I reminded myself, a man people thanked me for getting rid of. I wished I could turn off my thoughts, their endless bickering.

As I walked, I thought about the Whitelaw case. I'd been fresh out of training then, and wet behind the ears. I didn't work on what my colleagues called *the Lochrin rape case*, but I felt adjacent to it. That was my neighbourhood, after all: it was happening where I lived.

I was full of it. Full of having made it through the exams, having graduated. Full of being a policeman. Making a difference. Justice. The thought of that word on my own lips back then made me spit a thick, white star on to the wet Cameron Toll pavement. I'd gone on dates with women, spent whole evenings talking at length about responsibility, the difference I planned to make. All those women wanted to know was what we were doing about the Lochrin rapist. Had we caught anyone yet? No? How many more victims would it take? It shouldn't have bugged me, but that rained on my parade. I wanted to be proud of the institution I'd joined, but the open question of the Lochrin rapist made it pretty hard. When Lennox Whitelaw was finally caught, it felt important. It felt like I could start to be a policeman at last – like the difference I wanted to make would start to kick in. I felt stupid now – crossing Lady Road in the drizzling rain, dressed in my murder clothes – to think I'd ever believed that.

I found the street and walked its length. I'd attended this safe house before, more than once, but it had been a while. I stood under the tree on the far side of the road and looked at the dark house, thinking that once you knew what it was, how obvious it seemed. There were nick-nacks on the windowsills, but they were random: a model of a big white sailboat, a vase with faded plastic blooms. No one chose these objects, they catered to no one's personal taste. I wondered if they came from charity shops, or lost property, or the evidence room. They made the house look lived-in at a glance, and that was the extent of their purpose. The bedding plants in the garden were headache pink, tipped directly out of their plastic pack of six-for-the-price-of-four and still arranged in that same formation. No care had been taken, the way it would have been were this a real home. All attention was on security: the motion-sensor lights along the side of the house, the high fence, and no direct line of sight into the windows. This house wasn't so much a hiding place as a storage facility for witnesses – or, in Whitelaw's case, perps. It was a place you could put people and forget about them. Rather like prison, I thought. But I didn't want to think about prison.

The tree was huge and old, and probably the reason that no house had been built on this side of the road. It was a copper beech, with deep brown leaves that shushed in the drizzle. The lower branches stooped almost to the ground in places: if

I stood near the trunk, I knew I'd be practically invisible, and I was used to invisibility.

I hadn't been there long when a scene guard showed up, and I realised Lennox Whitelaw couldn't be far behind. The scene guard was a guy I vaguely knew, and as I stood listening to the rain in the wet leaves, I wracked my brain for his name. Grant, maybe? Graham? There was another person with him, a woman: he let her into the house, closed the door behind her, and took up his position. The woman wasn't in uniform, but she also didn't look like a civilian. A legal representative of some sort, perhaps – Whitelaw's lawyer, or someone. I didn't much care who she was, but I'd stay and watch until she left.

As time passed, the street seemed to settle in for the night. Takeaway delivery bikes came and went. Late-shift workers arrived home. Lights went on, and TVs – then they went off again. Dog walkers brought out their Labradors and spaniels for a final run around the block. One dog caught my scent and came right up to me: a monochrome collie with blue eyes that looked milky white in the darkness. I placed one hand on its head, enjoying the velvet of its fur and the feel of its strange dog skull beneath.

'Don't bark,' I whispered, and it cocked its head at me. Then the owner called its name, just once: *Fly, c'mere, girl.* And it was gone.

Lennox Whitelaw made an appearance not long after: my hand still felt warm in my pocket from petting the dog. The same unmarked saloon I'd seen on Castlehill purred up the street and stopped at the kerb. Amy Kato got out. Her false smile from earlier in the day was gone: she looked crumpled, tired, defeated. I refused to allow myself to feel sorry for her, but watched as she opened the car's back door and hooked Lennox Whitelaw out by the elbow. I almost gasped: his face

was banged up, like someone had punched him. I thought
of the protesters outside the concert and wondered if maybe
someone had. The front of his shirt was stained with blood,
and I realised the woman inside the house was likely a medic,
sent to patch him up so he wouldn't need to be taken to A&E.
I leaned against the tree trunk and grinned, wishing I'd been
there to see him get smacked around. Maybe it happened at
the cordon on the way out, I thought. It made me wish I'd
stayed there on the pavement, hiding in plain sight.

Kato's colleague got out of the driver's seat, and brought up
the rear as she half led, half dragged a protesting Whitelaw up
the house's front drive. The beech's whispering leaves made it
difficult, but I could hear the gist of their conversation.

'You think I won't bring charges, Sergeant Kato,' Whitelaw
was saying, 'but I promise you, I will. And you'll be named.'

My eyes widened. Had Amy Kato been the one to punch
Whitelaw in the face? The thought was kind of delicious.

'Keep your voice down,' the male officer was saying, while
Kato ignored them both. She made it to the front door and
addressed the scene guard.

'Evening, Greg.' Yes, that was it, I thought – Greg. Of
course. Greg Riley: his name like a light bulb going on in my
head.

Riley's voice was lower, more difficult to hear. I heard him
say the word *medic*, and my theory was confirmed.

'This is it?' Whitelaw asked. I saw him flinch away from
Kato's grip on his elbow, and use the few seconds before she
grabbed him again to make a melodramatic gesture. 'One
officer? This is who'll be protecting me through the night?'

Every other thought in my head fell silent. I simply itched
to hurt this man. Right then, I wanted to step out from under
the tree, walk over, and twist his neck until it broke.

'You've been shown where the panic buttons are?' Amy Kato asked this question in a way that suggested she already knew the answer, but also didn't care. She seemed only moments away from snapping Whitelaw's neck herself.

He began to protest, but Riley stepped forward and helped the other two officers bundle him into the house. They followed him, and Riley closed the door behind them. Moments before they'd arrived, he'd been scrolling through his phone. Now Riley took up the stance of an official scene guard: feet planted, hands behind the back, eyes front.

'Bootlicker,' I hissed.

Kato and her colleague weren't inside for long. They left the way they'd come, except this time, the medic was with them. I was almost disappointed by how quickly she seemed to have dealt with Whitelaw's face: his injuries couldn't have been serious.

'I'll soon fix that,' I whispered.

Once the black saloon had pulled away, there was nothing left for me to do but wait. Not long, now: it was already after one. I turned my back on the house and slipped away from the tree, moving in the opposite direction so as not to be seen.

Saturday, 24 July, 02:35

'Ye swear this cannae wait, hen?'

Jamieson was hammering the van along at well over the limit, and Birch wasn't about to stop him. There wasn't a soul around at this time of night. Against a backdrop of threatening cloud tinged pink by the streetlights below, Arthur's Seat and the city skyline loomed, black and spiked.

Birch had her phone to her ear. Her hair was a bird's nest, and the jumper she'd pulled on was inside out.

'It cannae wait until the morn?'

'No, Dad! Don't you understand? He's *police*, he's one of us. That's why he didn't show up at the concert tonight, why he didn't try anything. He's known what we've been up to this whole time.'

Jamieson braked hard and made a left.

'Aye,' he said, 'I get that. Bit why can ye no wait—'

'Because,' Birch cut in, 'Lennox Whitelaw goes back to jail tomorrow morning. If the Vampire is going to strike, he has to do it tonight. It might already be too late.'

Ahead of them, a traffic crossing switched from green to red. Jamieson glanced at his daughter.

'Run it,' she said, 'just do it. Jesus *Christ*, why is no one picking up their phones?'

'It's half two, hen. They're asleep.'

Birch smacked a hand, hard, against the dashboard.

'They're not, damn it! They've seen who's calling, and they're ignoring me. They've been *ordered* to ignore me.'

Out of the corner of her eye, she saw Jamieson's mouth twist. She hit the dashboard again. It made the heel of her hand throb.

'Dad! You have to believe me, this is serious. I have to do this *now*, before it's too late.'

'But hen – is Whitelaw no in a safe hoose?'

Birch pressed the same throbbing hand to her forehead.

'He is,' she said, 'but the Vampire is *one of us*. Don't you see? Anyone with a badge and a decent excuse could walk through the front door of that house.' She knew this wasn't strictly true even as she said it, but her father didn't, and she needed to convince him. 'He could be in there with Whitelaw *right now*.'

Edinburgh was wet and shining and full of gulls. Jamieson overtook a night bus, swerved around a double-parked bread lorry filled to the roof with crates of rolls.

Birch was back on her phone. This time – at last – someone picked up.

'Marm? Is everything okay?'

Amy sounded croaky.

'Kato! You picked up.'

On the other end of the line, Birch heard the rustle of a duvet.

'Yeah, well – you *kept* calling. Are you hurt? Has something happened?'

'No, I'm fine, but listen. He's a policeman, Amy. The Vampire, he's police.'

She heard her friend sit up in bed.

'What? What do you mean?'

'I mean,' Birch replied, 'that we haven't been listening to our witnesses. Alyona said when she first met Jay she assumed he was police. Dale McGill told me the very same thing. I just didn't listen.'

Amy was quiet for a moment.

'Helen,' she said, 'where are you?'

Birch raised her head.

'South Bridge,' she said.

'What the hell are you doing on South Bridge? And how did you get there?'

Birch glanced at Jamieson.

'My dad's driving me. We're heading to the safe house now.'

'What?' Amy's voice was almost a shriek. 'No, you can't – you mustn't.'

'Didn't you hear me? The Vampire is a policeman, Amy. He could be anyone. He could be – I don't know, *Crosbie*. And he could be inside that safe house with Whitelaw right now.'

Amy was moving around in her flat now. Birch could hear her shuffling over the laminate floor.

'Hang on for a second,' she said, 'let's just rewind. You're getting this new information from where?'

Birch pushed out a sigh.

'It isn't new information,' she replied. 'It's information we've had this whole time, and ignored. Crosbie really hasn't been *with it* at all. Alyona said she thought Jay was police, and she ought to know a polis, right? She'll have dealt with plenty of us in her time. Then after that, Dale McGill said to me—'

'Okay,' Amy cut in, 'let me get this straight. It's, what, 2 a.m.? You're at home, you're in a ton of pain, you've had a disappointing night with Operation Stake—'

Birch snorted.

'That's an understatement.'

'You're exhausted,' Amy went on, ignoring the interruption, 'and you start thinking about the case.'

'Yes! And I realise—'

'Helen, please.' Amy's voice was brittle, hard-edged. Birch fell silent. 'You have to stop this. I know you must be gutted about how things went with Whitelaw, but—'

'No, listen, I'm serious.'

Amy made a despairing noise.

'I know,' she said. 'I know you fully believe what you're saying, but honestly? It's starting to sound unhinged. I hate to say this, but I think McLeod's right. You need to put this case down – you need to put everything down – because it's taking over your life.'

'Amy—'

'And it's partly my fault,' Amy went on. 'I've encouraged you this whole time, when I ought to have put my foot down sooner. You're acting crazy, and you need a break.'

Birch looked at Jamieson. His mouth was a straight line, his eyes fixed on the road. He agreed with Amy. Birch's chest felt leaden.

'I can't believe you're saying this.'

She heard Amy flop into a chair.

'I can't believe I'm saying it either. But you have to admit, calling me at two thirty in the morning from some kind of wild goose chase in your dad's van – it's not great.'

Birch didn't know what to say. The certainty she'd felt sitting on the edge of her bed skipping through Alyona's recording was beginning to ebb. She let her vision blur, watching the headlights of the car behind swim in the nearside mirror.

'He could be there,' she said, and her voice cracked. 'He could be in the safe house right now. The Vampire.'

Amy sighed.

'I know you'd like that to be true,' she said. 'We'd all love it if he'd just turn up already. Listen, *I* have to go back into the office on Monday and face McLeod. Start the whole case over from scratch. I'd *love* it if instead of that, our vampire turned up and knocked on the door to say hey, I'm here to attack Lennox Whitelaw, and once I'm done, you can cuff me. But you and I both know that things don't work that way.'

Jamieson signalled right and turned. The car behind did the same.

'You really think I'm crazy.'

Amy was quiet for a moment.

'I think,' she said, 'that you're tired. You're exhausted. You're learning to live with chronic pain, and I can only imagine how hard that is. You've been so powerless these past few weeks, not being able to work – no wonder you want a result on this case. But trust me, I was just there – I was just at the safe house, not even two hours ago. Lennox Whitelaw is tucked up safe. Tomorrow he'll go back to jail, we'll go back to the drawing board, and I promise you, we'll find this perp. We will, Helen. I give you my word.'

Jamieson braked. Looking up, Birch saw his teeth clench.

'This bastart behind me,' he hissed. 'Ah hink he wants tae get in the van wi us.'

'But you really should go home now,' Amy was saying. 'You really should just put this down. Let us handle it.'

Birch wasn't listening.

'Dad,' she said, 'turn left here.'

Jamieson threw her a look, but did as he was told. Birch watched in the mirror as the car behind indicated left, then followed suit.

'I have to go, Kato,' Birch said, and ended the call.

Her father glanced at her, his face a mask of worry.

'Turn right,' she instructed, ignoring him as he opened his mouth to speak. 'We're being followed.'

'Hen, ye're—'

'Turn right!'

Jamieson complied.

'Ye are, though,' he said, as the car behind slid into the street behind them. 'Bein crazy. Amy's got a point.'

Birch closed her eyes. In her hand, her phone was ringing: Amy, calling back. Calling to try and talk her down some more. Birch threw her phone into the footwell.

'Stop the car!'

Jamieson jumped.

'I mean it,' she said, 'stop the car. If you stop, they'll have to pass you, and keep driving, otherwise they'll give themselves away.'

Her father shook his head, but hit his hazard warning lights, and then the brakes. It wasn't quite an emergency stop, but it was sudden. The car behind swerved, then sailed past, accelerating.

'Didn't want me to see who it was,' Birch said. She watched the car – a black saloon – dither its way to the end of the street and stop at the Give Way. Jamieson was watching, too.

'Go on,' she whispered. 'You have to turn one way or the other. We're on to you now.'

The driver of the other vehicle knew it, too – after a pause that was much too long for a silent, middle-of-the-night road, the right-hand indicator went on, and then the car drove out of sight.

'Right.' Birch's tone was urgent. 'He'll try to go round the block and end up back behind us, so we haven't got long.'

She looked at her father. Jamieson didn't move.

'Come on! Didn't you hear me?'

He twisted in his seat to face her, one forearm braced against the steering wheel.

'Can I no jist take ye hame, hen? Is it no possible Amy's right? This aw seems mental, ah cannae lie.'

Birch set her teeth. The dashboard clock said 02:48. She watched it tick over to 02:49.

'Anyway,' Jamieson was saying, 'who cares if this Vampire turns up? He's wantin tae kill a serial rapist. Ah widnae stop him, personally.'

Birch closed her eyes. She imagined the black car making another right turn, then another, coming back around in a square. How could she explain to her father what her job was like? How could she explain that justice didn't work like that? That often, justice was a fiction: there was no justice in this world of violence, powerlessness, anger, hurt. There was only mitigation. There was only the so-called thin blue line. She couldn't. There was no explaining it, because it had no logic. And yet here she was, careening around in the early hours of the morning after a perp they'd stupidly decided to call the Vampire. She was unhinged – that was the word Amy had used – chasing a fairy-tale character through the wet streets, all so she could keep her stupid, difficult, illogical fucking job.

'Dad,' she said, 'you're the only person these past few weeks who hasn't treated me like I'm totally mental. I know I *seem* totally mental, but – I need you to keep believing I'm not, just for the rest of tonight. Just for the next hour, even. Can you do that?'

Her father rubbed his neck, that familiar gesture.

'Hen, ye're worryin me a bit, ah cannae deny it . . .'

Birch opened her eyes again, reached over and took hold of his shoulder. She could feel the knobs and whorls of the bone against her fingertips. He met her gaze.

'Jamieson,' she said, and her voice was loud in the claustrophobic shell of the van. 'I love you. I'm so glad you've come back. But I just want to remind you: for the first forty years of my life, you were nowhere. Never there when I needed help. Now I need help, and you're here, and you owe me a hell of a favour. This is me calling it in, okay? I *need* you, Jamieson Birch. I can't do this without you.'

Her father didn't speak, but his eyelids fluttered. After a moment's pause, he wrenched the van into reverse.

'Ah've always fancied a bit o that James Bond driving,' he said. 'Let's see if yer auld da cannae lose this tail, eh?'

Saturday, 24 July, 02:35

I wandered the nearby streets for a while, the baseball cap still pulled low. The rain stopped, but the air stayed damp. My feet and clothes were wet, but I didn't much care. I stalked along the pavements, looking in at the few windows still lit at this hour – a hobby I'd been partial to since I was a kid. I loved seeing these little snapshots of other people's everyday lives, and the more mundane the scene, the better. Most folk were already in bed; others had closed their curtains, and I watched the colours from massive TV screens dance beyond the patterned fabric. But at one house I got to watch a woman at her kitchen sink, dabbing sadly at a spill on the front of her pristine white hoodie. In a darkened living room a few doors along, a man lay asleep in an armchair, illuminated by the sickly purple light of a fish tank. A while later, I looked up to see projected shooting stars tumbling over the ceiling of a little kid's room. A mini telescope was propped against the window, and I felt a small, strange pang of nostalgia for childhood enthusiasms, simplicity – all the mistakes to come, undreamed of and unmade.

But it was after two now, and I needed to focus. Luckily for me, this little maze of streets was essentially a cul-de-sac estate: though it had many branches, there was only one way out on to the main A701. Inside the Give Way was a little copse of saplings, landscaped there when the houses were built, I guessed. The trees were sparse but unlit, thick enough to hide in. I clambered as far into the treeline as the brambles would allow, kicking aside discarded beer cans as I went, and settled in for a little more waiting.

Since the night I met James Able – six days ago, I realised, though it felt much longer – my old life had been broken down, and a new one made that was built entirely out of waiting. Waiting in a cash-only hostel, trying to decide what to do next. Waiting to see a picture of myself – grainy, maybe, from CCTV – in the news. Waiting for the words *police are looking to speak to this man in connection with the murder.* Waiting to hear they'd found the car, to hear they'd traced it back to me. Waiting – once I'd read the news about Lennox Whitelaw's release in a discarded paper in the hostel's laundry room – for the stupid concert he'd been taken to. Waiting for it to be over. Waiting, hoping the knock at the door would come – or more likely, its being kicked down. I realised then, standing in the scratchy trees as the night buses rolled by on the distant main road, that I would never outrun that waiting. No matter what I did next, and no matter where I went, I'd always be waiting for that sound of heavy boots outside my door. For ever waiting for the consequences of my actions to catch me up. It made me want to laugh: when I'd joined the force, I'd been so committed to justice, and so pissed off when I saw how little of it was really doled out. Other people seemed to walk away from their crimes so lightly – I felt like I'd seen it happen so many times. Technically, I'd done the same: I'd murdered Able and got away. I was still free. There was nothing to keep me here, no reason I couldn't walk away. But I could never walk away from the waiting. I'd always be listening for the vans, for the sirens, for the first tooth-grinding crunch of the battering ram.

The relief scene guard – plain clothes, but unmistakable with his clean-cut hair and police-issue boots – walked round the corner at 2.55 a.m., bang on time. It was the thought of that – the thought of all that waiting, maybe for the rest of my life – that made me step out of the trees and get hold of him.

'Stop!'

Birch hit the dashboard with both palms, and the van's tyres screeched as Jamieson hit the brakes. Her crutch, wedged in the passenger footwell, clattered against her bad leg, but she barely felt it. For a brief second, out of nowhere, she was reminded of her first driving lessons – way before she joined the police or took the Advanced Driving Certificate – wherein the instructor would smack the passenger-side console with his clipboard, and Birch would inevitably stall the engine as she attempted an emergency stop. Back then she was just Helen: eighteen, newly out of high school, with a bratty kid brother and a dad who wasn't really around. Now she was officially middle-aged, her kid brother in jail, and that same dad had driven her here – to a silent suburban street in south Edinburgh at 3 a.m. – because she'd been shot and couldn't do it herself. This happened, occasionally: Birch would find herself in the middle of things and suddenly think, *what is my life?* She'd never found a straight answer, but increasingly, she didn't even like the question.

Jamieson was watching her.

'This is the street,' she said. 'Just ease on round the bend, nice and slow. The house is on the left.'

Her father was already moving the van.

'There'll be somebody there?' he asked.

Birch glanced at the van's clock. 03:04, it said. She hoped it was fast.

'There's a round-the-clock scene guard,' she said. 'Shift change is at three.'

Jamieson nodded, and crept the van round the corner. The houses all around were unlit, save an occasional string of solar garden bulbs or a porch light accidentally left on. The safe house was in the darkest part of the street. Across the road was an old tree, which threw a deep shadow across the road.

'Park there,' Birch said, pointing to it. On the front step of the safe house she could make out the figure of the scene guard, camouflaged in his black police-issue windcheater, but not invisible.

Birch had opened the car door before Jamieson had time to put the handbrake on. He reached out a hand towards her.

'Hen,' he said, 'ah'll help ye . . .'

But Birch was already swinging her feet out on to the wet road. Grabbing the roof of the van for support, she clawed her way to a standing position without the crutch, then reached back for it. Jamieson was holding it out to her, his face pale in the dim light.

'Helen,' he said, 'ye ken ah'd dae anythin fur ye.'

Birch blinked at him.

'I know, Dad. You're here, aren't you?'

'An Charlie, tae,' he said.

She slid the crutch out of his hands and over the passenger seat.

'I know,' she said again. 'Why are you saying this?'

'Because,' Jamieson replied, 'Amy's right, this is aw madness.'

'But you're here, nevertheless.'

He nodded.

'Aye.'

Birch stood astride the stick, feeling a familiar ache – in her hip, in her forearm, in the shoulder that supported her.

'Well, thanks,' she said, finding she meant it. 'I appreciate it. And anyway, if it's all a hiding to nothing, we're about to find out.'

'Be careful,' Jamieson called out, but Birch had already slammed the van door and set off, crutch clicking, across the road.

By the time she got halfway up the house's tarmacked drive, she was close enough to see alarm registering on the scene guard's face. As she reached the door, Birch peered at him. He wasn't an officer she knew.

'Evening,' she said.

'Marm.'

She saw him look her up and down.

'Oh,' she replied, 'you know me, then? I didn't think we'd met.'

The officer was stocky – he had a rugby player kind of build, and hair that looked sandy, maybe ginger, in the orange-grey streetlight. This wasn't the tall, thin man.

'We haven't,' he said. 'But I'm assuming you're DI Helen Birch? I was told to expect you.'

Birch snorted.

'By whom?'

His eyes shifted. He didn't want to look at her directly.

'I'm operating on orders from DCI McLeod.'

Birch's heart stuttered in her chest. McLeod had feared she'd come here. Perhaps he'd *known* she'd come here.

'Well.' It was important that she keep her composure, though it was tricky. She both hated McLeod in that moment and empathised with him. He'd been right, after all: he'd feared she'd do the stupid thing, and here she was doing it. 'I suppose that saves me getting my warrant card out.'

The scene guard was still looking her up and down. She remembered what she looked like: she'd pulled her work boots on below her PJ bottoms, and shoved on a jumper that was inside out. It hadn't mattered at the time, she'd just wanted to get here. Now she realised that it may well matter quite a lot.

'I'm afraid I can't let you into the property,' he said, 'if that's what you mean.'

Birch tried to draw herself up a little taller. The crutch made it difficult.

'What's your name, sunshine?'

The man had the audacity to sigh.

'It won't make any difference,' he said.

'Fine. But I'm asking you.'

He glanced around – a gesture so furtive that, under other circumstances, it might have been comical – before flipping back the windcheater to show Birch his lanyard and ID.

'PC Greg Riley,' he said.

Birch threw him a fake smile.

'Lovely,' she said, 'thank you, Greg. Now, tell me . . . you've just come on shift?'

'I really can't—'

She let out an exasperated noise.

'I'm not *asking* to get into the property, okay? I'm literally just asking if you're the relief shift.'

'I . . . can't disclose that information.'

'Oh, come *on.*'

'I can't. I was ordered not to engage with you if you showed up. We've all been told the same.'

Birch froze. McLeod had clearly issued some sort of all-staff bulletin. *No one talk to DI Birch, she's a crazy woman.*

'I'm a senior officer,' she said, trying to keep her voice level, 'asking a simple question.'

Riley was openly cringing now. He was clearly enjoying this about as much as she was.

'I was told— I mean, the order said . . .'

He tailed off.

'What? The order said what?'

He had the good grace to look down at his feet before he replied.

'The order said you'd been suspended.'

This shouldn't have been a surprise – she'd known this was the fate that awaited her if Operation Stake didn't work out. And yet, hearing it said by someone else – hearing that it was common knowledge among her colleagues already – made her feel like she might throw up, right there, on PC Greg Riley's shoes.

'That's news to me,' she said, then realised it was a lie and probably only made her sound more unhinged.

Riley looked up then, past her. He was looking along the street, towards the bend that she and Jamieson had driven round in the van. Birch turned her head.

'Did you see something?'

Riley's eyes snapped back. He looked at her face then, properly, for the first time. She decided to try a different tack.

'Okay, listen,' she said, hoping she could hold his gaze. 'I know what this looks like. I know I've turned up here in the middle of the night, mad and dishevelled-looking. I know you've had your orders, and Christ only knows what you think of me. But listen: I have reason to believe that the perp you're currently guarding is in very real danger, and all I've come here to do is ascertain that he isn't currently—'

Her voice faltered. She wasn't sure what she'd expected to find when she got to the safe house. Perhaps she'd hoped for a scene guard she knew, someone who'd let her poke around the place a bit, scratch the itch of her anxiety. Perhaps she'd hoped she could stay on the doorstep herself, until the morning came with its armoured van and uniforms to escort Lennox Whitelaw back to Saughton. She could tell PC Riley wasn't about to allow her to do any of those things.

'I dunno,' she said, 'that he isn't currently *being murdered*. I just want to set my mind at rest.'

Riley didn't say anything. He seemed to be scrutinising her, perhaps trying to figure out just how crazy she was – whether or not he needed to be worried. She winced: perhaps he was trying to work out whether or not he ought to be reaching for his cuffs.

'Just let me do that.' She realised she was pleading now: standing in the drizzle with her hair sticking up, suspended, a joke, pleading with some jobsworth uniform. 'Just let me set my mind at rest, and then I'll go away. I'll leave you be.'

Still, Riley didn't speak. Once again his expression changed, and he looked up, over her head, and along the length of the street, as though his attention had been caught by something. Birch turned her head once more and peered into the dark.

'At least tell me,' she said, 'why you keep looking over there. Have you seen something? Is there someone hanging around?'

Riley seemed to sag then, as though he'd let all the air out of his lungs.

'Fucksake,' he said, though his tone was gentle. 'You really do sound crazy, marm, I'm sorry. There isn't anyone there. I'm just waiting for my relief guy.' Riley glanced at his watch. 'He's more than ten minutes late.'

Birch felt that same flywheel in her brain begin to turn.

'So you've been on all night, so far?'

Riley closed his eyes for a moment. He'd let her have a crumb of information, and now he was regretting it.

'Yeah,' he said. 'And before you ask, absolutely nothing's gone on. One of the most boring shifts of my life, if that makes you happy.' He lifted both hands, and started to count off his own fingers as he spoke. 'I was here when they brought Whitelaw back, I was here when the medic came by to look at his face. I was here when the medic left, and then Sergeant Kato and the protection team left shortly after that. I've been here ever since, completely on my tod. There's been not a peep from Whitelaw, and nothing to report out here. There. Is your mind at rest?'

Birch frowned. It ought to be, she thought. I ought to be satisfied with that, but I'm not.

'Not quite,' she said. 'You're on your own, you say? No one at the back entrance?'

Riley sighed again, this time with greater exasperation.

'There *is* no back entrance,' he said. 'Not on this house. This is the only way in or out. And I'm telling you, there's been nothing. Not a peep.'

Birch looked behind her again, back down the street. As though he'd been waiting for an excuse to do so, Riley copied the action. The big tree rattled its leaves, and around the base of the streetlights, the shadows rearranged themselves. But there was no one there. Riley was right: all quiet.

'Your relief hasn't shown up, though,' Birch pointed out.

Riley shrugged.

'Three in the morning,' he said, 'it's hard to get out of bed. If he's not here in another ten or so, I'll radio in. But you should really go now, marm. If he turns up and I'm talking to you, he could feed it back, and then I'd catch hell.' Birch looked at his face. He looked like a man who needed a cigarette. 'I've already said way too much to you,' he added.

Birch tried for a grin. She still wasn't satisfied: the sense of unease she felt had only grown, standing there talking in half-whispers to a man who'd been told she was mad, a flight risk: *the suspect is dangerous, do not engage.* She realised too late that the fake smile might not look great, under the circum-stances: Riley's expression changed. All of a sudden he was wary again.

'Listen,' he said, his voice stern, 'I'm going to have to ask you to leave. You're on private property.'

'I'm on Police Scotland property.'

Riley fixed her with a look. He raised one hand and slipped his fingers inside the windcheater. Birch knew he was feeling for his radio, checking it was there.

'Marm,' he said, 'I get it. You don't seem well, and I know that when anxiety comes along, it's—'

'I'm fine,' Birch snapped, then wished she hadn't. She looked down at herself, and smiled weakly, trying to turn it into a joke. 'I mean, despite appearances, I really am fine.'

'What I'm saying is this.' Riley's hand hadn't moved from the radio. 'If you want to go back over there and sit in your vehicle all night, and watch this house, I'm not going to stop you. Sure, you say you're fine, but whatever – if doing that would make you feel better, you carry on. But if you don't get off this property, and I mean immediately, then I *am* going to have to follow orders, and radio in to tell them you're here. I don't really want to have to do that, and I'm pretty sure you'd also rather I didn't.'

Birch was already backing away – lurching, really, thanks to the crutch. Fine, she thought. Sit in the van all night, it is. If that's what it takes.

'Okay,' she said. She tried to imagine the rage McLeod would fly into if he found himself woken up at half three in the morning to hear she'd been meddling again – the very thing he specifically told her she must not do. 'I'm going. Thanks, though.'

She turned on her heel and clicked away towards the pavement, the metallic rattle of the crutch unnaturally loud in the dark, empty street. All the way across the road and back to the van, she felt Riley's eyes on her back. She opened the passenger door and arranged herself back down into the seat.

'So, can we head fer hame?' Jamieson asked.

Birch threw him a scowl so fierce she saw him flinch.

'Not on your life,' she said. 'This isn't over.'

Saturday, 24 July, 03:15

Hi James. Sorry, middle of the night. Just trying a text. Can't sleep and very worried about Client PS7. Please contact me as soon as you can? I'm in urgent need of advice. Thanks – and sorry. Jane R

Saturday, 24 July, 03:20

Birch nudged Jamieson in the ribs, and he jumped. She realised too late that her father had been nodding off: he let out a strangled snore and jolted upright.

'Look,' Birch hissed. She was peering in the passenger-side wing mirror. 'Look.'

Jamieson leaned over and looked in his own mirror.

'Ah cannae see,' he replied, 'fer these bastart branches.'

Birch was transfixed. She bent close to the mirror, trying to make out the person walking along the pavement towards the house. The figure wore a neon yellow overcoat, boxy and large.

'It's the relief scene guard,' Birch whispered. 'Who just happens to be a tall, thin man.'

Jamieson leaned over the car's central console to peer into Birch's mirror himself, and the van shuddered.

'Dad! I'd rather no one knew we were in here.'

Jamieson froze as though she'd yelled at him, though they were speaking in whispers.

'Sorry,' he hissed back. 'D'ye hink it's him?'

Birch shrugged, but she could feel the racing flywheel starting up again in her head.

'Let's see what he does,' she replied.

The tall, thin man drew level with the van. Jamieson eased back into the driver's seat, and without speaking, they both sank down in their seats to avoid being seen. But the shadows around them were deep: this looked every bit like the works van of a plumber or spark, parked up on the street after a late job. On the other side of the road, the tall, thin man strode up the safe house's driveway.

Carefully, Birch cracked the van's window. She gave thanks for the fact that Jamieson hadn't upgraded it: the windows were old-fashioned, handle-wound, silent. PC Greg Riley had been watching his colleague's progress along the street, and now he called out to him in a low voice.

'That you, Jamie?'

The tall, thin man raised a hand in greeting.

'Jamie,' Birch breathed. 'He has a J name.'

'Aye,' the tall, thin man called back. 'Sorry I'm late, pal. Not used to these middle-of-the-night starts.'

He arrived at the front door, and Riley reached out a hand, which he clapped on the tall, thin man's shoulder.

'Fucking hell,' he said, 'I haven't seen you in months, mate. We were all wondering what happened to you.'

Tall, thin Jamie seemed to flinch at this. He wriggled out of Riley's grip.

'Had to take some leave,' he replied, 'for personal reasons. You know how it is.'

Riley paused for a moment, as though he hoped the other man might elaborate.

'Yeah,' he said, when it became clear no more information would be forthcoming. 'Sure. But you're good? You're healthy?'

The man named Jamie cocked his head.

'Never better,' he said. 'Sorry again for being late, though.'

Riley grinned. Birch saw the tangerine gleam of the street-light on his teeth.

'Don't worry about it,' he said. 'Can't imagine how rough getting up for this gig must have been, when you've been relaxing on leave for bloody weeks.'

Jamie laughed a low, strange laugh.

'How's it been?' he asked: an obvious deflection from the other man's gentle prying. 'Tonight, I mean.'

Riley shrugged, and Birch held her breath, hoping he wouldn't mention her. *He could feed it back,* he'd said, *and then I'd catch hell.*

'Dull as shit,' he replied. 'Absolutely nothing doing.'

She allowed herself to exhale.

Jamie was nodding.

'Great. That's what we like.'

'Aye.' Riley seemed to draw himself up then, bouncing slightly on the balls of his feet. 'Well, it's all yours, pal. This your first posting back on the job? Graveyard shift?'

'Cheeky bastart,' Jamieson hissed, 'he really wants tae stick his neb in.'

Birch frowned, keen to listen, and held up a finger to her lips.

'Guess they want to ease me back in gently,' Jamie replied.

The *go away now* inflection was clear in his voice. In response, Riley zipped up his jacket and stepped away from the threshold. Birch watched as he dipped a hand into his pocket, and handed over the keyfob that would open the safe house's front door. As they switched positions, Riley pressed one hand on to the other man's shoulder once again.

'Listen,' Riley said, 'it's really good to see you back on the job, yeah? Back where you belong.'

Jamie jutted his chin up. He now had his back to the house for the first time, and Birch got her first proper look at him. His face wasn't especially familiar, and she realised she'd expected to recognise him. Surely they must have met before, worked together sometime, somewhere . . .

'Thanks, pal,' Jamie was saying. 'I appreciate that.'

Riley turned, and set off down the house's drive.

'Have a good night,' he called back over his shoulder. From the front step, Jamie raised one hand in response. He kept it raised – one flat palm at right angles to the ground, like a witness taking the stand – until Riley had rounded the bend, and disappeared out of sight.

'Jamie,' Birch whispered. 'A PC, I assume. PC Jamie . . . what?'

'How sure are ye,' Jamieson asked, 'that this is him? He disnae look much . . .'

Birch held up a hand.

'Wait,' she said.

The man on the doorstep was casting around now: looking up and down the street in both directions, tense and alert. Jamieson and Birch watched him stand very still for a few seconds, as though listening. The man still had the keyfob Riley had passed to him clutched tight in his fist. After a moment, he turned his back on the street, pressed the fob to its sensor, and the front door clicked open.

'I knew it,' Birch said, reaching for her crutch. 'This is the fucking Vampire.'

Jamieson shot a hand out and grabbed her arm. Across the street, Jamie stepped in through the door, and closed it behind him.

'Ye cannae be goin in there, hen.'

Birch spun round, her eyes wide.

'Of course I'm going in there! He's about to murder my perp!'

Jamieson's face was panicked. He looked down into the passenger footwell, nodding towards Birch's bad leg.

'Ye cannae,' he said again, 'no wi that leg.'

Birch wrenched her arm from her father's grip.

'I am so fucking *sick* of this leg,' she hissed. 'I can do this, Dad. I can.'

But Jamieson grabbed hold of her again.

'Can ye no call fer back - up? Send the cavalry in there?'

As he spoke, he leaned over her, and with his free hand, plucked up her phone from where she'd thrown it earlier. He held it out.

'Call Amy,' he said, 'or . . . someone. Ask fer help, hen.'

Birch glanced down at the phone. Jamieson's thumb had touched the screen, bringing it to life. *Missed call (4): Amy Kato*. She turned her head and looked towards the safe house. It could only have been a few seconds, but it felt like an hour already since the Vampire let himself in.

Birch snatched the phone from her father. Her hip throbbed, though it didn't hurt. She could still feel the effects of her missed painkillers, but adrenalin was coursing through her bloodstream.

'Fine,' she said. 'But not Amy. Amy can't do anything now.'

She thumbed her passcode into the phone, then dialled 999.

'This is CA38, Detective Inspector Helen Birch,' she said, as soon as the call connected. 'I'm off radio, but I'm at a crime scene and require immediate back - up. My location is—'

'DI Birch,' the dispatcher cut in. It was a male voice, young-sounding. 'I'm sorry, marm. I can't help you.'

'What? What do you mean, you can't help me?'

There was a pause on the line.

'We've received orders,' the dispatcher replied, 'to report any calls that come in from you direct to DCI McLeod. You've been blacklisted, I'm sorry.'

Birch felt her heartbeat snag.

'Blacklisted? Are you kidding me?'

'I'm sorry, marm. I'm just following orders.'

Birch punched the dashboard, making the whole van vibrate. She felt Jamieson's hand – still resting on her upper right arm – recoil.

'What's your name?'

There was silence on the end of the line.

'Tell me your name, you cowardly little shit.'

'I'm not obliged to do that,' the dispatcher replied. His tone was icy now. Official.

'Someone's about to be murdered,' Birch yelled, 'and it's going to be on your head, do you hear me? I will find out who you are, and make sure they throw the bloody book at you.'

The dispatcher coughed.

'I'm going to end the call now,' he said.

'Fine. You fucking do that.' Without hanging up, Birch flung the phone back into the footwell. She heard the screen splinter as it made contact with the van's floor.

'Bastard,' she hissed.

Jamieson was watching her, his eyes like saucers. She rounded on him.

'See? See how much good that did me? Now I'm going in, and you needn't try to stop me.'

Jamieson didn't speak, but unbuckled his seatbelt.

'Oh no, you don't. You needn't think you're coming too.'

He gawped at her.

'Ye cannae go in there alone, hen.'

'Better that,' she replied, pushing the van door open, 'than go in there with some civilian who has no idea what he's doing.' She saw from the way his face crumpled that she'd stung him, and modified her tone. 'You have to stay here. I need eyes on that front door, in case the Vampire decides to run. If he does, you're welcome to give chase, okay?'

She clambered out of the van the same way she had before, hauling herself up by the roof. This time, she turned and grabbed the crutch herself. Her pulse roared in her ears: for the first time in weeks, she felt like she was really doing it. She was doing her job.

'Helen,' Jamieson said, 'is that scumbag Whitelaw really worth ye getting hurt?'

Birch fixed him with a glare.

'He's the scumbag,' she said, 'that *I picked* as bait. I promised a lot of people that no harm would come to him. Just like I promised I'd catch the Vampire. I have to do this, Dad.'

Jamieson's mouth twisted, but she looked away, and slammed the van door.

'Stay there,' she shouted, through the passenger window's glass. Then she turned and clattered across the street.

The front door had locked itself behind the Vampire, and Birch had no fob. Breathing hard after her lopsided dash from the van, she bent to look at the lock panel, searching for some sort of manual override. But there was nothing of that kind on this side of the door – of *course* there wasn't. She half jogged along the front of the house, and rounded the corner into the back garden. Above her, all the motion-triggered floodlights came on.

The garden itself was a wide rectangle of grass, with a small, paved patio tacked up against the house. Lit by the eerie blue floodlights, it could have been the surface of another planet. The high fence rose all around her.

'Obvious safe house is obvious,' she muttered.

The patio had once had French windows that opened out on to it – presumably before the property had been obtained by Police Scotland. A cheap job had been done to block them off into a window, the central pane of which was unusually large. Birch barely registered the rest of the garden. There was no back entrance, Riley had said. She looked down at the crutch, her hand curled around the grip, her knuckles white.

'Finally a use for this godforsaken thing,' she said, swinging over the patio until she was less than a crutch-length away from the window. Birch shifted her weight on to her strong leg, hitching the stick upwards in her hand until she was holding the stopper end. She looked at the grip. It was coated in grey plastic, supposedly for comfort, but she knew from the weeks-old blisters on her hands that inside the handle was a formidable metal shank, built to take the full weight of a human being. She swung the crutch back in a wide arc, as though wielding an axe. Then, with all the strength her injured body had, she smashed it into the patio window. There was a loud snapping sound, and the glass crazed, but didn't break. Birch imagined lights going on along the street as she raised the crutch again, and let it fall. On the third impact, the glass gave out. The window fell away in a jagged sheet, and she was in.

Except she wasn't in. She'd made a hole to climb through, but she wasn't entirely sure she could climb. She'd need to stand, unaided, with her full weight on both feet to even start, she realised, and since the shooting, this was something she'd only done in physio, with the option to stop whenever she wanted. Swaying there, squinting into the darkened dining room of the safe house, she thought of Dr Jane, and Anjan, of Amy and her dad, even McLeod. She thought of all the people who'd urged her to rest and get better, told her – quite rightly – that if she didn't, her hip would never properly heal. She took a deep breath.

'Fuck it,' she said, and planted her feet. Swaying slightly, she chucked the crutch through the broken window, as far as it would go. 'Now I have to.'

As Birch boosted herself up through the window, she knew her wounded hip had to be hurting. She couldn't feel the pain, because her whole body was racing to get inside, to find the

Vampire. But she suspected that under normal circumstances, she'd have knuckled on to the ground by now. She swung her good leg in through the window first, so she could steady herself down on to it. Then she dragged the bad leg, bent weirdly, after it. Under her feet, nuggets of detonated glass crunched into the carpet. The house was silent, except for the sound of her own ragged breath. Outside, the floodlights flipped themselves off, and for a second, she could see nothing. The bad leg felt strange to stand on: she could feel the muscles were wasted and weak from lack of use. Her physio had told her this. She felt as though she might list over to that side if she walked too far, but she couldn't see where her crutch had fallen. Then, as her eyes adjusted to the gloom, her heart clutched. Standing in the doorway of the dining room – lit by the sickly peach light of the distant street – was the Vampire.

'Police!'

Birch had tried to shout, but her voice came out with a strange creak. She thought her knees might buckle.

Slowly, the Vampire reached round the door frame and switched on the light. Birch's eyelids flickered. The crutch was about a metre away, lying on the glass-strewn carpet.

The Vampire was looking her up and down, taking in the combat boots, PJs, wonky jumper, messy hair.

'What in the hell?' He looked almost amused.

'Police!' This time it sounded a little better. She reached into her pocket, pulled out her warrant card, and brandished it. For a moment, she felt like the victim in a horror movie – like she was holding up a crucifix in the face of a real vampire. 'Detective Inspector Helen Birch. You're under arrest.'

The Vampire laughed. He stepped over the threshold, into the room with her. She was able to look him up and down now, too. She could see that although he was thin, he was sinewy. Strong. *Do you say wiry?* Alyona had asked. *Is that correct?* It was. And the Vampire was young: he couldn't even be thirty. As if on cue, Birch felt the adrenalin begin to ebb, and a hot wire of pain tautened in her hip.

'I don't think so,' the Vampire said, stepping towards her. 'I'm kind of in the middle of something here.'

Birch stood her ground, though it was hurting, now, to do so. 'Where's Lennox Whitelaw?'

The Vampire took another step towards her. Above them, there was a sound – a sort of muffled thud.

'Upstairs,' he replied. 'I think I might have disturbed his rest.'

Birch glanced at the ceiling.

'Whitelaw?' she called out. The Vampire was still advancing.

'He's still alive,' he said, 'if that's what you're wondering. For now, at least.'

Birch was still holding the warrant card, but her hands were shaking. It slipped from her fingers.

'Don't come any closer!' she barked. The Vampire ignored her.

'I don't know what you think you're doing,' he said. He was only a few feet away now: she could smell the sharp edge of him, smoky and feral. His clothes were crumpled, like he'd slept in them. 'But it isn't going to work.'

'You're under arrest,' she said again, 'for the murder of James Able. You are not obliged to say anything, but—'

The Vampire lunged forward, swung, and punched her hard in the jaw. Birch felt her teeth bang up against each other inside her skull, then she fell like a tree, arms by her sides, in a neat, straight line. Her cheek hit the carpet, and she felt a prickling sensation as the shattered glass sank into her face. Her vision glitched, like she might pass out. *Do not pass out*, she commanded herself. Somewhere in the background, she felt a vague sense of relief that she was no longer standing on her bad leg.

The Vampire pushed one foot underneath her ribs. She allowed her body to be flipped face up, but as she went over, she felt more glass pieces lodging in her scalp, catching in her hair. If she reached out her right hand now, she could brush the fallen crutch with the tips of her fingers.

The Vampire stood over her.

'I thought *I* was the vigilante,' he said. 'What kind of batshit insane mission is this?'

Birch coughed. She could taste blood.

'The cavalry's right behind me, arsehole,' she spluttered. 'Any minute now you're going to have Kevlar-vested bastards lining up to snap you in half.'

The Vampire laughed.

'Big talk,' he said. He swung one foot over her body, then dropped to his knees, pinning her down. Her bad hip burned. 'I think I should shut you up.'

Birch stretched out her fingers and felt the cold metal of the crutch. The Vampire clamped one large, bony hand over her nose and mouth. The other one he placed on to her throat – not pressing down, but threatening to.

'That's a little better,' he said.

Birch kicked with her good leg, to little effect. If she could just get hold of the crutch . . .

He started to apply pressure to her throat. She felt her windpipe contract under the heel of his hand, and her vision flickered. She kicked again, but it was weaker this time. She could feel real panic beginning to set in as her lungs rapidly leaked their last bit of air.

Suddenly, there was a noise overhead: that same thud she'd heard before. It was followed by another, then something in the room upstairs – a piece of furniture, perhaps – crashed to the floor. The Vampire's grip loosened, ever so slightly, as his face shot up to look in the direction of the sound. Birch could see patterns on the edge of her vision. She knew she didn't have much time.

Using her very last shred of energy, she writhed enough to shift the Vampire's weight just a little and free her arm to stretch the extra inch she needed in the direction of the crutch. Her hand closed around its cold metal girth, but before she could lift it, the Vampire grabbed on to both her wrists and yanked them above her head. Her throat opened up and she hauled in a breath, then coughed and retched. The Vampire sat astride her, her hands pinned under his own, laughing.

'Feisty, aren't we?' he said.

Birch took another breath. This one hurt, too, but a little less. She coughed into his face, watching her spit fleck his lips. Her ears rang, and she could feel the nerves in her eyes pinging. She knew she had one chance at whatever came next, so she risked a third big breath, then arched her back as high as she could. As the Vampire bucked upwards, she shot her pinned hands down to her sides, raking them over the broken glass. The Vampire pitched forward, and she saw the shock in his eyes the moment before his forehead hit the floor. The usual conclusion of this particular move was to reverse the roles, end up on top of your assailant and able to cuff them. But Birch knew she didn't have the strength for that: he'd easily overpower her again. The main thing she needed to do now was get away.

She slithered from under the Vampire's weight, and pulled herself on to her knees. She retched again, and spat into the carpet. He was already rallying: up on his knees himself now, one hand pressed to his forehead where pieces of glass had stuck. Birch slapped a palm on to the edge of the dining table and dragged herself upright.

'You've been on leave a while, haven't you, constable?' she said. 'Forgotten a lot of your self-defence training, anyway.'

He looked at her with wide eyes.

'Yeah,' she said, 'I know who you are.'

This wasn't remotely true: she knew only what she'd over-heard from his conversation with PC Greg Riley on the door-step. Without getting up off his knees, he lunged at her, and as she side-stepped, grappling along the tabletop, she spotted the hideous cut-crystal fruit bowl someone had placed there. She wanted to drag her bad leg now: it felt like dead weight, atrophied. Hand over hand, she scooted the length of the din-ing table as the Vampire got to his feet and advanced. She lifted the fruit bowl.

'You must be joking,' he said, though the crowing tone from earlier was gone. He just wanted her neutralised now, and out of the way – she could see it in his eyes.

Her arms trembled as she hefted the fruit bowl above her head and lobbed it at him. He dodged it easily, and she heard it shatter against the wall behind him. She glanced around for something else to throw, anything else she could pick up and use to defend herself. But something was wrong: the Vampire should have been coming for her. He wasn't. Instead, he'd stopped as though frozen stiff, a question in his eyes, his focus now on something behind her. She didn't have time to turn and look before her head was yanked backwards, her neck crushed once again, this time in a headlock.

'DI Birch,' Lennox Whitelaw wheezed. 'So kind of you to drop in.'

Birch raised both hands and dug her fingers into the forearm Whitelaw had clamped around her neck, trying to prise it away.

'What the *fuck*, Whitelaw!' she screamed, though the scream came out twisted and hoarse. 'I'm here to help you!'

His face was close to hers, and on his breath, she could smell blood. His hands were slippery with it, and it was all over the T-shirt he was wearing. The Vampire had already messed him up, though she couldn't tell how much.

'If you think,' Whitelaw rasped, 'that I'm going to waste this chance to get away from you fucking people, then you're more stupid than you look.'

Birch rocked in his grip. If he was losing blood, she reasoned, he couldn't keep up this hold for all that long. But she was failing herself, her hearing stuttering in and out. The Vampire stood watching them, shifting his weight this way and that, clearly unsure what to do.

'You're trying to *escape*?' she croaked.

Whitelaw let out a laugh that sounded more like an ancient machine rattling to a halt.

'Once I've dealt with you,' he hissed, 'I'm going to deal with this little bastard, and then I'm getting the fuck away.' Birch's eyesight was faltering again, and she felt both legs – not just the bad one – losing the will to keep her upright. Though she was screaming internally not to give up, her eyelids began to drift shut. 'Yes, DI Birch,' Whitelaw whispered, his voice wet. 'I'm escaping.'

'Ye're fuckin dreamin, sunshine.'

Birch's eyes shot open. She was just in time to see Jamieson swing her dropped crutch at Whitelaw's face. She was close enough to hear the stick's grip break Whitelaw's nose as it made contact: a sickening crunch. He howled, and doubled over on to the floor.

'Dad!'

But now the Vampire was on top of Jamieson, piggy-backing on to him in a bid to push him to the floor. But

Jamieson Birch fought dirty. He spun round to face the window he'd just climbed into, then staggered backwards until both he and the Vampire collided with the table in the centre of the room: a real old-fashioned bar brawl move. Birch heard the air huff out of the Vampire's lungs as he landed flat on his back on the tabletop. She was coughing again; her lungs felt full of fibreglass thanks to Whitelaw's chokehold, and her legs had all but given way. Long strings of drool hung from her mouth, and spots of light – or perhaps just a blank white blindness – swam before her eyes. Lennox Whitelaw writhed and moaned on the floor at her feet, hands over his face, dark blood oozing out between the fingers. Her elderly father was dancing around on the glass-studded carpet, shadow-boxing, goading the Vampire – a man far taller, and at least half his age.

'C'mon, ya soft bastart,' he sang. 'Oan yer fuckin feet!'

Had pain not been wringing out her every nerve, Birch might have laughed. Instead she fell against the wall and staggered her way along it, one shoulder dragging against the Anaglypta. The Vampire was up now, as instructed, both fists raised but mainly trying to back away from Jamieson's erratic dance, towards the door. By the time Birch made it to the room's far corner, she realised that her strength had finally given out. As she let her legs give way, she reached out and hit the discreet red panic button that was set into the wall. She curled into an agonised knot, her hands flattened and tucked under her cheek like a sleeping child, and closed her eyes.

Sunday, 25 July, 14:00

Tiny nuggets of glass had taken root in her face, and been pulled out with tweezers by a very patient nurse. Birch's cheeks still stung from the antiseptic. She'd never appreciated before just how *everywhere* broken glass could get: hours ago, she'd been brushing little shards of it out of her hair in a hospital bathroom, hearing it sift on to the waxed floor like snow. Her jaw was bruised and swollen where the Vampire had punched her, but her teeth were intact. She didn't know what painkiller they'd given her, but it was delightfully strong: she'd been able to shower and change her clothes in a state of strange, drugged bliss. Beyond the flimsy hospital curtain, the beep and whirr of machinery seemed almost like music.

'Whatever this is,' she'd said to the frowning doctor who discharged her, 'I want it on an IV for the rest of my life.'

They'd loaned her a wheelchair, and it made her so happy that she thought she might cry. It was a strictly short-term deal: she'd most likely be back on crutches within a week. She decided to savour the wheelchair's every creak, rattle and stuck brake for all she was worth. The physio people were going to play hell anyway, so she might as well. The doctors told her that all her work in recovery thus far – all her small, hard-won victories – had been pretty much cancelled out. She'd thoroughly retraumatised her hip, and was going back to square one. She wasn't looking forward to seeing how it felt once the drugs wore off.

When she'd wheeled herself out of the lift and into the bullpen at Fettes Avenue, she felt for a moment like she'd walked into a room where everyone had just been talking about her and then suddenly shut up. Her cheeks burned: all her colleagues must have had the same order as PC Greg Riley and the dispatcher the night before: DI Birch is suspended and insane, please ignore or avoid her. It was Sunday, and the bullpen sparsely staffed, but one by one, every face turned towards her. One of those faces belonged to Amy Kato, who broke the silence by yelling, 'Helen!' and practically sprinting across the room.

'Please don't hug me,' Birch warned, as her colleague got close. 'I'm too fragile, I'm sorry.'

Amy skidded to a halt beside the wheelchair.

'Don't *you* apologise,' she said. 'If anyone ought to be apologising, it's me.'

Birch grinned.

'Don't be daft, you did good last night.'

Amy's nose wrinkled.

'I was terrible,' she said. 'I refused to listen to you, I called you crazy, and I left you to deal with everything on your own. It was bad behaviour from a colleague, and even worse behaviour from a friend.'

Birch cocked her head. Her neck hurt, in spite of the painkillers: between them, the Vampire and Whitelaw had bruised it pretty badly.

'You followed an order from McLeod,' she replied. 'That's your job. What's more, you did try to talk me out of it, and that was absolutely the right thing to do. If I had my time again, there's no way I'd have gone in there alone and unarmed. It *was* crazy.'

Amy snorted.

'Don't fib,' she said. 'You'd absolutely do it again.'

Birch was still grinning, but she also shrugged.

'Well,' she said, 'maybe. But I'd take my auld da with me next time. He really saved my bacon in there.'

Amy was allowing herself to smile now, too.

'He properly messed up Lennox Whitelaw's face,' she said. 'I mean, the man had already knocked his own teeth out on the Castle Esplanade, but your dad really finished the job.'

'Tell me,' Birch said, her mind turning to Whitelaw's victims, 'that the press got a photo of him.'

Amy fished her phone from her pocket, brought it to life, and then swiped around on the screen. She turned it to face Birch: the image was of Whitelaw being escorted out of a panda car and into the Edinburgh Royal Infirmary. It was blurry, but there was no escaping the fact that his face was a shattered mess. One eye was swollen shut, and his shirt was stiff with dried blood.

'Poor guy,' Amy said, the words like acid in her mouth.

'Bless his soul,' Birch replied, matching her friend's tone.

'He'll be in the Infirmary for a couple of days, probably,' Amy went on, 'before he's put back in Saughton. How would you feel about adding a charge of assaulting a police officer to his rap sheet?'

Birch pressed the tip of her index finger against her chin, as though thinking hard.

'Hmm,' she said, 'let me see, would I be okay with that?'

Amy was already laughing.

'I thought you'd be keen,' she said.

'What about our vampire? Where are we at with him?'

'Well, he's in a cell, if that's what you're asking.'

Birch laughed.

'I was looking for just a tad more detail than that.'

Amy scrunched up her face.

'Marm,' she said, 'you can't possibly be here to work? I assumed you were just coming in to see McLeod or something.'

'I am.'

'So . . . don't you want to just go get a cup of coffee 'til he's ready for you? You literally just got out of the hospital.'

Birch spread out her arms in a *look, I'm fine* gesture, but then caught sight of the angry grazes on the backs of her hands.

'I'm doing okay,' she said, dropping her hands again before Amy noticed. 'Cuts and bruises, that's all.'

Amy snorted.

'That, and having been shot a little while ago.'

Birch looked down at the wheelchair in mock surprise.

'Wait,' she said, 'when did *that* happen?'

Amy rolled her eyes, but then jerked her head in the direction of her desk.

'Come on, then,' she said, 'I'm just going over the file now.'

Birch wheeled herself across the carpet of the bullpen, trying to meet the eyes of her colleagues as she passed. Some acknowledged her, while others looked away. She wondered if they were ashamed of themselves, or if they just hadn't heard the final outcome of Operation Stake yet. Maybe they assumed she was still suspended, and here to collect her things.

'Here we are,' Amy said, as Birch drew level with her desk. 'James Lyndoe, better known as Jamie. Alias Jay, fondly known to us as the tall, thin man, and then later the Vampire.'

Birch looked at the photo of Lyndoe on Amy's screen. It showed him on graduation day at Tulliallan. She recognised the familiar college buildings in the background.

'Nearly three years as a fully - fledged constable with Police Scotland,' Amy was saying, 'until an incident back in January that saw him placed on paid leave pending formal investigation.'

'What was the incident?'

Amy was still standing, but now she bent towards the computer screen and clicked through the file.

'Lyndoe had an outburst while on the job,' Amy replied. 'He was working crowd control outside the Sheriff Court one day when a particularly nasty perp walked.'

'Anyone I know?'

'I'm still typing up the details,' Amy replied, 'but it wasn't anything you'd have worked on. A small-time guy trying to set up business as a pimp. He didn't treat his girls too well, so they shopped him.'

Birch rolled her eyes.

'But he had a good lawyer,' she said, 'and no one ever believes the girls. Same old, same old.'

'Pretty much. Anyway, Lyndoe started shouting about how it was all a fix, the injustice of it – you can probably imagine. There were some press around, so it got a little traction, though of course the wagons were circled at this end.'

'Circled pretty effectively,' Birch replied, 'given that this is the first I've heard of it.'

'I guess so,' Amy said. 'Anyway, Lyndoe was placed on leave, and told to attend compulsory counselling sessions while he waited for the investigation to get under way.'

'And did it? Get under way, I mean.'

Amy scrolled again.

'Not massively,' she replied. 'Lyndoe was obviously not much of a priority.'

Birch let her vision swim. She realised she was nodding.

'Which, if you're someone who joined the force because you care about injustice, and you want to be out there doing good,' she mused, 'is basically just going to make you climb the walls.'

Amy grinned.

'I know you know what that's like.'

Birch dipped her head towards her shoulder, a kind of sideways nod. It hurt.

'Sure,' she said, 'but I didn't go out and start killing people.'

Amy was still smiling.

'I dunno, marm,' she said, 'I think it was probably touch - and-go for a while, there.'

Birch snorted.

'I wasn't as close to it as you think, promise. One last question: what happened to the relief scene guard, last night?'

Amy's face turned grave.

'Lyndoe intercepted him,' she said, 'on his way to take up the shift. He was found earlier today in some woodland near the safe house.'

Birch felt the blood drain from her face.

'Found dead?'

Amy shook her head.

'Thankfully not,' she said, 'but he's in a pretty bad way. Lyndoe hit him over the head with something, multiple times, they think. He's been put in a medically induced coma.'

'Shit.'

'Yeah. I'm in touch with the hospital though. I can let you know if anything changes?'

Birch was about to reply, but then the atmosphere in the bullpen changed, and without turning round, she knew that McLeod had walked in.

'DI Birch?' he called out, across the room. She felt all the eyes that had been on him flick round to look at her, as though it were her turn to serve at a tennis match. 'Can you come with me, please?'

Birch let the brake off her wheelchair and performed an awkward three-point turn. Amy bent down close to her.

'His apology,' she whispered, 'had better be a doozy. Call me after and tell me everything?'

Birch reached out and patted her colleague on the arm.

'Like you have to ask.'

McLeod was waiting on the far side of the room, holding open the door that led back out to the lifts. Birch trundled off towards him, almost waiting for a chorus of high-school playground whispering to start up behind her.

★

On the other side of the one-way glass, Dr Jane was stating her name for the record. She looked far less put together than Birch had ever seen her: her brow was knit with worry, or perhaps it was guilt. McLeod stood next to Birch, stiff as a pillar. Her position in the wheelchair didn't help: he seemed unnaturally tall and painfully still.

'DI Alan Crosbie,' Crosbie said, on the other side of the glass, 'interviewing.'

Suddenly, McLeod spoke, making her jump.

'I'm aware,' he said, 'that Alan called you at home a few nights ago.'

She looked up at him, her mouth slightly open. He was watching Dr Jane, and didn't look back at her.

'How did you know about that?'

'He told me,' McLeod replied. 'On Friday night, at the concert.'

'Did he tell you he called me while drunk?'

McLeod's face didn't change. He knew, then.

'I inferred that,' he said.

'So you're aware? Of his drinking, I mean?'

'I am.' McLeod's gaze did shift then: he glanced down at the floor, but then snapped his head back up again. 'I had reason to raise some concerns with Alan a few weeks ago, but he assured me it was a one-off incident that would not be repeated. I now realise that wasn't true. I didn't understand the extent of the problem.'

Birch was quiet for a moment. In the other room, Crosbie was asking Dr Jane how she'd describe her relationship with Lyndoe.

'Crosbie's a good bloke,' she found herself saying. 'And a really good DI.'

McLeod gave a nod so slight, she wondered if she'd imagined it.

'Agreed,' he said. 'And I'm going to make sure he gets proper support. A thing I should have done when the issue first came to my attention.'

Birch didn't reply, simply because she wasn't sure what to say.

'Client PS7 attended every session,' Dr Jane was saying, 'without fail. On paper, he was a model client. But yes, I did have concerns. I raised them with my supervisor, in fact – but I wish now that I'd done more.'

McLeod cleared his throat.

'I feel,' he said, his voice strained, 'that I have a lot of amends to make.'

Birch cringed. She couldn't remember the last time she'd slept, and she really didn't want to be on the receiving end of a speech right now.

'Guv,' she said, 'you don't have to—'

'I do.' He looked at her now, for the first time since she'd entered the little interview anteroom. 'I need to apologise. I hampered your efforts last night, Helen, and it's my fault you were hurt.'

'The fault is mostly mine,' Birch replied. 'I should never have gone in on my own.'

'Probably not. But you called for help, and no one came. No one came, because I had told them not to.'

Birch was quiet again. Some strange part of her wanted to laugh, perhaps just to break up the atmosphere.

'Well,' she said, her mouth twitching at the corners, 'when you put it like that . . .'

'I mean, you are incorrigible, Birch.' He'd dropped his shoulders a little now, as though her small joke had given him permission to say what he felt. 'You were already almost killed during Operation Kendall. Is this some sort of adrenalin sport for you?'

Birch grinned.

'What, guv? Pissing you off?'

'Don't push your luck,' he snapped. But in spite of himself, he smiled.

Birch raised an eyebrow at him, the grin fading a little.

'I do have a question,' she said. She saw him set his teeth.

'Ask away,' he replied.

'Last night – and I might be wrong about this – when my dad was driving me to the safehouse, I could have sworn the van was being followed. Do you happen to know anything about that?'

McLeod closed his eyes.

'I suppose I ought to apologise for that, too,' he said. 'I stationed a surveillance unit outside your house.'

Birch's eyes widened, but she laughed.

'Well,' she said, 'I'm glad to hear I wasn't just imagining it. Let me guess – a couple of newish DCs, thinking they were getting an easy job for the night?'

McLeod rolled his eyes – not at her, she knew, but at the officers who'd failed at their fairly simple task.

'I didn't really believe you'd go anywhere,' he said. 'I need to remember to stop underestimating you.'

Birch smiled. She made a mental note to quote that line back to Amy later, then turned to look again at Dr Jane.

'I haven't seen enough of him,' Dr Jane was saying on the other side of the glass, 'to make a formal diagnosis, and honestly, I don't think it's really my place.'

Crosbie leaned forward, resting an elbow on the table between them.

'Okay,' he said, 'but . . . if pressed, you'd say there was something wrong there, wouldn't you? Surely no one sane takes the law into their own hands.'

Sunday, 25 July, 17:00

It was around 5 p.m. by the time Birch wheeled herself out of the front door of Fettes Avenue. The rain of the night before had been blown out to sea, and in front of her the long lawn of the police complex looked almost impossibly green. Beyond it, on the basketball court across the road, two teenage boys were practising their lay-ups. She could hear snatches of their bad music blasting from the speakers of a mobile phone. Edinburgh smelled of warm tarmac and barbecues and the brewery. She took a deep breath, and then laughed out loud, realising the extra - strong pain relief the hospital had given her could be the only possible reason for her feeling so zen.

She took out her phone and typed an *I'm outside* text to Anjan. As she hit *send*, she heard a voice.

'Helen.'

She turned: Dr Jane had followed her out of the building.

'Hey, doc. Good to see you.'

Dr Jane closed the gap between them and came to a stop beside the wheelchair. For about the fiftieth time that day, Birch twisted her neck to look up, and then regretted it.

'Good to see you, too,' Dr Jane said. 'Though . . . Helen, I am so, so sorry about what happened to you last night.'

Birch laughed. She knew it wasn't funny, but the drugs were making her loopy.

'What on earth could you possibly have to apologise for?'

Dr Jane looked down at her feet.

'He called me,' she said, 'James Lyndoe. Client PS7, as I've been calling him. Last night – he phoned me up, around half past midnight.'

Birch's eyes widened.

'I listened in to some of your interview,' she said, gesturing vaguely backwards towards the building behind them, 'but I must have missed that part. What did he say to you?'

Dr Jane was still examining the scuffed toes of her shoes.

'Not a great deal,' she replied, 'but he was very erratic. Disturbed. He sounded by turns very driven and focused, and then very nihilistic and depressed. It wasn't really a conversation, he just rambled at me, then hung up. Initially I thought he might just be blowing off steam. But the thought that he intended to do harm to himself or others wouldn't leave my mind. The more I thought about it, the more agitated I got. But I didn't act, and I should have. I'm so sorry.'

'Hey,' Birch said, her voice soft. She waited until Dr Jane shifted her gaze, and their eyes met. 'I don't think there's anything you could have done. It wasn't your responsibility.'

Dr Jane flicked her eyes away once more, focusing this time on the young men in the playground across the road.

'I felt frozen,' she said. 'You know the fight or flight response? It's actually not binary, there are other parts to it. One of them is *freeze*. I froze. I wanted to do something, but I was afraid to do the wrong thing. I reached out to my supervisor for help, but of course, it was the middle of the night, he was asleep. I tried to call DCI McLeod. But now I think I ought to have dialled 999. I ought to have taken it more seriously.'

Birch was still watching Dr Jane's face, even though the other woman was looking away.

'What would you say . . .' The words came slowly: Birch wasn't sure if it was her place to say this, or if what she was

saying would even be helpful. 'What would you say to someone else – to a client – if they were talking like this? If they'd
failed to – well, let's face it, if they'd failed to be sufficiently
psychic in a situation like this one. And if they were then blam-
ing themselves for a bad outcome that really, they couldn't
have controlled. What would you say?'

Dr Jane was quiet for a moment.

'I don't know,' she replied, her voice small.

Birch raised an eyebrow.

'I think you do know,' she said. 'It's just hard sometimes,
isn't it? Listening to that voice.'

It took a few seconds, but Dr Jane nodded, then pushed her
shoulders back and turned to face Birch properly. She smiled.

'You're hearing voices now, DI Birch? Maybe I should note
that down somewhere.'

Birch snorted.

'If anything,' she said, 'it's the exact opposite. I'm starting
to think maybe I haven't been hearing anything at all, these
past few weeks.'

Dr Jane cocked her head.

'What do you mean by that?'

Birch shrugged, and the shrug hurt.

'Well . . . everyone's been trying to help me, haven't they?
You. Anjan. Amy. Even McLeod, in his own weird and won-
derful way. People have been telling me over and over again
that I'm not better yet, that I'm doing too much, that the way
I'm going, I'll end up getting hurt. And then I end up getting
hurt. They were right. All of you were right. I just couldn't
hear you.'

There was a pause, in which Birch looked up and found
Dr Jane eyeing her with a look that contained more than
a little amusement.

'Is that true, Helen?' she asked. 'Is it true that you couldn't hear?'

This time, it was Birch's turn to look at her own feet. They looked weird, hitched in the stirrups of the wheelchair.

'*Okay,*' she said, injecting a degree of mock petulance into her voice. 'Maybe I heard you all fine. I just thought that I knew better.'

Dr Jane waved a hand as if to say, *and there it is.*

'How about now?' she asked.

Birch was quiet for a moment.

'Now,' she said, 'I'm not certain. I feel like nothing's certain, and that's not a feeling I like.'

'No,' Dr Jane said, 'I know.'

An impulse came, and Birch followed it, without thinking: she lifted her hand from the wheelchair's armrest and slipped it into Dr Jane's, then squeezed.

'I want you to know,' she said, 'that what happened to me last night had nothing to do with you. Not a thing. Lyndoe isn't your responsibility, and neither am I. I was rash, I got hurt, and that's it.'

Dr Jane bit her bottom lip.

'There was the other man, too,' she said. 'The scene guard Lyndoe attacked, he . . .'

Birch squeezed the other woman's hand again, and she fell silent.

'Doc,' she said. 'I'm serious. None of this was your fault.'

As she spoke, Anjan's Lexus rounded the corner and began moving along the street towards them.

'That's my ride,' Birch said. She dropped Dr Jane's hand and began scrabbling with the wheelchair's sticky brake.

'Let me.' Dr Jane moved round behind the chair. Birch felt the urge to object, to say she'd be fine, she'd manage – but

Dr Jane was already letting off the brake and beginning to push. 'I'll take you down to the kerb.'

Birch bit back the objection, as though swallowing a hiccup.

'Thank you,' she said.

'Thank you, too. I'm really glad we spoke.'

Birch smiled, though Dr Jane couldn't see her. The chair's wheels trundled on the uneven concrete of the path.

'Mind if I come by your consulting room tomorrow morning, as usual, and we can speak some more?'

Dr Jane trundled the wheelchair through the main gates, and out on to the kerb.

'I'll look forward to it,' she said.

Both women looked out along the road: Anjan was just a few yards away.

'You okay from here?' Dr Jane asked.

Birch squinted up at her, feeling every bruise on her neck.

'You don't want to hang about and meet Anjan?'

Dr Jane was already stepping away.

'Not yet,' she said, grinning. 'It might make things awkward if you ever want to trash him in therapy.'

Birch laughed, and watched as the other woman turned her back and walked smartly away.

Anjan signalled, and pulled the Lexus up to the kerb.

'Perfect timing,' she said, as he drew level with her, both front windows already rolled all the way down.

Anjan was watching Dr Jane disappear around the corner.

'Who was that?' he asked.

'That was my therapist,' Birch replied. 'The way things have been these past few days, I've got her on twenty-four-hour call.'

Anjan rolled his eyes.

'Very funny,' he said. His face was slightly twisted: Birch could tell there were things he wanted to say to her, but knew it wasn't the time.

'Listen,' she said, gesturing widely at her chair, 'we're maybe going to have a problem here. Getting me in the car, I mean.'

Anjan killed the engine and climbed out of the driver's seat.

'Don't you worry,' he said, rounding the front of the bonnet to open the passenger door. When he turned back to her, he bent down, and she lifted her face up, surprised, to receive a kiss. Instead, Anjan hooked one arm underneath her knees, and pushed the other between her lower back and the back-rest of the wheelchair.

'You are *not* serious,' she said, but Anjan was already lifting her. She yelped, and gripped her own arms behind his head. 'You're going to hurt yourself!'

Anjan puffed out air, but held her steady nevertheless.

'How many times,' he said, between breaths, 'have I said that to *you*, only to be ignored?' He was smiling at her as he added, 'For once in your life, Helen, just let someone *help*.'

Birch fought the idea for only a moment before relaxing in his arms. He placed her into the passenger seat, and she sank gratefully into the plush upholstery.

'I didn't argue then,' she said, 'did you notice? I didn't argue.'

Anjan laughed.

'I noticed,' he said, and then his face became serious again. 'Thank you.'

He scooted the wheelchair towards the car. There were beads of sweat on his brow, but she could see he was trying to carry on like lifting her had been no big deal.

'Just let me fold this thing up,' he said, 'and then I'll take you wherever you'd like to go.'

She watched him as he fiddled with the wheelchair's moving parts.

'Does that include your place?' she asked, her voice low and tentative for fear he'd say no. Instead, he looked up from his work, and beamed.

'I was hoping you'd say that,' he replied.

Acknowledgements

I am hugely indebted to Cath Summerhayes, Jess Molloy and everyone at Curtis Brown not only for their work on this book, but for everything they've done for me and for DI Birch over the past five years. To everyone at Hodder & Stoughton who's been involved with the series so far – thank you, you're the best team a novelist could ask for. Special mention to Jo Dickinson, my superhero editor – Jo, thank you for coming to my rescue every time this book threatened to overwhelm me. Also to Jenny Platt, publicist extraordinaire – Jenny, I can't thank you enough for giving me so many opportunities to reach readers and geek out about crime fiction. Charlotte Seymour, thank you for taking a chance on me, I hope I can do you proud.

I couldn't have written this book without the invaluable help, advice and support of Jane Claire Bradley, who helped me create the therapy storylines in this novel. Jane, I can't tell you what a privilege it is to be your friend and have your amazing brain to pick when I need it. I'm also indebted to Caroline Merz and Mal Jones for giving me my own experiences of therapy – I carry your words and tools around with me always. Thank you.

Special thanks go to Dominic Stevenson for advising me on the inner workings of Scottish news media, and all sorts of other things. Thank you to Paul Forster for giving me advice on how to effectively headbutt someone (vital information). Thanks to the brilliant Sean Caddell, who gave great advice for a scene that eventually ended up on the cutting-room floor – Sean, I always appreciate your support! I'm for ever grateful to Marjorie Lotfi, for giving me opportunities to work in Scottish prisons as part of the amazing Open Book project. Any errors in this book are, of course, mine.

As always, I need to thank my posse of writing supporters, without whom I am nothing. Stella Hervey Birrell, thank you for being my #WifeForLife. Alice Tarbuck, you make everything more magical. Kerry Ryan, Helen Sedgwick, Catherine Simpson, Jennifer Cornick, Julie Galante and everyone in the Very Chill Writing Group – writing this book was harder than you know, and you all helped so much in keeping me going. Thank you to Leon Crosby for the laughs and rants and cat photos. I love you all.

I have to mention my cousins, Julia and Lisa, for being *such* champions of me and of DI Birch – thank you for sending me so many excitable photos from bookshops! You're the best. My parents have given me more support over the past year than maybe ever before in my life, which is saying something – Mam and Fath, I don't have the words to thank you for everything you do. And I can't forget Nick, who dispenses wisdom and gives me a floor to sleep on whenever I need it. Team Askew, I love you.

I also love Al Smith, whose patience and understanding knows no bounds. Al, thank you for sticking around. I hope we get to go on many more adventures.